Blinding Rain

Also From Elisabeth Naughton

Eternal Guardians
(paranormal romance)
MARKED
ENTWINED
TEMPTED
ENRAPTURED
ENSLAVED
BOUND
TWISTED
RAVAGED
AWAKENED

Firebrand Series
(paranormal romance)
BOUND TO SEDUCTION
SLAVE TO PASSION
POSSESSED BY DESIRE

Against All Odds Series
(romantic suspense)
WAIT FOR ME
HOLD ON TO ME
MELT FOR ME

Aegis Series
(romantic suspense)
FIRST EXPOSURE
SINFUL SURRENDER
EXTREME MEASURES
LETHAL CONSEQUENCES
FATAL PURSUIT

Blinding Rain
By Elisabeth Naughton

Rising Storm
Season 2
Episode 7

Story created by Julie Kenner and Dee Davis

EVIL EYE
CONCEPTS

Blinding Rain, Episode 7
Rising Storm, Season 2
Copyright 2016 Julie Kenner and Dee Davis Oberwetter
ISBN: 978-1-945920-03-5

Published by Evil Eye Concepts, Incorporated

Foreword

Dear reader –

We have wanted to do a project together for over a decade, but nothing really jelled until we started to toy with a kernel of an idea that sprouted way back in 2012 … and ultimately grew into Rising Storm.

We are both excited about and proud of this project—not only of the story itself, but also the incredible authors who have helped bring the world and characters we created to life.

We hope you enjoy visiting Storm, Texas. Settle in and stay a while!

Happy reading!

Julie Kenner & Dee Davis

Sign up for the Rising Storm/1001 Dark Nights
Newsletter
and be entered to win an exclusive lightning bolt
necklace specially designed for Rising Storm by Janet
Cadsawan of Cadsawan.com.

Go to www.RisingStormBooks.com to subscribe.

As a bonus, all subscribers will receive a free
Rising Storm story
Storm Season: Ginny & Jacob – the Prequel
by Dee Davis

Chapter One

Standing behind the bar at Murphy's Pub, Logan Murphy reached back for a bottle of Jack Daniels from the glass shelves behind him and momentarily considered saying *screw it* to the patron waiting for his drink. He was in the mood for his own damn drink. More than one drink. In fact, downing the entire bottle of whiskey currently in his hand sounded pretty freakin' good right about now.

"I know that look." To Logan's right, a barstool scraped the old wood floor at the same moment Marcus Alvarez spoke. "That's the 'my life is fucked, I might as well get tanked and run for the hills look.' Don't do it, man. Trust me. It won't help."

Scowling, Logan pulled the bottle the rest of the way off the shelf and sloshed whiskey over the ice he'd already filled in a glass as he glared at his oldest friend. "My life *is* fucked when Marcus Alvarez, bad boy extraordinaire, has become the voice of reason."

Marcus chuckled as he sat on the barstool and rested his forearms on the gleaming bar top. Dark hair fell over his eyes, and he shook his head to force it back. "What can I say? I'm wise beyond my years."

Logan huffed and added Coke to the tumbler, then moved down the counter and set the drink in front of one of Murphy's regulars. Grabbing a dishtowel, he wiped his hands as he walked back to the computer, keyed in the order, then turned to stand in front of Marcus, more relieved than he wanted to admit that his friend had shown up at the perfect time and saved him from making yet another terrible decision. "It's two o'clock on a Wednesday. What are you doing in here? Shouldn't you be working?"

"I was." Marcus grabbed a pretzel from a bowl on the bar and popped it into his mouth. The bar was only sporadically filled, but in a few hours it would be hopping. "Took off early. I'm meeting Ian in a bit. We're heading out to look at some property."

Logan nodded and tossed the towel over his shoulder as he studied his friend. Marcus's family life might be shit in a hundred different ways now that his old man was back in town, but Marcus had something solid. He had Ian Briggs on his side—a man who was more of a father to Marcus than Hector Alvarez had ever been. Logan knew Marcus was stressed about what was happening with his mother and sisters now that his abusive father was back in the picture, but because of Ian, Marcus had a shot at a real future now—a partnership in a new ranch, land soon to build a home, freedom from the hell he'd grown up in. Heck, Marcus even had the perfect girl to start his new life—Brittany Rush. The prettiest girl in all of Storm, Texas.

Logan's chest pinched because he knew that wasn't true, at least not for him. The prettiest girl in Storm, Texas, wasn't blonde and blue-eyed like Brittany. She had dark curly hair, even darker eyes, and a belly that was rounder every time he saw her thanks to her pregnancy.

His mood took a serious nosedive, and he glanced

back toward the bottles on the shelves behind him. Man, he needed a drink. Standing here talking to his friend should make him feel better but all it was doing was making him relive the shitstorm that was his own life. Why couldn't he stop thinking about Ginny Moreno? He hadn't dated her that long. She'd already been pregnant when they'd gotten together. They'd never even slept together. That baby growing inside her was never going to be his, and he'd known that from the start. So what did it matter if she was carrying Jacob Salt's kid or Senator Rush's brat?

Bile swirled in his gut, edging its way up his esophagus. Because it mattered to him. It mattered that she'd slept with a married man. It mattered that she'd told the world she was carrying Jacob's baby so the truth about her affair with Senator Rush would never come out. But mostly, to Logan, it mattered that she'd lied to him. That during the months they'd dated when he'd thought they'd connected on a deeper level, the whole time she'd just been using him to make herself feel better.

That's what really burned. That he'd been a fool the whole time. That he'd been played. He'd shared everything with her—his time in Afghanistan, the friends he'd lost, even his fucking PTSD—and she'd shared virtually nothing. Nothing that the rest of the world didn't already know. Everything that mattered, everything intimate and secret and true about her she'd kept from him. And now he wasn't even sure who she really was.

"*I know she loved you.*" Ginny's sister's words from weeks ago echoed in Logan's head, making his heart speed up. "*She still loves you.*"

Could he believe Marisol? He wanted to, but there was too much crap between him and Ginny, too many lies. And even if he could get past it all, if he could somehow find a way to forgive Ginny, when she had Senator Rush's baby the prick would forever be a part of her life, reminding Logan time and again what an idiot he'd been.

"Seriously, dude," Marcus said behind him. "Alcohol is not going to fix what's bugging you."

"Yeah?" Logan glanced back at his friend. "And what will?"

Marcus eyed him across the bar. "Forgetting about her will."

Logan huffed, and that ache in the center of his chest he'd been living with the past few weeks seemed to grow wider instead of narrower. "Easier said than done," he muttered. "The only way I can forget about her is to get out of this miserable town."

When Marcus frowned like that was a stupid idea, Logan said, "Could you do it? If it was Brittany? Just forget about her?"

Marcus's jaw tightened. "Probably not. I'd wanna get shitfaced and run. But we're not kids anymore. Once the buzz wore off, the problem would still be there, and if there's one thing I've learned over the years it's that you can't get drunk enough or run far enough to escape your problems. They'll still be there when you sober up. Trust me, with all the crap going on with my dad, the only thing I wanna do is get the hell out of this town too, but I can't. And you can't either. We've got people here who need us. My mom and sisters. Your mom and dad, your brothers. Responsibility sucks, but it's part of life."

It did suck. And hearing about Marcus's family only made Logan feel guilty for whining about his love life—or lack thereof. "How are things at home?"

"Like shit. I can't get my mom to stand up to the bastard."

Logan's gut twisted. Yeah, he was a dick for moping about Ginny when Marcus was reliving the hell of his youth. "I'm sorry, man. Is there anything I can do?"

"Yeah, there is." The bell over the door jangled, and

Marcus glanced over his shoulder where Ian Briggs was stepping into the bar. Marcus looked back at Logan as he pushed off his stool. "You can be thankful for what you have. You've got a special family here, Logan. People who care about you and just want you to be happy. It's killing them seeing you so miserable. If you can't forgive Ginny, then let her go. Put her behind you and move on. If not for yourself then do it for them. Hell, do it for me. We all love ya, jerk."

Marcus turned away, greeted Ian with a handshake, and the two headed for the door. Behind the bar, Logan watched them go and thought about the things Marcus had said.

Let Ginny go. His head knew it was time. His heart, though—that ache in his chest grew so wide it felt like the Grand Canyon was swallowing him whole—wasn't sure that was possible.

Someone down the bar laughed and called, "I'll have another, bartender."

On a deep breath, Logan sighed and pushed his body into motion. Reaching for a glass, he scooped up ice and went to work making another kamikaze. Regardless of the ache, Marcus was right. He had to move on...for his family, for his friends, but mostly for himself. Because torturing himself like this was only prolonging his misery. He wasn't about to run. He wasn't about to abandon his family again. And he knew Ginny wasn't leaving town. Which meant the only way he was going to be able to get on with his life was to put her in the past where she belonged.

Along with every other mistake he'd ever made.

* * * *

"They're perfect," Ginny said, looking at the bouquet

Kristin Douglas had put together for her at Pushing Up Daisies. While Kristin was more a party planner than a florist, she'd been picking up more duties at Hedda Garten's shop since Joanne Alvarez had quit. "Marisol is going to love them."

Kristin leaned on the counter and eyed the arrangement of lilies. "It's sweet of you to get these for her."

"Well, she's been really great to me." Ginny fingered an orange blossom and shook her head, thinking about her older sister and everything Marisol had endured because of her. "I lied to her so much. I lied to everyone."

Her mind flitted to thoughts of Logan—to the hurt she saw in his eyes every time their paths crossed in town, to the way he couldn't even be in the same room with her anymore thanks to her lies. If there was one person she should have been honest with about the paternity of her baby, it was Logan. He'd been there for her when no one else had been. He'd been willing to be a father to Little Bit even knowing it would never be his biological kid. And he'd loved her when she hadn't been able to love herself. She'd fallen for the former soldier hard and fast after Jacob's death, and instead of being scared of the truth, she knew she should have shared it—with him.

Blinking back the burn of tears, she shook her head and told herself she was doing the best she could. He'd come around eventually. At least she hoped he would because living without him was all but killing her. "I can't change that, but I can try to make it up to Marisol. This isn't nearly what she deserves, but I want her to know how much I appreciate everything she's done for me." She placed a hand on her round belly. "And Little Bit. Plenty of people in this town just want to act like we don't even exist."

Kristin sighed. "Are the Salts still giving you the cold

shoulder?"

Thankful her new friend hadn't immediately thought of Logan, Ginny huffed and lifted her gaze from the flower to Kristin's russet hair. Behind Logan, the Salts were next on the avoid-Ginny-at-all-costs list. "More like the proverbial freeze out. They aren't even entertaining the possibility Little Bit could be Jacob's baby."

"And you are?"

Ginny heard the skepticism in Kristin's voice, and her first reaction was to say, "Yes, I am," but she bit her tongue. Ginny was sure Kristin was only trying to help her keep things in perspective, but her bluntness made Ginny miss her old friends Jacob and Brittany. Jacob was gone, and Ginny couldn't bring him back no matter how much she wanted to, but Brittany was still in Storm. And Ginny couldn't help but remember a time when Brittany would have defended Ginny to the ends of the earth. Before Ginny's lapse in judgment, Brittany would have sided with Ginny on everything. Now—because that lapse had involved Brittany's father—Brittany could barely look at Ginny.

Just like Logan.

Ginny glanced back at the flowers, her mood sliding south fast. Man, she'd made a giant mess of her life, hadn't she? "There's still a chance Little Bit could be Jacob's baby."

"A very small chance," Kristin said softly. "I just don't want you to get your hopes up, honey."

"I'm not. It's just—"

The bell above the door jangled, and Ginny turned to look then caught her breath when Celeste Salt stepped into the shop with her daughter Sara Jane. Both women were halfway into the store before they saw Ginny and realized their mistake.

Celeste drew to a halt and went rigid as she stared at

Ginny with wide, unreadable eyes. At her side, Sara Jane glanced from Ginny to her mother and back again with a worried expression. Placing a hand on her mother's arm, Sara Jane whispered something Ginny couldn't hear.

Tension filled the room like thick smoke. Ginny's heart rate shot into the stratosphere. In Ginny's belly, Little Bit jumped around as if he or she sensed the excitement, and all Ginny wanted to do was run, but Kristin's voice at her back, whispering, "Just act normal," kept her still. At least for the moment.

Long, silent seconds passed where all Ginny heard was the rush of blood in her ears. Finally, Celeste blinked and lifted her chin. With her purse hooked over her forearm, she continued walking toward the counter as if she owned the town, her daughter at her side. But as she drew close, Ginny couldn't help but notice that Jacob's mother looked terrible—thinner than she'd been the last time Ginny had seen her, pale, with dark circles under her eyes as if she'd barely slept in weeks.

Celeste stopped a foot away from the counter. "Ginny. Kristin. Good afternoon."

The situation couldn't be more awkward. Ginny swallowed the sickness threatening to consume her and tried to smile, but even she knew it came out looking more like a scowl. "Hi, Celeste. Sara Jane."

Ginny nodded at Jacob's older sister. For her part, Sara Jane sent Ginny a pitying smile and shrugged, telling Ginny loud and clear that she not only hated this moment as much as Ginny, but that she felt sorry for her.

"Kristin," Celeste said, no longer looking at Ginny. "I need a bouquet for my sister, Payton. Something sunny and fun. She's going through a difficult time and could use some cheering up."

At the mention of Senator Rush's wife, a woman Ginny had betrayed by sleeping with her husband, Ginny's stomach completely pitched. Especially when Celeste glanced Ginny's way with a very disapproving glare.

Dear God, she was never going to get away from the misery she'd caused. It was still spiraling, months after the fact. Closing her eyes briefly, Ginny said the same silent prayer she'd been reciting since the moment she'd found out she was pregnant: *Please, please, please let this baby be Jacob's.* But in the bottom of her soul she knew she didn't deserve to have that prayer answered. She deserved to suffer for all the lives she'd ruined because of her stupidity.

"Uh, sure." Kristin glanced from Celeste to Ginny and back again. "I can do something like that. Do you want me to have it delivered to Payton's house?"

"No, my house is fine," Celeste answered.

When she didn't elaborate, Sara Jane added, "Aunt Payton, Brittany, and Jeffry are staying with my parents for the time being. At least until they can find their own place."

The Rushes were separating? Ginny's eyes shot open, and she looked at Sara Jane, wondering immediately how Brittany was handling the news...if she was relieved or upset or worried or...

Her heart picked up speed. Whether Brittany agreed or not, Ginny still considered Brittany a friend. The oldest friend she had in Storm now. They'd been friends since they were kids. No one understood Brittany's conflicted feelings regarding her parents more than Ginny. Brittany would need someone to talk to about all this. She'd need someone on her side now who understood the—

"Does that thrill you, Ginny Moreno?" Celeste's icy eyes shifted Ginny's way and narrowed. "Knowing the senator is free now? It makes your life and that of your *baby's* much easier, doesn't it?"

Kristin gasped behind the counter.

At Celeste's side, Sara Jane said, "Mom, don't."

But Celeste didn't seem to be listening. She turned fully to face Ginny, her eyes like frigid daggers. "You can all be a happy little family now, can't you?"

Ginny's mouth fell open, and her face flamed.

"Mom," Sara Jane said harshly. "This is not the time or place."

"No, it's not." Celeste's eyes simmered with both pain and fury. "It's never the time or place for lies." Lifting her chin but not looking away from Ginny's eyes, she said, "Kristin, put the order on my account. Travis will take care of it."

She turned for the door.

Still standing near the counter, Sara Jane looked at Kristin, then at Ginny. "I'm sorry," she said in a low voice. "She's going through a really rough patch right now. I talked her into getting out of the house for a bit to get flowers for Aunt Payton. I-I didn't know this was going to happen."

"It's okay," Kristin said softly.

But it wasn't okay. Anger flared inside Ginny as she watched Celeste walk toward the door. Anger and a sense of self-preservation she knew she needed to start listening to—if not for herself then for Little Bit.

"Celeste, wait." She hustled—okay, waddled—after Celeste and reached Jacob's mother just before the woman pulled the door open. Stepping in front of the door so Celeste couldn't leave, she pinned the older woman with her eyes, not letting Celeste strike out and run away this time. "I know you don't want to hear this but I'm going to say it again anyway. I'm sorry I hurt you. I'm sorry I hurt everyone. I made a mistake. I'm human. Humans make mistakes. If I could go back and change what I did, I would. But I can't. All I can do is try to be a better person now. No one feels worse about what happened than I do."

Celeste's eyes narrowed. "I find that very hard to believe."

"It's true." Protectively, Ginny placed a hand on her belly to settle Little Bit, who was still flopping around like a Mexican jumping bean. "I know you don't want to believe it, but I loved your son. He was my best friend. He looked out for me. He kept me grounded. Even when I made stupid choices or got myself in trouble, he was always there for me, lifting me back up and making sure I knew someone cared."

Tears burned Ginny's eyes, and it took everything she had to blink them away instead of letting them fall down her cheeks as she forced herself to go on. "I wasn't perfect, but neither was Jacob, and no one knew that better than he did. I don't know what would have happened between me and Jacob if he hadn't died, but I do know what he'd say to me now if he were here. He'd tell me I was a complete idiot for what I let happen with the senator but he wouldn't want to crucify me for it. He'd want me to do exactly what I'm trying to do now—which is to pick up the pieces I let shatter and make things right for this baby. Jacob had the biggest heart I've ever known. Deep down I know he would have forgiven me eventually, especially knowing there's a chance this baby could be his. And whether you want to believe it or not, there *is* still a chance this is his baby. One I'm holding on to with everything I have in me."

Celeste stared at her long minutes in silence. At the counter, Kristin and Sara Jane didn't move. Ginny wasn't even sure they breathed. She herself was having trouble breathing as she waited for Jacob's mother to say something—anything.

"And what if that child inside you is not Jacob's?" Celeste finally said. "What then?"

Ginny swallowed hard because she didn't want to

think about what would happen if this baby wasn't Jacob's. But she had to. She had to start thinking about the future and how she was going to protect Little Bit from the senator should the paternity test confirm her greatest fear.

Reflexively, she smoothed her hand over her belly, trying to settle herself and Little Bit at the same time. "Then I'll still love it because that's what Jacob would want me to do. He'd want me to be the best mother I could be. Just like you were a great mother to him."

Celeste's eyes filled with tears, and her lip quivered. Looking quickly away, she blinked rapidly and cleared her throat. In a raspy voice, she said, "Sara Jane, I'm ready to go. Kristin, thank you."

She looked back up at Ginny and for a moment, as their eyes held, Ginny thought she saw...understanding. If not that then at least acceptance. "I hope for your sake..." Celeste's voice wavered again, and she cleared it once more. "I hope things turn out the way we both want."

Celeste reached around Ginny for the door handle. Heart still pounding, Ginny moved aside so Jacob's mother could leave. Sara Jane headed for the door but paused when she reached Ginny.

"For what it's worth," Sara Jane said softly, "Jacob would have liked what you just did. He would have liked it a lot." She smiled sadly, then pulled the door open and hurried after her mother.

As soon as the two were gone, Ginny's adrenaline waned. She exhaled and leaned against the wall, but her big body swayed and she nearly knocked a card display over in the process. Kristin hustled around the counter to right the display before it hit the ground.

"Well," Kristin said on a slightly hysterical laugh, sliding cards that had tipped back in their slots. "That was pretty impressive. You put Celeste Salt in her place. Too bad it didn't happen at the Bluebonnet Cafe. It'd already be all over town if that were the case, which by the way, I think it should be. Good job standing up for yourself, little mama."

Ginny's hands shook as she sagged against the wall. "I can't believe I just did that."

"It's about time you did." Kristin placed her hands on her hips and pinned Ginny with a look. "I understand Celeste is grieving over her son, but that doesn't make it okay for her to treat you like crap. People in this town give that woman way more leeway than they should."

As Ginny studied her newest friend, she didn't miss the bite in Kristin's words. And even though she appreciated having someone on her side again, she couldn't help but get the feeling there was something simmering beneath the surface between Kristin and Celeste—at least on Kristin's side.

The bell above the door jangled before Ginny could ask about it, and Kristin looked away, fixing a smile on her face. "Can I help you?"

A slim, tall, twenty-something woman with dark hair pulled back into a neat tail, olive skin golden from the sun, and wide green eyes smiled as she stepped into the shop wearing jeans and a long-sleeved tee. "Hi, actually, yes you can. I saw the Help Wanted sign in the window. Are you still hiring?"

Relief washed over Kristin's face, and she crossed to shake the woman's hand. "Yes, we are, Ms...?"

"Phelps." The woman returned the handshake. "I'm Delia."

"Delia Phelps..." Kristin's eyes narrowed. "That name is very familiar."

"That's because I grew up here. My last name used to be Bruce. I recently got divorced and need to change it back but..." She waved her hand. "Well, it's a huge process and I just haven't had time."

"Delia Bruce Phelps," Kristin muttered. Her eyes flew wide. "Oh, I know why that name sounds so familiar."

So did Ginny. Unease rolled through Ginny's gut as she pushed away from the wall and took a better look at the cute, athletic woman with perky breasts and a flat stomach who'd just breezed back into Storm. Delia Bruce had dated Logan Murphy back in high school, and Ginny suddenly remembered how ga-ga Logan had been for the star volleyball athlete before he'd graduated and gone off to the military.

"Yeah." Delia's blush deepened. "I'm the girl who ran off with her teacher and got married. That was a major mistake, let me tell you. Thank God some things can be explained away by the stupidity of youth, right?" She smiled. "Anyway, I'm looking for a job, and I'd love to fill out an application if you have one."

"Sure." Kristin headed for the counter and motioned for Delia to follow. "We're only looking for someone part time to help out at the counter. If that interests you, you can fill this out and leave it for Hedda Garten, the owner."

"That sounds perfect. Thank you." Delia took the pen Kristin handed her and looked down at the application on the counter. "It's really great to be home, let me tell you. This town never changes. I can't wait to catch up with all my old friends. I heard Marcus Alvarez and Logan Murphy are back in town too."

"That they are," Kristin said. "Looks like you picked the perfect time to come back to Storm."

Ginny didn't agree. Eying the woman's slim back from where she stood near the door, Ginny couldn't help but think this was the absolute worst time the perky, perfect Delia Bruce could roll back into Storm. Because Ginny had a feeling as soon as Logan took one look at his gorgeous ex-flame, any lingering thoughts he had about

Ginny—assuming he even had any anymore—were going to fly right out of his head.

And then any hope Ginny had for a reconciliation with the man she'd grown to love would be nothing but a fantasy.

Chapter Two

By eight o'clock, Murphy's was hopping.

Logan worked the bar with his dad, making drinks and refilling pints while his mom manned the kitchen. Every time she rang the bell and said "Order up," he grabbed plates of steaming food from the high counter and delivered them to waiting customers. Tending bar at the family pub wasn't a bad job—it sure as hell beat baking in full camo gear in one hundred and twenty degree heat in the desert—and he hoped to one day run the place when his folks finally retired, but lately any joy he'd found falling back into the familiar swing of Murphy life was gone. And he knew it was all thanks to one person he couldn't seem to stop thinking about.

"You're an idiot," he muttered to himself as he wiped his hands on his apron and reached for a pint glass under the counter then pulled on the tap to fill another order. So he was never going to work the bar with Ginny and their kids like his parents did with him and his brothers. He could let go of that little fantasy. He had to, right? God knew, holding on to it was only making him miserable.

The bell over the door jangled, and Logan glanced over noisy patrons laughing and drinking to see Marcus pull Brittany into the bar after him. Marcus waved Logan's way, and Logan lifted his chin in acknowledgment as he continued to pull the tap and fill another pint, but inside his stomach twisted with a familiar feeling of discomfort.

That twisting intensified as Marcus and Brittany headed toward the bar. Logan was happy for his friend, happy Marcus and Brittany were doing well especially considering all the shit pulling at them from both sides of their families, but seeing them together only reminded Logan of everything he didn't have. And even though he knew it made him an ass, lately Logan wanted to tell Marcus to find another bar for his dates with Brittany, just so he didn't have to watch the two of them being so in love.

"Hey." Marcus stopped at the end of the bar and wrapped an arm around Brittany's waist as she moved up at his side. "You workin' all night?"

Duh, what does it look like? Logan checked that response and filled a highball with ice. "We're short staffed tonight."

Someone slipped money in the jukebox, and Keith Urban's voice filled the bar, crooning about the heat of summer. Brittany turned to look over her shoulder.

"Does that mean you don't get a break?" Marcus asked.

Logan tipped the vodka bottle upside down and eyeballed a shot into the glass. "Not until Patrick or Dillon get off work and get here to help."

"Bummer." Marcus watched him drop the vodka bottle back on the counter with a clink and reach for a pitcher of fruit juice. "We were hoping we could tempt you into having dinner with us."

Be the third wheel on their date? No way in hell.

Logan reached for a maraschino cherry and slid it into the glass. "Sorry. Not tonight."

Marcus frowned.

At Marcus's side, Brittany whispered, "I don't see her yet."

A tingle rushed down Logan's spine as he set the drink on a tray and went to work filling another glass with ice. He hoped like hell they weren't talking about Ginny. Seeing her tonight when he was already feeling depressed was the last thing he needed. "You lookin' for someone?"

"No." Brittany faced him and grinned. "No one special."

Logan could tell by the way she wouldn't meet his eyes that she was full of crap. But before he could call her on it she looked at Marcus and said, "How about that booth in the back?"

"That works. I'll be over in a minute."

"Okay." She pressed a quick kiss to Marcus's cheek— one that turned Logan's stomach—then smiled Logan's way and said, "Try not to work too hard."

Unease rolled through Logan's gut as he fixed another drink and watched her cross the bar. He looked back at Marcus, caught the nervousness in his friend's eyes, and knew the two were up to something.

After setting the second drink on the tray, he grabbed a pint glass and moved to the taps. "Whatever you two are planning, knock it off."

"Who, us?" Marcus flashed a quick smile. "We're not planning anything."

Logan huffed. "I might be screwed in the head from my time overseas, but I'm not dumb. I'm not in the mood for seeing Ginny."

"Brittany isn't either." Marcus's expression sobered. "She wasn't looking for Ginny."

"Then who was she looking for?" Logan topped off the beer and set it on the tray.

"Don't know." That mischievous look filled Marcus's

dark eyes again. He tapped a hand on the bar. "Come over and join us when you get a break. And try to keep an open mind. That's the only thing I ask."

Logan's gaze followed his friend as he wove through the bar and joined Brittany at the booth in the back. He didn't sit across from her as he normally did when they came in. He sat next to her, both facing the door as if waiting and watching for someone.

Logan's discomfort kicked up even more, but he barely had time to wonder what the two were up to. His mother called, "Order up" again just as he was about to deliver a tray full of drinks. He didn't have time for romance and silliness. He had a job to do, even if that job was a helluva lot less enjoyable than it had ever been.

An hour later, Logan was still having trouble getting his mind off Ginny. Marcus and Brittany hadn't left. They sat in the same booth, their burgers now finished, nursing their drinks as they flirted and didn't even try to keep their hands off each other. The sight was more than Logan could handle, and when his brother Patrick showed up and offered to relieve him at the bar so he could take a break, he untied his apron, desperate for fifteen minutes out back to clear his head and check his attitude. He was just about to turn for the kitchen when the bell above the door jingled again and a familiar face walked into the pub.

His feet stilled and his eyes widened as Delia Bruce, his high school girlfriend and the first woman he'd ever said *I love you* to, stopped and glanced over the booths and tables.

She was prettier than he remembered, with high cheekbones and creamy skin. Taller, too, though she'd always been tall and insanely athletic. Tonight her lean body was covered in ripped jeans that hugged her long legs and a loose sparkly black tank that showed off her toned shoulders and pert breasts. Her thick mahogany hair was longer than he remembered, hanging sleek and straight to the middle of her back, but when her eyes shifted his way he saw they were the same. Still green and gorgeous and as mesmerizing as they'd been when he was sixteen.

A warm smile spread across her face when she spotted him. And before he knew it she was heading straight for him.

"Logan Murphy." Her silky voice caressed his name exactly as it had when they were teenagers. "I heard you were back in town."

"Hey, Delia." When she pushed to her toes and wrapped her arms around him without pretense, he returned her hug and realized his heart was racing because being surrounded by her again felt both awkward and familiar at the same time. "This is a surprise."

She dropped to her heels and let go of him, and he couldn't quite tell if he was disappointed or relieved by that fact. "I just got home. First night back in Storm. Gosh." She glanced around the bar. "This place hasn't changed, huh? Remember the time we stole a bottle of vodka when your dad wasn't looking and drank it up at the lake?"

Logan glanced over his shoulder and caught his dad's gaze where he stood filling pint glasses. "Yeah, probably shouldn't mention that too loudly. My dad still gives me shit about the morning he found me passed out in the front yard."

Delia laughed. "God, those were crazy times. My mom still claims that was the night I turned to the devil. Stayed out 'til four in the morning and came home a wild woman."

The corner of Logan's mouth inched up, and he realized it was the first time he'd smiled in weeks. The first time he'd had anything to smile about since Ginny.

His smile quickly died, but when Delia placed a hand on his arm, the heat of her touch distracted him from his looming depression and brought his attention back to her. "Hey, can you get a drink with me or are you working?" She glanced over her shoulder. "I'm meeting Brit and Marcus." Spotting them, she waved.

So this was what those two had been up to. Logan's gaze darted to their table and the sheepish grins on their faces as they watched him with Delia. "Actually," he heard himself say, "I was just about to take a break."

Delia looked back at him and grinned. "Great." Turning toward Marcus and Brittany's booth, she wrapped both of her arms around his and practically pushed him across the bar. "I can't wait to hear all about what you've been doing since you broke my heart and ran off to join the military."

Logan huffed. "Word was you weren't that broken hearted. You skipped town with Mr. Phelps not long after."

Delia rolled her eyes and smiled in that cute, lighthearted way of hers that had always made him crazy. "What can I say? I was lost without you and had to get out of town. Mr. Phelps looked like an easy ride."

Logan nearly choked. "Okay, that's an image I don't need in my head."

Delia giggled. "Trust me, it wasn't all that good a ride. Did you know older guys can have erectile problems?" She shuddered. "Seriously should have considered that part of the whole ride thing beforehand. Would'a saved me a hell of a lot of time and money. Brit!" she squealed as they neared the booth. "Look at you! I think the last time I saw you I was babysitting Jeffry!"

Brittany jumped out of the booth and both girls let loose those high-pitch girl screams women do when they see an old friend and wrapped their arms around each other. And as he watched, Logan's chest filled with something light—or maybe it just didn't feel so damn heavy anymore. He knew Delia had been teasing him a few minutes ago. She hadn't loved him back in high school any more than he'd loved her—which was only as much as he'd needed to love her to get in her pants. But seeing her again felt good, familiar, easy in a way nothing had felt easy in a long time. And as he slid into the booth next to her and the four of them launched into stories about the good old days, he found himself smiling and laughing and barely thinking of Ginny at all.

He glanced at Delia and caught her gaze. And as she smiled and nudged her shoulder against his, for the first time in forever he thought...maybe. Maybe Marcus was right and he really could move on with his life. Because if he had someone like Delia Bruce in his life again, distracting him and keeping him busy, he just might be able to let go of Ginny Moreno for good.

* * * *

Brittany watched Logan closely as the four sat in the back booth long after Logan was supposed to go back to work, feeling both happy and guilty at the same time.

She wasn't betraying her friendship with Ginny by encouraging some kind of rekindling between Logan and Delia, was she? No. She and Ginny weren't friends anymore. She didn't even know if Ginny was upset over her breakup with Logan. For all she knew, Logan Murphy had just been another notch on Ginny Moreno's bedpost.

But even as the thought hit, Brittany's mood sank lower. Regardless of Ginny's shortcomings, Brittany knew the girl was a wreck over losing Logan. It was as plain as the nose on her face anytime the two ran into each other in town. Though, that wasn't Brittany's fault, now was it?

Logan was the one who'd called things off with Ginny. Logan, like Brittany, had been devastated by Ginny's lies. The guy deserved to have fun and find someone else just as Brittany deserved to move on with her life with Marcus and try to forget the fallout from the storm that Ginny Moreno had unleashed on all of them.

"Well," Logan said with a sigh when laughter at their table died down. "I hate to break up this party, but I'm getting the evil eye from the kitchen so I'd better get back to work."

Brittany glanced toward the bar and the open kitchen counter where Sonya Murphy was watching them. Brittany lifted her hand and waved. Sonya smiled and shook her head, looking back down at whatever food she was prepping behind the half wall.

"Oh, really?" Delia reached for Logan's hand as he slid out of the booth. "Are you sure you can't stay just a little longer?"

"Yeah, I'm sure." Logan glanced over his shoulder toward the bar but didn't, Brittany noticed, try to pull his hand away from Delia's. His gaze drifted back to Delia. "I may get fired if I don't get my ass over there soon."

"You're breaking my heart all over again, Logan Murphy." Delia crossed her arms over her chest in a mock pout.

Logan chuckled and ran a hand through his hair.

"The only thing that will make it up to me is dinner tomorrow night. The four of us. And no working."

Logan's smile wobbled, and he looked to Brittany, then Marcus. "Uh..."

"I'm free tomorrow night." Marcus glanced Brittany's way. "Can you make that work, babe?"

Another whisper of guilt washed over Brittany but she pushed it away. "Yeah. Sounds like fun."

Delia grinned and looked up at Logan expectantly.

"Well?"

Logan's nervous eyes skipped from face to face. He seemed unsure. Brittany's whisper turned to a full-on rush. "Just dinner?"

"Well, dinner and whatever," Delia said with a wink.

Unease flashed in Logan's eyes, but it quickly faded when he blinked. He smiled down at Delia. "Yeah, that sounds good."

"Awesome." Delia bolted out of the booth and planted a kiss on Logan's cheek. "You can pick me up at six. I'm staying with my folks. Use the door. You're older now. I don't want you breaking any bones trying to climb through my bedroom window like you did when you were seventeen."

Logan looked a little dazed when she drew back, and Brittany realized he'd just been ambushed into a date he might not be up for so soon after breaking things off with Ginny. "Okay," Logan said. "I guess I'll see you at seven. Marcus. Brit. Later."

He still looked a little stunned as he wandered back to the bar.

"God, he is way cuter than I remembered." Delia dropped back into the booth with a sigh. "Why the hell did we break up?"

Brittany remembered. She'd been a few years younger than Delia and Logan, but Delia Bruce's affair with Mr. Phelps had been the talk of the town. Word was Delia had been making eyes at the teacher long before Logan had left for the military, though no one knew for sure if that was true. No one but Delia.

"Well, this was super fun," Delia said. "But I gotta get going. I should probably be the good daughter and get home before my folks fall asleep in their recliners." She slid out of the booth. "It was so awesome to catch up with you both." When Marcus stood she gave him a hug, then did the same with Brittany. "I feel like dancing tomorrow night so pick someplace fun. Bye, you two."

She swept out of the bar the same way she'd swept in, like she owned the place. As she reached the door, she caught Logan's gaze and shot a sultry smile his way before disappearing into the dark.

"Well," Marcus said with a lift of his brows as he turned Brittany's way. "She is exactly the same as she was in high school."

"And what is that?"

"Exhausting."

Brittany laughed and easily moved into Marcus's arms when he reached for her. "I'm so glad I'm not the only one who felt that way. That woman is high energy. I could barely keep up with all her stories."

"That's because you weren't drunk. Trust me. Gets easier when you're drinking." Marcus's lips curled as he pressed a kiss to her neck then drew back. "She liked to party. Which, now that I think about it, is probably the reason Logan ran off and joined the military. It was either get the hell out of town or turn into an alcoholic."

Brittany chuckled. "You are so full of it."

Marcus closed his hand around hers and led her toward the door. "I'm totally serious. You saw the three vodkas she sucked back while we were chatting. Did she seem drunk to you?"

"No."

"To me either. That woman's got a high alcohol threshold. She always did. Dangerous for a guy. And expensive."

Brittany smiled. "And we both encouraged him to go out with her. We're terrible friends."

Marcus shook his head as she tossed Logan a wave and opened the door for her. "In all fairness, we didn't know it was a date until after we agreed to dinner with them tomorrow. And actually, that makes us good friends because we're saving him from being alone with her."

They walked to his car, and he pulled the passenger door open for her. She hesitated before getting in. "In all seriousness. Do you think it's a good idea? Logan and Delia going out?"

Marcus considered for a moment then shrugged. "It's not a terrible idea. They dated for over a year. I know she was his first. While I don't think they were ever madly in love, they cared about each other once. If there wasn't still something between them he wouldn't have been laughing and smiling tonight."

Brittany wasn't so sure. Yes, Logan had seemed to be having a good time, but there'd been something missing in his eyes. Some spark of happiness she'd seen in him not that long ago.

"I'd just hate for us to, you know, encourage him to date if he's not ready."

"Babe." Marcus slid an arm around her waist and drew her against all his firm, masculine heat. "The only way Logan's going to get over Ginny and what she did is to move on. And if he can do that with someone fun like Delia, then why the hell not? No one's saying he has to marry her. No one's saying he has to fall in love with her. He just has to get out there and start living again. I, for one, think it's a good thing Delia's back in town. She might be exactly what Logan needs right now."

Brittany rested her hands against Marcus's strong chest and looked down at the three buttons on his henley. "You use that word love like it's a bad thing."

His finger nudged her chin up until her eyes met his. "For Logan, who fell hard and fast for someone who betrayed him? Yeah. Love is a bad thing. For me? It's exactly what I want. You are everything I want, Brittany Rush."

Warmth spread through her chest, stinging her eyes with a wave of emotion. Lifting to her toes, she pressed her lips against Marcus's then groaned when he opened to her and drew her into his mouth.

"Get a room, you two." Dillon Murphy's voice drifted to Brittany's ears. Tugging her lips away from Marcus's, she glanced over his shoulder toward the sheriff, who was pulling the door to the pub open with a wry smile. "I don't want to get any calls about indecent exposure in the parking lot of my family's establishment."

Marcus's lips curled as he turned to look toward the sheriff, not letting go of Brittany. "We'll try not to keep it decent, Sheriff."

Dillon laughed and disappeared into the bar.

As the door closed behind him and the laughter and music from inside faded, Marcus finally released her. "Come on. We should probably get you home. I won't win any bonus points with your aunt and uncle if I bring you home too late."

Brittany sighed as she climbed into the car and Marcus closed the door for her. "I doubt they'd notice," she said when he slid into his seat next to her. "Uncle Travis is barely around and Aunt Celeste spends most of her time in her room."

"Not exactly the happy home you hoped you were moving into, huh?"

Brittany rolled her eyes. "Not even. At least Mom is happy. And Jeffry is so much more relaxed away from my dad. He's like a whole different person."

"Then it's all good." He lifted their joined hands and kissed the back of her hand as he drove.

All that warmth she'd felt when he kissed her came steamrolling back, and when he laid their hands on her knee, she tightened her fingers around his wishing they could have another night together like the one they'd spent at the motel. She rested her head against the seat and watched his profile as he drove. God, she was crazy about him. She just hoped everything with her parents and his parents settled down so they could be together again like that soon.

He pulled to a stop in front of the Salt home and killed the engine. And as she glanced at the warm glow in the windows, all that warmth inside her grew cold.

"Hey." Marcus squeezed her hand. "You okay?"

Brittany's gaze held on Jacob's dark bedroom window—what had been Ginny's bedroom window when she'd lived with the Salts just after Jacob's death. "Yeah, I'm fine."

He tugged on her arm, drawing her gaze his way. "I know fine, baby, and you're not it. You've been sad all night. Is it your mom and dad?"

She huffed, feeling like an idiot. "No. I'm happy they finally split. It was way past time."

"Then what?"

"I don't know." She glanced back at the house. "I guess it's being here. And maybe having drinks with Logan. It's all familiar, you know? Except..."

Her chest pinched, and the words died on her lips.

"Except Ginny's missing," Marcus said softly.

Tears Brittany knew she shouldn't be feeling burned the backs of her eyes. "Yeah. That." She looked back at Marcus. "Stupid, huh?" She swiped at a useless tear that didn't want to stay in her eye.

"Not stupid. Not at all. You two were close."

They had been. Until Ginny ruined everything. "It makes no sense. She's the one who betrayed me and Logan and everyone, and I, for some reason, am the one who feels guilty."

"For what it's worth, I'm pretty sure she's the one who feels worse."

Brittany knew that. But it didn't make her feel any better. Closing her eyes, she fought back the futile sadness and told herself she should be angry, not sad.

"Do you want to talk to her?" Marcus asked quietly.

Brittany's eyes floated open and she stared through the windshield at a tree down the street. Did she? Her chest tightened at the thought, but just as quickly her skin prickled with a heat that told her the answer. "No. Not yet, and I don't know when or if I'll ever want to talk to her." She turned to Marcus. "Does that make me a bad person?"

"Not at all." Emotions softened his features as he let go of her hand and wrapped his arms around her. "You're the best person I know." His lips brushed her temple. "When and if you're ready to talk to her, you'll know. And if you never are, then that's okay too. There are plenty of people who love you right here."

She wrapped her arms around his waist and held on tight. Tears burned her eyes again, and she turned her face against the soft skin of his neck and breathed him in. She was so thankful for him, for everything he was and the way he cared for her. No one else had ever been there for her like him.

"I love you," she whispered.

His arms tightened around her, and he pressed his lips to her temple. "Not nearly as much as I love you. I know I'm not the same as Ginny, but you've got me. You've always got me."

She closed her eyes as her heart swelled. A few months ago, she hadn't realized how lonely she really was. Then Marcus Alvarez had walked back into her life and everything had changed. Things that were dull suddenly became vibrant. Her heart had felt as if it had finally started beating. Now, she couldn't imagine living without him, and she never wanted to go back to a world where he didn't exist. He was her everything, and she would do anything to hold on to him.

Her eyes slid open, and her thoughts drifted to Ginny. And before she could stop it, she wondered if that was why Ginny had told so many lies. So she could hold on to the one thing that had given her a reason to live.

Chapter Three

Lacey Salt looked from her mother, seated on the couch studying her clasped hands in her lap as if they held the mysteries of the world, to her father, sitting tense across the room in his favorite recliner with a perturbed look on his face.

Lacey sighed. Yeah, they were really the picture of the perfect family these days, weren't they?

After her sister Sara Jane had come home from her trip to the florist with their mother and told Lacey what had happened, Lacey had decided enough was enough. If their parents wanted to ignore each other, fine, but it was way past time they stopped ignoring Lacey.

She glanced toward Sara Jane, seated beside her on the love seat. Sara Jane lifted her brows and shrugged, telling Lacey she felt just as frustrated. Lacey drew in a breath and looked at both her parents again. "Thanks for sitting down with us," she started. "It's been forever since we had a Salt family meeting."

It had been forever—since before Jacob's death. Lacey pushed that thought aside and sat up straighter. "Sara Jane and I want to talk to both of you about how things are going here at home. We know you're both dealing with your grief in different ways but"—she glanced at her sister, and when Sara Jane nodded, she said—"we want you to remember that you have two other children who are still alive."

Lacey's father tensed even more but he didn't speak. Lacey didn't think it was possible but her mother seemed to sink further into the couch cushions. "We know that, dear," her mother said softly.

Lacey nearly huffed. They had a funny way of showing it. "Yeah, see"—she scratched the back of her head—"we don't think you do." She glanced toward her mother. "Hiding in your bedroom doesn't make me or Sara Jane feel like you know we're around." She looked toward her father. "Neither does working twenty-four seven."

"That is entirely unfair," her father finally said in a harsh voice. "I'm working to provide for you, Lacey. You make it sound as if I'm working to escape from this family."

Wasn't he?

"What Lacey is trying to say," Sara Jane piped in, "is that neither of you is here for her. Throwing money at her doesn't make her feel valued as your daughter. I should know, Daddy. You've been doing it to me lately as well. I might not live here anymore but that doesn't mean I haven't noticed what's going on. Upgrading my cell phone was very nice of you, but instead of a new phone, I'd rather have you around for Sunday dinners or to go out to the range and hit a bucket of balls with me on a Saturday afternoon. All the things you used to do before Jacob died."

Their father pursed his lips and sat back in his chair, clearly irritated.

Lacey sighed, sensing they were getting nowhere. And the way her parents wouldn't even acknowledge each other sent a ripple of worry down her spine. "We're not trying to tell you you're bad parents—"

"Sounds like you are," their father muttered.

Lacey ignored that comment. "We're just trying to tell you that we realize neither of you are acting normal. I wasn't acting normal either for a while and it didn't help me move on or ease the pain of losing Jacob. We're all hurting because of that. And although we understand our new normal without Jacob is going to be very different from our old normal, we"—she glanced at Sara Jane again for encouragement—"both feel it's time we all started acting like a family again instead of this...fractured household."

Neither of their parents looked at them. Their mother continued to study her hands and their father stared down at a spot on the carpet. Any hope Lacey'd had about this family meeting fixing things took a serious nosedive.

Sara Jane frowned. "Lacey's right. And both of you could learn something from her. It took a lot of maturity for her to realize acting out after Jacob's death wasn't doing anything to help her grief." She glanced Lacey's way. "I'm proud of you, baby sister."

Lacey's cheeks heated. She had a lot of regret over the things she'd done after Jacob's death, but hearing Sara Jane say she was proud of her filled her with warmth. "Thanks," she whispered.

"As for you two." Sara Jane looked back at their parents. "I'm not proud of either of you. It's been months since Jacob's death and you're both still acting like it just happened."

Their father's jaw clenched down hard and his enraged eyes shot their way. "What would you have us do? Act like it didn't happen? You both have no idea what it's like to lose a child."

"No, we don't," Sara Jane said. "We only know what

it's like to lose a brother. And what it's like to lose both our parents. You both have pulled away from us. And while we've been sympathetic to it until now, we're not anymore. It's time you both started acting like the parents you are."

"And," Lacey cut in before either could respond, "it's time you both put aside your feud with Ginny Moreno." When her mother's wide eyes shot to Lacey's face, Lacey said, "I know what happened at the flower shop today. Sara Jane told me. You had the chance to do the right thing, Mom, but you didn't."

"That girl—"

"What happened at the flower shop?" Their father sat forward, his brows drawn low, showing interest in the conversation for the first time since they'd started.

"Mom and I went to buy flowers for Aunt Payton and we ran into Ginny there. She was chatting with Kristin. I would have pulled Mom out of there if I'd known Ginny was there, but by the time I spotted her it was too late. Instead of being civil, Mom actually accused Ginny of being happy Aunt Payton and Uncle Sebastian separated."

Their father huffed and sank back into his seat. "I'm sure she is."

Lacey'd had enough. She pushed to her feet, unable to sit still any longer. "That's what I'm talking about. Whether or not you both want to admit it, there is still a chance Ginny's carrying your grandchild, but you're both so hellbent on punishing her that you can't even act like human beings. She made a mistake, but so did Uncle Sebastian, only I don't see either of you vilifying him. I was plenty mad at her too, but I know how grief can make you do things you wouldn't normally do. Yes, she lied to us, but she didn't do it to be mean. She did it because she cared about Jacob and all of us. You've both treated her like a daughter her whole life, only now when she really needs someone you're acting like she's the devil. Well, you know what? I've told plenty of lies over the last few months. I hurt people just like Ginny did. If you're going to treat her like garbage then you better treat me the same way."

Their father's face turned red, but he didn't speak. Across the room, their mother sighed and lifted her gaze. "Lacey, dear. What you did is very different from what Ginny did."

"You're right. It is. I told lies because I was hurting and I wanted others to hurt too. Ginny lied because she knew what she'd done was wrong and she was trying to protect you from more hurt. And because she wanted to give you both something to live for after you lost Jacob."

Their parents were both silent, and Lacey looked from one to the other, willing them to speak. At her side, Sara Jane placed a hand on Lacey's arm, and when Lacey looked down at her sister she saw the compassion in her sister's eyes and more pride.

Their father pushed out of his chair, his face still red and angry. "You all believe what you want to believe. I need some air."

He stalked out of the room without another word. And feeling like a failure, Lacey sank back on the love seat next to Sara Jane. Seconds later the front door opened and slammed shut.

Yep, the picture of the perfect family. Their dad couldn't even stay in the same room with them. He was always walking out. Lacey's gaze shot toward the entryway where he'd just left, and that shiver of unease turned to a warning all across her skin. Something was going on with him. Something more than just his grief over losing a child. Lacey wasn't sure what it was, but she sensed it was something bad.

"I'm sorry, girls." Their mother's soft voice drew Lacey's attention. "I hear what you're both saying. It's just..." Her eyes filled with tears. "All of this is harder than I thought it would be."

Guilt swamped Lacey for being such a hardass. She looked at her sister, and when Sara Jane nodded, they both rose and moved to the couch to sit on either side of their mother.

"We know, Mom," Sara Jane said, reaching for Celeste's hand.

"We definitely know." Lacey wrapped an arm around her mother's shoulder. "But none of us can go back in time, and maybe..." She gathered her courage. "Maybe the only way we're all going to get through the pain is to let go of the anger and hurt feelings once and for all. I want that. Sara Jane wants that. I know Ginny wants it too."

Her mother drew a steadying breath and blinked several times, fighting back her tears. With a shaky hand, she squeezed Lacey's knee and pressed a kiss to Lacey's cheek. "You're a sweet girl, Lacey." With her other hand, she tightened her fingers around Sara Jane's hand. "So are you, Sara Jane. I am very lucky to have both of you girls, and I'm sorry I've been so useless lately. I'll try to be better. I can't make any promises about your father—"

"We know," Sara Jane said. "We just love you both and want you to be happy."

"Yeah, we do," Lacey added.

Celeste's eyes filled with tears again and she shifted, wrapping both of her thin arms around her girls, pulling them in for a group hug. "I love you both as well. And I couldn't be more proud of both of you. I know what you did here wasn't easy, but I'm glad you spoke up. We'll find a way through this, I promise."

Celeste kissed both of their heads, and as Lacey laid her cheek on her mother's breast just as she'd done when she was little, she had hope for the first time in months. Hope that maybe she could get her family back. It would never be the same. They would always miss Jacob, but something in her heart told her their mother had heard what they'd said, not just about their family, but about Ginny as well.

One out of two wasn't bad. Lacey would just go on hoping her father eventually came around as well.

* * * *

Mary Louise Prager frowned as she walked down Main Street and stared at her phone. She only heard from her father about once a year. Today, obviously, was the day her dear old dad decided to take a break from his guitar and check in on how she was doing. Probably only because the holidays were sneaking up and he felt guilty for being such a slacker parent.

She hit delete on the e-mail and shoved the phone back in her pocket, hating the way that one e-mail could ruin her entire day. She was a grown woman in her thirties, for crying out loud. She'd gotten by just fine without a father all these years. She didn't need one now.

Trying to push aside the guilt she felt for deleting that e-mail without responding, she rounded the corner toward the Bluebonnet Cafe, but drew to a stop when she spotted Tate Johnson across the street, leaving Cuppa Joe with a box in his hands. Just as he stepped down onto the sidewalk, his brother Tucker, holding Hannah Grossman's hand, smacked into him, sending the box flying to the concrete.

Both Hannah and Tucker jerked back. Tucker's shoulders stiffened, and he quickly stepped in front of Hannah. Tate looked up to see who'd hit him, and when he spotted the two, his entire face hardened and shifted from the handsome man she recognized to one who was consumed by rage.

Mary Louise couldn't hear what the two brothers said to each other as Tucker bent down to pick up Tate's box, but even from this distance she could see the hard line of Tate's spine beneath his suit jacket and the slice of steel that was his jaw.

She glanced right and left. A few other people had slowed their steps on the sidewalks and were now staring at the face off happening in broad daylight.

Her pulse sped up, and her skin grew tingly. Tate's angry words drifted toward her ears, telling her he didn't realize people were watching. Unable to sit back while he damaged the rest of his political career, she rushed across the street and caught Tate by the arm just as he was moving toward his brother in an aggressive way.

"What the hell?" Tate's furious eyes darted down at her.

Mary Louise smiled up at him, but quickly shifted her gaze to Tucker and Hannah. "Hey, Tucker, Hannah. Sorry to interrupt. Can I steal Tate away from you for a bit? I've been trying to catch him all morning."

"Tate?" She looked up at the man who made her pulse race and tried like hell to keep it steady, but nothing worked. She hated that he had this effect on her after all this time, especially knowing he only had eyes for the woman across from her who'd chosen his brother. "There's something I need to talk with you about."

Tate's brows drew together to form an adorable crease between his eyes. "Right now?"

"Yes, right now." She tugged on his arm, desperate to pull him away from what could be an explosive situation. Reaching for the box of pastries from Tucker, she stepped back and drew Tate with her. "It won't take long, I promise."

Thankfully, Tate moved with her, stepping away from his brother, but Mary Louise wouldn't breathe easier until they were on the next block. "What's in the box?" she asked, still keeping one hand wrapped around his arm as she walked. "Smells good."

"Cupcakes. Was cupcakes," he grumbled beside her. "For my staff. What's so important you had to interrupt me back there?"

Mary Louise pulled him around a corner and spotted Murphy's Pub down the road. She suddenly felt like having a beer. Or a stiff shot. It was four o'clock on a Thursday, and she was done with work for the day. She had a strong hunch Tate could use one as well, and if he couldn't, well, she'd force him to have one. Lord knew he needed to chill out a bit before he did something he'd regret.

"I feel like a drink," she said, pulling him with her toward the pub. "How about you? Wanna get a drink? Because I think we could both totally use a drink right about now."

"Mary Louise, what the heck is going on? You're acting like a lunatic."

She huffed because she was not the one acting like a lunatic. He was.

Reaching the pub, she tugged the door open and pulled him in after her. A quick scan of the bar told her the dinner crowd hadn't hit yet. With a wave toward Sonya Murphy, standing behind the bar drying out a glass, she headed for an open booth near the back.

"Sit," she said to Tate, finally letting go of him as she set his cupcake box on the table. "And tell me what you want to drink."

He dropped into the booth and frowned up at her like she'd grown a second head. "I don't know. A pint of whatever they have on tap, I guess."

"Gotcha." She turned for the bar. "I'll get two."

She knew he was watching her with both confusion and dismay as she crossed to the bar and stopped near Sonya to order their drinks, but she didn't care. He needed to pull his head out of his ass, and she was tired of watching him throw his career away over a woman who wasn't worth his time.

"Hey, Sonya," she said as she drew close. "We'll take two attitude adjustments."

Sonya smiled and reached for clean glasses from below the bar, glancing past Mary Louise toward the booth where Tate—hopefully—still sat. "An attitude adjustment sounds exactly like what that boy needs."

Mary Louise sighed and propped her elbow on the bar so she could rest her chin in her hand. "You have no idea. I just broke up an almost fight between the two Johnson brothers right on the street."

"That would explain the irritated look on his face," Sonya said, filling two glasses with ice.

"Yeah, but not why he insists on being such a jackass," Mary Louise mumbled. She didn't get it. Why the heck couldn't he see that Hannah Grossman wasn't worth being upset over? The woman clearly hadn't loved him if she'd so easily dropped into bed with his brother. Tate Johnson was an incredible man. There were hundreds of women who'd be thrilled to be in a relationship with him—her included. But she didn't even stand a chance with him because he couldn't see any woman besides Hannah.

Sonya grinned as she added a multitude of alcohols to the glasses, then topped them off with sweet and sour mix, followed by a splash of cranberry. "Sadly, I know how men think. Got myself a houseful of men, and they're all jackasses from time to time. Only way that boy's gonna stop acting stupid is to mend fences with his brother."

"Yeah, good luck with that. The only way that will happen is if Tucker stops seeing Hannah. But we all know *that* won't happen. Those two are crazy about each other."

"Yeah, they are." Sonya set both drinks on the bar, added two straws, then leaned a hip against the counter and eyed Mary Louise across the space. "Tate over there isn't upset things ended with Hannah, he's upset she left him for his brother. Sibling rivalry's a terrible thing. I've watched it happen with my own boys a few times. I saw Tate and Hannah together numerous times in here before all this nastiness with Tucker happened. They were like two friends who hadn't realized that's all they'd ever be. Trust me, Tate didn't love her any more than she loved him. He's just forgotten that fact because his pride's been bruised. Once he and Tucker work things out, he'll realize it."

Mary Louise's frustration ebbed as she stared at the older woman and realized what she needed to do. "Thank you, Sonya. That makes perfect sense."

"Does it?" Sonya laughed. "Aiden thinks I tend to ramble."

Mary Louise smiled as she lifted the drinks from the bar. "Tell your husband he's wrong. And if he doesn't believe you, I'll help you knock some sense into him."

Sonya laughed. "I'll do that, honey. Enjoy your drinks. And good luck trying to make that man see what a sweet little thing you are."

Mary Louise's face heated. Was it obvious to everyone in town but Tate that she was hung up on the man? Apparently it was.

Tate's scowl deepened as Mary Louise drew close and he spotted the drinks in her hands. "Those don't look like beers."

"They're not. They're attitude adjustments." She slid onto the seat across from him. "You could use a big one.

Sadly, this is the only size they make."

He glared at her across the table as she leaned forward and sucked back a sip through her straw. "Very funny."

He took his own sip and coughed. "Dear God, that's awful."

Mary Louise stirred her drink with her straw. "Expand your horizons, Tate Johnson. In fact, expand them in all areas."

"What the heck does that mean?" He obviously didn't think the drink was too awful. He was taking another sip. "I'm running for mayor, aren't I? I'd say that's expanding my horizons."

God, he was dense. "In your career, maybe. But if you don't learn to cool your jets with your brother, you'll never win the election."

He tipped his head and stared at her. "I don't need—"

"Yeah, actually, you do. You need someone to tell it to you like it is because you're not getting it on your own. So here it is. You're mad at your brother. I get that. What he did was a dick move. But being angry isn't going to change anything. It's not going to make him break up with Hannah, and it's not going to make her run back to you. And let's be honest, here, shall we?"

Tate leaned back against the booth and crossed his arms over his chest, clearly not liking her bluntness, but she didn't care. "Sounds like you already are."

"Hannah Grossman obviously didn't love you if she so easily fell into bed with someone else."

"I already know that," he said between clenched teeth. "You don't have to state the obvious."

"Clearly I do, because you're acting like she broke your heart. She didn't break your heart and we both know that. Face it. You wouldn't be this upset if she'd cheated on you with anyone else. You're ticked because she did it with your brother."

"Of course I'm pissed she did it with my brother!" When Mary Louise eased back and looked around the bar, Tate's gaze followed, and he realized several heads were turned their way. Frowning, he leaned toward her and tried to quiet his voice when he said, "If you had any siblings you'd understand why I'm so mad, but you don't, so don't try to act like you know what I'm feeling."

"You're right," she said softly, trying to calm her own frayed temper. "I don't have any siblings. So maybe I don't know what it's like to have a brother or sister betray me, but I can sure as hell tell you that I know what it's like not to have a sibling at all. Or parents, for that matter."

The fight seemed to slide right out of him. Tate's shoulders relaxed and the fire she'd seen flare in his eyes moments before died down. "Sorry. I didn't mean to make you feel bad about your own family."

"Thank you." Mary Louise reached for her drink and took a small sip. She wasn't sure how they'd gotten off on this tangent, but she had a feeling maybe it was for the best. "And I'm not trying to sound ungrateful. I love my aunts and everything they've done for me. It's just... I'd give my left arm for the kind of family you have, Tate, but you're so blinded by your anger you can't see what you're about to throw away. *All over a woman you wouldn't even want back.* Would you take her back right now if you could?"

"No."

"Do you love her?"

He scowled and reached for his drink. "No."

"Did you ever?"

He lifted his drink and sucked through the straw until his drink was gone and all that remained was a slurping sound from the bottom of his glass. "I don't know." He set his drink down. "I thought so. Now I'm not so sure."

"What about your brother? Do you love him?"

"Not at the moment."

Mary Louise tipped her head and pinned him with a look. "Come on, Tate. Just because you're mad at a family member doesn't mean you stop loving them. I can admit that I harbor a lot of harsh feelings toward my dad for being absent from my life, and that I am not always the greatest when he tries to make an effort with me, but deep down I still love him. Even when he hurts me, I love him. Because screwed up or not, he's still family."

He stared at her for several heartbeats, then finally rested his hands on the table and shook his head as he glanced toward the ceiling. "Fine. I love the jerk, okay? I just don't particularly like him very much right now. What he did..." He looked down at his hand. "I never would have done that to him."

That was the crux of what was bothering him. Mary Louise reached across the table and laid her hand over his. Warmth seeped into her skin, but she ignored it and tried to be the friend he needed, not the woman he wasn't interested in. "That's because you're the better man."

He frowned. "You really don't think that. If you thought that, you wouldn't have rushed over and intervened on the sidewalk."

"I intervened because I don't want to see you throw away this election. I think you'll make a wonderful mayor. I think you're smart and funny, when you're not upset with your brother, and that you're just what this town needs in a leader. I also think you're too good for Hannah Grossman."

He blinked at her. "You really think all that?"

Her heart skipped a beat, and she smiled. Maybe she looked like a fool for putting her heart on her sleeve but she didn't care. He needed to know he was more than just the jilted ex-lover. "I really do. I also think Hannah

Grossman is a total fool for ever having let you go."

He looked down at her hand over his but he didn't pull away. "A fool, huh?"

"A total fool. Huge. Gigantic. "

One corner of his lips turned up. "I could go with that."

She smiled, because this was the Tate she remembered. The confident, easy-going one, not the angry man he'd been of late. "Do you think you could maybe go with, I don't know, forgiving them? If not Hannah, then at least your brother."

His smile faded, and he looked up at her again. "That's asking a lot."

"Maybe. But remember you are the better man. Just think about it, okay? I have a feeling if you can get past this thing with Tucker, you'll feel a whole lot better. And then...watch out, Storm. The new Mayor Johnson will be in town."

His eyes skipped over her features, and as he looked at her, her stomach tightened. Because she had the oddest sense he was seeing her for the first time.

"I'll think about it."

Mary Louise supposed that was a beginning. She started to pull her hand away from his, but Tate flipped his palm up and captured hers before she could get away.

"On one condition," he said, lifting two fingers on his other hand and catching Sonya's attention at the bar. Sonya nodded, and he looked back at Mary Louise. "You have to have another attitude adjustment with me."

Mary Louise smiled and relaxed her hand against his, loving the way his fingers wrapped around hers, trying not to read too much into the gesture, hoping—for the first time in forever—that maybe there was something there. "I could probably do that."

"Good." Tate frowned but didn't show any sign of

wanting to let go of her. And she liked that. Boy, did she like that. "Because I have a feeling I may need two or three more of those awful drinks for liquid courage. You know, if I'm really going to consider forgiving that jackass."

Chapter Four

Tate wasn't sure how he'd been talked into this.

Now that the buzz from his two drinks had worn off, he suspected he could blame the alcohol. One glance across the front seat of his car though, told him he was wrong. He was on his way to talk to his good-for-nothing brother all because one very pretty strawberry blonde had looked at him as if she saw something in him no one else did.

He forced his gaze back to the road. Forced his hands to stay curled around the wheel so he wouldn't reach for Mary Louise again. He'd liked touching her in the bar. He'd liked holding her hand. He'd liked it a hell of a lot more than he'd thought he would and he wanted to do it all again. He'd always thought Mary Louise was pretty, he just hadn't realized they had a lot more in common than he'd known. Or that underneath all that sweetness she was a take-charge kind of woman.

He *really* liked that about her. Hannah had never looked at him the way Mary Louise had. She'd never told him he was being an idiot or tried to talk any kind of sense into him. In fact, thinking back, Hannah hadn't ever taken any kind of initiative in their relationship. He'd been the one to do all the courting. He'd been the one to always check in on her, not the other way around. He'd been the one pushing for more in their relationship, right from the start, and she'd just sat back and let it happen.

He rested his elbow on the open window and brushed his fingers over his mouth as he thought back to Mary Louise's questions in the bar. Had he ever really loved Hannah? He'd thought they made the perfect couple. On paper she was everything he'd always wanted. But he couldn't deny that he'd felt more of a spark sitting with Mary Louise for an hour at Murphy's than he'd felt with Hannah in all the time they'd been together. He glanced her way and couldn't help but feel an increase in his pulse as he took in the soft curve of her jaw and the gentle slope of her nose. If he'd had someone like Mary Louise by his side these last few years, how different would his life be now?

"Um, Tate?" Mary Louise braced a hand on the door at her side. "You're drifting."

"Huh?"

"The road. You're drifting!"

Tate glanced back at the road and quickly corrected the wheel to keep from driving onto the gravel shoulder. "Sorry."

Mary Louise breathed easier and pressed her hand against her chest. "It's okay. You're nervous. I get that."

He was nervous. But not about talking to his brother. He was nervous about *her*. He hadn't expected her to say yes when he'd asked her to go out to the ranch with him so he could talk to Tucker, but he really liked that she was here now. Everything just seemed easier with her. More relaxed. And he was almost afraid of fixing things with his brother because he didn't want to give her any reason to leave.

He turned down the lane to his parents' place and

pulled to a stop behind Tucker's truck. This time of day, Tucker was probably in the barn. Tate glanced past Mary Louise toward the massive structure and frowned.

"Hey." Mary Louise's hand covered his on his knee. "You got this. Just remember what we talked about. She's the fool, not you. And you're the much better man."

He looked down at her and felt a tug toward her, followed by an overwhelming urge to kiss her. Right here. Right in front of his parents' place. Right where anyone could see.

His gaze drifted to her lush, pink lips. He *really* wanted to kiss her but he wasn't sure if he should. Would he look like an ass if he did? A couple hours ago he'd been ranting and raging about his ex with his brother. Would Mary Louise think he was mental if he so quickly changed his mind about what he wanted?

"Will you come with me?" The words left his mouth before he could stop them.

Mary Louise smiled and squeezed his hand. "I think this part you should probably do on your own."

He nodded and looked down at her hand covering his. Man, she had great hands. Long fingers, delicate nails. He really liked the look of her hands. They weren't callused or rough from working outdoors or with animals. They were soft and perfect.

"Tell you what," she said softly. "I'll be right here when you get done. And after, if you're up for it, I'll cook you dinner back at my place. If, that is, you don't already have plans."

His gaze lifted to hers. Was she asking him out? His heart picked up speed as he studied her. The nervous look in her eyes told him yes.

"Okay," he said slowly, savoring that knowledge. "Don't steal my car while I'm gone."

Mary Louise smiled as he popped his door and

climbed out. "I will try not to, Mr. Johnson."

Tate was actually smiling as he crossed toward the barn, about to meet with his brother. He never in a million years would have predicted *that*. But his smile faded as soon as he stepped into the barn and heard the unmistakable sounds of kissing.

A familiar burn cut across his chest, and his first reaction was to retreat, but before he could make it back to the door he remembered what Mary Louise had said to him at the pub. That he wouldn't be nearly as upset if Hannah had cheated on him with another guy. Mary Louise had been right of course. Now that he could look at his relationship with Hannah objectively, he knew she hadn't been right for him and he hadn't been right for her. Neither of them had been able to admit it, though. So instead of breaking up months ago as they should have done, their relationship had deteriorated to this.

He frowned as he moved back into the barn, toward the sound of kissing instead of away from it, as he wanted. Mary Louise was right about something else. His anger had little to do with Hannah and everything to do with his brother. But for the sake of the family, he could be the better man, couldn't he? He sure the hell hoped so since he was about to come face to face with two people he'd rather not see.

He rounded a corner toward the stalls, and just as he expected, the two lip-locked in front of the horses were Tucker and Hannah. His gut tightened, and his feet itched to turn and run, but he stopped where he was and slid his hands in the pockets of his slacks instead.

Neither heard him. And though he definitely wasn't happy with the scene in front of him, it didn't hurt him. At least not in the way it should if he really had loved Hannah.

He cleared his throat, anxious just to get this over

with. Hannah's eyes opened, and when she spotted him over Tucker's shoulder she lurched back and gasped. "Tate."

Tucker whipped around and immediately stepped in front of Hannah.

"Relax," Tate said, inwardly cringing because, geez, had he really been that bad that his brother thought he had to protect Hannah from him? "I'm not here to cause any trouble. I just want to talk."

"Okay," Tucker said warily. "About what?"

Tate rolled his eyes. Hannah must have nudged Tucker or pinched him because he whispered, "Sorry. I don't know what to say."

"Well, I do," Tate said. "I've been a little bit of a bear—"

"A little?" Tucker asked.

When Tate frowned, Tucker said, "Sorry. Go on."

"I probably didn't...handle things as well as I could have," Tate went on. "The two of you together is..." He waved a hand, trying to find the right word, coming up absolutely blank. "Well, it's not anything I ever expected."

"Listen, Tate." Tucker stepped forward. "I know we didn't go about this the right way—"

Tate held up a hand. "Let me finish." He wasn't really in the mood for excuses. Wasn't sure he was ready to hear them. He just needed to say what he'd come to say so he could leave. He looked at Hannah. "I'm not so upset about us. The more I've thought about it, the more I've realized we didn't make a whole lot of sense." He glanced at his brother. "I've mostly been upset because you're the last person I expected to go behind my back."

"I know." Tucker's face fell. "Shit, I know and I'm sorry. If I could change what happened, I—"

"No." Tate waved a hand again. "I don't want to hear any excuses. That's not why I came here. I just came to tell you I realize I've been an ass lately and that you two don't have to worry about me anymore. Someone made me see things in a different way, and I'm...bowing out gracefully and admitting defeat. If I run into either or both of you in town, I won't make a scene."

Neither said anything. They just stared at him as if he'd grown a third eyeball. And even though he felt like an idiot, Tate figured that was probably for the best. He'd said what he'd come to say. He'd been the bigger man. Now it was time to go.

He rounded the corner and turned for the barn doors. Stepping into the early evening light, he drew a deep breath and knew he'd done the right thing. Only he didn't feel a whole lot better.

But the moment he spotted Mary Louise leaning against the hood of his car, studying her phone, that pressure in his chest eased. He took two steps toward her before he heard shuffling at his back, followed by his brother's voice.

"Tate, wait."

Drawing a breath for patience, he turned to face Tucker. Thankfully, Hannah wasn't with him. "What?"

Unease passed over Tucker's face as he stepped into the light and slipped his hands into the pockets of his worn jeans. "I know you don't want to hear apologies or excuses so I'm just gonna say...I love you. You're my brother, and I love you, and I know it doesn't change anything but somehow I'll find a way to make it up to you."

Shit. He just had. Something light replaced all the anger inside Tate that had been weighing him down. Something he didn't know how to define and wasn't even sure he *could* define. He frowned because...yeah, he wasn't ready to do much more just yet. "I love you, too. I just don't really like you very much right now."

Tucker grinned, looking more like the annoying kid brother he'd been Tate's whole life than the man he'd grown into. "I can live with that."

So could Tate. If nothing else, it was a start. He glanced toward the barn where Hannah was standing just inside the shadows. He wanted to tell Tucker to be better to her than he'd been, but he wasn't there yet either. The most he could do was nod her way. She answered with a sad smile and a wave, and as Tucker turned and headed back to her, Tate took a deep breath that felt a helluva lot like...freedom.

Mary Louise was waiting at the car with a warm smile on her pretty face when he reached her. She'd been watching him with Tucker. He could see it in her eyes. He wasn't sure where her phone had gone, but he didn't care. In the fading light of dusk, on the farm where he'd grown up, she looked absolutely perfect.

"Are you okay?" she asked as he drew close.

"Yeah," he answered, meaning it. "I'm good."

"Really?" She lifted her brows and looked up at him.

He nodded. "And I have you to thank for it."

"I didn't really do anything."

"Yeah, you did. You talked some sense into me. Pretty sure my old man would say you're the only person who's ever been able to do that."

A wide grin spread across her face. "Well. Yay, me, huh?"

He felt himself smiling for the first time in weeks. "Yay, you." He moved closer, until they were only a breath apart. "I want to kiss you, Mary Louise Prager. Would that be too forward of me or would it be okay?"

Her smile wobbled, and her chest rose and fell with her increased breaths. "No. I mean, yes. I mean...I would love for you to kiss me."

Those breathless words touched his heart in a way

nothing had for a really long time. Lifting his hands to cradle her face, he leaned down and brushed his lips against hers. And the moment he did, he felt something inside him finally come to life.

They were both breathless when he drew back. Her eyes sparkled as she looked up at him, and the way she licked her lips and glanced back at his mouth made him want to kiss her all over again. But this time he wanted to do it where no one else could see. "Are you still up for feeding me?"

A wide, gorgeous smile spread across her face. "I am. How do steaks sound?"

He opened the car door for her and helped her in. "Steaks sound great."

He closed her door, moved around the car and climbed into the driver's seat. Just as he was about to start the ignition, Mary Louise put a hand on his arm. "Just one question, though."

He looked at her. "Yeah?"

"Assuming you like my, uh, cooking..." She bit her lip, looking nervous and gorgeous and perfect. "I was just wondering...how do you like your eggs in the morning?"

Heat rushed through his body, electrifying him in ways he hadn't felt in way too long. From any other woman that would have sounded dirty and presumptuous. From her, it sounded absolutely right. Letting go of the ignition, he slid a hand in her hair, unable to keep from touching her. "I think after everything you've done for me today, I'm the one who owes you breakfast. Hopefully in bed."

Her eyes went all soft and dreamy the way he'd always wanted a woman to look at him. "I am not about to turn down that offer, Mr. Almost Mayor."

Neither would he. He pulled her to him and kissed her again. And this time he didn't care who saw.

* * * *

"So, then," Delia said, smiling at Logan in a familiar way that tightened his stomach before glancing back at Marcus and Brittany seated across the table from them. "My father comes barreling into my bedroom, sure he heard a male voice. I shrieked and jumped off my bed, doing my best to sound shocked and appalled that he didn't trust me and tried to push him out the door. Meanwhile, Logan here's pinned under my bed in nothing but his boxers, trying not to make a sound because he knows if my father sees him, he's dead."

Marcus chuckled. Brittany rolled her eyes and tried not to smile as she sipped her wine. All Logan could do was shake his head and say, "Teenage hormones. I've got no excuse but that."

Laughing, Delia leaned against him in the booth at the Italian restaurant Brittany had picked and patted his knee under the table. "I'm sure I was to blame for that. As I recall, you were nervous about my parents being home and wanted to leave long before my father rushed in. I'm the one who convinced you to stay."

A memory of that night, when Delia had tempted him to stay with her fingers and lips, flashed in his mind. But it didn't bring the rush of heat he'd thought it would. "So you're the bad influence," he said, trying not to read too much into that fact.

"I'm always the bad influence, don't you know that?" Delia sat up and reached for her wine. "Part of the reason I left."

"So are you back to stay?" Britanny asked.

"Yep." Delia set her wine down. "Newly divorced and back home with the folks again. It's like a bad country song."

"I don't know too many country songs that include a teacher-student romance," Marcus muttered, lifting his wine to his lips.

Brittany must have kicked him under the table because he flinched, looked her way, and said, "Ow, that hurt."

Brittany's eyes widened and she angled her head toward Delia.

Frowning, Marcus looked across the table at Delia and said, "Sorry. I didn't realize I said that out loud."

"It's okay." An amused expression crossed Delia's face, and she waved a hand. "I've heard it all, believe me."

Delia seemed happy enough, but Logan couldn't tell if it was an act, and part of him wasn't sure if he wanted to ask if she was really okay. She'd obviously been through something big to walk out on her husband and come back to Storm. And while he was happy to see her again and was having a good time tonight, he didn't particularly want to hear all about her sob story. At least not when he was still trying to get past his own.

"What about work?" Brittany asked. "Have you started looking for something yet?"

"Yeah, I actually put in an application at Pushing Up Daisies, but they're only looking for something part time. I'd like to get something with more hours so I can get a place of my own sooner rather than later. I love my parents but..." She rolled her eyes. "You know how parents can be."

"Unfortunately, I do," Marcus muttered.

"I did notice Murphy's is way understaffed." She glanced toward Logan. "I left a message with your dad about it. I've done a ton of waitressing. Wouldn't that be fun? You and me working there together?"

Logan's stomach tightened, and he pictured what she was describing. But she wasn't the girl he'd always envisioned working the bar with him. The one he'd thought would be there with him was pregnant with someone else's kid.

His mood went south, just that fast, and he heard himself say, "Sure," as he reached for his wine. But he didn't mean it. And he knew from the pitying look Marcus sent him across the table that his friend sensed it too.

Delia launched into a story about her last job waiting tables at a bar in Dallas, and relieved they were on to another topic, Logan refilled his wine glass from the bottle in the middle of the table, ignoring the pointed looks Marcus kept sending him. He was doing what his friend had told him to do, right? Moving on? So what if he was drinking a little more than normal. People drank when they went out and had fun, didn't they?

He laughed at something Delia said, laid his arm over the back of her chair, and for the rest of the evening acted like he was having the time of his life. Because that's what people did when they moved on. It's what Marcus and his folks and everyone had told him to do after Ginny had wrecked him. So in an attempt to push Ginny out of his head and heart forever, he forced himself to do exactly that.

And it worked. Delia smiled and flirted with him. Brittany laughed at his jokes. Even Marcus eased up and seemed to enjoy himself. Everyone had a great time. Everyone but Logan.

He hated every single minute of it.

Chapter Five

Ginny hadn't planned to end up at the cemetery when she'd gone for a walk in the waning light of early evening, but she wasn't surprised when she found herself standing outside the iron fence, staring through the rails toward the headstones beyond.

Sometimes, as a teenager, when she'd been struggling with something heavy, she'd wound up here. Her parents were both buried in this cemetery, and just sitting beside their graves had calmed her when she'd been fighting with Marisol or worrying about boys, or even when she'd been arguing with Jacob.

She moved through the gate and into the cemetery, following a familiar path, but instead of veering to the right where her parents were buried, she found herself heading left, stopping when she came to Jacob's polished headstone.

It wasn't a flat marker like others around it. It was an upright arched gravestone on a concrete base, roughly three feet high and two feet wide, with the years of his birth and death etched into the granite stone beneath the words:

In Our Hearts Forever
Jacob Andrew Salt
Beloved son and brother

Ginny's chest tightened, and tears stung her eyes as she sank onto the new grass in front of the headstone. Swiping at the tears on her cheeks, she stared at Jacob's name and fought back a hysterical laugh.

"Oh, man," she said aloud. "I can only imagine what you'd say if you were here right now." Through her watery vision, she glanced up at the sky. "I really hope you're getting a laugh out of everything up there, because someone should be enjoying themselves right now."

Sighing, she looked back at the marker, feeling like an idiot, feeling a little better just by being here and talking to him. "I know you probably won't believe this, but I was trying to do the right thing after you...after you left."

She placed a hand on her belly. "I didn't lie to protect myself. I lied because..." Even now the words felt pathetic, but she forced them out. "Because your mom overheard I was pregnant and she just assumed you and I, that we..."

A lump formed in her throat, and she swallowed hard. "And the thing is, I wanted that. I was in love with you for a very long time, Jacob Salt. The night you and I spent together, it was like...perfect. If it had been up to me, there would have been a lot of other perfect nights between us. I only started seeing the senator because I was depressed that you and I, that we weren't...that you weren't interested in me like that. The first time with him, I was feeling self-destructive because I couldn't have you. It's not an excuse but it's the truth. After that..." She shrugged. "After that, it was nice to feel wanted, you know?"

She swiped at the stupid tears again. "But I knew it

was wrong. And I'd already broken it off with him the night you found me upset. I wanted to tell you about it but I felt wretched. And I was still so in love with you. I was afraid you'd be disgusted by what I'd done. And then you kissed me, and it was like none of it mattered. Everything was right for one perfect night."

She drew in a shuddering breath. "The whole way home from college, the night I was driving, just before the accident, all I wanted to do was tell you I loved you and beg you to give me a chance. And then that deer stepped into the road and everything changed in an instant."

The tears flowed faster down her cheeks, and she swiped at them again, forcing herself to go on, needing to purge the words once and for all. "I shouldn't have lied to everyone in the hospital. I know that. But I was devastated after they told me you were gone. I wanted to die too. And then when I found out I was pregnant, it was like...like a tiny miracle in the middle of Hell. I didn't even think. I just said the words."

She rubbed her belly again and choked back a sob. "This baby is yours, Jacob. It has to be yours. I have to believe it's yours because the alternative is just...it's too awful to comprehend. I love you. You were my best friend. You are still my best friend, and I would give anything to have you back right now, even yelling at me and telling me what an idiot I am."

Emotions overwhelmed her, and she dropped her face into her hands and cried. She cried over her lost youth, over her mistakes, over losing her closest friend. But mostly she cried because she knew she had to stop hiding behind excuses. She had to stand up for herself so she could stand up for her child—whoever its father might be. And she had to let go of Jacob, once and for all, so she could have a shot at happiness and some kind of future, even if that future wasn't at all what she'd planned.

Sniffling, she swiped at her nose and eyes and stared at Jacob's headstone again. "You must think I'm totally pathetic." She drew in a deep breath and slowly let it out, until she knew the sobfest was over. "I think I'm pathetic. Though...did you see me talk to your mom yesterday in the flower shop? I don't know what got into me."

She sighed again, feeling steadier, knowing Jacob would have gotten a kick out of that scene with his mother. A wry smile tugged at her lips. He would have told her "Good job. Way to finally stand up for yourself." And he would have meant it.

"I'll make things up to your mom," she said softly. "I don't know how, but I will. And I'm trying to make things right with Marisol. But the one person who won't give me a chance is Logan."

She felt a little strange talking to Jacob about Logan, especially now when she was pregnant, but she pushed the feeling aside and reminded herself she'd talked to Jacob about a lot of guys, and that Jacob had always been right there for her when she'd needed advice.

"I love him," she whispered. "I love him in a way that is very different from the way I loved you, and I don't know why. I just know...he came into my life at the moment I needed someone, and I can't help but think that you sent him. I know that sounds silly but you always knew what I needed. You were always the one person who could tell me the truth and make me listen. And I felt good about dating him because I knew you'd have told me to go for it. But now..."

Her heart pinched as she thought of Logan. "I miss him. And I don't know what to do to fix things with him. I never should have lied to him. He's the one person I should have trusted, but I'm scared he's never going to give me another chance."

A wave of emotions washed over her—pain, regret,

heartache, and sadness—and though it didn't leave, it did ease enough so she could look up at Jacob's headstone and frown. "You could say something encouraging, you know. I'd be up for anything right now. Even just a sign that says I'm not a total loser and that everything's going to be okay. It would help a lot if I knew you were on my side and that you believe I'm going to make it without you." She placed a hand on her belly. "That *we're* going to make it. Because, honestly"—she shook her head—"sometimes I'm just not sure anymore."

The wind whistled through the trees around her. A bird cried somewhere in the sky. But otherwise there was no sound. No answer. Nothing but her sitting silently in front of the gravestone of the boy she'd loved and lost.

Her heart sank, and she closed her eyes. And just when she was ready to get up and leave, Little Bit kicked hard, right at her belly button.

Blinking damp lashes, she glanced down and watched her shirt move as the baby kicked out again.

Her gaze shot up to Jacob's gravestone, and something light and hopeful filled her chest. Something that hadn't been there moments before.

Her eyes filled with tears again, this time not from sadness, but from joy, and she couldn't stop the smile pulling at the corners of her lips. "I hear you," she whispered. "I hear you loud and clear, Jacob."

Her legs ached as she pushed to her feet and headed back toward the gates of the cemetery. Dusk was fading to early evening, and the streetlights were just flickering on as she stepped onto the sidewalk and headed home. Some people might say Little Bit kicking at that moment was a coincidence, but she knew it wasn't. No matter what the paternity test said, she believed this baby was Jacob's. It was Jacob's baby, and through it he was telling her that everything was going to work out all right. It might not work out the way she wanted. It might not be the perfect happily ever after she'd always dreamed of. But it would all be okay in the end. She'd survive. She and her baby would thrive.

She headed back into downtown Storm and was just about to turn toward home when the door of the new Italian restaurant off Main opened at the end of the sidewalk and Brittany and Marcus stepped out in front of Logan and...

Delia.

Tall, slim, gorgeous Delia Bruce Phelps. Logan's ex-girlfriend. Who, with her arm wrapped around Logan's as they moved onto the sidewalk, was laughing and smiling up at Logan as if he were the center of her universe.

As if he weren't an ex any longer.

* * * *

Brittany drew to a stop when she spotted Ginny standing still at the end of the block, staring at the four of them with wide eyes.

Wide, heartbroken eyes.

Something in her chest tightened, just as it had the other night when Marcus had driven her home and they'd talked about Ginny. At her side, Marcus squeezed her hand, and behind her, Delia's laughter died down, and she sensed Logan and Delia draw to a stop. Ginny's gaze shot from Brittany to Logan then back to Brittany, then in a rush she turned back around and disappeared around the corner, heading away from her house instead of toward it.

That pressure in Brittany's chest increased because she knew what betrayal looked like. And even though she knew she had nothing to feel guilty about, she did. Her heart sank.

"Was that Ginny Moreno?" Delia asked. "I saw her

the other day at the florist shop but didn't realize it was her. I heard about her little scandal all the way in Dallas. Now there's someone who's a worse influence than I am."

Brittany ignored Delia's comment and turned toward Marcus, an urgency she didn't quite understand but needed to listen to pushing at her. "I'm sorry to do this, but do you mind if I cut our date short?"

"I don't mind at all." Marcus smiled down at her and squeezed her hand again. "Do you want me to go with you?"

She rose on her toes and kissed his cheek. "I think I need to do this on my own. Thank you for understanding."

"Call me after."

She smiled at him once more, then turned toward Delia and Logan. Delia looked confused. Logan looked...conflicted.

"Sorry, guys. I gotta go. Dinner was fun." Brittany glanced toward Logan and caught the uneasy look in his eyes, but she didn't care what he thought. This wasn't about him and Ginny. It was about her and Ginny. It was about that broken look she'd seen in her friend's eyes just before she'd turned away. A look she knew well because she'd seen it in her mother's eyes for years.

With one last smile at Marcus, she let go of his hand and moved away from the group, following Ginny around the corner. She didn't know where Ginny was heading, but she had a hunch, and considering how slow Ginny was these days, Brittany figured she should be able to catch up with her before she got too far ahead.

The lights were on when she reached the park. It wasn't dark yet, but it would be soon. She scanned the playground but didn't see Ginny. Her heart sped up as she narrowed her gaze and looked across the grass and through the oak trees. And when she spotted Ginny sitting at the base of one, leaning against the large trunk, her feet moved forward all on their own.

Ginny didn't hear her as she approached, and Brittany wasn't sure how she felt about that. She wasn't sure about anything at the moment—not what she wanted to say or why she was here—she only knew it was time. Time to stop ignoring each other and talk.

"Hey," she said when she drew close.

Startled, Ginny looked up and blinked damp lashes in the fading light. "Brittany. What...?" Her gaze skipped past Brittany, searching for the rest of the group she'd seen, Brittany realized.

"I'm alone." Brittany glanced down at the grass. "Mind if I sit?"

"Um. I guess."

Brittany sank to the grass and folded her legs in front of her. As Ginny watched her with confusion and unease, Brittany's nerves kicked in. Now that she was here, she wasn't sure what to say. Biting her lip, she glanced up at the oak above them. "Remember all the times we sat in this park under these trees?"

"Yeah."

Silence hung between them. Brittany cleared her throat. "Speaking of trees, did you hear that Lacey wants to put a bench under the Storm Oak? She's starting a fundraising campaign to have one built in his honor."

"I know. That's really great of her."

Yeah, it really was. Especially considering how off-kilter Lacey had been acting the last few months. Brittany knew a lot of that acting out had been a result of losing her brother. But Lacey was really pulling it together. Even Jeffry had told Brittany how impressed he was by Lacey's maturity lately. People reacted to tragedy in very different ways. As Brittany looked back at her friend, she knew that wasn't an excuse for any of the things Ginny had done—

especially regarding her affair with Brittany's father—but the lies after Jacob's death...could Brittany really blame her for those?

"Are you okay?" Brittany asked.

"Me? Yeah, I'm fine." Ginny swiped at her cheeks and tried to put on a tough-girl face, but Brittany knew her too well to buy it.

"I'm not," Brittany said with a sigh, figuring honesty was the only way to go at this point.

Ginny turned concerned eyes her way. "I heard about your parents. I'm sorry. I hope..." She swallowed hard. "I hope that wasn't about me."

"It wasn't."

Ginny nodded and looked down at her hands, and the awkward silence settled between them once more. One Brittany didn't know how to bridge. She thought about getting up, about leaving, but she hadn't come here just to walk away. She pulled up her courage and decided if there was ever a time to lay it all on the line, now was that time.

"So I don't think I'm ever going to be able to understand or forget what you did with...my dad." She closed her eyes because just saying the words brought up images she didn't want to see. "I mean, my dad. Ew. I get that some women think he's attractive but...he's my dad."

"I know," Ginny said in a quiet voice laced with guilt. "And I don't have any kind of explanation except that I was vulnerable and stupid and not thinking."

"Yeah." Brittany's eyes shot open with a mixture of disgust and anger she couldn't hold back. "You were." But just as quickly as the anger hit, she looked at Ginny and realized being vindictive wasn't going to change anything. All it would do was make them both continue to feel awful.

Brittany sighed. "But I also know that it takes two to do...what you did, and I know my father isn't innocent.

I've seen him with girls our age before. I know how he is. If you were feeling vulnerable like you said, he would have used that to his advantage."

Ginny blinked several times and looked back down at her hands. And even though it was none of Brittany's business, she couldn't stop herself from asking, "What were you feeling vulnerable about? Was it Jacob?"

Ginny released a sound that was half groan, half laugh and closed her eyes as she ran a hand through her hair. "About the fact I'd been in love with him forever and he had no idea? Yeah, you could say that." She sighed. "I know it doesn't mean much now, but if I could go back and change what I did, I would. It was the biggest regret of my life, and not just because of what people think of me now but because of the way I hurt you." She looked up at Brittany, and tears shimmered in her eyes when she said, "I'm so sorry I hurt you."

Brittany's heart contracted, and she wanted to reach out and hug her friend, but she wasn't sure if she could. Or even if she should. "I know."

Blinking quickly, Ginny looked back down at her hands.

Long seconds passed in silence, and Brittany knew it was still none of her business, but she had to ask. "Did you and Jacob really sleep together?"

Ginny lifted a shaky hand and swiped at her cheeks with a nod. "After the Turbo Fruit concert. It just happened the one time, and after, I was afraid he wasn't in love with me the way I was in love with him, but...that one night was perfect. He made me feel special. Like all the stuff I'd done wrong didn't matter. That the only thing that mattered was...us."

Brittany studied Ginny, and in the dim light, she saw truth in Ginny's expression. The rest of her anger slowly seeped out of her.

"What are you going to do if this baby isn't Jacob's?" Brittany asked softly.

Ginny drew a deep breath and let it out slowly. "I don't know."

"Now that my parents have split, my dad won't have much to lose by admitting to the affair. If he can use your baby politically, he will."

Ginny drew another deep breath and lifted her gaze to Brittany's. "I know," she said softly.

"What will you do if he does that? What if he tries to get custody?"

Ginny placed a protective hand on her belly. "Then I'll fight him."

The resolve Brittany heard in Ginny's voice echoed around her. "And that doesn't scare you?"

"It scares the hell out of me. But there's nothing I can do about it right now." She smoothed a hand down her round belly. "All I can do is continue to pray that this baby is Jacob's."

"So will I."

Ginny held Brittany's gaze for several seconds, and emotions swirled in her eyes—regret, heartache, but mostly sadness. A sadness Brittany felt all the way in her own heart.

When Ginny looked down at her belly, that pressure in Brittany's chest intensified all over again. "Look, Ginny," she said, "I don't think I'll ever understand why things happened the way they did but I do know that you're not the only one who made mistakes. I made mistakes, too."

"What kind of mistakes?" Ginny's head came up. "You didn't do anything wrong."

"Yes, I did." Brittany sighed. "I knew you were in a funk last spring. I knew you were upset about your relationship with Jacob, and I told myself that it wasn't my business and that I shouldn't get involved. But maybe if I'd been there for you things wouldn't have gotten so crazy. Maybe if I'd been the friend you needed then, you wouldn't have turned to someone else."

Ginny faced Brittany. "My mistakes are not yours, Brit. And I won't have you feeling responsible for them. None of what happened was your fault."

Brittany frowned. "What's happened between us since then is, though. Instead of looking at things from your perspective, I've been wallowing in my own anger."

"You have every right to be mad at me."

"Yeah, but I heaped the blame solely on you, and I shouldn't have. My dad's just as much to blame. More so because he should know better. Plus, it was easy to stay mad at you because I made it about me. But I know what happened between the two of you had nothing to do with me. And I just want you to know..."

She drew a breath. Did she want to say the words?

Yes. Yes, she did. Because they were the truth.

Brittany exhaled. "I'm here for you. No matter what happens. I'm here for you because if the roles were reversed, I know you'd be here for me."

Tears filled Ginny's eyes. "You don't have to say that to me."

"Yes, I do. Because regardless of everything, you're my best friend. And the truth is..." Her heart contracted, and tears filled her own eyes. "I was jealous of Jacob. I was jealous of your friendship with him because it was different from ours. And when you were upset because the two of you weren't a couple, I didn't get involved because I didn't want you with him like that. I thought you wouldn't need me anymore. When you started acting strange last spring, I knew you were seeing someone. I knew whoever it was wasn't good for you, but I didn't try to stop you because I figured anyone was better than

Jacob. Not for you, but for me."

Ginny tried to blink back the tears but they slipped past her lashes. "Even if something had developed between me and Jacob, you and I would have still been close."

"I know that now. But then..." Brittany shook her head. "I was stupid. Can you ever forgive me?"

"I'm the one who needs forgiving, not you."

Tears filled Brittany's own eyes. "How about we both just admit we made mistakes and move on?"

The corners of Ginny's lips tipped up as she stared at Brittany. "I think I can do that."

"Me, too." They stared at each other for several seconds, then Brittany said, "Would it be too awkward if I gave you a hug?"

Ginny's smile widened, and her eyes sparkled through the tears. "Not at all. And I would love that."

Brittany moved onto her knees and wrapped her arms around Ginny. The two friends held each other in the fading light for several moments, and even though things between them would never truly be the same, Brittany knew this was the start of something new. And that the road to reconciliation was paved now with good intentions.

Brittany finally released Ginny and sank back on her heels. Swiping at her cheeks, she pushed to her feet and held out her hand. "Come on. It's getting dark and I'm sure Marisol will start to wonder where you are before long. I'll walk you home."

Ginny slid her hand in Brittany's and let Brittany pull her to her feet. Her growing belly made it awkward, but she finally made it.

"How are you feeling?" Brittany asked as they moved out of the park and onto the illuminated sidewalk. "With the pregnancy, I mean."

"Good." Ginny rested a hand on her stomach. "Ready to be done, though."

"I bet."

They passed the Italian restaurant, and Brittany couldn't help but notice the way Ginny stiffened. There was something else they needed to talk about, Brittany realized.

"It wasn't a date," she said, glancing sideways at Ginny. "Logan and Delia. It was just dinner. She knew both Logan and Marcus back in school."

"Oh. Well. She's very pretty. They dated back in high school, didn't they?"

Ginny was saying all the right things, but Brittany knew her friend too well. "Yes, but I don't think he's interested anymore."

Hope shone in Ginny's eyes when she looked Brittany's way. "How do you know?"

"I could just tell. He looked like he was having a good time but I got the feeling he was acting. I saw what he was really feeling when I told him and Marcus I was leaving to come after you."

Ginny tensed. "And what did you see then?"

"Hurt. Confusion. Anger."

Ginny's gaze darted down to the sidewalk and her shoulders fell.

"He's still angry with you because he cares," Brittany said. "You know that, right? The fact he still feels that way is a good thing in the long run. It means there's hope."

"Hope for what?"

"That you two can work things out."

Ginny's eyes fell closed. "I want to believe that, but..."

Brittany reached for Ginny's hand, drawing her friend to a stop. When Ginny turned and looked at her, Brittany said, "Believe it. I came around. If I can do it, so can he."

Ginny stared at her, but instead of hope, Brittany saw doubt in her friend's eyes. A doubt she hoped wouldn't prevent Ginny from taking a second chance on happiness if and when it ever came back around.

Chapter Six

Logan's chest ached with a mixture of disgust and guilt he didn't like.

The look of betrayal he'd seen in Ginny's eyes when she'd stood at the end of the sidewalk, watching him and Delia walk out of the restaurant replayed in his mind, making him feel even worse. He had nothing to feel guilty about, dammit. He wasn't the one who'd lied to the entire town. He wasn't the one who'd had an affair. He wasn't the one who'd stabbed daggers through multiple hearts—his included.

He had every right to go out to dinner with a pretty girl. With an old *friend*. He and Ginny hadn't been married. They hadn't been engaged. Hell, they hadn't even slept together. He'd been a fool to think she was so innocent and sweet when in reality she'd been nothing but a slut.

He winced at that thought. No, that was too harsh. If she really were a slut, she would have tried to sleep with him when they were dating and she hadn't. She'd been the one who'd wanted to take things slow. Yeah, she'd been stupid and foolish and had made really bad decisions, but that didn't make her a slut. It made her...

Human, he realized, not liking the way that realization felt in his gut.

"So," Delia said, slowing her steps at his side where

she was still clinging to his arm. "This is me." She stopped in front of her parents' white scalloped yard fence and turned to look up at him. "Are you sure you don't want to go somewhere and get a drink? It's still early."

"No, I need to head home. I have to work in the morning."

Delia's eyes darkened, and she inched closer. "My parents are already asleep, you know." She trailed her fingers down the sleeve of his shirt and across his bare forearm. "You could come in if you want. Stay the night. I promise to be quiet so they don't know you're there and to wake you when you need to get up for work."

Logan looked down at her in the shadows in front of her parents' house and tried to feel something—anything for her. God knew, if he could put Ginny Moreno out of his heart and fall for someone else, his life would sure as hell be a lot easier. He'd thought he'd loved Delia once, but that feeling had faded so fast, he'd realized long ago it hadn't been love. It'd been the lust of a teenage boy and not much more. He tried to pull up that lust now, hoping if he could feel even that, it'd be a good sign. But he couldn't. All he felt for Delia was the warm rush of shared memories and nothing else.

He drew a half step away, letting her know he wasn't interested. "I don't think I'll be ready for that anytime soon." When her face fell with the bite of rejection, he added, "I just got out of a relationship."

"With the pregnant girl?" When his eyes widened at her brashness, she said, "I heard the rumors. I just didn't believe them until right now. How could you of all people have gotten involved with someone who lied and cheated the way she did?"

The hair on Logan's nape tingled, and he glared down at her. "Careful, Delia. It wasn't that long ago you were the girl at the center of Storm's rumor mill, lying to everyone about your indiscretions. If anyone should feel sympathetic to what Ginny's going through, it's you."

Delia's mouth snapped closed, and she glanced down at his shirt. "You're right," she said quietly. "That was bitchy of me."

Now he felt like a douche for calling her out on it. That guilt swirled inside Logan.

Delia lifted her gaze to his and studied him for several seconds. "So you and Ginny. Are you still in love with her?"

"No," he huffed.

"You denied that awfully quick there, Logan Murphy. Sounds to me like there's still something between the two of you."

"Well, there's not." He crossed his arms over his chest, but even to his own ears, that declaration sounded lame.

He wasn't still in love with Ginny. He was trying his best to get over her and move on with his life. It wasn't his fault this was a small town and he kept running into her every damn place he went.

"If there's one thing I know a lot about," Delia said softly, interrupting his thoughts, "it's regret. I made my fair share of mistakes here and in Dallas, but the regret...that lives with a person. It's why I came back here. It's why I'm trying to fix things with my parents. It's not easy to ask people to give you a second chance, but everyone deserves that, regardless of what they've done. Me included."

She hesitated and looked up at him. "Maybe that's what you need. A second chance with Ginny."

He frowned because that was not what he'd expected her to say after that little diatribe. If anything, he'd expected her to talk about a second chance between him and her. "You don't know anything about me and Ginny."

"I know you still love her. I saw it in your eyes when you looked at her. And I heard it in your voice just now. That doesn't bode well for me at the moment but...life is short. You of all people should know that from your time in the military. People make mistakes. Happiness, though...true happiness...that's very hard to come by. If you have a chance to be happy with Ginny, I think you should ignore everything else and go for it. Because trust me, happiness like that doesn't come around all that often."

His pulse sped up, and his heart beat hard and fast as he stared at her and tried to tell himself she didn't know what she was talking about. But his brain was spinning too fast to convince himself of that. And when she moved close, lifted to her toes, and kissed his cheek, he was too dazed to try to stop her.

"You're a good man, Logan Murphy. You have a very big heart, and I'm sure I'm going to regret this in the morning but..." She lowered to her heels and looked up at him. "Go to her. Give her a second chance. We both know that's what you really want."

She turned away and pushed the gate open. Still too stunned to move, he watched her walk up the short walk, climb the three steps of her porch and reach for the door handle. She flicked him one last smile then disappeared inside her house. And alone in the dark, all Logan could do was stare after her and try to settle his racing pulse.

Because he was even more confused than he'd been before. And he had absolutely no idea what he should do next.

* * * *

The story continues with Episode 8, Blue Skies by Dee Davis.

About Elisabeth Naughton

Before topping multiple bestseller lists—including those of the New York Times, USA Today, and the Wall Street Journal—Elisabeth Naughton taught middle school science. A voracious reader, she soon discovered she had a knack for creating stories with a chemistry of their own. The spark turned into a flame, and Naughton now writes full-time. Besides topping bestseller lists, her books have been nominated for some of the industry's most prestigious awards, such as the RITA® and Golden Heart Awards from Romance Writers of America, the Australian Romance Reader Awards, and the Golden Leaf Award. When not dreaming up new stories, Naughton can be found spending time with her husband and three children in their western Oregon home. Learn more at www.ElisabethNaughton.com.

Sign up for the Rising Storm/1001 Dark Nights
Newsletter
and be entered to win an exclusive lightning bolt
necklace
specially designed for Rising Storm by
Janet Cadsawan of Cadsawan.com.

Go to www.RisingStormBooks.com to subscribe.

As a bonus, all subscribers will receive a free
Rising Storm story
Storm Season: Ginny & Jacob – the Prequel
by Dee Davis

Rising Storm

Storm, Texas.

Where passion runs hot, desire runs deep, and secrets have the power to destroy...

Nestled among rolling hills and painted with vibrant wildflowers, the bucolic town of Storm, Texas, seems like nothing short of perfection.

But there are secrets beneath the facade. Dark secrets. Powerful secrets. The kind that can destroy lives and tear families apart. The kind that can cut through a town like a tempest, leaving jealousy and destruction in its wake, along with shattered hopes and broken dreams. All it takes is one little thing to shatter that polish.

Rising Storm is a series conceived by Julie Kenner and Dee Davis to read like an on-going drama. Set in a small Texas town, *Rising Storm* is full of scandal, deceit, romance, passion, and secrets. Lots of secrets.

Look for other Rising Storm Season 2 titles, now available! (And if you missed Season 1 and the midseason episodes, you can find those titles here!)

Rising Storm, Season Two

Against the Wind by Rebecca Zanetti
As Tate Johnson works to find a balance between his ambitions for political office and the fallout of his

brother's betrayal, Zeke is confronted with his brother Chase's return home. And while Bryce and Tara Daniels try to hold onto their marriage, Kristin continues to entice Travis into breaking his vows...

Storm Warning by Larissa Ione

As Joanne Alvarez settles into life without Hector, her children still struggle with the fallout. Marcus confronts the differences between him and Brittany, while Dakota tries to find a new equilibrium. Meanwhile, the Johnson's grapple with war between two sets of brothers, and Ian Briggs rides into town...

Brave the Storm by Lisa Mondello

As Senator Rush's poll numbers free fall, Marylee tries to drive a wedge between Brittany and Marcus. Across town, Anna Mae and Chase dance toward reconciliation. Ginny longs for Logan, while he fights against Sebastian's maneuvering. And Hector, newly freed from prison, heads back to Storm...

Lightning Strikes by Lexi Blake

As Ian Briggs begins to fall for Marisol, Joanne and Dillon also grow closer. Joanne's new confidence spreads to Dakota but Hector's return upends everything. A public confrontation between Marcus and Hector endangers his relationship with Brittany, and Dakota reverts to form. Meanwhile, the Senator threatens Ginny and the baby...

Fire and Rain by R.K. Lilley

As Celeste Salt continues to unravel in the wake of Jacob's death, Travis grows closer with Kristin. Lacey realizes the error of her ways but is afraid it's too late for reconciliation with her friends. Marcus and Brittany struggle with the continued fallout of Hector's return, while Chase and Anna Mae face some hard truths about their past...

Quiet Storm by Julie Kenner

As Mallory Alvarez and Luis Moreno grow closer, Lacey longs for forgiveness. Brittany and Marcus have a true meeting of hearts. Meanwhile, Jeffry grapples with his father's failures and finds solace in unexpected arms. When things take a dangerous turn, Jeffry's mother and sister, as well as his friends, unite behind him as the Senator threatens his son...

Blinding Rain by Elisabeth Naughton

As Tate Johnson struggles to deal with his brother's relationship with Hannah, hope asserts itself in an unexpected way. With the return of Delia Burke, Logan's old flame, Brittany and Marcus see an opportunity to help their friend. But when the evening takes an unexpected turn, Brittany finds herself doing the last thing she expected—coming face to face with Ginny...

Blue Skies by Dee Davis

As Celeste Salt struggles to pull herself and her family together, Dillon is called to the scene of a domestic dispute where Dakota is forced to face the truth about her father. While the Johnson's celebrate a big announcement, Ginny is rushed to the hospital where her baby's father is finally revealed...

Rising Storm, Midseason

After the Storm by Lexi Blake
In the wake of Dakota's revelations, the whole town is reeling. Ginny Moreno has lost everything. Logan Murphy is devastated by her lies. Brittany Rush sees her family in a horrifying new light. And nothing will ever be the same...

Distant Thunder by Larissa Ione
As Sebastian and Marylee plot to cover up Sebastian's sexual escapade, Ginny and Dakota continue to reel from the fallout of Dakota's announcement. But it is the Rush family that's left to pick up the pieces as Payton, Brittany and Jeffry each cope with Sebastian's betrayal in their own way...

Rising Storm, Season One

Tempest Rising by Julie Kenner
Ginny Moreno didn't mean to do it, but when she came home to Storm, she brought the tempest with her. And now everyone will be caught in its fury...

White Lightning by Lexi Blake
As the citizens of Storm, Texas, sway in the wake of the death of one of their own, Daddy's girl Dakota Alvarez also reels from an unexpected family crisis... and finds consolation in a most unexpected place.

Crosswinds by Elisabeth Naughton
Lacey Salt's world shattered with the death of her brother, and now the usually sweet-tempered girl is

determined to take back some control—even if that means sabotaging her best friend, Mallory, and Mallory's new boyfriend, Luis.

Dance in the Wind by Jennifer Probst
During his time in Afghanistan, Logan Murphy has endured the unthinkable, but reentering civilian life in Storm is harder than he imagined. But when he is reacquainted with Ginny Moreno, a woman who has survived terrors of her own, he feels the first stirrings of hope.

Calm Before the Storm by Larissa Ione
Marcus Alvarez fled Storm when his father's drinking drove him over the edge. With his mother and sisters in crisis, Marcus is forced to return to the town he thought he'd left behind. But it is his attraction to a very grown up Brittany Rush that just might be enough to guarantee that he stays.

Take the Storm by Rebecca Zanetti
Marisol Moreno has spent her youth taking care of her younger siblings. Now, with her sister, Ginny, in crisis, and her brother in the throes of his first real relationship, she doesn't have time for anything else. Especially not the overtures of the incredibly compelling Patrick Murphy.

Weather the Storm by Lisa Mondello
Bryce Douglas faces a crisis of faith when his idyllic view of his family is challenged with his son's diagnosis of autism. Instead of accepting his wife and her tight-knit family's comfort, he pushes them away, fears from his past threatening to undo the happiness he's found in his present.

Thunder Rolls by Dee Davis
In the season finale ...

As Hannah Grossman grapples with the very real possibility that she is dating one Johnson brother while secretly in love with another, the entire town prepares for Founders Day. The building tempest threatens not just Hannah's relationship with Tucker and Tate, but everyone in Storm as dire revelations threaten to tear the town apart.

Blue Skies
Rising Storm, Season 2, Episode 8
By Dee Davis
Now Available

Secrets, Sex and Scandals …

Welcome to Storm, Texas, where passion runs hot, desire runs deep, and secrets have the power to destroy… Get ready. The storm is coming.

As Celeste Salt struggles to pull herself and her family together, Dillon is called to the scene of a domestic dispute where Dakota is forced to face the truth about her father. While the Johnson's celebrate a big announcement, Ginny is rushed to the hospital where her baby's father is finally revealed…

* * * *

Ginny closed her eyes for a second, the senator's threats coming back full center. She hated to burden her family. But then what else was family for? She knew they'd stand by her. And peripherally Mal was family too, and hadn't she just been hoping the same about Ian? Her gut clenched again, her back still aching.

She blew out a breath and opened her eyes. "It was Senator Rush." It seemed weird to be so formal. The guy had in all probability knocked her up. But Ginny realized she'd never really thought of him in any other way. How sick was that?

"What about him?" Marisol asked her voice tight with anger. Ian reached over to lay a soothing hand on her shoulder. Yup. The man had it bad.

"He threatened me." Ginny's voice came out on a

whisper, and she shuddered with the memory. "I think he was trying to get me to reconcile with him. Give him access to the baby."

"And you told him no," Luis said, crossing his arms over his chest, his expression thunderous.

"Of course I did. But that's when he threatened me." After another sip of tea and a wince from the pain in her gut, she told them everything the senator had said.

"I'll talk to him," Ian said, anger glittering from his eyes.

"No," Marisol shook her head. "This isn't your battle."

"The hell it isn't." Again he reached out to touch her, and for a brief moment Marisol leaned into the touch.

"No one is going to do anything." The pain had let up a bit, the tea and the proximity of her family easing her panic. "We don't even know if the baby is his."

"Ginny," Marisol began, but Ginny cut her off.

"I know the odds, Marisol. But I'm not giving up. And even if Little Bit turns out to be the senator's, I'm not just going to hand him or her over. This is my child. And he or she belongs here with me." Her gaze moved to encompass them all. "With us."

"And we'll do everything in our power to make sure that happens," Marisol said.

"Damn right," Ian echoed, with Luis and Mallory nodding behind him.

Ginny felt the warmth of her family surround her and started to relax, but then the pain was back, stronger now, almost robbing her of breath. She leaned forward clutching her belly.

"So what do we do now?" Luis was asking.

Marisol's arms came around Ginny, holding her close. "We get Ginny to the hospital. I could be wrong, but I think that was a contraction."

1001 Dark Nights

Welcome to 1001 Dark Nights... a collection of novellas that are breathtakingly sexy and magically romantic. Some are paranormal, some are erotic. Each and every one is compelling and page turning.

Inspired by the exotic tales of The Arabian Nights, 1001 Dark Nights features *New York Times* and *USA Today* bestselling authors.

In the original, Scheherazade desperately attempts to entertain her husband, the King of Persia, with nightly stories so that he will postpone her execution.
In our version, month after month, each of our fabulous authors puts a unique spin on the premise and creates a tale that a new Scheherazade tells long into the dark, dark night.

For more information about 1001 Dark Nights, visit www.1001DarkNights.com.

On behalf of Rising Storm,

Liz Berry, M.J. Rose, Julie Kenner & Dee Davis would like to thank ~

Steve Berry
Doug Scofield
Melissa Rheinlander
Kim Guidroz
Jillian Stein
InkSlinger PR
Asha Hossain
Chris Graham
Pamela Jamison
Fedora Chen
Jessica Johns
Dylan Stockton
Richard Blake
The Dinner Party Show
and Simon Lipskar

Made in the USA
Middletown, DE
08 June 2017

Contents

Foreword

Because producing a book for a professional readership is a lengthy process – from writing the first outline to actual publication – it must always be the authors' (and publisher's) nightmare that by the time it is in the catalogue and on the shelves it will be obsolete and outdated. Not so for this book – *The Good Consultation Guide for Nurses* is needed even more now than when it was first conceived. Not only do we have large numbers of nurse practitioners in primary care, walk-in centres and emergency departments, and nurse consultants running nurse-led clinics in numerous different clinical specialisms, but we now also have community matrons – all these nurses need to improve their skills in the process of consulting with patients, which is what this book is designed to do.

In his Foreword to the Department of Health policy document *Supporting People with Long Term Conditions*,[1] Dr David Colin-Thomé, the National Clinical Director for Primary Care in the English National Health Service, stated the government's intention to reduce emergency bed-days and improve outcomes for vulnerable people with long-term conditions (such as diabetes or asthma) through the provision of personalised care plans. The document goes on to explain how case management, utilising care plans, will be spearheaded by Community Matrons, a new breed of advanced practice nurses drawn from a variety of nursing backgrounds (but particularly district nursing), who will 'anticipate, co-ordinate and join up health and social care' to reduce the number of acute hospital admissions. Amongst the many competencies required by community matrons are 'physical examination and history taking, diagnosis and treatment planning, independent and supplementary prescribing and medicines management'.

It is encouraging that in the UK in 2006, the Nursing and Midwifery Council (NMC)[2] is concerned to regulate a level of practice beyond initial registration; this is a long-awaited step recommended originally by the previous statutory body (UKCC)[3,4] more than a decade ago, thus ensuring that nurses registered at the higher level (called Advanced Nurse Practitioners – ANPs) do demonstrate enhanced clinical judgement, knowledge and accountability. The NMC have proposed an expanded definition to enable patients, carers and other health professions to know what can be expected of ANPs.[3] They are highly skilled nurses who can, amongst other things:

- take a comprehensive patient history
- carry out physical examinations
- use their expert knowledge and clinical judgement to identify the potential diagnosis
- refer patients for investigations where appropriate
- make a final diagnosis
- decide on and carry out treatment, including the prescribing of medicines, or refer patients to an appropriate specialist.

This definition fits very neatly with the competences framework for case management for the care of people with long-term conditions set out in 2005 by the NHS 'Skills for Health' working group.[5]

All the key elements of a consultation between nurse and patient are systematically examined in this book, illuminated by vignettes to bring the process to life and supported by educational guidance and assessment strategies. It will help those who are new to the art of consulting, but will also refresh the knowledge and skills of more experienced nurses and those who teach them.

This book is destined to meet the needs of nurses and especially Advanced Nurse Practitioners and those who educate them and employ them. Hopefully by making good use of it, nurses and those of allied professions who are also advancing their practice will confound the observation made by Florence Nightingale in 1859:[6]

> 'How few there are, who by five or six pointed questions, can elicit the whole case and get accurately to know and to be able to report where the patient is.'

Susan Read MBE, FRCN
Professor in Nursing Research
University of Sheffield School of Nursing and Midwifery
May 2006

References

1 Department of Health. *Supporting People with Long Term Conditions. An NHS and Social Care Model to support local innovation and integration* [online]. Leeds: Department of Health. 2005. Available from: www.telecareevents.co.uk/docs/Supporting%20people%20with%20long%20term%20conditions.pdf (accessed June 2006).
2 Nursing and Midwifery Council. *The Proposed Framework for the Standard for Post-registration Nursing* [online]. London: NMC. 2006. Available from: www.nmc-uk.org/aArticle.aspx?ArticleID=82 (accessed 28 April 2006).
3 United Kingdom Central Council. *The Council's Standards for Education and Practice following Registration.* London: UKCC. 1994.
4 United Kingdom Central Council. *PREP and You.* London: UKCC. 1995.
5 NHS Modernisation Agency & Skills for Health. *Case Management Competences Framework for the Care of People with Long Term Conditions* [online]. Bristol: Department of Health. 2005. Available from: www.dh.gov.uk/assetRoot/04/11/81/02/04118102.pdf (accessed 28 April 2006).
6 Nightingale F. *Notes on Nursing.* London: Harrison & Sons. 1859. (See also Van der Peet R. *The Nightingale Model of Nursing.* Edinburgh: Campion Press. 1995.)

About the editors

Adrian Hastings is a general practitioner (GP), who has been a principal in a practice serving an inner city area of Leicester since 1984. Before coming to Leicester he worked in Mozambique where he was responsible for developing a training course for primary care health workers in the diagnosis and treatment of common illnesses. Since 1991 he has taught consultation skills to medical students, and more recently GP registrars in his own practice, and in seminar groups at the University of Leicester. In developing the CAIIN as an assessment and teaching instrument he worked with nurses with a wide range of previous experience using direct observation, small-group teaching, analysis of video-recorded consultations and simulated patients. He has gained a high regard for the consultation skills demonstrated by these nurses and acknowledges their role in helping him expand the ideas in this book.

Sarah Redsell is a Principal Research Fellow at the School of Nursing, University of Nottingham. Initially, she trained as a nurse and worked in secondary care settings throughout the UK; she then trained and worked as a health visitor in Nottingham. From 1997–2000 she undertook a doctorate in health psychology which involved developing and evaluating an intervention for children with bedwetting ('All about nocturnal enuresis'). Sarah has worked as a Lecturer at the Universities of Nottingham and Leicester teaching behavioural sciences, audit and consultation skills. She has carried out both quantitative and qualitative research in a wide range of health service settings. Her research interests centre on improving the quality of nursing care.

Sarah worked with Adrian Hastings at the University of Leicester to develop and validate two instruments to assess and improve nurses' consultation skills (Consultation, Assessment and Improvement Instrument for Nurses). Together they developed and ran a number of workshops teaching consultation skills to practice nurses, health visitors and first-contact care managers.

About the contributors

John Fowler is a Principal Lecturer in Nursing at De Montfort University Leicester and honorary Education Consultant to Leicester City West PCT. He has edited several books on clinical supervision and professional development in nursing.

Rhona Knight is a GP, undergraduate and postgraduate medical educator in Leicester. She has been a GP principal for a number of years and now works as a portfolio GP. This includes working as a GP in a nurse-led practice. It also includes medical education in a variety of spheres.

RK McKinley is Senior Lecturer in General Practice and Director of the Clinical Consultation Research and Development Unit, University of Leicester. He has a long-standing interest in the evaluation and enhancement of the skills of health professionals and has produced 60 publications and international conference presentations in the field.

Acknowledgements

The Editors would like to thank the primary and secondary care nurses who assisted in the development of the CAIIN; Chris Otway, senior lecturer in nurse prescribing; the other teaching staff and students on the nurse prescribing courses at De Montfort University and the practice and community nurses of the Saffron Group Practice whose invaluable comments in discussions have helped the Editors to develop the ideas presented in this book.

Introduction

Over the past decade substantial changes have taken place within health service structures, staffing arrangements and nursing practice. Whilst many nurses develop their clinical and psychosocial skills and expand their roles, others break traditional boundaries and undertake tasks previously performed by doctors. Increasingly nurses working in primary and secondary care are the first point of contact for patients seeking healthcare. Nurses are leading healthcare provision for some patient categories in walk-in centres, NHS Direct, A&E and minor illness units and in general practice. Patients attending hospitals now regularly consult with nurse specialists or nurse consultants rather than medical consultants, particularly for chronic and terminal illness management. The majority of nurses working autonomously in primary care also independently prescribe medicines routinely used within their specialist area.

Although practice has changed dramatically little is known about the quality of care provided by nurses working in these advanced roles. Some professionals have expressed concerns that nurses undertaking work previously the preserve of doctors are doing so without adequate preparation [1,2] education or support.[3] In order to achieve a successful outcome, nurses working in first contact or nurse-led services need to be able to make an accurate assessment of why the patient has attended, originate a working diagnosis of their problem and engage them in an evidence-based management plan. These activities require nurses working at the front line of clinical practice to consult with patients autonomously in a similar way to doctors. To do this successfully nurses need advanced consultation skills, some of which are different from those they have traditionally learned to use.

The aim of this book is to improve nurses' understanding of the skills and knowledge required to consult effectively with patients. The book follows the model the editors have used when undertaking consultation skills training with nurses at all levels. We intend it to be used as a tool for professional development purposes. The first part of the book looks at the 'nursing consultation' in detail and will be useful for individuals wishing to improve their own practice (*see* Chapters 1–5). Some nurses will wish to use it to learn about consultation skills during their pre-registration training. Much benefit will be gained by the experienced nurses who are already consulting with patients autonomously, and who wish to develop or improve their skills. This includes nurses undertaking post-registration training to prepare them for new, autonomous roles, such as independent prescribing. During the course they will need to learn more about solving problems and making a diagnosis. Chapters 6–8 look more widely at the educational issues likely to arise in organisations employing nurses who consult autonomously and are likely to be of greatest interest to nurse lecturers, learning and health service managers who wish to implement curriculum/organisational changes. However, aspects of the earlier chapters will be vital reading for any nurse leader trying to implement change and Chapters 6–8 are undoubtedly of interest to reflective practitioners trying to improve their consultation skills.

Chapter 1 supports the concept of nurses working in new and extended roles and discusses how nurses working autonomously might enhance their understanding of the consultation process. It outlines the development of the

Consultation Assessment and Improvement Instrument for Nurses (CAIIN). Chapter 2 examines the consultation models described in the medical literature and assesses their suitability for autonomous nursing consultations. It also looks at how consultations are organised and proposes a model for nurses based on the relative strengths of the models used in general practice. The third chapter outlines the component competences of the CAIIN and provides a brief description of how each competence might be challenged and assessed. Examples from nursing practice are used to demonstrate the components have 'real life' applicability. Chapter 4 covers in more detail so-called 'problem solving' but which might also be termed 'making a diagnosis'. Although making a diagnosis is a key skill needed by nurses working in front-line care and nurse prescribers, the ability to diagnose complications and secondary problems is an important attribute for nurses working in a specialist area. Chapter 5 examines how a care plan might be implemented once a diagnosis is made. It includes advice on reaching a shared understanding with the patient, giving advice, negotiating treatments, supporting lifestyle changes and applying evidence to individual patients.

Chapter 6 focuses on learning and assessment. It begins by looking at how we learn and then in detail at the nature of assessment. Chapter 7 is devoted to giving and receiving feedback. It describes the key features of feedback and the impact different ways of giving feedback can have on the learning outcomes. Tools to help the assessor provide effective feedback are discussed in detail. Chapter 8 looks at how an individual nurse can formulate and put into action a learning plan. This includes sections on reflection, identifying and addressing knowledge gaps, peer interaction and strategies for improvement and will be of particular use for nurses teaching and mentoring learners. Finally Chapter 9 provides practical advice on how to use the CAIIN and will be useful for anyone interested in assessing nursing consultations.

The English language does not allow for gender neutral writing in the singular person. We have used the terms she and hers when referring to nurses, as the majority of nurses are female. However, in our examples we make reference to nurses who are male and to surgeons who are female because we know that neither occupation is the sole preserve of men or women.

Some disciplines in nursing prefer to use the term 'client' to 'patient'. We have chosen for simplicity to refer to 'patients' throughout this book as this is still the most widely used term in nursing practice.

References

1. Williams A, Sibbald B. Changing roles and identities in primary health care: exploring a culture of uncertainty. *J Adv Nurse.* 1999; **29**, 737–45.
2. Watson R, Stimpson A, Topping A *et al.* Clinical competence assessment in nursing: a systematic review of the literature. *J Adv Nurse.* 2002; **39**(5), 421–31.
3. Norwood SL. A course in nursing consultation: promoting indirect nursing activities. *Nurs Educ Today.* 1998; **23**, 16–20.

New roles for nurses and consultation skills

Sarah Redsell

A short history of new nursing roles

The nurse practitioner role emerged in the US in the 1960s in response to an increased specialisation of physicians, fewer general medical practitioners, difficulties with out-of-hours care and a highly mobile population.[1] In the UK, nurse practitioner roles have developed in an *ad hoc* way in response to service need and employer interest.[2] Plans to support changes in nursing practice were outlined over a decade ago[3] by the United Kingdom Central Council (UKCC) for Nursing, Midwifery and Health Visiting in 1992 and then the UKCC in 1994 formally recognised two higher levels of practice, namely 'advanced' and 'specialist'.[4] The UKCC continued to examine the regulation of post-registration practice until it was succeeded by the Nursing and Midwifery Council (NMC) in 2002. However, it looked broadly at standards for a higher level of practice, rather than specifically at nurse practitioner or specialist nurse roles. Whilst the title 'specialist practitioner' was formally recognised by the UKCC in 1994, the NMC are only now moving forward with regulating a level of practice beyond registration for 'advanced nurse practitioners'.

The government is keen for nurses to expand their role and develop skills to undertake tasks previously performed by doctors. In 1998 it launched *Agenda for Change* a policy document that outlined how nursing roles could be expanded further to address the National Health Service's (NHS) priority to provide prompt and patient-centred care.[5] In 1999 the government issued a strategy document specifically for nurses that explicitly acknowledged the need to improve nursing roles and nurses' career structures. *Making a Difference* acknowledged the changes that had already taken place in nursing practice and set out a strategy for workforce development to ensure that new roles and role developments are implemented by all NHS organisations.[6] In order to strengthen nursing leadership and provide a new career opportunity to help retain experienced and expert nurses in the clinical field the 'nurse consultant' was introduced into the NHS in 2000.[7] The plans for new and extended roles for nurses are set to continue.[8]

There is evidence to suggest that policy intervention was needed to support further developments of the nurse practitioner role, because locally agreed arrangements place restrictions on professional autonomy and there is no national guidance on educational preparation for the role.[1] However, there are those who believe that these nursing developments are service rather than professionally driven.[1] Although new and extended roles have been created to help with nurses' individual development and the development of the profession as a whole these changes need to be viewed within the wider context. In the past nurses at the top end of the salary scale had very little opportunity to stay in the clinical field and many left to pursue other careers with greater job satisfaction. This left a workforce deficit in terms of the numbers of nurses required to deliver care. There are also fewer doctors available to provide healthcare due to a short-fall in general practitioner (GP) recruitment, the implementation of the European Working Time Directive and subsequent reduction in junior doctors' hours, and the difficulties in recruiting doctors to provide services in socially deprived areas. Furthermore, the demand for health services from the public has never been greater. To cope with this ever-increasing demand the government launched *The NHS Plan*[9] that outlined a new delivery system for the NHS including changes for all staff groups. It also sets out plans for cutting waiting times, clinical priorities and reducing inequality. Many of these targets are motivated by the need to deliver healthcare quickly and efficiently to as many people as possible, which places particular pressures on doctors and the wider workforce. One 'solution' has been to develop 'new' and extended roles for nurses which help retain nurses at practice level to cover the deficit in the number of doctors available to provide care. However, a dilemma exists between the interests of nurses wishing to advance their own (and the professions') practice and the plan for nurses to undertake tasks previously undertaken by their medical colleagues. Although it is undoubtedly beneficial for nurses to develop their skills and knowledge thereby enhancing their career opportunities, if the pace of change is too rapid some nurses will inevitably take on tasks for which they have not been ade-quately prepared.[10] The Royal College of Nursing (RCN) began its Nurse Practitioner Training Programme in 1992 and has undertaken considerable work looking at the role, competencies and standards of a nurse practitioner.[11] Nurses, in conjunction with their professional bodies, need to guide the pace of change and appropriate training for additional responsibilities is essential. Furthermore, nurses cannot keep taking on additional tasks without reducing their original workload and the question of who undertakes the remaining tasks within the current workforce has not yet been considered.

Substituting nurses for doctors

Several research studies have examined whether nurses can undertake activities previously performed by doctors. There is growing evidence that nurse practi-tioners can substitute for at least some of the functions of GPs[12] but nurse practitioner care may differ from GP care in a number of important respects. Patients requesting 'same day' appointments report significantly greater satisfac-tion with nurse practitioner than with GP consultations.[13, 14] Nurse practitioners also provide significantly more information than GPs.[13] In contrast, after seeing a nurse or a GP patients state a preference to see a GP on the next occasion despite being satisfied with a nurse consultation.[13, 14] Nurse practitioners also carry out significantly more tests and ask patients to return more often than GPs.[15] Nurse practitioners conduct significantly longer consultations[13, 14] although one study found that patients are more satisfied with nurse practitioner consultations even when consultation length was taken into account.[15]

These studies all examined patient satisfaction with the consultation and it appears that nurses have a greater impact on this dimension of a consultation than do doctors. However, these studies did not look at the relationship between patient expectations and patient satisfaction and whether appropriate clinical care was given to the patient for the presenting condition. Patient satisfaction is determined by a number of factors including:

- expectations (which can in turn be determined by prior experience)
- patient characteristics
- psychosocial determinants.

These factors are different from the components of care delivery.[16] Patients bring different expectations to their consultations with nurses. For example they may expect nurses to pay more attention to the psychosocial aspects of their problem and doctors to have a greater understanding of the complexity of their medical problem. Furthermore, it may be that because nurses tend to give more time to the patient and invest in building rapport, patients are more satisfied even if the nurse does not achieve correct diagnosis or treatment. Importantly these studies did not examine what happened to the patient after the consultation and to what extent the patients' problem improved following the nurse consultation. These questions suggest that nurses and doctors may have different effects on patients within the consultation and it is not possible to conclude with certainty that one can substitute for another in all situations.

The results of these studies are unsurprising given the way nurses and doctors are trained in the UK. Historically, nurses' and doctors' training traditionally reinforced the idea that 'nurses care' and 'doctors cure' patients. In the past, medical students were predominantly required to learn about the biomedical or disease model of illness whilst student nurses approached health using models strongly influenced by psychology, sociology and social policy. The scope of undergraduate education is now broader so student nurses learn clinical skills and medical students a patient-centred approach to clinical practice. However, since it remains unclear whether one group can fully substitute for the other, it could be argued that those whose practice is based on traditional models might find it harder to work across boundaries. If nurses are to take on roles previously undertaken by doctors they will need a good understanding of the clinical aspects of patient care. This relies not only upon nurses being able to gain and give appropriate information within a consultation so the patient's problem is managed effectively but also to understand fully the disease processes of the conditions they most commonly encounter.

The nursing consultation

Nurses work within a diverse range of clinical and psychosocial areas that require different skills, knowledge and approaches. The roles of nurses who work autonomously are vast as shown by the different nurse consultant posts that have been introduced, for example:

- domestic violence
- midwifery
- respiratory care
- homeless families
- primary care.

As nurses we like to celebrate our differences as an example of the diversity of our profession and often fail to see that our colleagues working in different areas have similar approaches to patient care. There are good cultural and historical reasons for this. Nurses tend to develop their expertise within a specialist clinical area such as 'diabetes' or within an area where different models of health are used, such as health visiting. Once nurses get beyond a certain level they tend to stay within their chosen specialism and are rarely required to work outside their area of expertise. This approach drives nurses to develop their skills and knowledge from within their specialism rather than generally. Therefore, their knowledge of the conditions they regularly encounter and the most appropriate treatments for these conditions is usually high. However, even nurses who are 'super-specialised' still require up-to-date generic skills and knowledge in order to recognise conditions other than those of their specialty.

A different approach is to examine the skills and knowledge nurses working in all areas share and how these can be improved. Most nurses have been trained in a broadly similar way, which includes learning about different approaches to health, the importance of communication and the provision of information. Most nurses consider themselves better at dealing with the psychosocial issues associated with patient care than doctors. Most nurses conduct face-to-face meetings with patients and the conversation usually follows a structure that includes 'making an assessment of the patient's problem' (whether new or existing) and managing the problem using a patient-centred focus. Most of these face-to-face meetings will draw on nurses' ability to consult effectively and it is these skills which we believe are generic to all.

What should nurse–patient meetings be called?

What term would you use to describe the face-to-face meeting between yourself and a patient? Patients attending general practice or outpatients' clinics often refer to their 'appointment' with the doctor or nurse but this terminology refers to a scheduling arrangement and does not accurately describe what happens when the individuals meet face to face. Health visitors refer to 'visits' that might occur within the home or clinic setting and involve conducting need assessments with vulnerable families. Nurses working on surgical wards refer to 'pre-operative assessments', whilst those working in other parts of the hospital refer to 'admitting patients'. Nurses working in first contact settings often talk about 'triage' and making initial assessments of the patient's condition. General practitioners refer to the interaction between themselves and a patient as a 'consultation' but there is no common terminology to describe the process that occurs when a patient meets face-to-face with a nurse to discuss a healthcare need.

If you are still not convinced then consider the following. Within every face-to-face meeting between a nurse and a patient a set of rules operate, which are usually implicit and not discussed, but form a vital part of the interaction. At the beginning there is an introduction (or re-introduction if the individuals already know each other); followed by clarification (often initiated by the nurse) as to the reason the meeting is taking place. Once this has occurred a discussion will take place around the 'problem' that might take the form of a conversational assessment through to a formal structured enquiry.

Conversational assessment or structured consultations?

- Conversational assessment might be used within the palliative care setting where the patient and nurse know each other well and a new or existing problem has arisen. In this scenario the patient may mention to the nurse that something requires attention and the nurse will use a few focused questions to determine how to proceed.
- Structured consultations are likely to be more useful in a pre-operative assessment where the nurse knows little about the patient but a substantial amount of information must be elicited.

Once the nurse has determined the nature of the problem and how she or he might help the patient a discussion occurs where the nurse gives their version of how they see the situation and allows the patient to correct any misinterpretations and to give their views. Finally the nurse and patient try to agree on what is going to happen next and when they need to meet again (if at all).

A consultation with a patient is probably one of the most challenging encounters for nurses working in autonomous roles. The nurse is required to successfully identify the patient's problem whether psychosocial or biomedical (or both). To do this they require knowledge of a range of psychosocial and biomedical conditions and their associated symptoms. Patients will often wish to talk about other related or unrelated matters and whilst nurses need to give them time to do this using an open questioning style they also need to focus their questions around the likely diagnostic areas. For example a patient may present with a two-week history of a viral upper-respiratory infection. As well as determining whether or not this is a self-limiting minor illness, the nurse has to find out why the patient is consulting at this time. There may be underlying psychosocial issues that need to be carefully identified and addressed as appropriate. In contrast patients may spend their time during the consultation discussing well-established psychosocial problems when they have an underlying biomedical complaint that they are afraid of disclosing. A high level of sensitivity can be required for some patients to feel sufficiently comfortable to disclose the real reason for a consultation.

Decision-support tools

Nurses use a number of different tools to enable them to make an appropriate assessment of a problem. These include:

- admission forms
- assessment forms
- protocols
- NHS CAS (the decision-support system used by staff in NHS Direct).

These can be useful as they prompt the practitioner with the questions to ask and some computer-based systems are able to 'calculate' a probable diagnosis based on the responses. Although telephone services such as NHS Direct are based on the use of these tools there are problems with excess reliance on them. Often nurses pay too much attention to the need to complete all the 'boxes' and too little attention to what the patient is saying and how it is being said. This can result in the patient losing confidence in the nurse and withholding vital information. Nurses, who rely on the tool, rather than improving their consultation skills together with their knowledge of disease, might not be developing their own professional practice. For a nurse to consult autonomously with a patient considerable skill and knowledge are required.

The nurse needs to ensure that they and the patient have the same understanding about the patient's condition. If they do not, further explanation is required before treatment can be successfully initiated. For example a patient with a history of anxiety and depression may present with restlessness, low mood and loss of energy asking for treatment. The patient may believe that these symptoms are associated with chemical changes in the brain and can only be treated by tablets. However, the nurse may believe that the patient's symptoms can be better treated by counselling and lifestyle changes. If the nurse tries to manage the patient from her perspective without considering the patient's point of view, the consultation is unlikely to be successful and the treatment plan may not be followed. Patients are entitled to treatment for diseases based on the best available scientific evidence. Many conditions have been subject to rigorous research to determine the most effective treatment option. The nurse needs to be up-to-date with the clinical evidence for the conditions they encounter regularly. Nurses will be unable to achieve a shared understanding within every consultation and under these circumstances a referral may be necessary.

To do all of this a nurse is required to have a high level of clinical knowledge and interpersonal skills as well as an understanding of how their own behaviours within the consultation might have an impact on the eventual outcome. Nurse practitioners, specialist nurses and nurse consultants working within clinical areas need to learn enhanced consultation skills to help with problem definition and diagnosis, care planning to include pharmacological, psychosocial and nursing interventions and negotiating management plans in partnership with patients.

Assessment of consultation skills

There is increasing acknowledgement that nurses require high-level consultation skills in order to undertake autonomous roles. Consultation skills training is an essential requirement of the nurse-prescribing course.[17] Nurse practitioners are required to 'analyse and interpret history, presenting symptoms, physical findings and diagnostic information to develop appropriate differential diagnosis'.[11] Despite this, Robb, Fleming and Dietert (2002) in a review of the international literature conducted in 2001, were unable to find a competency framework for the assessment of nurse consultation skills that had been validated as acceptable to the nurses on whom it might be used.[18]

In the field of medicine, it is now accepted that consultation performance can only reliably be assessed by observation.[19] Proxy measures such as patient satisfaction surveys or clinical audit may raise concerns about a practitioner's performance but cannot identify the specific difficulties that give rise to low scores for these measures. If consultation skills are to be assessed by direct observation it is vital that the nurse being observed understands what is meant by a successful consultation and how their consulting performance is to be judged. A useful starting point is to use a set of valid and reliable criteria of consultation competence. The use of standard criteria ensures that any differences in the view of different observers (inter-rater reliability) are minimised. Consulting criteria should explicitly describe the interpersonal, practical and thinking skills the nurse is required to possess for successful consultations, that are acceptable to the nursing profession and that are feasible to use in a healthcare setting. However, until recently no such criteria existed. Bond *et al.* (1999),[20] in a study to assess the performance of trained nurse practitioners had to use, without modification, an instrument designed to assess the performance of GPs in videotaped consultations.[21] The instrument focuses principally on the behavioural characteristics of the doctors and does not include, for example, problem-solving skills, record keeping or preventative care. Furthermore, its use in this study was limited to nurse practitioners undertaking the work of GPs and any instrument designed to measure nurses' consultation competence needs to be useful in a wider range of settings where nurses work autonomously or semi-autonomously.

Consultation Assessment and Improvement Instrument for Nurses (CAIIN)

In the absence of any robust tool to measure nurses' consultation competence we have developed and validated two sets of criteria. The first set is designed for the work of primary care nurses.[22] The second has been adapted for nurses working in a secondary care (hospital-based) setting.[23] We believe these criteria describe the important features of a 'nursing consultation'. The remainder of this chapter describes the development of the first set of criteria for nurses working in primary care.[22] The process of adapting these criteria to describe the work of secondary care nurses is outlined in a separate paper.[23] Both sets of criteria have now been incorporated into training packs that can be used to assess and improve the consultation skills of nurses.[24, 25] The Consultation Assessment and Improvement Instrument for Nurses (CAIIN) training pack also includes a users' guide, a recording form for the observer to make notes on each consultation seen, feedback summary forms, descriptors of levels of performance, which facilitate the reliable allocation of grades or marks and guidance on giving feedback. The CAIIN briefing pack also contains questions that can be asked of nurses being observed to directly test their problem-solving skills and recommended strategies for improvement that are directly linked to each of the criteria. Observers can use the strategies as a guide when developing feedback or as an educational prescription of the nurses' consultation performance. The information contained in the CAIIN training pack is given in Chapter 9 of this book.

Development and validation of CAIIN criteria

A literature search revealed no suitable set of criteria of consultation competence for nurses. However, criteria of consultation competence exist for GPs and a pragmatic decision was made to adapt these to the work of primary care nurses rather than start anew. The Leicester Assessment Package (LAP)[26] has been demonstrated to be a reliable[27] and valid[28] instrument to facilitate the assessment and improvement of the consultation competence of GPs. It has been successfully adapted for use with other clinicians including medical undergraduates and hospital doctors.[29] We therefore believed it would be a useful starting point in the development of criteria of consultation competence for primary care nurses. However, we recognised that it would require considerable modification.

The LAP contains seven categories of consultation competence as follows.

1. Interviewing/history taking.
2. Physical examination.
3. Patient management.
4. Problem solving.
5. Behaviour.
6. Relationship with patients/anticipatory care.
7. Record keeping.

Within each of these categories are a number of further criteria, which describe the activities that take place within each category. For example the category interviewing/history taking has components such as 'puts patients at ease, listens attentively, uses silence appropriately, recognises patients' verbal and non-verbal cues'. There are 39 further criteria spread across the seven categories of consultation. Three distinct stages of work were required to modify these criteria for the work of nurses. The first involved examining the criteria to determine whether they fitted the work of primary care nurses who consult autonomously with patients and making appropriate amendments. The second stage involved video-taping volunteer nurses consulting with patients in primary care; comparing the observed activities with the proposed criteria and making further amendments as necessary. The third stage was to conduct a national validation survey to determine the suitability of the criteria for nurses working in primary care.

For the first stage the criteria in the LAP were reviewed to exclude those not applicable to the work of primary care nurses, and to add appropriate extra criteria. As the work of primary care nurses often involves using clinical protocols (e.g. sexual health/family planning clinics or chronic disease management) the category 'problem solving' was thought to be challenged more frequently during patient-initiated consultations. For this reason this category was revised with movement of four criteria between the 'problem solving' category and 'patient management'. Two new criteria were generated: 'performs reagent tests correctly' and 'applies diagnostic protocols correctly'. Three criteria were re-worded to make them more appropriate to the work of primary care nurses. This process produced six categories, with a seventh optional category 'problem solving', and a total of 34 criteria.

The second stage involved testing the criteria by observing a number of nurses consulting with patients. The nurses were video-recorded undertaking consultations with patients and the observed activities were compared with the proposed criteria. The video-recording sessions took place between October 1999 and January 2001. Seven volunteer primary care nurses were shown the proposed criteria and invited to allow consultations representative of their usual work to be video-recorded. The nursing activities observed were classified using the criteria in the modified version of the LAP. The strengths and areas needing improvement of each nurse's performance were also recorded. Activities that were not classifiable using the criteria were noted. At the end of the observation phase the team met to agree the categories of consultation competence and the related criteria, to be used in the subsequent validation study.

The third stage was to ensure the proposed criteria adequately described the consultations between primary care nurses and their patients. To do this the proposed criteria were sent to a representative sample of nurses to seek their opinion as to whether they were an accurate description of what they did.[22]

The national validation survey was conducted in two parts. The proposed categories and criteria were sent to 1126 health visitors, district nurses and practice nurses who consented to participate in the study. Respondents were asked to indicate their level of agreement with the proposed consultation categories and criteria using a four-point scale (strongly agree, agree, disagree or strongly disagree). They were given the opportunity to reject any of the proposed categories and/or criteria, to suggest additional categories and/or criteria that they considered important attributes of consultation competence and to provide free text comments. The respondents were invited to participate in the second part of the study, which aimed to establish what proportion of marks should be allocated to each category when the criteria were used to assess the level of consultation competence of a nurse. Those who consented ($n=387$) were sent a further questionnaire in which they were asked to indicate their level of agreement for our suggested weightings or to suggest alternatives. They were also asked their opinion about changes to the criteria proposed as a result of the first part of the study.

The level of support for the inclusion of each of the seven categories of consultation competence varied from 93–98%. This was also true for all of the 39 criteria (88–98%). The categories and the criteria are described in Chapter 3. Fewer than 1% of respondents suggested removing or altering specific criteria. Ninety-five percent of respondents agreed with the principle that the marks allocated to each category of consultation competence should vary with its importance and 58% agreed with the suggested weightings. Of those who disagreed there was no consensus regarding an alternative allocation of priority weighting.

There were 425 comments suggesting that the wording of some categories and criteria should be changed, but there was little consensus regarding alternative language. For example 206 respondents suggested that the term 'patient' should be replaced by the term 'client'. During the second part of the study respondents were asked to indicate whether they preferred the term 'patient' or 'patient/client' and 70% indicated a preference for 'patient/client'. Over 90% of health visitors and nurse educators were strongly in favour of the wording changes, with only 50% of district nurses and practice nurses wishing to see this change. These proportions reflect the different philosophical paradigms the nurses work within. Practice and district nurses tend to deal with ill patients in primary care and the activities they undertake to care for patients fit within a disease model of health – hence their preference for the term patient. Health visitors work with the 'well' population and utilise sociological and self-empowerment models – hence their preference for the term client.

General observations about nurses' performance

The process of viewing the video-recorded consultations by the study team led to some interesting observations. The listed criteria provided a common language for the observers, which facilitated a focused discussion about behaviours, which might otherwise be seen as impressions. For example several nurses were noted to be having difficulties with problem solving. On occasions it was thought the primary difficulty for the nurse lay in knowing what relevant information to elicit from the patients and their records. For another nurse it was apparent that she was unable to identify the patients' reasons for attendance and the associated concerns and expectations. Although in both cases this led to patients' problems being incompletely addressed the feedback required to help these nurses improve in the future is very different.

The nurses whose consultations were viewed in this study were seen in general to have particular strengths in their behaviour with patients. They maintained friendly, professional relationships with their patients, listened attentively and were able to use their relationship to gain patient agreement with their advice. However, we also observed many consultations that lacked effective time management. These were often 'patient-led' encounters in which the patient introduced several different issues to be discussed. Nurses lacked strategies for prioritising these. There were a number of different reasons why these consultations became prolonged, including missing cues, failing to recognise the probable reason for attendance and not eliciting key features of particular conditions which would allow a secure assessment of the problem to be made.

In a large number of observed consultations, nurses working to protocols appeared to have difficulties in achieving effective prioritisation. For example, during a new patient 'welcome' clinic several opportunities to discuss lifestyle were identified but not followed up. The need to ask every question in the protocol conflicted with the task of responding to cues. In answer to the question, 'Do you smoke?', the patient replied, '20 a day, I know it's too many', but this indication that he may have been contemplating giving up smoking was ignored. During a 'drop-in baby clinic' every child was weighed, even when this was not an issue, and this task consumed valuable time that would have been better spent addressing expressed parental concerns about sleep problems and managing coughs, which were ignored.

Nurses, working in every setting, demonstrated problems with the organisation of their consultations. With the exception of the 'drop-in baby clinic', all the clinics were pre-booked and the nurse knew many of the patients beforehand. The prior information available at the outset of the consultation was rarely utilised effectively. Examination or diagnostic testing was carried out before necessary information had been gathered from the patient record or from the history. There was a notable tendency to move prematurely to care planning before adequate definition of the patients' problem(s), which resulted in unduly prolonged consultations. For those clinics where the patient record was available to the study team, several opportunities for opportunistic health promotion were overlooked.

Summary

As a result of this work we were convinced that the CAIIN could make a valuable contribution in helping all nurses to improve their consultation skills. There is currently a greater awareness of the need for all healthcare practitioners to be more accountable for their actions and to seek to improve the quality of healthcare they deliver. The emergence of new roles, such as nurse consultant, specialist nurse and nurse practitioner has led to a drive for nurses to work more autonomously with patients. Nurse–patient consultations are a key event in the delivery of patient care and, whilst many nurses have excellent content expertise in their specialty, many have not had the opportunity to develop high-level consultation skills to enable them to work autonomously. The CAIIN has been designed specifically to facilitate the initial assessment and subsequent enhancement of the quality of the consultation performance of nurses, and the remainder of this book explains how this can be done.

References

1. Marsden J, Dolan B, Holt L. Nurse practitioner practice and deployment: electronic mail Delphi study. *J Adv Nurse*. 2003; **43**(6), 595–605.
2. Read SM, Jones NMB, William BT. Nurse practitioners in accident and emergency departments: what do they do? *Brit Med J*. 1992; **305**, 1466–70.
3. United Kingdom Central Council for Nursing, Midwifery and Health Visiting. *The Scope of Professional Practice*. London: UKCC. 1992.
4. United Kingdom Central Council for Nursing, Midwifery and Health Visiting. *The Standards for Post-registration Education and Practice Project*. London: UKCC. 1994.
5. Department of Health. *Agenda for Change*. London: The Stationery Office. 1998.
6. Department of Health. *Making a Difference: strengthening the nursing, midwifery and health visiting contribution to health and health care*. London: The Stationery Office. 1999.
7. NHS Executive Health Services Circular 217 Nurse, Midwife and Health Visitor Consultants. 1999. http://www.christie.nhs.uk/profinfo/departments/nursing/nursing_developments/usefuldocs/Hsc217nurseconsultants99.pdf (accessed March 2005).
8. Department of Health. *Liberating the Talents*. London: The Stationery Office. 2002.
9. Department of Health. *The NHS Plan*. London: The Stationery Office. 2000.
10. Exploring New Roles in Practice. University of Sheffield. http://www.shef.ac.uk/snm/research/enrip/index.html (accessed June 2006).
11. Royal College of Nursing. *Nurse Practitioners: your questions answered*. London: RCN. 2002.
12. Horrocks S, Anderson E, Salisbury C. Systematic review of whether nurse practitioners working in primary care can provide equivalent care to doctors. *Brit Med J*. 2002; **324**, 819–23.
13. Kinnersley P, Anderson E, Parry K *et al*. Randomised controlled trial of nurse practitioner versus general practitioner care for patients requesting same day consultations in primary care. *Brit Med J*. 2000; **320**, 1043–8.
14. Shum C, Humphreys A, Wheeler D *et al*. Nurse management of patients with minor illness in general practice multicentre randomised controlled trial. *Brit Med J*. 2000; **320**, 1038–43.
15. Venning P, Durie A, Rowland M *et al*. Randomised controlled trial comparing cost effectiveness of general practitioners versus nurse practitioners in primary care. *Brit Med J*. 2000; **320**, 1048–53.
16. Sitzia J, Wood N. Patient satisfaction: a review of issues and concepts. *Soc Sci Med*. 1997; **45**(12), 1829–43.

17. National Prescribing Centre Maintaining competency in prescribing: an outline framework to help nurse prescribers 2002. http://www.npc.co.uk/nurse_pres.htm (accessed August 2004).
18. Robb Y, Fleming V, Dietert C. Measurement of clinical performance of nurses: a literature review. *Nurs Educ Today.* 2002; **23**, 299–306.
19. McKinley R, Fraser RC, Baker R. Model for directly assessing and improving clinical competence and performance in revalidation of clinicians. *Brit Med J.* 2001; **322**, 712–15.
20. Bond S, Beck S, Cunningham W *et al.* Testing a rating scale of video-taped consultations to assess performance of trainee nurse practitioners in general practice. *J Adv Nurse.* 1999; **30**(5),1064–72.
21. Cox J, Mulholland H. An instrument for assessment of videotapes of general practitioners' performance. *Brit Med J.* 1993; **306**, 1043–6.
22. Redsell SA, Hastings AM, Cheater FM *et al.* Devising and establishing the face and content validity of explicit criteria of consultation competence in UK primary care nurses. *Nurs Educ Today.* 2003; **23**(4), 299–306.
23. Redsell SA, Lennon M, Hastings AM *et al.* Devising and establishing the face and content validity of explicit criteria of consultation competence for UK secondary care nurses. *Nurs Educ Today.* 2004; **24**(3),180–7.
24. Hastings AM, Redsell SA, Cheater FM *et al. Consultation Assessment and Improvement Instrument for Primary Care Nurses (CAIIN1).* University of Leicester. 2002.
25. Redsell SA, Hastings AM, Lennon M *et al. Consultation Assessment and Improvement Instrument for Secondary Care Nurses (CAIIN2).* University of Leicester. 2004.
26. Fraser RC. *Assessment of Consultation Competence. The Leicester Assessment Package (2e).* Glaxo Medical Fellowship, University of Leicester. 1994.
27. Fraser RC, McKinley RK, Mulholland H. Consultation competence in general practice: testing the reliability of the Leicester Assessment Package. *Br J Gen Pract.* 1994; **44**(384), 293–6.
28. Fraser RC, McKinley RK, Mulholland H. Consultation competence in general practice: establishing the face validity of prioritised criteria in the Leicester Assessment Package. *Br J Gen Pract.* 1994; **44**(380), 109–13.
29. McKinley RK, Fraser RC, van der Vleuten C *et al.* Formative assessment of the consultation performance of medical students in the setting of general practice using a modified version of the Leicester Assessment Package. *Medical Education.* 2000; **34**, 573–9.

Chapter 2

The consultation

Adrian Hastings

Introduction

In Chapter 1 the pivotal role of the consultation in clinical practice was discussed, together with how nurses are taking on new roles in a wide range of fields that require them to undertake consultations without supervision. The consultation challenges that a nurse may encounter can be as broad and as deep as those experienced by doctors – in primary care and in hospital. Although many writers have recognised these new roles there has been very little research into nurse consultations (and not a great deal more into consultations between hospital specialists and patients, with the exception of particular fields such as psychiatry and palliative care). Consequently most research and writing about consultation in the UK has been done by general practitioners (GPs), or others observing their work. It is a central contention of this book that consultation skills are generic – that is whenever a health professional from any discipline meets with a patient the competences required are the same. For this reason the understanding that general practice has gained of the nature of the consultation is valuable to all health professionals.

The history of the UK medical profession from the end of the 17th Century, until the foundation of the NHS in 1948, is of three divided and often antagonistic branches of physicians, surgeons and apothecaries. Physicians saw themselves as the aristocrats of the healing professions, charging fees for their services from those who could afford them. If they treated the poor it was either from cold charity, or more usually to develop their professional reputations by describing previously unrecorded diseases. The roots of surgery lay in the work of barber surgeons feared because the work usually involved inflicting much pain, and there were high mortality rates after their operations. They gained full recognition as doctors at the start of the 19th Century, and with the discovery of anaesthesia and antisepsis, surgeons were the first people in the profession to treat disease effectively. Apothecaries, who in the 17th and 18th centuries were largely dispensers of herbal remedies, gained proper recognition some 30 years later with the foundation of the Society of General Practitioners in 1830. It was not until the 20th Century that the College of Physicians finally gave up its opposition to the title of doctor being awarded to GPs.

Very slowly the work of GPs became more effective with the discovery of a wide range of new drug treatments and increasing access to laboratory facilities to support them in making diagnoses. The unique structure of British general practice after the war had a major impact on the development of the relationship between doctors and patients. The absence of commercial considerations in the transaction freed patients from the fear that any interventions were designed to enrich the doctor. As importantly, doctors were liberated from the need to make unrealistic claims for their treatments, to justify the fee being paid. Patients registered with one doctor, usually for as long as they lived in the area, which fostered a long-term relationship developed over many short encounters. General practitioners gained detailed knowledge of many aspects of the lives of their patients, and an understanding that a simple biomedical model of disease could not explain many symptoms they experienced.

The new academic disciplines of psychology and sociology influenced ideas about the nature of illness and disease, and these ideas chimed powerfully with GPs seeking to describe the complex patterns of symptoms displayed by patients, when a single disease label to explain these proved elusive. Innovative doctors formed alliances with psychologists and sociologists to study and discuss the nature of the interaction between doctor and patient – the consultation. Academic departments of general practice were gradually established in medical schools from the mid-1960s onwards. The doctors who worked in them focused much of their teaching and research endeavour on the consultation – in part because of its critical importance, and in part because research into bio-medical fields in primary care is complex and expensive to conduct.

Models of the consultation

The introduction of incentives to undertake health promotion, and the shift from treating acute illness towards chronic disease management, brought about a large expansion in the numbers of nurses consulting independently with patients in primary care – a trend further reinforced as they now undertake first contact care. The validation work outlined in Chapter 1 describes how the LAP, initially developed to assess the consultations of GPs, only required minor modifications for primary care nurses to regard it as a suitable description of their work. In the same way that GPs have benefited greatly from insights from other disciplines into how they work, nurses can draw on the store of knowledge and experience GPs have developed, to further enhance the skills they already possess. A very similar trend is occurring in secondary care as nurses with additional skills perform tasks previously the preserve of specialist doctors. When secondary care nurses were invited to consider whether the version of the CAIIN developed in primary care described their activities they again saw little need for change.

For these reasons, and in the absence of alternative models for nurse consultations, it is not necessary to 'reinvent the wheel' – all health professionals can benefit from sharing the insight GPs have gained into the essence of the consultation. Several models have been described to analyse it.[1–4] They were developed for a number of different functions, and some serve more than one purpose as shown in the following list.

- Give doctors insight into the nature of the consultation.
- Guide doctors to change their personality.
- Aid researchers in categorisation of activities within the consultation.
- Teaching and training of students and doctors in consultation skills.
- Assessment of consultation competence.
- Explain patients' experiences of the interaction.
- Understand interaction between patient beliefs and professional views.
- Describe the different power relationships that exist between doctors and patients.

The different strands of thinking about the consultation between GPs and patients have been reviewed and summarised by Bower *et al.* in a paper that describes four domains for consultation research in primary care.[5] Although they are writing about the GP consultation in primary care, our work (in assessment and teaching of consultation skills to undergraduate medical students, GPs and experienced nurses and in running training workshops in assessment of consultation skills for hospital doctors) confirms that all the important consultation skills are generic. We therefore believe that their classification is also relevant to nurses and to hospital doctors.

The four domains are subdivided into internal (psychodynamic and clinical observational) and external (sociological and social-psychological). The internal domains are determined by, and arise from the consultation itself. The external domains refer to the application of pre-existing theories and methods from outside that are applied to the consultation. The psychodynamic domain emphasises the importance of emotions: those that the patient brings to the consultation and the interaction between these and the practitioner's response. It is dependent on a long-term relationship developing between practitioner and patient, with the focus of treatment on various forms of psychotherapy, and training in its use was designed to bring about personality change. This domain is the one that is most specific to primary care, and given its emphasis on the psychological dimension it is of more limited relevance to the treatment of acute illness and chronic, physical disease. The second internal domain, the clinical-observational, stresses the distinction between patient- and practitioner-centred consultations. The practitioner brings special skills and knowledge, which determine the issues they believe to be important. The patient has thoughts and feelings, which need to be revealed in order to bring about negotiated decision-making. The focus is on the behaviours of the practitioner that result in practitioner- or patient-centred consultation styles. These constitute the clinical method of the practitioner and can be taught. The training will teach specific skills, rather than aim to bring about global personality change as in the psycho-dynamic domain.

The social-psychological domain examines the attitudes, thoughts and beliefs that patients have about health and illness. It seeks to understand their health beliefs and how they explain illness. For this reason it is classified as 'external'. Whilst patient ideas are shaped by professional behaviour, they largely arise from life experiences that occur outside the consultation. The sociological domain views the consultation as a *social process* to be understood in terms of concepts like 'power' and 'knowledge'. The socio-economic status of the participants, gender and ethnicity are factors that help to explain why patients and practitioners behave in certain ways.

These four domains give us insight into the complexity of the consultation, and the vast array of variables that influence its outcome. The remainder of this chapter focuses on the clinical-observational domain, as our aim is to help readers develop their skills – their own clinical method that will determine the effectiveness of what they do.

Do nurses and doctors consult in the same way?

One issue that arises repeatedly is whether there are fundamental differences between consultations held by doctors and nurses. A secondary issue is whether practitioners in primary and secondary care consult with patients differently. In other words, are consultation skills truly generic? The clinical challenges faced by practitioners are very varied. Surgeons hold far fewer consultations in a week than GPs or nurse practitioners and any judgement over their general competence must be founded first and foremost on their ability to perform operations safely. This is not to say that it does not matter whether they consult well with patients. In order to make the correct judgement about the best treatment they are as dependent as any practitioner on their clinical skills, and if a patient cannot feel at ease with, and trust, their surgeon the outcome will be less favourable. Within the same setting, practitioners from the same discipline can have markedly different patterns of work. In the same general practice one nurse may perform treatment room procedures, whilst a colleague is dealing with diabetes and asthma care, and another is offering a 'minor illness' clinic. The nature of the problems they are dealing with is different, and this will affect the degree to which particular skills are needed. The treatment room nurse will be tested in the examination, diagnostic testing and procedures category of the CAIIN in almost every encounter, the nurse providing chronic disease management in care planning and the 'minor illness' nurse in problem solving. Despite these differences, at some point in their working day, they will all encounter patients that require them to exhibit every competence. If you are unsure about the truth of this argument, consider your own most recent working day, read each of the CAIIN competences listed at the start of Chapter 3 and recall instances where you had to be able to perform as described.

Our evidence for believing that there are no fundamental differences between medical and nursing consultations is derived from our studies, described in Chapter 1, to validate the consultation competences of the CAIIN with nurses. However, when our first workshops to teach nurses how to use the CAIIN to assess consultation skills were devised we encountered significant opposition to the idea that nurses diagnose illness. We were aware that for managerial and legal reasons nurse leaders would not concede that they do. Hence a term such as 'makes correct diagnoses' does not appear within the CAIIN as a consultation competence.

However, we do expect nurses to elicit relevant information from the history, look for relevant signs on examination and discriminate in the use of diagnostic tests. We also require them to interpret the information gathered and use their knowledge to identify the patient's problem. It would be the height of sophistry therefore for us to agree with the proposition that nurses do not diagnose, as the competences just given describe very precisely the thought processes that go on when a practitioner makes a diagnosis. It is therefore indisputable that nurses can, and do, diagnose. The range of diseases that any single nurse is likely to be called on to diagnose may be small, as is the case for many hospital specialists. Nevertheless, the fact that the number of likely diagnoses may be small does not diminish the need for competence in problem solving. Furthermore, many nurses work in settings where the number of potential diagnoses is very large.

It is often asserted that nurse education, in contradistinction to medical education, places high value on a holistic, patient-centred approach to clinical practice. In the absence of any systematic study of the curricula of schools of nursing and medicine to test the truth of this assertion, can we find evidence to support the view that nurses have better inter-personal skills than doctors? During the preparatory phase of the study to validate the CAIIN a nursing colleague and I watched 56 video-recorded consultations from seven nurses to determine what skills they were required to show. We concluded that the nurses concerned demonstrated considerable variation in the degree to which they were patient-centred and their ability to relate to the patient in a holistic way. This small sample cannot be seen as representative, but our observation is in tune with a 'common sense' view that all nurses could be placed at some point along a spectrum of 'patient-centred practice'. At one extreme the nurse simply orders her patient to obey instructions, at the other she is so 'in tune' with the patient that she overlooks the need to fulfil her professional role. Doctors could be placed along the same spectrum, and it would then be possible to see if the medical or nursing profession was more patient-centred (*see* Figure 2.1).

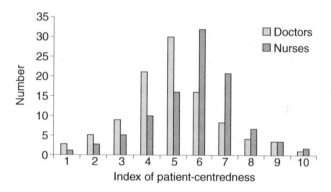

Figure 2.1:   Theoretical results of a study into patient-centredness of doctors and nurses.

To perform a study to test this view would be complex, time-consuming, expensive and pointless. Patients are concerned that *all* the practitioners they encounter are able to be as 'patient-centred' as the situation demands. If a surgeon examines a patient on the ward and believes her to be suffering from a ruptured ectopic pregnancy she needs the surgeon to advise surgery, without question. If the same patient returns 10 years later, to meet the same surgeon in connection with a cancer of the ovary she will probably want her to discuss in detail and negotiate the different treatment options available, using very high level inter-personal skills. The extent to which nurses are patient-centred depends upon the job they are doing. Nurses running a day-case unit where the emphasis is on getting patients through the procedure safely and home at the end of the day have organisational constraints put upon them that prevent them from being as patient-centred as say, palliative care nurses whose role is to form a relationship with patients and work in partnership with them to find the best way to manage their terminal illness. However, we should not confuse being patient-centred with possessing good interpersonal skills. The degree to which a consultation should follow the patient or professional agenda is dependent on context, but the use of good inter-personal skills by the practitioner is always desirable.

There is limited evidence, through direct comparison of the work of nurse practitioners and GPs, that patient satisfaction is higher amongst patients attending for 'first contact' care when seen by a nurse.[6,7] The small number of controlled studies has been limited to the diagnosis and treatment of acute minor illness, which is now a lesser part of the work of primary care practitioners. It has been suggested that an important reason for higher satisfaction with nurses is that consultation times are on average longer than with GPs. However, the only study that took this into account showed that the difference persisted.[8] There are, however, other potential biases, which were not taken into account. The studies did not control for the gender of nurses and doctors, nor did they consider the effect of 'burn out' from long experience. There is some evidence that patients of female doctors are more satisfied than those of male doctors.[9, 10] There is also evidence that older male GPs achieve lower patient satisfaction than younger male GPs.[11] Given that the biases of gender and age are likely to have been present in these studies it is unsafe to conclude that it is intrinsic to the role of the nurse that their patients will be more satisfied than those of a doctor.

There is one difference between medical and nursing consultations that is always present regardless of the setting in which they take place. This is the label 'nurse' or 'doctor' given to the practitioner the patient is seeing. These differences are likely to be external to the consultation and belong to the sociological domain described by Bowers et al.[5] The concepts of power and knowledge are relevant, as the patient will bring to the encounter preconceptions about the knowledge and skills of doctors and nurses and their respective roles.

Organisation of the consultation

In preparatory work to develop the CAIIN it was noted that nurses faced particular difficulty in the organisation of their consultations. In some cases a wish to be patient-centred resulted in the nurse following every twist and turn of the patient's story and thus lost sight of the direction and purpose of the encounter, which became patient-led. There were several examples of nurses gathering appropriate information to make a correct conclusion about the nature of, and best treatment for, the problem, and then encountering difficulty in gaining the patient's acceptance of their suggestions. In other cases nurses were providing care according to a predetermined formula. In these instances they were unable to either detect signals from patients that they needed to explore other issues, or had problems in responding appropriately when they recognised this need.

The available models of the consultation were reviewed in order to determine whether any would be suitable for use by nurses, regardless of the setting in which they work. None of the existing models appeared to be wholly suitable. We therefore developed a model that draws on the best elements of some of the existing models. It is designed to be applicable in any setting and for any practitioner consulting with patients. It is firmly in the clinical-observational domain of the taxonomy of Bower et al.[5] and it focuses on behaviours to be demonstrated by the practitioner, but it also incorporates the patient perspective and acknowledges the importance of the patient re-assuming responsibility for the problem at the close of the consultation.

It is not intended that the sequence of steps should be followed rigidly, but they do have a logical order. The model has been devised to complement the CAIIN and in particular to serve as a guide to practitioners who find that their consultations lack focus. We have prepared four clinical scenarios to demonstrate how the model helps to produce an effective consultation, incorporating the needs of the patient in different clinical settings.

A model of the consultation for all practitioners

The following list outlines the consultation model.

- Interpret prior knowledge about the patient.
- Set goals for the consultation.
- Gather sufficient information to make a provisional 'triple diagnosis'.
- Discover the patient's ideas, concerns and expectations about the problem(s).
- Carry out appropriate physical examination and near-patient tests to confirm or refute the diagnosis.
- Reconsider your assessment of the problem.
- Reach a shared understanding of the problem with the patient.
- Give the patient advice about what they need to do to tackle the problem.
- Explain the actions to be taken.
- Summarise and close.

Interpret prior knowledge about the patient

The amount of information available before the consultation starts varies hugely with the setting in which you work. It is rare not to know the age, gender and usually address before meeting with the patient. These three pieces of information alone hold valuable messages about the diagnostic probabilities and possible responses of the patient. In many settings the amount of information can be overwhelming. We are all familiar with the 'thick notes' problem when it would take several days to read everything. As a minimum a practitioner should review the most recent consultations. Properly ordered record systems should also allow you to see at a glance the main active problem(s) of patients and a list of current medication.

Set goals for the consultation

Goals too will be very dependent on the context of the consultation. It is worth taking a few moments before bringing the patient in to the consulting room to set your goals. In out-of-hours care the goal will usually be to define the problem causing the patient to seek a consultation and solve it efficiently. All other issues can be left to a future encounter. In chronic disease care you may have established these with the patient at the close of the previous consultation. In some instances it will be necessary to abandon your goals at the outset when the patient mentions a problem that must take precedence. In most encounters you will negotiate how many of your goals can be achieved, and what issues from the patient's agenda will be tackled.

Gather sufficient information to make a provisional 'triple diagnosis'

At this stage in the consultation you will be aiming to gather from the patient's history the correct amount of information you need to define the problem. The diagnostic process and the importance of the concept of the 'triple diagnosis' are described in Chapter 4. By the time you have finished taking the history you should have a reasonable idea of the scope of the problem, or if a new issue has arisen, the most probable cause. The diagnosis at this stage is provisional because it may require confirmation by examination, and in some cases the eventual diagnosis may not emerge until a future occasion.

Discover the patient's ideas, concerns and expectations about the problem(s)

At times the patient's ideas, concerns and expectations will be stated directly at the outset. More usually they will give some hints about their worries, but may be reluctant to admit to fears that they believe will cause the practitioner to label them as unduly anxious. They may have no prior expectations for treatment and be willing to accept whatever suggestion is made. In other instances they may want something to be done that the practitioner does not believe to be correct. It is difficult to reach a properly formulated diagnosis without knowing the patient's ideas, concerns and expectations, and it is impossible to formulate an acceptable care plan without this understanding.

Carry out appropriate physical examination and near-patient tests to confirm or refute the diagnosis

An essential skill for an effective clinical problem solver is to know the diagnostic value of signs on examination, or tests that will give you a result during the consultation such as pregnancy test. In many instances you will be using the *absence* of a sign (e.g. red ear drum) to rule out a diagnosis (acute otitis media). Physical examination does have a second function, which is to reassure patients that you have considered their problem seriously. This is particularly important for patients when verbal communication is limited by lack of a shared language.

Reconsider your assessment of the problem

After completing an examination and/or test(s) you will have further information, positive or negative, that you must incorporate into your thinking about the problem. When the problem is complex you may need to take some extra time to do this, on other occasions you will be confident about your assessment of the problem before the patient has finished dressing. It is essential you do not move to the next stage until you have properly reconsidered.

Reach a shared understanding of the problem with the patient

At times it is straightforward – you simply need to confirm that the patient's belief about the cause of the problem is correct. Alternatively, it can be very challenging. There are a number of techniques for reaching a shared understanding, which are described more fully in Chapter 4. It is vital to realise that proceeding to the next stages before you have done so is almost always a mistake.

Give the patient advice about what they need to do to tackle the problem

When practitioner and patient are in agreement about the nature of the problem, this is the most opportune moment to discuss the steps the patient needs to take. Having accepted your view, the patient is then cued to listen further. Most clinical problems depend on the patient doing what the practitioner proposes – self-treatment and lifestyle change are the cornerstone for management of a wide range of self-limiting illness and chronic disease. This stage also helps to achieve an essential goal for most consultations, which is that the patient re-assumes responsibility for the problem at the end.

Explain the actions to be taken

A number of facets of the care plan are for the practitioner to determine. These include whether to prescribe, what investigations (laboratory tests and images) are needed and if referral to a colleague is indicated. Although the patient may have strong views about a potentially harmful course of action (e.g. being given slimming tablets) reluctantly acceding to such a demand does not exonerate the practitioner from responsibility for the harmful outcome (addiction to amphetamines). Ordering excessive investigations or making unnecessary referrals is both wasteful and harmful and should not be done at the request of the patient. If the patient insists it is usually because the practitioner has failed to reach a true, shared understanding.

Summarise and close

Research shows that there are usually important differences between the recall of patients and practitioners when interviewed immediately afterwards. The forgotten items may be of less significance – or they might be essential. Every consultation with a patient must end with a summary of the key points. This should always include a discussion about follow up. Chapter 4 discusses this stage in more detail.

Organisation of the consultation – four examples

Each example is taken from a different clinical setting. It is unlikely that the reader will be familiar with all four settings but reading through each example will give better insight into why a model for organisation of the consultation can be so helpful in practice.

First-contact care: Health visitor 'drop-in' clinic

Carrie Ann is a three year old. Her family joined the practice list six months ago. She has a five-year-old brother and a six-month-old sister. You have met her mother and sister once when giving the third immunisation. Carrie Ann's records show that she was diagnosed as having asthma last year but that she has had no further contact or prescription for this condition since then.

- *Interpret prior knowledge about the patient*
She may be consulting with a problem related to her asthma. The mother's knowledge or understanding of the diagnosis could require checking because of the lack of subsequent treatment, or the diagnosis may need to be reconsidered.

- *Set goals for the consultation*
Discover the reason for consultation. If unrelated to the history of asthma, explore mother's understanding of the condition. Review need for health promotion activity including any concerns about development.

- *Gather sufficient information to make a provisional 'triple diagnosis'*

You learn that Carrie Ann has had a cough for one week. It started with a cold, but has now become 'chesty'. She has woken twice each night for three nights and last night she vomited after a prolonged coughing bout. Her mother mentions that she is 'getting worn out' and has taken time off from her part-time job as a school cleaner. Carrie Ann has felt hot to the touch on occasions during the last week, but her temperature has not been measured. Her mother tried using her inhaler again but it produced no improvement in her symptoms. You conclude she probably has a viral URTI (although asthma and a chest infection still need to be considered) and that this is imposing stresses on her mother.

- *Discover the patient's ideas, concerns and expectations about the problem(s)*

Her mother believes that Carrie Ann has a chest infection, which could result in her admission to hospital. She is expecting that a course of antibiotics will prevent this.

- *Carry out appropriate physical examination and near-patient tests to confirm or refute the diagnosis*

Carrie Ann has a runny nose, and during the consultation has coughed twice. She is alert but looks mildly unwell. You ask her mother to remove her T-shirt. She is breathing comfortably with no in-drawing between her ribs. Her respiratory rate is 20. Her temperature is 36.8 °C.

- *Reconsider your assessment of the problem*

You conclude that Carrie Ann has a viral upper respiratory tract infection.

- *Reach a shared understanding of the problem with the patient*

You explain the URTI to her mother. She asks whether this means you will be arranging for her to receive an antibiotic prescription, so you explain the nature of a viral infection, and the risk of side-effects and bacterial resistance from the overuse of antibiotics.

- *Give the patient advice about what they need to do to tackle the problem*

You advise Carrie Ann's mother on the importance of maintaining fluid intake, and relief of symptoms using paracetamol.

- *Explain the actions to be taken*

You recommend that Carrie Ann and her mother attend the Asthma Clinic at the practice to review her diagnosis and inhaler use.

- *Summarise and close*

You explain the symptoms that could indicate the development of a secondary chest infection and which should prompt a further consultation should they arise. You check that her mother has understood and accepted your conclusions.

Chronic disease management: Hospital diabetes clinic

Duncan Hamilton is a 56-year-old diabetic patient coming to see you for review. He takes gliclazide 80 mg per day. At a previous consultation three months ago he admitted he was not following his diet correctly since his wife had left him. His glycosolated haemoglobin then was 7.9% (4.5–6.3%). There is no record of an eye examination in his notes.

- *Interpret prior knowledge about the patient*
The break up of his marriage is likely to have resulted in poor eating habits, which is producing unacceptably high blood sugar levels.

- *Set goals for the consultation*
It will be necessary to take a detailed dietary history, and give practical advice. An appointment for retinal photography is needed.

- *Gather sufficient information to make a provisional 'triple diagnosis'*
You discover that his mood has been low, but is improving since starting a new relationship. You learn that before his wife left him he depended on her knowledge of correct eating habits. He is learning to prepare meals for himself, and his new partner. Your 'triple diagnosis' is that his loss of diabetic control resulted from a bereavement reaction, but recent changes in his social situation offer an opportunity for improvement.

- *Discover the patient's ideas, concerns and expectations about the problem(s)*
Mr Hamilton knows that his diet is unhealthy, and tells you that he is worried you will recommend that he needs to start insulin. His mother was diabetic and went blind in her early 70s. He expects you to check his eyesight.

- *Carry out appropriate physical examination and near-patient tests to confirm or refute the diagnosis*
You elect to check his blood pressure but no other examination is due at this time.

- *Reconsider your assessment of the problem*
His blood pressure is 132/70 so you conclude no alteration to his treatment is needed.

- *Reach a shared understanding of the problem with the patient*
You decide that the priority is improving Mr Hamilton's diet and he is ready to agree to this. You can reassure him that if he improves his diet he will not need to use insulin in the foreseeable future.

- *Give the patient advice about what they need to do to tackle the problem*
You arrange for retinal photography to take place. You also reinforce previous dietary advice and recommend a book he can obtain from the British Diabetic Association to support this.

- *Explain the actions to be taken*

You recommend an increase in the dose of gliclazide, and explain the need for a glycosylated haemoglobin test in three months.

- *Summarise and close*

You check he is willing to follow your advice, and has no other issue he wishes to discuss, before arranging to see him in three months to discuss the results of his next blood test.

Preventive health care: Family planning clinic

Sharlene is 19, she last attended six months ago for a review consultation having started the combined pill one year ago. She was satisfied with the pill at that time. Her records show that her BP was 118/70, her height was 1.6 m and her weight was 74 kg.

- *Interpret prior knowledge about the patient*

This is likely to be a straightforward consultation. She is slightly overweight (BMI 29).

- *Set goals for the consultation*

Check whether Sharlene is motivated to lose weight. Discuss the invitation she is due to receive soon for her first cervical smear.

- *Gather sufficient information to make a provisional 'triple diagnosis'*

You ask about Sharlene's periods and she tells you that they are fine, but in the last few days she has been worried because she has developed an unusual discharge. You discover it is creamy white; she has soreness of the vulva and it burns when she passes water. You decide thrush is the most likely diagnosis.

- *Discover the patient's ideas, concerns and expectations about the problem(s)*

You explore her use of the word 'worried', and she tells you that her friend sent her a text last month to say her boyfriend had been seen kissing another girl in a night club. He denied doing anything more, but she is not fully convinced. On learning this information you elaborate her diagnosis to include her fear of a sexually transmitted infection, and insecurity in her relationship with her boyfriend.

- *Carry out appropriate physical examination and near-patient tests to confirm or refute the diagnosis*

You check her blood pressure, which is 116/70. You examine her and note the typical appearance of thrush. In recognition of her concerns you take triple swabs to investigate whether she has a sexually transmitted infection.

• *Reconsider your assessment of the problem*
You conclude that she has *candida vaginitis,* because of the findings on history and examination. There is a small risk she may also have a sexually transmitted infection. Although she remains overweight you decide this is not an appropriate time to discuss dieting with her.

• *Reach a shared understanding of the problem with the patient*
You explain the nature of thrush, and reassure her that the risk of a sexually acquired infection is low.

• *Give the patient advice about what they need to do to tackle the problem*
You provide her with a patient information leaflet about thrush to reinforce your explanation and help her to prevent a reoccurrence in the future. If she is unsure about her boyfriend's fidelity she should avoid intercourse, or use a condom until she returns for the swab test results.

• *Explain the actions to be taken*
You provide her with a prescription for a clotrimazole pessary, and explain the nature of the swab tests you have taken. You ask her to return to see the clinic doctor in one week for the results.

• *Summarise and close*
Although you have arranged for the problem with her discharge to be followed up by a doctor, you will still need to advise her to return in six months for a review of her contraception. You check her understanding, and whether you have succeeded in allaying some of her fears.

Treatment room care: District nurse clinic

Geoffrey is 76. He has been coming to the clinic weekly for two months for dressings to his leg ulcer, which is a result of long standing varicose veins.

• *Interpret prior knowledge about the patient*
This is likely to be a straightforward procedure as no difficulties have been noted previously, although the ulcer had not diminished in size when last dressed.

• *Set goals for the consultation*
Check on the progress of the ulcer. If it remains the same size, discuss changing the type of dressing with the patient.

• *Gather sufficient information to make a provisional 'triple diagnosis'*
You ask Geoffrey how he has been over the last week. He tells you that his leg has been uncomfortable. The dressings appear to be tighter than before and his leg throbs at the end of the day. Despite this he is cheerful in

himself, although he admits that because his bedroom is so cold he has been sleeping in his armchair in the living room. You are concerned that he may have developed an infection in his affected leg.

- *Discover the patient's ideas, concerns and expectations about the problem(s)*
You ask Geoffrey what he feels might be causing the problem and he says he is concerned he might have a blood clot because he was warned that people with varicose veins can get a DVT.

- *Carry out appropriate physical examination and near-patient tests to confirm or refute the diagnosis*
You remove the dressings and inspect his leg carefully. The base of the ulcer looks more inflamed than before and there is an area of redness and swelling of the skin on the leg from the top of his ankle to the middle of his shin. He is not ill, and his temperature and pulse are normal.

- *Reconsider your assessment of the problem*
You conclude that the examination confirms your initial view that he has developed localised cellulitis.

- *Reach a shared understanding of the problem with the patient*
You explain that he has developed an infection in his ulcer, which is potentially serious.

- *Give the patient advice about what they need to do to tackle the problem*
You explain the importance of elevating his legs when he is seated in his chair and of sleeping in his bed at night.

- *Explain the actions to be taken*
You tell him you will ask the doctor to see him before re-dressing the ulcer as you believe he requires treatment with antibiotics. You also sensitively enquire whether he needs additional financial help to enable him to keep his bedroom warmer.

- *Summarise and close*
After the doctor has seen him you apply the dressing. You check that he understands how to take his antibiotic treatment, and that he is aware of the danger signs that could indicate the infection is spreading. You explain that until the infection has cleared he will need to be reviewed twice a week.

References

1. Kurtz SM, Draper J, Silverman J. *Teaching and Learning Communication Skills in Medicine (2e)*. Abingdon: Radcliffe Medical Press. 2004
2. Fraser RC. *Clinical Method: a general practice approach (3e)*. Oxford: Butterworth-Heineman. 1999.

3. Neighbour R. *The Inner Consultation: how to develop an effective and intuitive consulting style (2e)*. Abingdon: Radcliffe Medical Press. 2004.

4. Stott NC, Davis RH. The exceptional potential in each primary care consultation. *J Roy Coll Gen Pract*. 1979; **29**(201), 201–5.

5. Bower P, Gask L, May C, Mead N. Domains of consultation research in primary care. *Patient Educ Couns*. 2001; **45**(1), 3–11.

6. Bond S, Beck S, Derrick S, Sargeant S, Cunningham W, Healey B *et al*. Training nurse practitioners for general practice. The EROS Project Team. *Br J Gen Pract*. 1999; **49**(444), 531–5.

7. Shum C, Humphreys A, Wheeler D, Cochrane MA, Skoda S, Clement S. Nurse management of patients with minor illnesses in general practice: multicentre, randomised controlled trial. *Brit Med J*. 2000; **320**(7241), 1038–43.

8. Kinnersley P, Anderson E, Parry K, Clement J, Archard L, Turton P *et al*. Randomised controlled trial of nurse practitioner versus general practitioner care for patients requesting 'same day' consultations in primary care. *Brit Med J*. 2000; **320**(7241), 1043–8.

9. Delgado A, Lopez-Fernandez LA, Luna JD. Influence of the doctor's gender in the satisfaction of the users. *Med Care*. 1993; **31**(9), 795–800.

10. Roter DL, Hall JA, Aoki Y. Physician gender effects in medical communication: a meta-analytic review. *JAMA*. 2002; **288**(6), 756–64.

11. Wensing M, Vedsted P, Kersnik J, Peersman W, Klingenberg A, Hearnshaw H *et al*. Patient satisfaction with availability of general practice: an international comparison. *Int J Qual Health Care*. 2002; **14**(2), 111–18.

Chapter 3

The Consultation Assessment and Improvement Instrument for Nurses (CAIIN)

Sarah Redsell and Adrian Hastings

Introduction

In Chapter 1 the new roles that nurses are undertaking were discussed and how the recognition of these led to the need to develop a means of assessing and teaching consultation skills to nurses. Chapter 2 included a discussion of whether nurse consultations are uniquely different from those performed by doctors. The final section proposed a model for the organisation of the consultation. In this chapter the Consultation Assessment and Improvement Instrument for Nurses (CAIIN) is examined and the reason for its division into categories and the meaning of the competences are considered.

Categories and component competences of the CAIIN

Interviewing

This category includes the range of competences that a nurse needs to gather information from talking to the patient.

- Puts patients at ease.
- Enables patients to explain situation/problem fully.
- Listens attentively.
- Seeks clarification of words used by patients as appropriate.
- Demonstrates an ability to formulate open questions.
- Phrases questions simply and clearly.
- Uses silence appropriately.
- Recognises patients' verbal and non-verbal cues.
- Considers physical, social and psychological factors as appropriate.
- Demonstrates a well-organised approach to information gathering.

Examination, diagnostic testing and practical procedures

This category includes the competences that a nurse needs to elicit physical signs; to use instruments (e.g. sphygmomanometer) or to undertake practical procedures (e.g. passing a naso-gastric tube or urinary catheterisation).

- Elicits physical signs correctly and sensitively.
- Uses instruments in a competent and sensitive manner.
- Performs technical procedures in a competent and sensitive manner.

Care planning and patient management

This category includes the competences that a nurse needs to develop a care plan by working in partnership with patients to negotiate its content and agreeing goals.

- Formulates and follows appropriate care plans.
- Reaches a shared understanding about the problem with the patient.
- Negotiates care plans with the patient.
- Uses clear and understandable language.
- Educates patients appropriately in practical procedures.
- Makes discriminating use of referral, investigation and drug treatment.
- Arranges appropriate follow-up.

Problem solving

This category includes the competences that a nurse needs to decide about the nature of the patient's/client's problem(s) and the associated care plan. It concerns the cognitive (thinking) skills required to decide what information is needed and how it should be interpreted.

- Accesses relevant information from patients' records.
- Explores patients' ideas, concerns and expectations about their problem(s).
- Elicits relevant information from the patient.
- Seeks relevant clinical signs and makes appropriate use of clinical tests.
- Correctly interprets information gathered.
- Applies clinical knowledge appropriately in the identification and management of the patient's problem.
- Recognises limits of personal competence and acts accordingly.

Behaviour and relationship with patients

This category includes the competences that a nurse needs to establish a professional relationship with the patient.

- Maintains a friendly but professional relationship with patients.
- Conveys sensitivity to the needs of patients.
- Is able to use the professional relationship in a manner likely to achieve mutual agreement with the care plan.

Health promotion/disease prevention

This category includes the competences that a nurse needs to identify and act appropriately on opportunities for health promotion/disease prevention.

- Acts on appropriate opportunities for health promotion and disease prevention.
- Provides appropriate explanation to patient for preventive initiatives suggested.
- Works in partnership with the patient to encourage the adoption of a healthier lifestyle.

> **Record keeping**
>
> This category includes the competences that a nurse needs to make an appropriate and accurate record of the consultation.
>
> - Makes an appropriate and legible record of the consultation.
> - Records care plan to include advice and follow-up arrangements as appropriate.
> - Enters results of measurements in records.
> - Provides the names(s), dose and quantity of drug(s) prescribed to the patient together with any special precautions.

Category divisions within the CAIIN

The first three categories of 'interviewing'; 'examination, diagnostic testing and practical procedures'; and 'care planning/patient management' follow the usual sequence of a consultation. The amount of time spent within each category will vary greatly, depending on the setting. If Brian, a district nurse, is re-dressing a leg ulcer for a patient he knows well, almost all the time he spends will be in performing a practical procedure and maintaining rapport. However, he will still need to check the patient's progress since the last visit and to consider the social and psychological impact of the problem. There may be very little problem-solving if no new developments have arisen, but if the patient reports more pain and swelling since the last visit Brian will have to consider the possibility of a new diagnosis. Even if there are no new developments the care plan should be briefly reviewed. Each time Brian meets with this patient he will need to develop their relationship and make a record of the encounter. If the patient's lifestyle is contributing to the problem he may do some health promotion by encouraging the patient to lose weight. In a review consultation for chronic obstructive pulmonary disease (COPD) the nurse and patient might agree that the only goal to be tackled on that occasion is to work together to help the patient adopt a healthier lifestyle by giving up smoking.

In most consultations the nurse will demonstrate the skills in the first three categories in sequence. Although it is desirable to organise the consultation in the way that is suggested, it may also be appropriate to return to interviewing after examining, if the patient unexpectedly mentions a new symptom. The 'problem-solving' category is challenged continuously within the consultation. There are detailed discussions in Chapter 4 of how experienced practitioners use their reasoning skills to make a diagnosis and in Chapter 5 of how decision-making depends on accessing and interpreting knowledge from memory and information sources.

Similarly the category 'behaviour and relationship with patients' is a continuous activity. The depth of challenge to the nurse's skill can quickly change. The patient may begin a consultation by saying that he expects an antibiotic for a sore throat. If the nurse does not challenge him about this expectation then he will remain at ease whilst the nurse asks him some further questions and examines his throat. However, when the nurse has to explain that antibiotics are not necessary she is likely to encounter a very strong challenge to her ability to maintain a good relationship with the patient.

Health promotion and disease prevention can arise as an important activity in two ways. It may form the central aspect of the patient's reason for consulting – for example discussing the need to perform an overdue smear test at a contraception clinic, or diet change for a patient with angina and high cholesterol. Alternatively, the nurse may note an important health promotion opportunity unrelated to the problem. In a 'walk-in' centre on a quiet afternoon a patient attends with a sprained ankle, which is quickly sorted out. However, the nurse has heard the patient cough several times and seen that her fingers are nicotine stained. Encouraging her to give up smoking on this occasion has the potential to be the most valuable encounter she has with a health professional in her entire life.

Record keeping is an essential activity in every consultation. The means by which information is recorded is subject to many factors. The professional imperative for keeping good records is to remind yourself of facts you will forget, and if necessary to allow a colleague to deal with the problem if you are not available. Managers require records to measure professional activity and they form the basis for determining if targets have been met. The record must also provide evidence that you are practising to required standards should an allegation of negligence about your actions, or inactions, arise. The methods of recording clinical information are immensely varied – they can be free text on blank paper, tick boxes on forms, free text on computer or data in fields that can subsequently be searched. The nurse is faced with an important dilemma during the consultation – should she record information as the patient is talking, or wait until the end. The tension is between not paying full attention to the patient whilst writing or typing, and failing to record an important fact.

Component competences in the CAIIN

In the following section the competences in each category are considered and how nurses are challenged to demonstrate their skills, and some appropriate ways of responding are also discussed.

Interviewing

Putting patients at ease

The start of the consultation is very important. First impressions count. If you have not met the patient before, introduce yourself by name and explain your role. Some nurses like to call patients in from the waiting room and escort them to their chair. A handshake might be expected by an extrovert professional person, but would be very inappropriate if offered by a male nurse to a veiled Muslim woman. If this is a review consultation if may be appropriate to discuss the patient's understanding of the previous meeting. Although the start is important, patients can quickly become uncomfortable if an embarrassing topic is being discussed. At this point particular care will be needed to cause them to relax again. Even if you get off to a good start being distracted by the computer or telephone, or failing to maintain good eye contact and body posture will result in patients feeling uncomfortable.

Enable patients to explain situation/problem fully

The stories patients tell carry most meaning if they use their own words. It is important to start the consultation in as open a way as possible. Often it is not necessary to ask a question to start. Simply nodding and saying, 'yes' and nothing more will allow the patient to begin. Alternatively you could say, 'How can I help?'. As the consultation proceeds there will be opportunities to encourage the patient to elaborate – prompts such as, 'I see'; 'Tell me more about that'; 'How did that make you feel?' are very effective. At some point it is usually appropriate to move to a more practitioner-centred style. If this is done too quickly much useful information can be lost, and patients will not have the opportunity to give the verbal cues that are so valuable in understanding their ideas about the problem. If patients start to repeat information already provided, or stray from the problem it will then be necessary to use closed questions to move the consultation forward.

Listen attentively

The way you respond to patients will often determine how much they reveal to you. A patient who has plucked up the courage to come for an appointment about something that has been bothering them for a while wants you to listen to them. It is not helpful if you are distracted from the task of listening by external interruptions such as the telephone or a knock on the door. Obviously some distractions are unavoidable but you should try and arrange your clinic to be as free from interruptions as possible. It is also helpful to think about how you listen to patients in terms of using appropriate body language and eye contact and whether it is necessary to interrupt their flow by entering data on the computer or writing. Whilst patients are explaining their symptoms to you it is important to pay attention to what they are actually saying rather than think about the next question or how their problems might be managed. If you miss information that the patient has previously given, you will need to ask the question again and the patient will lose confidence that you are listening attentively.

Seek clarification of words used by patients as appropriate

Patients will sometimes use language where the meaning is unclear. For example they might use medical or technical terms to describe their condition but they may not have the same understanding of the term as you. For example a patient may say, 'I have constipation' by which he means he hasn't used the toilet for two days but which you may understand as hard, dry stools that are infrequently passed. Patients may also use other language that is local or cultural and make assumptions that you understand them. If patients use words, the meaning of which is unclear to you ask them to explain.

Demonstrate an ability to formulate open questions

At the beginning of the consultation it is essential that you keep all your opinions open about why patients have attended. Many practitioners make decisions about what they think the patient's problem is too early in the consultation. Therefore, although you may already have an idea about what is going on it is important that your questions show you still have an open mind. Questions such as, 'How did that affect you?' and 'How did that happen?' will help you to explore all the possible options.

Phrase questions simply and clearly

In order to formulate an appropriate diagnosis, clarification of the patient's current symptoms is required. Remember they may find it difficult to comprehend complex questions so keep sentence structure simple and tailor questions to the patient. Try to avoid using leading questions such as, 'You haven't passed any blood have you?'. These can lead patients to give an incorrect response. If a patient is in denial about the significance of rectal bleeding he may respond by saying, 'Umm, no...'. It is easy to miss the significance of this hesitation and a key piece of information is lost. Also, try not to use 'double' or 'nested' questions such as, 'What is your pain like and how long have you had it?'. Patients are likely to answer only the second part of the question and are unlikely to respond to the first. Ideally your questions should not contain jargon but if the patient is comfortable using clinical terms to discuss their condition ensure you both share an understanding of their meaning before proceeding.

Use silence appropriately

Silence is important within the conversational flow to allow you and the patient time to think. If patients do not respond immediately to a question allow them time to think before repeating or re-phrasing the question. Try not to keep talking within the long silences. If patients have difficulty telling their story or are distressed it is important to maintain the silence until they have regained their composure. If patients tell you something distressing it is usually helpful to acknowledge it and then keep silent for a while to demonstrate respect for what they have said.

Recognise patients' verbal and non-verbal cues

Patients will frequently provide cues for you to pick up which can help with the process of determining what is going on. A cue from a patient is an invitation to explore further something of concern to them. Try to develop your awareness of statements that may indicate the need to probe further for example, 'My husband's at home all day now'. Cues are sometimes not direct statements but take the form of an unusual remark or body language that does not match what the patient is saying. Non-verbal cues can also provide important information – for example if a patient laughs when you are discussing something serious there may be a problem. Sometimes the cue is given by body language. If you know that a patient has a partner who is violent with an alcohol problem, the fact that they fail to mention this during the consultation but appear edgy may be relevant. Try and develop sensitivity to patients' demeanour or mood. If they appear happy, sad, sensitive, anxious, or depressed ask yourself whether the reasons need to be further explored.

Consider physical, social and psychological factors as appropriate

All problems patients bring to practitioners will have physical, psychological and social dimensions. The physical dimensions are likely to be the most obvious as these will present with disease symptoms. The psychological dimensions may be less obvious and will include the attitude of patients to their illness and the distress they feel about being unwell. The social dimensions are those that impact on their social life such as caring for relatives or coping with work. Developing an awareness of how these factors interact will help you plan appropriate care for your patients. For example a female patient being offered major cardiac surgery may need considerable time to prepare because of her role as the head of the household and the family's ability to manage in her absence.

Demonstrate a well-organised approach to information gathering

Before patients arrive it is important that you have some understanding of who they are and why they might be presenting today. This will give you a plan for the start of the consultation. When the patient enters it is important to check early in the consultation whether your plan is appropriate or if the patient has a different agenda. If a patient's agenda is different then consider it, returning to aspects of your plan as appropriate. For example, a nurse running a hypertension clinic will have specific targets to achieve with patients. A patient may arrive and want to discuss their stress. The nurse should deal with this, but also return to the matter of treatment of hypertension as appropriate. If patients bring several issues to the discussion it is often helpful to identify these towards the beginning of the consultation and deal with each in turn. If you run out of time acknowledge this with patients and ask them to make another appointment indicating that you will deal with other topics during the next appointment.

In order to make the consultation run smoothly it is helpful to elicit all the information you require from the symptoms patients describe before you begin to tell them what you think is going on and develop management plans. If you begin to manage a patient's condition too early in the consultation this can result in the patient revealing new information and you will have to restart the consultation. For example, a teenage girl may present with symptoms of frequency and urgency in emptying her bladder. You may decide there and then that she has a urinary tract infection and send her off to pass a urine sample. However, if the urinalysis test proves negative you then have to go back to her and ask more questions about vaginal discharge, periods and sexual behaviour.

Examination, diagnostic testing and practical procedures

Elicit physical signs correctly and sensitively

To become competent in examining patients you will need to practise your technique on healthy people to learn what normal looks, feels and sounds like. In order to learn to detect abnormal physical signs you should take every opportunity to examine patients with these, within the constraints of behaving ethically. These skills can only be learnt by practice under supervision so ask a colleague to demonstrate them if you are uncertain.

Use instruments in a competent and sensitive manner

Exactly the same principles apply to learning to use instruments as those suggested above for eliciting physical signs.

Perform technical procedures in a competent and sensitive manner

Nurses are called upon to perform a very wide range of practical procedures, and the details of how these are to be done are different. However, there are some general issues that must also be considered, including gaining consent and providing an explanation. Gentleness is necessary to minimise discomfort, but excessive caution can prolong a procedure unnecessarily. If in doubt about your competence to undertake the procedure you must not do so.

Care planning and patient management

Formulate and follow appropriate care plans

Once all the information has been gathered from the patient you will have to consider an appropriate care plan. This should be formulated as best practice for that particular condition and address the patient's needs. The plan will almost always incorporate some advice to patients about actions they need to take themselves (for example, losing weight, smoking cessation). You will also need to consider if a prescription is required and whether investigations should be ordered. Referral may be necessary to another health professional or to a different agency such as social services or a voluntary counselling service. The future stage in the care plan will involve a decision about follow up. Preparing the care plan can be very quick if the problem is straightforward. In other cases it can be complex and may require one or two minutes of careful thought before speaking to the patient.

Reach a shared understanding about the problem with the patient

Patients and nurses need to have a similar understanding of the nature of the problem if a care plan is to be successful. It is important to share your views about what you think is going on with patients and to pause to allow them to clarify specific issues. If there is disagreement try and resolve this through discussion. It is often the case that patients have not been given sufficient information, in terms they can comprehend, to understand the problem properly. However, on occasions you will acknowledge that it is not possible to reach a shared understanding and you may need to ask patients to return on another day to discuss things further, or refer them to another health professional. There are several ways that you might improve patients' understanding about their problems. These include asking them to sum up their understanding of what you have said and giving them opportunities to question you. When appropriate, patient information leaflets and good quality Internet information provide excellent reinforcement of your explanation and advice.

Negotiate care plans with the patient

Although you may formulate appropriate evidence-based care plans patients are unlikely to comply with them if you haven't explained your proposals fully and incorporated their views. In order to do this effectively you must have discovered their concerns and expectations. The process will involve you explaining what you think needs to be done and your rationale for this decision. If patients have different ideas consider whether these can be accommodated. It is important that they have sufficient information to make informed decisions; particularly in relation to areas of disagreement. Patients have a right to follow a less effective course of action than the one supported by best evidence, but you must have provided them with an explanation of the risks and benefits of each strategy. Patients who take an active role in formulating their care plan are more likely to follow it than those who have been instructed what to do.

Use clear and understandable language

When you are explaining things to patients remember that they may not take in much of what you are saying. This might be because they feel emotional about their condition or because they cannot understand what you are saying or both. Try and tailor your explanations to both the emotional state of patients and their level of understanding. Breaking down the information into small chunks may be beneficial as well as reinforcing the information in future consultations as appropriate.

Educate patients appropriately in practical procedures

Examples of practical procedures that patients perform are self-administration of insulin, charting peak-flow readings and intermittent self-catheterisation. Before you start find out the patient's current understanding of the procedure and tailor your explanation accordingly. Demonstrate the procedure to them and ask them to practise under supervision. It may be necessary to allow additional time to clarify areas of misunderstanding and to offer further consultations to check their technique and explain missing components in their understanding. Providing written information can sometimes be useful but if leaflets are used it is important that you have checked their content for consistency.

Make discriminating use of referral, investigation and drug treatment

Errors of omission (in this instance not referring, failing to do a test or not prescribing a drug) are often seen to be worse than unintended harm arising from a decision to do something. However, it is important to remember that an unnecessary referral wastes the time of patients and colleagues, and can cause much anxiety for the patient and family. Furthermore, another patient with a more serious condition may be delayed in their treatment. Investigations can be an expensive and scarce resource. No diagnostic test is completely reliable so even if it is cheap a false-positive result will require further tests to establish the true facts. It may seem safer to prescribe an antibiotic for a patient with a sore throat 'just in case' but if the evidence suggests limited benefit and the possibility of harm through side-effects, interactions and drug resistance then not prescribing becomes the correct course of action. Discrimination in prescribing includes checking for important interactions with other medication, explaining likely side-effects to patients and how the items should be taken.

Arrange appropriate follow-up

If the problem is likely to resolve, or you consider that further advice would not be helpful at this stage then use 'open' follow-up. This means letting patients decide when to return but requires you to provide guidance as to the circumstances when this is necessary. If follow-up is essential indicate the time during which likely changes will take place and arrange a time for the follow-up appointment. In particular if patients are sent home on new medication it is important to let them know when their symptoms are likely to subside and any potential side-effects are likely to appear that require more urgent re-consultation. When patients are being transferred from one level of care to another it is important they are clear who to contact if they have a problem before they are due to be seen again.

Problem solving

Access relevant information from patients' records

Before patients arrive it is important that you have some understanding of who they are and why they might be presenting today. In the case of a new presentation consider the patient's age, gender and other demographic information. Read carefully any referral information available. In review consultations as a minimum you should always look at the summary details of the last consultation and be aware of the main active diagnoses. If time permits, a more detailed consideration of the record is almost always worthwhile. During the consultation it is important to refer back to the patient's records to guide you. You may also need to refer to the records to help you understand the history of the patient's illness, particularly if factual details are unclear.

Explore patients' ideas, concerns and expectations about their problem(s)

In each consultation you must be satisfied that you have established the patient's reason(s) for the consultation. Even when the appointment is for review of a continuing problem ensure you have understood their ideas about what is going to occur. When the patient presents with multiple problems try and find out what their main concerns are. This may require direct enquiry about their view of the nature of the problem, its cause and possible effects. Verbal cues from patients often provide an indication of their underlying concern. 'I wouldn't have come but my sister had one last year', could be a cue to discuss a family history of breast lump. Consider when is the most appropriate time to ask about a patient's expectations for treatment. If there is still a significant element of diagnostic uncertainty it is probably better to wait until you know what the problem is and how you think you are going to manage it, before exploring what the patient wishes to be done.

Elicit relevant information from patients

A diagnosis can usually be made from a patient's symptoms. Once patients have had an opportunity to explain the problem in their own words, identify the key features of the problem and concentrate your questions on these. If you do not have sufficient information focus your questions on the specific areas that concern you and fill in the information gaps by asking specific and tailored questions.

Seek relevant clinical signs and make appropriate use of clinical tests

Before embarking on a physical examination of the patient it is worth thinking through which signs, if present or absent, will help you to decide between competing diagnoses. The examination should not be used to look for abnormal physical signs that might be incidentally present. This will impose an unjustifiable burden on patients, particularly if elderly, very young or ill. Clinical tests should be used in the same way. These are tests that can be undertaken during the consultation, whilst the patient is present. Be aware of the specificity and sensitivity of each test you use. For example, a urine dip test for pregnancy has very high specificity (i.e. if it is positive it almost always confirms that the patient is pregnant). Other tests have high sensitivity. A urine dip test that is negative for protein, red and white blood cells and nitrites rules out a diagnosis of urinary tract infection.

Correctly interpret information gathered

The information you gather from patients can only be used effectively if it is correctly interpreted. Once you have gathered the information take sufficient time to consider what it means and how you can apply it. Sometimes it is helpful to organise your thoughts by summarising them and reflecting back to patients what they have told you. This has two benefits: it will confirm to them you have understood the problem and it will clarify your thoughts. To make correct diagnoses you will need to be familiar with the evidence base for the problems you encounter frequently. If there is a feature present in the history or examination that you do not understand check with books, reference papers, on-line data sources, or a colleague. It is a common source of diagnostic error to focus on the features that support a conclusion that has been reached before sufficient information has been gathered. When patients provide information that contradicts the initial diagnosis practitioners find it difficult to assimilate this and one of two responses may occur. The practitioner may ignore the conflicting information and reach an incorrect conclusion, or the practitioner heeds the new information and is then required to start the diagnostic process again. If you recognise a pattern of signs and symptoms that almost matches a diagnosis, consider very carefully any feature that does not fit, as this may be the pointer to an alternative possibility.

Apply clinical knowledge appropriately in the identification and management of a patient's problem

An adequate knowledge base is indispensable to make a diagnosis. If an experienced nurse moves to a new field, she will almost certainly need to spend a substantial amount of time learning relevant facts about the diseases she will encounter. However, basic clinical knowledge of anatomy can help if in doubt. For example a pain in the calf might come from a muscle, blood vessel or nerve. Understanding pathological mechanisms can also aid diagnosis. For example, considering differences in the way in which patients become ill from an acute infection and from cancer often assists you in working out the true diagnosis. In managing patients' problems you will need to know the most effective management and be aware of alternatives you can offer if patients reject your preferred treatment. It is in this area that knowledge changes most rapidly so you will be challenged to keep up to date.

Recognise limits of personal competence and act accordingly

A vital feature of being a professional is developing a level of self-awareness that enables you to acknowledge that there is much that you do not know. There are no healthcare practitioners in the world that know everything, even in the field in which they are expert. The minimum standard is that we understand enough about our everyday work to practise safely. It is therefore an excellent professional attribute to recognise the limits of your competence. When you recognise that you have reached the limits of your competence do not guess – seek appropriate help by asking colleagues or consulting the many information sources available. Patients are likely to recognise when you do not know something. Do not be afraid to tell them that you do not know. They will usually appreciate your honesty and you can always follow-up by saying that you will find out.

Behaviour/relationship with patients

Maintain friendly but professional relationship with patients

The degree to which you are friendly with patients largely depends upon the nature of the relationship they require from you and your reaction to them. It is unlikely that you will be able to establish and maintain 'easy' relationships with all your patients. As a basic standard adopt a friendly demeanour relevant to the circumstances of the individual patient. Remember that individuals from different cultural groups differ greatly in their needs. Whilst some prefer an open, friendly style others wish you to be more reserved. A professional approach implies that you are polite, that you demonstrate concern and consideration, but also that you avoid inappropriate emotional engagement with the patient.

Convey sensitivity to the needs of patients

It is important that you consider what it would be like to be the patient receiving the information that you are giving them. The psychological state of sympathy is closely linked with that of empathy, but is not identical to it. Empathy refers to the ability to perceive and understand another person's emotions, but does not necessarily imply a *sharing* of these emotions. Patients usually respond well to sensitive expressions of empathy. This becomes most effective when linked with a process of problem definition that assures the patient their concerns have been acknowledged. If a patient becomes upset with you respond appropriately within your professional boundaries. Try not to allow your emotional reaction to comments to enter into the discussion. If a patient becomes angry an appropriate response might include, 'I can see that you are upset about this'. If a patient becomes distressed, allowing silence, slowing the pace of the consultation and the appropriate use of touch demonstrate sensitivity.

Be able to use the professional relationship in a manner likely to achieve mutual agreement with the care plan

Patients are far more likely to agree with care plans if they feel they have actively participated in them. To enable this to happen you need to reach a shared understanding with patients about their problem. If there is uncertainty about the nature of the problem you may need to explain the process by which you have reached your conclusions. The patient's views about the problem and its management should be explicitly acknowledged and decision-making shared, as appropriate.

Health promotion/disease prevention

Act on appropriate opportunities for health promotion and disease prevention

Some interventions will be dictated by the nature of the problem. It is mandatory to consider how a patient with asthma be helped to give up smoking. In other consultations an observation (for example of a hand tremor and smell of alcohol on the breath) may lead to a preventive intervention unrelated to the reason for consultation. Before embarking on health promotion issues, establish a patient's motivation to change and be sensitive to their circumstances and beliefs. Once you have identified preventive opportunities, select and prioritise these according to the evidence for their effectiveness and the circumstances of the patient. Remember that there may be circumstances that might make a preventive intervention harmful, even though otherwise indicated. Pressurising one person in a family to switch to a different diet, when the other members are unwilling to do so is likely to produce nihilism rather than change.

Provide appropriate explanation to patients for preventive explanations suggested

Before you initiate your choice of preventive actions ask patients what they have tried previously and their perceptions of success. Talk to them about why you think it is important that they try this particular intervention and work towards setting objectives for their undertaking. Continually check their responses and if they do not appear to be listening they probably are not. Remember that you may need to see them again to check their understanding and consent before initiating any intervention.

Work in partnership with patients to encourage the adoption of a healthier lifestyle

Establish patients' level of motivation to change and then agree an action plan. The action plan may involve a series of achievable interim targets, which move towards an overall goal. When working with patients undertaking lifestyle changes, be consistently positive about their benefits. Try and adopt a supportive approach and provide encouragement and reinforcement. Offer patients continuing support and review of their progress through regular follow-up consultations. Remember there is no point in repeatedly trying to alter the behaviour of an informed patient who rejects your intervention.

Record keeping

Make an appropriate and legible record of the consultation

The information recorded needs to be sufficient for another nurse to be able to continue the care as planned (or adjusted as necessary). The minimum information set is date, summary of key findings, significant examination findings, a diagnosis or problem definition (which should also be coded if using computer records).

Record care plan to include advice, prescription and follow-up arrangements as appropriate

Once you have reached agreement with patients about the problem and plan for treatment you will need to record this in their records. In circumstances where patients can take action themselves to improve their situation it may be helpful to draw up a contract with agreed targets. Where you have made an agreement with patients about when they should return, this should be recorded. You also need to record any investigations requested and referral elsewhere together with the date these were undertaken.

Enter results of measurement in records

The results of tests undertaken during the consultation, such as weight and blood pressure, should be recorded immediately as they can be quickly forgotten. A useful way of doing this is to record the numerical values on a jotting pad for later referral. If possible you should avoid searching the patient's record or computer for a specific place to enter the results until an appropriate moment arises. Otherwise the focus of the consultation is likely to change and the patient is likely to either remain quiet or to provide you with important information when you are not sufficiently focused to heed it. Once the patient has left you can review the record you have made to ensure the important measurements have been recorded in the appropriate place.

Provide the names, dose and quantity of drugs prescribed to patients together with any special precautions

When a prescription is issued you should inform the patient of the drug name, the dose to be taken and at what times of day. The duration of treatment and specific information about important side-effects should be given. This information must be recorded in the notes.

Conclusion

In this chapter the meaning and the importance of each of the consultation competences within the CAIIN have been discussed. Once the chapter has been read it would be useful to observe a consultation and to recognise many of the competences in action. This consultation could be one of your own recorded on videotape or a colleague you are teaching or mentoring. You will find that your judgements about the performance, whether good or poor, will be more focused, and that it will be clearer what steps should be taken to ensure improvement.

The use of CAIIN in formal assessments has not been covered. This description is given in Chapter 9 'Using the CAIIN for assessment'. It includes the documentation for undertaking a formal assessment and preparing written feedback. It also contains recommended strategies for improvement, which are a summary of much of this chapter in a tabulated form, to assist an assessor in giving specific advice.

In Chapters 4 and 5 clinical problem solving (which includes making a diagnosis and choosing a care plan) is discussed in depth. The majority of the readers of this book are expected to have reasonable confidence in their interviewing skills and their ability to relate to patients. However, for most practitioners the most challenging part of their role is clinical problem solving.

Chapter 4

Making the diagnosis

Adrian Hastings

Introduction

The dictionary definition of diagnosis is, 'the act or process of identifying or determining the nature and cause of a disease'. In consultations where patients present with new problems determining an accurate diagnosis is an essential goal. The diagnosis informs in what way the normal functioning of the body has been disrupted and clinical knowledge indicates how it can be restored. It is very important to understand that many clinical terms are misused. Constipation is frequently given as a diagnosis, but it is not – it is a symptom. Although constipation is a disorder of the function of the large bowel it can result from many different disease processes. On occasion it is simply due to lack of fluid and fibre in the diet, alternatively it can be the first symptom of bowel cancer. The consequences of treating undiagnosed constipation with a laxative could either be ineffective treatment or avoidable death from cancer. A diagnosis tells us which pathological process has produced the illness. We will return to this idea later when considering how to make a diagnosis.

Extending the diagnosis

However, we must go beyond the concept of diagnosis as a simple disease 'label'. In Chapter 2 we saw how some models of the consultation contrast the bio-medical with the psycho-social domains. An alternative concept is the 'triple diagnosis', which involves looking at how physical, social and psychological factors interact and contribute to a patient's problems. This term has gained widespread acceptance amongst GPs. It is sometimes referred to as the bio-psychosocial model of disease. The triple diagnosis helps in understanding that every disease episode we deal with as practitioners is unique. A fracture of the wrist is a straightforward biological problem and its treatment is long established and the same for every patient. However, the impact on different patients can be very diverse. An elderly person may become anxious and fearful about leaving the house; a self-employed decorator may face losing his house if unable to pay the mortgage; a professional sportsman may become depressed through losing contact with members of his team and suffer a major loss of income. Although surgeons fixing fractures cannot change these outcomes directly, they need to be aware of them and refer the patient for appropriate help.

The triple diagnosis is more useful than making us consider how to treat the disease. It also helps us to develop a deeper understanding of why the disease occurred. If an elderly lady is admitted to hospital with shortness of breath, it is a straightforward matter to diagnose iron-deficiency anaemia on a single blood test, and to send her home after a blood transfusion with some iron tablets. But if the practitioner making the diagnosis fails to consider the psychological (she is depressed because her husband died six months previously) and the social (her son has been abroad for four months so she has only been able to get to the corner shop to buy food) dimensions of the diagnosis she will be readmitted with the same problem later.

Although the diagnosis is a label that imparts the nature of the disease it is necessary to be aware of how it is reached, the context in which it occurs and the consequences that follow once it has been made. To help you develop your awareness of the central importance of the diagnosis in clinical practice the following is a useful exercise. Take a sheet of paper and write the term diagnosis in the centre.

DIAGNOSIS

Think about diagnosis in its broadest terms, write ideas in boxes on the paper and link these to the central box and to each other to create your own 'mind map' of your understanding of the term diagnosis. A diagnosis mind map created by a group of students during their training is given in Appendix 1 on page 60.

How do practitioners learn to make diagnoses? Is it a skill that can be taught, or is it an attribute that they acquire mysteriously with experience? Traditionally medical students have been taught to make a differential diagnosis after taking a full history using a defined 'checklist' of questions that have to be answered in a predetermined sequence and examining every single body system. The process takes an hour if done correctly and assumes the patient is well enough to endure the course. When completed the student is expected to consider the information gathered and write a list of diagnoses that might explain all the findings and to list these in order of probability that each diagnosis is correct.

This approach to the task of reaching a diagnosis has many flaws:

- It is time consuming and many questions asked and examination findings sought are irrelevant to the problem.
- It hinders patients from telling the 'history' of the illness in their own words (i.e. it is practitioner-centred rather than patient-centred).
- It is prone to error as it is difficult for the practitioner to listen carefully to the answers to questions asked by rote.
- When patients already have an illness it can be hard to know if a feature that is present is due to the pre-existing or the new disease.

Most importantly this is not how diagnoses are made in practice. This chapter is an explanation of how experienced doctors reach a diagnosis and discusses whether 'novice' diagnosticians can learn to do so more quickly by being taught or if this skill can only be acquired with experience.

Do nurses make diagnoses?

Until recently nurses have been taught they should not make diagnoses, as they have not been trained to do so and diagnosis is a medical function. Yet all nurses who consult with patients know that they are frequently challenged to make a diagnosis. In a family planning clinic a patient attending for a pill check might say, 'I have an itchy white discharge again, I know it is thrush because the pessary worked last time I had it'. The nurse has a dilemma – she might be required by a protocol to say, 'I'm just the nurse, you will have to come back to see the doctor next week'. The patient is likely to be annoyed by the inconvenience and the nurse is likely to be frustrated by procedures that prevent her using her knowledge and skills to deal with the problem there and then. Similar issues will arise time and again in clinics where nurses offer systematic care of continuing disease, for example the patient whose COPD is worse because of a chest infection or the diabetic patient with a urinary tract infection.

The introduction of nurse prescribing has made it even harder to sustain the view that to diagnose is a medical, not a nursing, task. When nurses prescribe a drug from the Extended Nurse Formulary they assume responsibility for any adverse outcome. Although many drugs in the formulary are also available as over-the-counter remedies to relieve symptoms, the prescription of others implies that a diagnosis has been reached. In prescribing trimethoprim to a patient with a three-day history of burning pain and passing urine frequently it is indisputable that the nurse has made a diagnosis of urinary tract infection by a bacterium. Even when a symptomatic remedy such as paracetamol is prescribed to a child with a cough and fever, a competent nurse will have concluded the illness is a viral infection and not due to pneumonia.

The 25 nurses in the first group undertaking the Consultation Skills module of the Extended Nurse Prescribing course at De Montfort University were asked to list the ways in which they thought their patients might be harmed when they undertook their new role. They gave 57, which are listed in Table 4.1. Subsequent cohorts of students made a very similar pattern of response. The reason most frequently cited was reaching an incorrect diagnosis through lack of knowledge and/or interpretation and the second commonest was gathering insufficient or incorrect information from patients. Concerns about errors in prescribing were only cited 16 times. These nurses therefore identified that the central issue to ensure safe prescribing is diagnostic accuracy.

Table 4.1: Ways in which patients may be harmed during nurse consulting as listed by 25 nurses attending the Extended Nurse Prescribing course, De Montfort University.

Reason for harm	Number of citations
Incorrect diagnosis	14
Insufficient/wrong information from patient	8
Inability to gain agreement, understanding or compliance	7
Incorrect drug	7
Dosage error	6
Failure to recognise the severity of the problem	4
Follow-up (incorrect, or problematic due to service)	3
Referral difficulties (including lack of availability)	3
Drug interactions	3
Recognition of limits of competence	1
Poor communication with colleagues	1
Total	**57**

In a number of first-contact care settings such as hospital emergency departments, NHS Direct, out-of-hours centres and minor-illness clinics in general practice, nurses are consulting with patients who potentially have any illness. Some of these settings use strict computerised protocols, which require nurses to ask a set of questions in a particular order for the computer to calculate the likely diagnosis. Does such technology result in less error? In 1972 a similar system proved to be more accurate in the diagnosis of the cause of abdominal pain in an A&E unit than the doctors working there.[1] In this setting abdominal pain is likely to indicate serious disease and misdiagnosis is potentially lethal. Despite this success such technology is not widely used. There are a number of reasons apart from the practical difficulty of data entry in a busy unit. The system is dependent on the accuracy of the information gathered which has to be done by a doctor or nurse, from a patient who may be confused, angry or drunk. Interpretations of particular words such as 'gripping' need to be made; hesitations by the patient may indicate information is being withheld; pre-existing disease may produce confounding symptoms. Judgements about these and similar issues require considerable levels of knowledge and skill. Professionals who have attained this level of ability can make diagnoses more quickly and with acceptable levels of error by drawing on their experience.

All practitioners make diagnostic errors throughout their careers. In many cases these are trivial, either because the illness is minor or because the correct diagnosis is reached as the illness evolves, before harm is caused to the patient. Because diagnostic accuracy improves with experience, it is when first practising independently that serious diagnostic error is most likely to occur. In a study reported in 1999, 10 recently qualified doctors in the US reflected on an average of four instances each when they had made the wrong diagnosis in the preceding year.[2] The reasons they gave are listed in Table 4.2 in order of decreasing frequency. In analysing these replies some important conclusions about how practitioners diagnose were made.

Table 4.2:   Why did I miss the diagnosis?

Why did I miss the diagnosis?
It never crossed my mind
I paid too much attention to one finding, especially lab. results
I didn't listen enough to the patient's story
I was in too much of a hurry
I didn't know enough about the disease
I let the consultant convince me
I didn't reassess the situation
The patient had too many problems at once
I was influenced by a similar case
I failed to convince the patient to investigate further
I was in denial of an upsetting diagnosis

Pattern recognition

This method of diagnosis is fast and accurate, provided the practitioner is experienced. It depends on being able to match the features of illness in the patient with other instances of the same diagnosis that the practitioner has encountered previously. It is not a method that novices can use easily. We usually learn about the symptoms and signs of disease from reading books. The description of any disease in a textbook will include those features present when it is fully established and they are not usually presented in a sequence of evolution through time. Few textbooks indicate the likely prevalence of one feature compared with another. Furthermore, most textbooks have been written by specialists who do not normally encounter disease when it first presents. Therefore, novices will have knowledge organised in their memory as a series of lists headed 'pneumonia' or 'angina'. However, a patient with pneumonia may simply say, 'I feel very ill' making it difficult for the novice practitioner to match this patient against their understanding of pneumonia. Experienced practitioners can make the diagnosis in a few seconds in a process that appears intuitive, and they can find it difficult to explain how they have done so. In reality these diagnosticians are noting the key features from observing the patient, asking highly focused questions in the history and searching for those few additional features that are necessary to obtain a good match to recognise the pattern. Even for experienced practitioners error can arise. Some common reasons for mistakes in diagnosis by pattern recognition are cited in Bordage's paper as follows.[2]

- *Paying too much attention to one finding* can lead to 'premature closure' on a diagnosis.
- *Failing to listen carefully to the patient's story* results in missing a feature that does not fit the pattern and which should cause reconsideration of the diagnosis.
- If *in a hurry* the practitioner may not seek out sufficient features to ensure a good match.
- Many patients have coexisting disease when presenting new symptoms and *having too many problems at once* clouds the picture.

A further source of error to which experienced practitioners are prone is that unusual events are remembered more easily. A GP sees a child who is unwell with symptoms of a virus illness in the morning. Next day he learns the child was admitted to hospital late the previous evening with meningitis and that the parents want to make a complaint about the GP's 'missed diagnosis'. In reality he did nothing wrong – the symptoms of meningitis develop very quickly and the disease often arises after a viral illness. At the time he saw the child he made the correct diagnosis. However, it is likely that this doctor will find it much harder correctly to diagnose viral illness in the future and may admit many more children to hospital than necessary.

Example: Pattern recognition

Sandra is 23 and presents with the following symptoms.

> 'It's cystitis again. It burns when I pee, I can't hold it long and I seem to spend all my time in the loo just doing little dribbles. Can you do me a prescription for antibiotics; they worked for me last time?'.

Now consider the following questions.

- What is the *single* most likely diagnosis?
- Are there other possibilities?
- What is the next step?

Think how you would answer these questions and note your thoughts on paper. My answers are given on page 57.

Analytical thinking

This is the method by which practitioners reach a diagnosis when the pattern is not quickly recognised. It depends on both identifying features and making an interpretation of these.[3] At a very early stage in the consultation a number of propositions or hypotheses are considered that can explain the patient's presentation. These hypotheses are tested and refined through the collection of more data. As this extra data is interpreted some hypotheses will be rejected, until a working diagnosis is reached. This can often be achieved using information from the history alone.[4] In these cases physical examination and investigations serve to confirm what is already believed.

Norman and others studied how students and experienced physicians picked out the diagnostic features in a case.[5] He found that they paid heed to the existing features of the correct diagnosis much more readily (59% of features detected) if they were considering this as their most likely diagnosis. If the correct diagnosis was on their list of differential diagnoses, but not thought of as the most likely, 50% of features were noted. If they gathered information in a checklist approach, by rote they only detected 44% of the features, and if they were considering the wrong diagnosis as the most likely the detection rate fell to 40%. The conclusion is that we see what we are looking for. Therefore it is important that we look for the right thing. When consulting with patients we must always know the reason for asking a question or looking for a physical sign on examination. This process of thinking about the information being gathered and interpreting it as the consultation proceeds will produce higher levels of diagnostic accuracy. It also has the useful benefit of reducing the amount of unnecessary information being sought. This will result in more time to focus on what really matters to the patient.

Example: Analytical thinking

Maureen is 42 and presents with the following symptoms.

'I have got pains in my legs, I am short of breath and I feel distant.'

Now consider the following questions.

- What is the *single* most likely diagnosis?
- Are there other possibilities?
- What is the next step?

Think how you would answer these questions and note your thoughts on paper. My answers are given on page 58.

Problem representation

There are a number of techniques that can be used to help explore the problem to be solved and to find explanations that fit the facts. These help us to search the networks of concepts and examples stored in our memory. The first is to practise translating features from the history into abstractions that have diagnostic meaning. 'It started last night' becomes 'acute'; 'It's a really bad pain, that doubles me up every five minutes' becomes 'colic'; 'I get out of puff climbing up one flight of stairs' becomes 'short of breath on exertion'.

The second technique is to use mental pictures. A patient limps into the walk-in centre 24 hours after a football injury. How do we work out what is the cause of the problem? Thinking of a diagram of the main anatomy of the knee joint is very helpful and the structures that can be damaged – kneecap, cartilages, cruciate ligaments, etc. – enables us to be more systematic in reaching the diagnosis. This example illustrates how to ensure that the physical examination detects abnormal findings. Unless the practitioner consciously thinks about each structure and how it may have been disrupted, when palpating or examining it, any positive findings can easily be missed. The best example I have witnessed is a medical student in an examination being asked to demonstrate how to palpate a patient's abdomen. She had taken a history but failed to realise that the diagnosis of polycystic kidney would produce enlargement of the kidneys. She went through all the motions correctly and reported there was nothing to find. She was asked to do the examination again and still said she found nothing. It was only when their examiner told her what to find that she recognised both the patient's kidneys were enlarged five times their normal size.

The third technique is to create an interim summary of information obtained so far. This can be helpful at an early stage in taking the history if the problem is complex. In creating the summary concepts and instances are likely to come to mind and thinking about these will flag up important features that are present and those that need to be sought. If the summary is given back to the patient this technique has the additional benefit of checking the facts and confirming to the patient that the story has been understood by the practitioner.

Example: Problem representation

Harold is 60 and presents with the following symptoms.

> 'I feel as though my food has not been going down properly. The Gaviscon I have always taken for heartburn isn't helping now, and I don't fancy my food like I used to.'

Now consider the following questions.

- What abstract terms can we use to translate the findings?
- What further enquiry should we make?
- What is the likely diagnosis?
- Should other diagnoses be considered?

Think how you would answer these questions and note your thoughts on paper. My answers are given on page 58.

Clarifying the presenting problem

This is the most important skill to develop to become a good diagnostician. The symptoms the patient is reporting hold the key to what is wrong and unless the practitioner can build for themself a clear picture of the patient experience, diagnostic error is likely. A very useful mnemonic to help us do this with the symptom of pain is 'SQITARS'. The letters stand for:

Site and radiation
Quality
Intensity
Timing
Aggravating factors
Relieving factors
Secondary symptoms

I am not advocating that we should therefore revert to a practitioner-centred style of consultation whereby the patient is asked these questions in a set order. It is essential to encourage patients to describe their pain experience in their own words and in the order they choose. I use the metaphor of someone sorting post into pigeonholes to explain how I use this mnemonic. I let the patient tell me about the pain and as the information is given I slot it into the appropriate place. This is George's story, a patient the receptionist asked me to see before the start of morning surgery.

George:	'I woke up this morning with a kind of pain in my chest (places hand over sternum). I have not had anything like it before. It's still there.'
Practitioner:	Thinks: Site – central chest, need to ask about radiation; Quality – kind of pain, need to ask more about this; Timing – new problem, only had it two hours. Says: 'Tell me more'.
George:	'I thought it was a bad attack of indigestion but Settlers made no difference, when I told the missus that I felt clammy and short of breath she rang the surgery straight away.'
Practitioner:	Thinks: Relieving factors – not relieved by antacids; Secondary symptoms – cold sweats and breathlessness. Says: 'Yes?'
George:	'Well, at first I just had to sit on the bed, but it has gone off a bit, although it was worse coming up the stairs. It's not really a pain, more like a weight pressing down.'
Practitioner:	Thinks: Intensity – initially severe, now lessened; Aggravating factors – made worse with exertion; Quality – dull heavy. Still need to know about radiation. Says: 'Have you noticed if the pain has travelled anywhere?'
George:	'Oh yes, it did go up into my jaw to begin with.'

Try to create a summary of the information we have learnt so far using abstract terms. My summary is on page 58, including my most likely diagnosis.

This approach can be used with only minor modifications for any symptom. Diarrhoea does not have a Site, but every other letter in the SQITARS mnemonic applies.

Quality:	Colour and consistency of faeces
Intensity:	Volume and frequency of opening bowels

Timing:	When did it begin and is it getting worse
Aggravating factors:	Eating meals or particular foods
Relieving factors:	Use of over-the-counter remedies
Secondary symptoms:	Vomiting, abdominal pain, blood in faeces

Making a diagnosis – key concepts

Janet Gale published some of the earliest descriptions of how doctors make diagnoses in a study of 22 final-year medical students and 22 registrars with an average of over five years of clinical practice.[6] Her subjects were recorded as they conducted a diagnostic clinical interview with a patient. Immediately afterwards it was played back to them in short sections and they were asked to explain their thinking.

As a result of her work, and that of others,[2,5,7,8] some forms of thinking can be identified that are used to make a diagnosis when the process of analytical thinking is used. They are:

- preliminary interpretation
- identifying key features
- reinterpretation of information
- active elimination
- seeking specific features.

Some critics suggest that nurses cannot use these forms of thinking in their practice and that this method of consulting with patients is largely used by busy GPs who need to take 'short cuts'. Although this form of thinking has not been tested on nurses, the fieldwork was undertaken with hospital doctors demonstrating that these techniques are transferable to other settings.

As research studies have shown that the most accurate information is gathered when the practitioner is considering the correct diagnosis at the start of the consultation it is important to make a preliminary interpretation. At first this need not be a specific diagnosis. For example, 'I've been dizzy and short of breath' can be interpreted by thinking that a psychological, cardiovascular or respiratory problem is more likely than one from the gastrointestinal or urinary system. Using other information such as the age of the patient and visual cues practitioners may then choose to focus their enquiry on a particular system. If the patient is young and appears anxious it would be appropriate to explore a psychological diagnosis, if the patient is elderly and short of breath a cardiovascular or respiratory problem would be considered. This is an example of using the 'systems sieve' to aid the practitioner in generating possible diagnostic explanations for the problem.

In this example the presenting problem would then be clarified. For example, it is established that the young patient, looking anxious, was short of breath on waking up this morning and felt light headed after breakfast before leaving for work. The key features of an anxiety disorder would be that the symptoms were short lived and precipitated by some incident, seen to be stressful. If these are present we can conclude that the most likely diagnosis is an acute anxiety attack. We can rule out a respiratory illness such as chest infection if the patient has no symptoms of cough, chest pain or fever. Our most likely diagnosis would be confirmed if the patient had also experienced a churning feeling in the stomach and pins and needles in the hands, at the same time as feeling light headed.

> **Example: Making a diagnosis**
>
> **Parveen** is 56 and presents with the following symptoms.
>
> > 'I have had a cough for two months and it has been getting worse. My brother says it might be asthma as he has it.'
>
> - What clarifying enquiry needs to be made of his presenting problem?
>
> Think how you would answer this question and note your thoughts on paper. My answers are given on page 58. Once you have considered the information try to answer the following questions, returning to each question after reading the answer to the previous one.
>
> - What are the key features for the most likely diagnosis?
> - How is this information reinterpreted?
> - What features would help us to eliminate an alternative diagnosis?
> - What specific features need to be sought?

This way of making diagnoses depends on the practitioner developing a number of 'rules of thumb' about the clinical problems she confronts most commonly. In the jargon these are known as 'heuristics'.[9] They go beyond the factual knowledge learnt from reading books and depend on experience of using this knowledge in practice. Some heuristics are general. For example: 'bacterial infections are acute and symptoms become progressively worse from their onset'. Heuristics are not universal laws but they do increase or decrease the probability of the outcome they predict. Although there are a number of very useful general heuristics, many are specific to clinical problems in a particular specialty. If a practitioner moves from working in one specialty to another it is necessary to discover these new heuristics quickly. For example a nurse might start work in a primary care walk-in centre having previously looked after patients in a medical admissions ward. If she uses the 'rules of thumb' from the admissions ward she is likely to refer far too many patients presenting with chest pain because she thinks they might have a myocardial infarction, pneumonia or pulmonary embolism.

Developing diagnostic skill

A useful exercise to help recognise the heuristics used in making diagnoses in a specific specialty area is shown below. Read through the worked example for the diagnosis of bacterial tonsillitis and then use the form given in Appendix 2 on page 61 to construct your own examples.

> **Worked example: Diagnosis of bacterial tonsillitis**
>
> - *Competing diagnoses:* viral URTI, glandular fever.
> - *Key features* of diagnosis: (rank these and list duplicate features on the same line).
>
> 1. Exudates on the tonsils (red pharynx, enlargement of tonsils).
> 2. Temperature > 37.5 °C (general malaise).

3. Tender, enlarged sub-mandibular lymph glands.
4. Pain on swallowing or talking (palatal speech).

- *Features that help to eliminate competing diagnoses:*

Feature	Diagnosis made less likely
Absence of cough, dry or productive	Viral URTI
Absence of runny nose, sneezing	Viral URTI
Duration of illness less than one week	Glandular fever
No enlarged lymph glands in axilla/groin	Glandular fever

* A 'feature' is a symptom, examination finding or test result.

The example given above is firmly evidence based. The diagnostic criteria for bacterial tonsillitis have been well researched and published as the Centor criteria.[10] However, there are many heuristics used that are less validated. A good example is the belief that the colour of sputum predicts if a cough is due to a viral illness or bronchitis. The heuristic is, 'green sputum – bacterial; clear white sputum – viral'. In reality many patients with bronchitis that may need antibiotic treatment have clear sputum and others with viral illness have purulent sputum. The best available evidence suggests that this rule is only true for a minority of patients with productive cough.[11,12] It is wise therefore to question the validity of heuristics in use. Even when the evidence is strong, as for the Centor criteria, it is important to realise that it only applies to the population in which it has been validated (in this case, first-contact care patients in a developed country). The criteria have not been established in developing countries where disease patterns are very different.

This exercise has been undertaken by groups of nurses from a wide range of different specialties on a nurse-prescribing course. All of them have been able to identify a diagnosis they commonly consider and the competing diagnoses that must be ruled out. Many nurses work in situations where the primary diagnosis is known but they can be challenged to make secondary diagnoses. For example, community mental health nurses are rarely required to make a primary diagnosis of schizophrenia but must be capable of recognising when schizophrenic patients they are seeing develop depression. Although nurses working in first-contact care require good diagnostic skills, all nurses will benefit from understanding how diagnoses are reached and a consideration of how to apply this in their own work setting. Table 4.3 shows the diagnoses chosen by small groups of nurses working in particular specialty areas.

Table 4.3: Diagnoses chosen by small groups of nurses working in particular specialty areas.

Diagnosis chosen	Work setting for nurses
Conjunctivitis	First-contact care
Vaginal *chlamydia* infection	Well-woman clinic
Schizophrenia	Community mental health
Opiate dependency withdrawal	Substance abuse
Staphylococcal skin infection (pubic area)	GU clinic

Table 4.3 (Continued)

Diagnosis chosen	*Work setting for nurses*
Childhood asthma	Paediatric specialty nurse
Type II diabetes	Chronic disease clinic (primary care)
Myocardial infarction	First-contact care
Oral *candidiasis*	Palliative care
HIV AIDS (paediatric)	Paediatric specialty nurse
Type I diabetes	Diabetes specialist (secondary care)

In analysing the worksheets a number of issues emerged about which it is helpful to be aware.

Prevalence of disease

Common diseases occur frequently and practitioners are more often challenged to recognise the unusual presentation of a common disease than the typical presentation of a rare disease. This implies that if a practitioner is unsure of the diagnosis it will be more fruitful to consider common conditions and not to be concerned to rule out the improbable possibility of an unusual presentation of a rare disease. Remember that the diagnostic probabilities are strongly influenced by the setting in which practitioners work. This is particularly important when they move to a new field.

Be clear about what is a diagnosis

For example conjunctivitis is not a diagnosis. It is a *symptom* (redness of the white of the eye). It can be produced by infection, trauma or allergy. These different possibilities can be distinguished by *secondary symptoms* such as itch or purulent discharge. Unless you are clear about the exact diagnosis it will not be possible to choose the correct treatment. Other examples, such as anaemia and constipation have been given earlier in the chapter.

Aim for optimum diagnostic precision

Chest infection is commonly recorded as a diagnosis in both primary and secondary care and a prescription is written for a broad-spectrum antibiotic. This is poor clinical practice as none of the important infections of the lower respiratory system infects the chest. Tracheiitis, bronchitis, bronchiolitis, pneumonia and pleurisy are all chest infections but each one occupies a defined part of the lungs; the clinical features of each are different and it is straightforward to distinguish between them. This is an essential task because the best treatment of each one is different. Without the required degree of diagnostic precision the patient may be given an incorrect treatment.

Ranking the diagnostic possibilities

At some point in a consultation it can happen that several possible diagnoses are being considered. In this situation it is useful to stop and create a list and rank the items in order of probability. From the available information choose the 'most likely diagnosis' and then list the alternatives in order of probability as 'less likely but important to consider'.

Competing diagnoses may have several key features in common

Two groups of nurses considering diabetes generated lists of six key features for type I and seven for type II diabetes. For these, five were common to both lists. The only feature on the first list that favoured type I diabetes was the presence of ketones in the urine, and in the second list, type II was repeated infection with *candida*. In practice, distinguishing between the two forms of diabetes is usually straightforward on the basis of the age of the patient and the acuteness of the illness.

Clarification of the timing of a symptom is often the key to eliminating a diagnosis

For example a chest pain that comes and goes over a period of several weeks is unlikely to be a myocardial infarction. The important causes of headache have very different patterns of occurrence with time. A tension headache builds up over minutes or hours, a brain tumour causes pain that is worse on waking, a migraine comes on quickly.

Additional symptoms may not increase the probability of the eventual diagnosis

If a patient is thought to have hypothyroidism, dry hair is a common feature, but the presence of dry skin also adds no additional diagnostic certainty. Enlarged tonsils and red pharynx as features of a throat infection do not double the probability of this diagnosis if there are exudates to be seen on the tonsils. If a patient has dysuria and frequency the diagnosis of UTI is not made any more likely if they also have urgency.

Elimination of a diagnosis is often easier than confirmation

In trying to distinguish whether the symptoms of general malaise, shaking and vomiting are due to withdrawal from opiate drug use or hepatitis it is useful to recognise that hepatitis A is an unlikely diagnosis if the patient has no fever or jaundice. In trying to decide if a patient has staphylococcal infection or herpes simplex causing soreness of the pubic area, the absence of any lesions on the mucus membranes of the labia make herpes much less likely.

Some features, often enquired about, can be over-interpreted

It is usual in considering the diagnosis of asthma in a child to ask about a family history of the disease. However, whether or not a child has a close relative with asthma is of little diagnostic significance. If the practitioner is considering bronchiolitis as a possible diagnosis the fact that the child's brother has asthma does nothing to rule out bronchiolitis. Similarly many children who develop asthma do not have close relatives with the disease, so a negative answer to the question does not rule out asthma as the diagnosis. If undue weight is given to these features then the true diagnosis may be overlooked.

Conclusion

For the practitioner the diagnosis is a label that defines the pathological process resulting in disease. For individual patients this must encompass the physical, psychological and social aspects of the illnesses they experience. Nurses are challenged to make diagnoses when they consult independently with patients and therefore understanding the principles of how practitioners diagnose will improve their decision-making.

References

1. de Dombal FT, Leaper DJ, Staniland JR, McCann AP, Horrocks JC. Computer-aided diagnosis of acute abdominal pain. *Brit Med J.* 1972; **2**(5804), 9–13.
2. Bordage G. Why did I miss the diagnosis? Some cognitive explanations and educational implications. *Acad Med.* 1999; **74**(10 Suppl.), S138–43.
3. Groves M, O'Rourke P, Alexander H. Clinical reasoning: the relative contribution of identification, interpretation and hypothesis errors to misdiagnosis. *Med Teach.* 2004; **25**(6), 621–5.
4. Hampton JR, Harrison MJ, Mitchell JR, Prichard JS, Seymour C. Relative contributions of history-taking, physical examination, and laboratory investigation to diagnosis and management of medical outpatients. *Br Med J.* 1975; **2**(5969), 486–9.
5. Norman GR, Brooks LR, Regehr G, Marriott M, Shali V. Impact of feature interpretation on medical student diagnostic performance. *Acad Med.* 1996; **71**(1 Suppl.), S108–9.
6. Gale J. Some cognitive components of the diagnostic thinking process. *Brit J Ed Psychol.* 1982; **52**(Pt 1), 64–76.
7. Leblanc VR, Brooks LR, Norman GR. Believing is seeing: the influence of a diagnostic hypothesis on the interpretation of clinical features. *Acad Med* 2002; 77(10 Suppl.), S67–9.
8. Bordage G, Lemieux M. Semantic structures and diagnostic thinking of experts and novices. *Acad Med.* 1991; **66**(9 Suppl.), S70–2.
9. Elstein AS. Heuristics and biases: selected errors in clinical reasoning. *Acad Med.* 1999; **74**(7), 791–4.
10. Centor RM, Witherspoon JM, Dalton HP, Brody CE, Link K. The diagnosis of strep. throat in adults in the emergency room. *Med Decis Making.* 1981; **1**(3), 239–46.
11. Lautenbach E, Metlay JP. Managing upper respiratory tract infections: practice without evidence. *J Gen Intern Med.* 1999; **14**(3), 203–4.
12. Jonsson JS, Sigurdsson JA, Kristinsson KG, Guthnadottir M, Magnusson S. Acute bronchitis in adults. How close do we come to its aetiology in general practice? *Scand J Prim Health.* 1997; **15**(3), 156–60.
13. Medina-Bombardo D, Segui-Diaz M, Roca-Fusalba C, Llobera J. What is the predictive value of urinary symptoms for diagnosing urinary tract infection in women? *Fam Pract.* 2003; **20**(2), 103.

Answers

Sandra

The most likely diagnosis is cystitis. It is a common infection in young women. Dysuria, urgency and frequency are usually present in cases of cystitis and not common in other problems. I would not consider other diagnoses *at this stage*. Pregnancy may cause frequency, but the volume of urine is usually nearer to normal and dysuria would not be present. The next step is to do a urine dip test checking for red and white blood cells and nitrites. If these are present Sandra has cystitis beyond any reasonable doubt.[13] However, if there were only a trace of protein and a small quantity of white blood cells then I would reconsider. At this stage other possible diagnoses such as *chlamydia* or thrush should be explored, by taking a more detailed history. This would be an example of how paying too much attention to one finding (the typical symptoms) might lead the practitioner to ignore a feature that does not fit (the unusual dip test result).

Maureen

The most likely diagnosis is not apparent. Could she have had a deep vein thrombosis (DVT) with a pulmonary embolism? She may be seriously ill with a systemic infection. A psychological problem might be indicated by the unusual term 'I feel distant'. The next step is to gather more information and in particular to clarify the presenting symptoms. How do the three symptoms relate to each other? What is the duration of the problem – is it acute or chronic? Where are the leg pains? If bilateral a DVT becomes unlikely. What is the degree of shortness of breath? Does she also have chest pain as an associated symptom of pulmonary embolism?

Harold

The abstract translation I have made is: 'An older male patient, with long-standing reflux oesophagitis presents with dysphagia and anorexia'. When this summary has been created it should prompt the practitioner to further clarify the difficulty in swallowing and loss of appetite. The need to ask about weight loss is also highlighted. At this stage we must conclude that the most likely diagnosis is carcinoma of the oesophagus and until this has been confirmed or ruled out we do not need to entertain any other diagnoses.

George

Central chest pain, radiating to the jaw, dull, initially severe but now easing, single acute episode starting two hours ago, made worse by exertion and not relieved by antacids, associated with cold sweats and breathlessness. I need to ring the Coronary Care Unit and tell them I want to admit a patient who is likely to be experiencing an acute myocardial infarction.

Parveen

- *Clarifying enquiry:* In clarifying the presenting problem the framework of the SQITARS mnemonic can be used, adapted for cough. When you have considered the information gathered return to the next question.

Quality:	Productive, clear sputum
Intensity:	Initially mild often dry, now constant and always productive of two teaspoonfuls sputum
Timing:	Cough started three months ago, now present day and night, progressively worse, no days free of symptoms
Factors:	No aggravating or relieving factors noted by patient
Symptoms:	No chest pain. No shortness of breath

- *Preliminary interpretation:* This could be tuberculosis (TB). The symptoms fit and the disease is more common in the Asian community. We need to think about cancer because of duration of illness and his age. Asthma is unlikely unless he has had it when younger and the cough is worse at certain times of day.
- *Key features of most likely diagnosis:* TB typically causes a productive cough, with haemoptysis, weight loss and night sweats. When asked Parveen says he has had no night sweats, no haemoptysis but has lost half a stone in weight.

- *Reinterpretation:* TB is still the most likely diagnosis but there is still not a definite, clear pattern.
- *Eliminating features:* There is no history of wheeze and he did not have asthma as a child, so we can rule out asthma at this stage. He has never smoked so lung cancer is very unlikely.
- *Specific features to be sought:* We must ask about possible contacts or recent travel to an area where TB is common.

Appendix 1: Diagnosis mind map

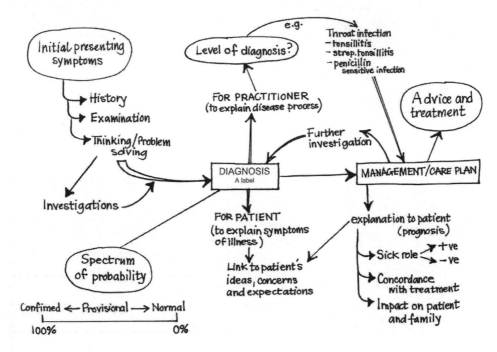

Figure 4.1: Diagnosis mind map.

Appendix 2: Making a diagnosis – developing 'rules of thumb'

- *Diagnosis:*

- *Competing diagnoses:*

- *Key features* of diagnosis:* (rank these and list duplicate features on the same line).

1.	
2.	
3.	
4.	
5.	

- *Features that help to eliminate competing diagnoses:*

Feature	Diagnosis made less likely

---

* A 'feature' is a symptom, examination finding or test result.

Chapter 5

Implementing the care plan

Adrian Hastings and Sarah Redsell

Introduction

In Chapter 4 the importance of making a diagnosis, not simply as a disease label, but also in consideration of the impact upon the individual patient, whose problem you are helping to solve, was discussed. In this chapter the second phase of problem solving is considered – deciding what to do. In the medical world this is traditionally referred to as patient management, but this language seems inappropriate in an era of patient-centred practice. In reality it is the problem, not the patient, that requires managing, so care planning is a better term. Even so, this is not an ideal form of words as it downplays the importance of the patient taking responsibility for their problem once the consultation is over. A model is provided to help organise individual care plans and the implementation of care plans is discussed with examples taken from practice.

Formulating a care plan to address the needs of an individual patient

Before speaking to the patient, it is worth taking a few moments to think. Review the information you have available and ask, 'Does it match up?'; 'Am I confident I know what the problem is?'. When the patient has presented a new problem, you will need to check that your diagnosis is supported by the evidence you have gathered. There are four stages that you should consider in formulating the care plan for patients.

1. Reach a shared understanding.
2. Provide advice about self-care.
3. Actions decided by health professionals.
4. Summarise and close.

The amount of time taken discussing each stage with the patient, and in some cases the order in which they are tackled, will vary. Rehearse quickly in your mind what you think the patient should do to help themselves, and what actions you need to take. Before you embark on an explanation consider what you believe to be the ideal outcome. You may need to modify this in the light of what the patient says. It is better to accept compromises through negotiation than respond 'off the cuff' to suggestions and requests from the patient. The stage of reaching a shared understanding is the most critical and it would be unusual to start with a different stage. It can be helpful to use the technique of 'sign-posting'. For example, 'Let's start by agreeing what the problem is, and after that we'll discuss what you can do about it'. By alerting the patient to the topic to be discussed you increase the likelihood they will engage with what you are saying.

Reach a shared understanding

> To write prescriptions is easy, but to come to an understanding with people is hard.
>
> Franz Kafka (1919) *A Country Doctor. Selected Short Stories*

If the consultation has been well conducted and the patient has a straightforward clinical problem you could consider an opening which invites the patient to restate what they believe is wrong. Nurse: 'You said earlier you thought you might have appendicitis'. This gives the patient an opportunity to frame the discussion and to create opportunities for the nurse to build on his understanding. Stephen: 'Well the pain was in the right place but I didn't know if you get bad diarrhoea with appendicitis'. The nurse can then explain: 'You are right that it causes tummy pain, but actually you have just a little tenderness all over. With the type of diarrhoea you have had I think it is more likely to be a tummy bug'. In this example the nurse has been able to refer back to ideas the patient expressed earlier in the consultation about the cause of their problem. This is likely to reassure the patient, the nurse has listened carefully and is concerned to incorporate Stephen's thoughts into the care plan.

However, the task can be much more challenging. The following box gives an example taken from a consultation in a first-contact clinic in primary care.

Example 1: Reaching a shared understanding

David is 35 and began the consultation by asking for an ECG because he was worried he was getting angina. The features of the chest pain and the examination made the nurse confident that the pain was muscular in origin. However, the records show he attends frequently with minor symptoms and usually imagines they are caused by life-threatening disease. In the last five years he has been referred to three different hospital specialists with no significant disease found on each occasion. Although the clinic has an ECG machine the nurse practitioner knows the ECG is usually normal in cases of angina and therefore will not rule out the diagnosis.

Take a few minutes and think about how you would approach the problem. Note down what you anticipate the patient might say and how you would respond. Some suggestions are given on page 83 to help you. When you have recorded your strategy read the outcome in our example.

Nurse: 'David, you said you were worried this chest pain could be from your heart, because your father has had a heart attack, but he was a lot older than you wasn't he?' (This opening acknowledges David's concerns but also cues him to expect that the nurse is going to discuss his request rather than accede to it.)

David: 'Yes he was, but I know they can happen to men of my age.' (The nurse cannot challenge the truth of the statement, but she also knows that they are rare. If the nurse agrees and offers investigation and referral she is in danger of further reinforcing his high level of anxiety about his physical health. Excessive worry, whilst the matter is being resolved will impair David's psychological health and may have a serious impact on his social life, including work avoidance and giving up beneficial exercise.)

Nurse: 'That is true, but I think the explanation for your pain is much simpler and less serious.'

David: 'How can you be so sure?'

Nurse: 'Well the pain you get is made worse when you have been using your arm a lot. When I tested your chest and arm movements I found out that the pain was coming from where the big muscle that moves your left shoulder attaches to your ribs.'

David: 'But that's also where your heart is, isn't it?'

Nurse: 'I asked you if the pain ever comes on when you get out of breath and you said not. You also said that it was sharp and stabbing. If it was your heart I would expect it to be like a pressure feeling spreading right across your chest and down your left arm.'

David: 'OK, I agree it's not very likely, but can't you do an ECG just to prove it?' (This request places the nurse in a difficult position. She knows it can be done quickly and cheaply and is likely to be normal. However, she also knows that over 20% of tracings show minor abnormalities that are not of clinical significance, but which will worsen patients' anxiety if they result in further investigations. It is also possible that if the nurse requests an ECG David will later discover that most patients *with angina* have a normal result.)

Nurse: 'No, I don't think it is necessary – your problem is typical of muscular pain and not like heart pain in any way.'

David: 'Well, with all respect – and I know you have taken me seriously – diagnosing heart disease is for doctors isn't it?' (At this stage the nurse may conclude that the only way of convincing David is to refer him to his GP, explaining her reasoning to the GP, with the expectation that the doctor will support what she has done.)

In the next example the nurse is working in a family planning clinic.

Example 2: Reaching a shared understanding

Kylie-Ann is a rather truculent 16-year-old girl who has attended for a repeat prescription of the combined oral contraceptive pill. She has also complained of erratic vaginal bleeding. From the history and examination the nurse is satisfied that irregular pill taking is the most likely reason, rather than infection, pregnancy or endocrine disease.

Take a few minutes and think about how you would approach this problem. Note down what you anticipate the patient might say and how you would respond. Some suggestions are given on page 84 to help you. When you have recorded your strategy read the outcome in our example.

Nurse: 'You've been on the pill for over a year now, haven't you? Do you understand how it works?'

Kylie-Ann: 'Well, like, you know it stops you getting pregnant don't it'. (The nurse recognises that this flippant response probably indicates poor knowledge and embarrassment.)

Nurse: 'Well, yes it does. And if you take it regularly it is very effective because it stops your body from releasing eggs.'

Kylie-Ann: 'Are you saying I don't know how to take it? I'm not stupid you know, I don't want to have a baby; me Mam'd kill me!'

Nurse: 'No, but it isn't easy to remember to do something every day, I know I sometimes forget my blood pressure tablets.' (The nurse has been willing to show empathy and disclose something of herself to put Kylie-Ann at ease. Kylie-Ann's aggression is most likely to be due to discomfort in an unfamiliar setting.

Kylie-Ann: 'Yeah, well I suppose I do miss one or two a month, especially if I've been sleeping over at Sharan's.'

Nurse: 'What do you do then?'

Kylie-Ann: 'I take two the next night once I get home.' (The nurse has now created an opportunity for a discussion with her about how to take the pill and how to cope with missed doses. During the discussion the nurse may also be able to explore whether or not Kylie-Ann has a regular partner and her understanding of risk in relation to sexually-transmitted diseases. The nurse might also recognise an opening to explore whether Kylie-Ann has problems at home.)

Nurse: 'Do you sleep over at Sharan's often?'

Kylie-Ann: 'Now and then, usually after a row with me step-dad – he's really creepy.' (The nurse has demonstrated high quality consultation skills. She has been able to create a rapport with her patient, listened carefully to the verbal cues and responded to them in such a way that the term 'creepy' can now be followed up, to check whether Kylie-Ann is the victim of any form of abusive behaviour at home.)

The nurse in the following example is a respiratory nurse specialist working in the chest clinic of a hospital.

Example 3: Reaching a shared understanding

Derek is a 64-year-old man with severe lung disease. Despite his condition deteriorating rapidly he continues to smoke heavily. During the consultation he has asked the nurse to prescribe antibiotics, steroids and a 'stronger puffer' to relieve his shortness of breath. The nurse does not believe any of these solutions to be appropriate at the moment.

Take a few minutes and think about how you would approach this problem. Note down what you anticipate the patient might say and how you would respond. Some suggestions are given on page 84 to help you. When you have recorded your strategy read the outcome in our example.

Nurse: 'Now that I have explained why I think you are already on the best treatment, we should discuss what you can do to look after your lungs.'

Derek: 'You mean smoking don't you?' (The nurse nods but remains silent.)

Derek: 'Well I have thought about it often and tried once or twice as I know the doctor's always going to ask me about it.'

Nurse: 'Yes, how can we help you do it?'

Derek: 'I do realise that smoking doesn't help, but I believe my chest was started off by working in the pit.'

Nurse: 'I agree, but you haven't worked underground for 20 years and since you started coming to the clinic your lungs have got a lot worse.'

Derek: 'So it's too late then … .'

Nurse: 'No, we can't make your lungs young again, but we can stop them from getting worse. When you smoke the mucky phlegm gets trapped in the lungs and makes it likely you will get an infection.'

Derek: 'I get so irritable when I don't smoke and I am always raiding the fridge, last time I tried, I put on half a stone in two weeks.'

Nurse: 'That does happen, but with time most people lose it again. One of the reasons is that food tastes so much better when you don't smoke.'

Derek: 'Last time I tried to give up I bought the patches but they were so expensive.'

Nurse: 'These days we can prescribe them for you and then you can save the money you are spending on cigarettes. In six months you would have enough for a two-week holiday abroad.'

Derek: 'If you can give me the patches, I'll have another go.'

Nurse: 'That's great, can you get your family to help?'

Derek: 'Emily will as she hates me smoking in the house, but most of our friends at the Bowls Club are smokers.'

Nurse: 'You need to explain to them why it's so important for you to give up and ask them to help you.'

It is very tempting to take refuge in the principle that patients are autonomous and responsible for their own health, so that when they choose not to comply with the best advice given by practitioners we have done all that is required. In our examples the nurse has taken an approach aimed at gaining concordance.[1] This emphasises the importance of incorporating the patient's views into explanations, offering alternatives and providing support.

We have focused in our examples on consultations where only the nurse and patient are present. Many consultations include a third party, most commonly a parent of a child as patient and spouse or carer of an elderly person. However, there are many other circumstances where consultations take place with third parties. One of the most challenging is where the third party is acting, either informally or professionally as an interpreter for a patient who does not speak English. Third parties can help the practitioner but they can also make the consultation much more difficult if they are bringing their own 'agenda'. It is therefore always important to clarify the precise relationship and role of third parties at the start if this is not self-evident and to involve the third party as appropriate throughout. On some occasions you will decide that you need to speak to the patient alone. Achieving this can be difficult, but in most circumstances a direct approach with an explanation to the third party of why you believe this is necessary is best.

Key principles in reaching a shared understanding

In the above examples, some of the general principles that should guide your approach to reaching a shared understanding are illustrated. In summary these are as follows.

- Acknowledge patients' views and show respect for them. This is particularly important if there is likely to be disagreement between you and the patient.
- Provide sufficient explanation to enable patients to make informed decisions about their care.
- Be prepared to extend the explanation by providing more detail if patients are unsure.
- Tailor your explanation of the problem to the reason for consulting.
- Do not assume that patients understand concepts you believe to be common knowledge (e.g. the differences between viruses and bacteria, the action of insulin in the body or the meaning of high blood pressure as a risk factor for a stroke).
- If patients want a course of action that you do not believe is correct you are entitled not to accede to the demand. Most patients will respect your point of view if you explain your reasons. A good understanding of the signs, symptoms and evidence-based management of the conditions you encounter regularly will help here.
- Repetition of key messages is usually necessary to ensure that patients have taken them in, provided you have made due allowance for their ability to understand you.[2]
- Breaking down the information you need to give into smaller 'chunks' will aid understanding if the message is complex. If you combine this with the technique of 'sign-posting' at the start of each chunk this will further improve patients' recall of what you have said.

It is vital to realise that proceeding to the next stages before you have achieved a true, shared understanding is almost always a mistake. Without this, it is unlikely that patients will take the prescribed treatment correctly and improbable that they will follow advice that requires major changes in their lifestyle. If you do not have sufficient time or feel you and the patient are not making progress in reaching a shared understanding it may be helpful to advise them to make a further appointment rather than treat them for something about which they are unconvinced. The intervening time before the next appointment may allow both you and the patient to reflect upon the problem and tailor your discussions accordingly.

Providing advice about self-care

When nurse and patient are in agreement about the nature of the problem, this is the most opportune moment to discuss the steps the patient needs to take. Having heard and accepted your explanation for the problem, the patient is then cued to listen further. Most problems depend on the patient following advice from the nurse – lifestyle change and self-medication are the cornerstone for the management of a wide range of chronic diseases and self-limiting illness. This stage also helps to achieve an essential goal for most consultations, which is that the patient re-assumes responsibility for the problem at the end. Patients who feel that they are active participants in decisions about their care are more likely to express satisfaction[3] and to follow the advice given,[4] which is particularly important when this concerns how they can help themselves. Skilful use of third parties can be very effective in achieving the necessary ends. If the patient is a child, or an elderly person with confusion the carer will be responsible for carrying out your recommendations. In other circumstances, for example dietary advice to a man who relies on his wife to do the cooking at home, it may be necessary to ask a third party to attend a future consultation.

Lifestyle change

One of the commonest challenges nurses face is to give patients advice to stop an addictive behaviour. In the UK 25% of adults are smokers[5] and the harm that smoking causes is central to most common, chronic illnesses. Smokers and their children also experience more frequent episodes of infection. A very helpful aid in thinking about how people give up a harmful, addictive behaviour is the 'Spiral of Change' model proposed by Prochaska and DiClemente.[6]

Figure 5.1: The 'Spiral of Change Model' helps to explain the stages that a patient passes through when giving up an addictive behaviour.

The five stages are illustrated in the box below during an interview with a patient who has just had a heart attack.

Example: The five stages of giving up an addictive behaviour

Interviewer: 'What's next?'

Patient: 'I've started on the pills and been to see my GP for a sick note and check- up.'

Interviewer: 'What did he say?'

Patient: 'He seemed only to be interested in whether I was going to give up smoking. Before the heart attack, I hadn't given it a thought.' (**Precontemplation**) 'Most of my family smoke and no one has ever had heart disease. Maureen doesn't smoke and she has often nagged at me to give up because of the cost.'

Interviewer: 'Did she ever smoke herself?'

Patient: 'Yes, until about 10 years ago. Her mother died of lung cancer and that shook her up. She decided at the funeral that she would give up herself but it was at least another two years before she did.' (**Contemplation**) 'She was always making New Year resolutions, or trying to stop on her birthday, but the next day she was back to the fags.'

Interviewer: 'Do you think you will be able to give up?'

Patient: 'I don't know, I have already cut down and I wait 'till after breakfast before I have the first cigarette of the day. (**Preparation**) I do want to, as I know it is important.'

Interviewer: 'How did Maureen manage it?'

Patient: 'She finally made her mind up that she was going to do it, and chose her birthday as the day. She wrote lists of reasons for giving up and stuck them around the house. We decided that we would make the front room in the pub a non-smoking bar and serve the meals there. She usually runs that bar and I stay in the back bar as much as possible. All the regulars were asked to help by not offering her cigarettes.' (**Action**)

Interviewer: 'And did that work?'

Patient: 'She stuck with it for over three weeks and then our son had a road accident. He wasn't badly hurt but it was waiting around the hospital for him to come out of the operating theatre that did for her.' (**Relapse**)

Interviewer: 'But she doesn't smoke now?'

Patient: 'Yes, she had another go a few months later and this time she stuck with it. It wasn't easy for me as she got very mardy at times, but when she was about ready to give in, we all stepped in to remind her why she wanted to give up.' (**Maintenance**)

This model can be usefully applied to other addictions such as the misuse of alcohol and overeating. How it is applied in practice with these behaviours should be adjusted to take important differences into account. There is no 'safe' level of smoking so you can give a simple message that patients must aim to give up. Alcohol drinking within the current recommended levels of 21 units for women and 28 units for men is believed not to be harmful (although the beneficial effect of drinking alcohol in moderation has probably been overstated by doctors who enjoy the occasional glass of red wine!). However, the alcohol-related death rate in the UK has more than doubled from five to 11 per 100,000 population between 1979 and 2003 and continues to rise particularly amongst young people.[7] Advising patients about reducing alcohol intake is a common challenge to nurses who treat chronic disease such as diabetes and cardio-vascular disease. For some patients complete abstinence is appropriate, for others harm reduction by limiting intake is more appropriate. Using the Spiral of Change Model can help you to choose the best strategy for patients.

Regarding overeating as an addictive behaviour is more controversial although research into brain function has shown close parallels with drug addiction.[8] As obesity levels are rising rapidly almost all nurses will require the skills of counselling overweight patients about how to control their eating behaviours. It is much more useful to regard obesity as a disease state resulting from a disorder of appetite than a problem of 'slow metabolism'. Understanding the conflicting motivations that result in patients overeating and becoming obese when they hate being fat is essential. The model can help you to avoid confrontation with patients who are not ready to change and to instead focus your efforts on those who are. In order to increase your effectiveness you will need to suggest a range of strategies to reduce food intake and to increase exercise levels. These will have to be carefully tailored to the circumstances of individual patients.

Advice – general or specific

A common failing by practitioners in giving advice to patients is to be general rather than specific. There is limited research evidence to support the common-sense view that patients are more likely to follow advice that is specific to them, rather than general.[9,10] Some examples of advice that is given thousands of times everyday are: 'keep his temperature down', 'take enough exercise', 'drink plenty of fluids'. If you are unsure about the value of being specific, imagine yourself to be a mother, whose first baby is six months old and is unwell with a high temperature for the first time. Now put yourself in the shoes of a 60-year-old man who was discharged from hospital after a myocardial infarction two months ago and who is attending a rehabilitation clinic before returning to work. Alternatively, think about a student who has come back from a holiday in Thailand with acute vomiting and diarrhoea. How could the general advice be made specific for each of these patients? Note down exactly what you would say to each one and compare your advice with the suggestions we give on page 84.

Nurses are often expected to teach patients how to do practical tasks such as measuring their blood sugar using test strips and a meter, inserting a bladder catheter and using an inhaler. Whilst a minority of people can learn such a skill by following written instructions most will require an explanation of why it is necessary, followed by a demonstration of how to do it. The patient will then need an opportunity to show the nurse how to do the task, with appropriate feedback and further supervised practice.

Self-medication

The concept of the 'symptom iceberg' was developed when research showed that less than 5% of symptoms experienced by people resulted in a consultation. The iceberg under the water represents self-care and only the 'tip' is illness reported to a health professional.[11] That people are willing to self-care when they feel unwell is vital for first-contact services. If everyone who felt unwell attended the services they would be overwhelmed, so teaching patients to make appropriate use of self-medication is essential. The desire to take a medicine to relieve symptoms of disease is ancient and self-treatment for illness long predates the establishment of health professions. Every pharmacy has several shelves of preparations to relieve symptoms such as pain, indigestion, diarrhoea and cough and the range of prescription-only drugs transferred to over-the-counter status has grown rapidly in recent years.[12] If a practitioner prescribes unnecessary antibiotics for minor illnesses this will result in more consultations in the future,[13] creating dependence on professional advice with the attendant waste of resources of time and money. Most patients prefer self-care because it is easier than arranging to see a nurse or doctor and because they realise this will result in more time being available to treat more serious illness.

Self-medication also has an important role in the treatment of more serious and chronic illnesses. The doses of many drugs supplied on prescription are best decided by patients. Examples include analgesics for arthritis, restarting preventive (steroid) inhalers for asthma, nitrate sprays for angina and so on. If patients with these types of illnesses understand the way their treatments work and the indications for starting and stopping them they will feel more responsible for looking after themselves and less dependent on professional advice.

Actions decided by health professionals

'First, do no harm'

A widely quoted saying by Hippocrates, the doctor who wrote about healing practices in Ancient Greece is 'Primum non nocere'. In a literature search we found 139 papers in which it is included in the title of the paper and a further 142 with the English translation 'First, do no harm'. Almost all of these papers were examining the possible harmful effects of diagnostic testing or prescribing of treatments. The potential to do more harm than good is the reason that many tests and treatments can only be authorised by particular health professionals. A large part of the history of medicine and nursing concerns the abandonment of treatments confidently recommended as essential to cure by one generation of practitioners which are then seen as potentially lethal to patients by the next. Blood-letting was used for many centuries to treat a wide range of conditions including fever and mental illness. As scientific understanding of human physiology developed in the 19th Century it fell out of favour. There are many reasons why a practice that was so harmful to most patients on whom it was practised persisted for so long. It is useful to be aware of them for they still operate today.

Most patients attending physicians in a pre-scientific era felt a sense of despair. Lifespans were short and communities lived with the expectation that disease was poised to kill even young people in good health. The physician offered hope of recovery and the more elaborate the rituals surrounding a procedure such as blood-letting the more convincing it would be. Most physicians were not charlatans – they genuinely believed they were doing good. There was a process of connivance between doctor and patient in which neither party wanted to question the value of the procedure, as to do so would eliminate the hope of recovery. This interaction was further reinforced by the power relationship between physician and patient – most physicians would be wealthier and better educated than their patients. In a hierarchical society figures of authority were rarely challenged.

There are several further reasons that help to explain the continuation of useless treatments. Blood-letting has an incidental effect of reducing circulating blood volume, which will provide temporary relief from the symptoms of oedema and breathlessness in cases of heart, liver and kidney failure and this will further reinforce the belief of physician and patient that the treatment is helpful. In some conditions, particularly pain and depression, there is good evidence for the placebo effect – if you believe in the treatment it can make you think and feel better but it is not actually *making* you better. Remember also the most important phenomenon of all, which is that much disease and injury ends as a result of natural healing processes. If the time span of these coincides with the application of the treatment then physician and patient will be confirmed in their belief that the treatment works.

Many forms of alternative medicine depend on these phenomena to create the illusion that they are effective, which is why it is important that the cures they claim are scientifically assessed. Practitioners of alternative medicine are often better at using empathy than orthodox health professionals and this skill allied to the longer time available in the consultation can explain most of the apparent benefits of their treatments.

Before we criticise doctors from a previous era too harshly we should reflect on changes that we have made in our own practice. Bed rest following surgical operation was confidently asserted to be an essential process for rapid recovery until very recently, yet we now believe patients should be mobilised as early as possible[14] and bed rest for very elderly patients is probably detrimental. Consider how much harm would occur each year if we continued to enforce bed rest in terms of disease (thrombosis, muscle wasting and infection), wasted resources and delayed return of patients to normal function.

Prescribing

The advent of nurse prescribing is a very significant step. Nurses are now personally responsible in law if harm should occur as a result of a prescribing error. The first stage in taking on this role is to acquire sufficient knowledge about the drugs they prescribe. Beyond this is a duty to become more aware of the evidence in favour of using a treatment and the potential risks of so doing. In addition to the reasons we described for the continued use of ineffective treatments such as blood-letting, is the influence of commercial interests, which will use a wide range of generously funded methods to persuade practitioners of the merits of their company's product. It is essential to question the claims made for such products carefully and to learn about them from independent sources.

There exist now several useful resources that you should be aware of and learn how to use to aid you in making treatment decisions. Most of these can be accessed via the Internet using the portal: http://www.library.nhs.uk These include Clinical Evidence which is also published six monthly and made widely available in most settings. It summarises briefly the evidence for benefit and harm of treatments for many common diseases and gives clear guidance as to whether they should be used. Other information sources available from the same portal are the Cochrane Database of Systematic Reviews, the Drug and Therapeutics Bulletin and Bandolier. Many chronic diseases are the subject of nationally recommended guidelines to treatment. As these change regularly it is necessary to become familiar with those that apply to your work and to keep up to date with the changes.

Although most prescribing decisions are uncontentious patients can have strong views about a harmful course of action. Despite recent changes to drug licensing there still exist a number of prescribed treatments with little evidence of benefit and a high risk of harm. Patients often request benzodiazepine drugs for chronic insomnia and, despite careful explanation of the alternative approaches, continue to insist they will benefit from using a sleeping tablet. Reluctantly acceding to such a demand does not exonerate the practitioner from responsibility for the harmful outcome of the patient becoming dependent on the drug.

Evidence-based treatment

The definition of evidence-based medicine (EBM) is the integration of best research evidence with clinical expertise and patient values.[15] It is beyond the scope of this book to teach you EBM and there are a number of good books that will do this. The book we used whilst writing this chapter was *Evidence-Based Medicine* by David Sackett *et al.*[16] However, there are some very useful concepts you should understand when thinking about treatment. Those relevant to diagnostic investigations are discussed later.

Effect size is a useful way of thinking about how good a treatment is for a particular disease. A study might show that a new drug produces lower blood pressure than the placebo after four weeks of treatment and that because it was studied in a large group of people the difference is highly significant, statistically. However, if the reduction in average systolic blood pressure was from 196 to 190 in the study group and from 196 to 193 in the control group you would be right not to want to use the treatment. The effect size is so small it is not worthwhile and even less so if the treatment is expensive or has important side-effects. By contrast a small effect size for reduction in blood pressure by reducing excessive alcohol intake is very worthwhile, as the intervention has many other positive benefits.[17]

Many of the papers and reviews quoted in sources such as Clinical Evidence use the term NNT (number needed to treat). This is the number of patients that need to be treated to prevent one bad outcome. As applied to acute ear infection in children the NNT is given as seven in a study quoted in Clinical Evidence.[18] This means that for every seven children given the treatment only one will benefit from it. How do you judge whether to prescribe an antibiotic? You will need to know more that just the NNT. How did the study define benefit? Without treatment acute ear infection in children will heal naturally. The benefit was that for one in seven children there was significant increase in the rate of resolution of symptoms with antibiotics after 7–14 days of treatment compared with a placebo. In this situation there is no definitive course of action that must be recommended. Sharing the evidence with the child's parent and negotiating the best course of action will help. Some parents have strong views that antibiotics should only be given when essential, others have great faith in their power.

However, it is important to remember that prescription drugs do harm as well as good and to make an informed decision the parent must also be told of these. The NNH (number needed to harm) for antibiotic treatment of ear infection is given as six in one review.[19] This means that for every six children given an antibiotic rather than placebo there was one child who experienced a significant side-effect (in this example vomiting, diarrhoea or rash). Even for conditions that have been thoroughly researched the evidence can be conflicting as in our example. Clinical guidelines can be helpful as they are written by experienced practitioners who have reviewed the evidence and applied it to the relevant setting. Those written for the UK can be found on the website: http://libraries.nelh.nhs.uk/guidelinesFinder/ By January 2006 it contained over 1400 guidelines so many of the treatment dilemmas in your setting are likely to be described. In our example the advice is not to use antibiotics routinely as the initial treatment but to give advice on symptom relief and to offer a delayed prescription for the parent to collect after 72 hours if the child has not improved.

Investigations

In writing this book we have drawn a distinction between a 'near-patient test' and an investigation. A 'near-patient test' is done during the consultation and its results are immediately available to the nurse. In this sense a finger-prick blood glucose measurement as a sign of diabetes is equivalent to seeing exudates in the throat as a sign of tonsillitis. The difference between an investigation and a near-patient test is that the results of the investigation will only be available at a follow- up consultation. This might take place a short time afterwards (e.g. seeing an X-ray in the Emergency Department), or could happen many months later if the condition is not urgent and there is a waiting list for the test (e.g. MRI scan for chronic back pain). There are four major modes of investigation.

1. Analysis of components of body fluids (e.g. urea and electrolytes in venous blood).
2. Examination of body tissues (e.g. microscopy of a biopsy sample).
3. Imaging of internal organs (e.g. ultrasound of the gall bladder).
4. Measurement of function (e.g. nerve conduction study).

There are thousands of investigations in use in clinical practice and even a primary care generalist will only use a small proportion of these regularly. Nevertheless, the principles that govern how they should be used can be applied to every investigation. It is essential that you are can do so for the investigations that you use, as errors in deploying them can be just as harmful as mistakes in prescribing.

Roles of investigation

Confirming the diagnosis

The most obvious role for an investigation is to confirm a diagnosis the practitioner has made by interpreting the information from the history and examination of the patient. However, if there is little doubt then the investigation is a waste of resources – both the cost of the test itself and the time of the practitioner to review the result and explain it to the patient. Therefore, judgement is called for in deciding whether to do the test. A patient with a fever, enlarged neck glands and exudates on the tonsils has a probability of suffering from bacterial tonsillitis of greater than 70%. David Sackett recommends that if the probability of the patient having the disease that you have diagnosed on clinical grounds is greater than 65%, there is no need to test to confirm this – you should get on with treatment,[16] and in this example prescribe penicillin without ordering a throat swab.

Refuting the diagnosis

You will often be in the situation of thinking one diagnosis is most likely, but want to rule out another, often more serious, diagnosis. For example a patient may complain of a pain in the left side of the chest, which has been diagnosed as a pulled muscle but the practitioner wishes to rule out a chest infection. However, it is not feasible to order a chest X-ray on every patient with chest pain. Judging when to do so requires experience, but a useful rule of thumb is that if the probability of the patient having a less likely diagnosis is below 25%, testing for it is unnecessary, it is better to get on and treat the more likely diagnosis.

Pre-test and post-test probabilities

The key question to be able to answer when deciding whether to do a test is: 'Will the result of this test change the care plan for the patient?'. As suggested by the examples above if the pre-test probability is less than 25% of finding the disease, or the probability is already greater than 65%, the test will not change what you think. Therefore, tests to confirm or refute diagnoses are most useful if the pre-test probability of the disease being present is between 25 and 65%. In this situation a good test will either raise the *post-test* probability above the 'get on and treat' threshold of 65%, or lower it below the 'treat the more likely disease' threshold of 25%. Unfortunately, there is only good research evidence to help calculate these probabilities for a limited range of conditions (in primary care settings: urinary tract infection, tonsillitis and depression are examples of where this does exist). A significant part of gaining expertise as a practitioner is developing your own awareness of the probabilities for the conditions you normally treat.

Sensitivity and specificity

These terms are important to understand in relation to diagnostic tests. The ideal test will be 100% sensitive and 100% specific. This means that it is always positive for the condition being tested (it never produces a false-negative result) and no other condition can cause the test to be positive (it never produces a false-positive result). Less experienced practitioners often regard tests as being 'perfect' and will ignore strong clinical evidence to the contrary and rely solely on the test result. You will find it very helpful to know something about the sensitivity and specificity of the tests you order. Sackett describes a simple rule to aid interpretation of test results – '*SpPin*' and '*SnNout*'. The first stands for a: 'Specific test that is Positive rules *in* the diagnosis'. That is, it will not produce many false-positive results. The second stands for a: 'Sensitive test that is Negative rules *out* the diagnosis'. A test with this quality will not miss many cases. His example of a specific test is the appearance of the face of a child with Down's syndrome – there are no other diseases that produce the typical combination of features. A test with high sensitivity is the ESR (erythrocyte sedimentation rate – in some areas a similar test is used called C-reactive protein) and is used when considering the diagnosis of acute rheumatoid arthritis. It is rare for the test to be negative in this condition, so if it is negative it is much more likely another condition is responsible for the problem. A word of caution is needed here, sensitive tests such as ESR and CRP often have low specificity so they can be positive for a wide range of reasons and false-positive tests produce anxiety for patient and practitioner, as well as further testing to establish exactly what is happening.

Patient safety

The most usual reason given for doing tests even when the pre-test probability is very low is, 'I did it just in case, I didn't want to miss anything'. This way of thinking is often reinforced by risk-averse managers who provide practitioners with lists of tests to do for a particular symptom that often do not take into account factors such as the age of a patient, which make a particular diagnosis extremely unlikely. This type of policy might be justified if every test was very cheap, did not result in any discomfort for the patient, gave an immediate result and had very high sensitivity and specificity. Such tests are rare indeed and there is a further factor to be considered. In every clinical setting practitioners encounter patients with high levels of anxiety that they have serious disease. Over-investigation of such patients causes immense damage as it reinforces, rather than relieves their anxiety and risks producing somatisation disorder, which is a serious and disabling condition.[20] In discussing sensitivity and specificity we indicated the potential for harm resulting from a false-positive result but false-negative results can be equally misleading, delaying the eventual diagnosis.

It is sometimes argued that, 'no one ever got sued for doing an unnecessary test'. This is a dishonourable argument if you accept that indiscriminate testing can do harm and is not factually correct. In the US a number of clinics were established to offer whole body CAT scans to well people to screen for disease. Around half the people having a scan were found to have an abnormality that required further work up before being reassured it was not significant.[21] As the evidence for benefit of such testing is lacking it would be reasonable for them to sue the screening clinic to recover these costs. The fear of future litigation has caused many of these clinics to close. A further reason for avoiding indiscriminate testing is that patients are unlikely to have given informed consent. For example, a practitioner decides to do a range of blood tests for a man who is tired all the time, although the clinical diagnosis is very likely to be minor depression. If the test indicates the patient has pre-symptomatic liver disease and he is in the process of applying for a mortgage loan, he could reasonably seek to recover the additional insurance premiums by arguing he had not been told of the consequences of this testing.

Patient reassurance

Are tests a useful way to reassure patients who are concerned about a more serious diagnosis, but not unduly anxious? This strategy can be effective, particularly if the true illness resolves through natural healing or as a result of treatment. I find that I am much more likely to order tests if I am working under time pressure, or if the patient seems unconvinced by my explanation. This helps to buy time as the patient expects to return at a later date for the results but doing so leaves me with a sense of a job not done well. A test commonly ordered in such circumstances is a full blood count to rule out anaemia in a patient with no energy. The likely diagnosis is depression, but the patient has rejected this and is expecting iron tablets to restore their energy. The advantages of a normal test are that the patient is more likely to accept the clinical diagnosis and a wasteful prescription is avoided. The disadvantage is that borderline changes in haemoglobin levels are very common and often of no clinical significance. In this situation the test may make it harder for the patient to accept the diagnosis and start effective treatment. An alternative approach is to take the time needed to provide a better explanation and bring the patient to a shared understanding. Few practitioners are convincing actors able to persuade patients of something they, themselves, do not truly believe.

It may appear that we have focused on the negative aspects of diagnostic testing. However, if tests are ordered for the correct reasons they play a vital role in guiding diagnosis and care planning decisions. Understanding their limitations as well as their strengths will make us more thoughtful and effective practitioners.

Referral

Introduction

The dictionary defines referral as, 'directing to a source for help or information' or more narrowly as, 'to transfer care from one clinician to another'. The possible reasons for making a referral are several. When you have seen a patient and are uncertain of the diagnosis, referral to a colleague will be an appropriate step, if arranging investigations or allowing time for the clinical picture to develop are not safe alternatives. In many cases you will be confident about the diagnosis, but want advice about the best form of treatment – for example achieving good control of blood pressure in a patient who is already on two different antihypertensive drugs. Other referrals will be for a specific procedure to be performed that requires specialist skills – for example assessment by an occupational therapist for aids to daily living.

Referral destinations

When a nurse has decided that she needs to refer a patient the options open to her will vary widely according to the setting in which she works. These can include a colleague, with similar qualifications but who has gained additional experience. For example, a nurse in primary care seeing patients with hypertension may send a patient who also has asthma to see the respiratory nurse. Most nurses conducting autonomous consultations will be part of a team including doctors and the majority of their referrals will be to the medical practitioner with whom they work. For example, a health visitor may advise the mother of a child with constipation to consult a GP. The third referral destination is to other health professionals with specialist skills, for example a diabetic nurse referring a patient to a dietician. Although few nurses are likely to make direct referrals to complementary practitioners they may well be asked by their patients about the possible benefits of using alternative medicine. It is necessary to have an awareness of the most common forms of complementary and alternative medicine and their limitations. If the patient should come to harm through delayed diagnosis or from unsafe treatment the nurse may be open to litigation if the patient believes they have recommended seeing a complementary practitioner.

Referral mechanisms

Before you refer a patient there are some important considerations. How will you communicate with the person to whom you are referring your patient? A certain way to create resentment is to use the patient. 'I saw the nurse and he told me to come and ask you for some antibiotics for my infected ulcer', is an example of this approach. The colleague is in a difficult position. How reliable is the patient's account? If the nurse really did say this, how did he reach this decision? Did he make a full assessment of the problem, perhaps including a wound swab to identify the bacterium and sensitivity? The best communication method is in a face-to-face meeting with the person to whom you are referring the patient. This is usually only a practical proposition for referrals between members of the same team, although in almost all cases a telephone conversation is feasible. This form of communication allows for a dialogue and the person whose opinion is being sought has the opportunity to ask for extra information, suggest actions that might be taken before the patient is seen or even spare the patient the inconvenience of attending for an unnecessary consultation. This will also make it more likely that the patient is seen with the most appropriate degree of urgency.[22] When a referral is made verbally it is good practice to follow-up with written information. The majority of referrals are made by written communication – either electronically or by letter. Despite the importance of providing sufficient, reliable information this is often lacking.[23] The most serious and common problems are omitting enough detail about the problem and not providing results of previous investigations. Structured, pro-forma letters may be preferred by those making and receiving referrals.[24]

Referral information

An example of the kind of letter *not* to write is:

> Dear Dr,
> Re: John Smith.
> Chest Pain. Please see and advise.
> Yours,

The single most important piece of information wanted by colleagues is the reason for referral. Does this referrer want a diagnosis or advice on how to manage the problem? There is no history of the problem given, making it impossible to judge how urgently the patient should be seen. Does the patient have any relevant or important medical history? What investigations have been done and which drugs have been prescribed for the chest pain? What does the patient believe to be wrong and what does he expect to be done? Are there any relevant social or psychological factors in the patient's background? A better letter about John Smith is shown in the following box.

Dear Doctor Brown,

Re: John Smith, 27 The Rise, Newtown. NN5 6QE. Tel: 01234 567 890

Thank you for seeing this patient and advising on the treatment of his chest pain. I saw him first a month ago, with a burning pain around the left side of his chest. He said he had had a rash in the same area and when I looked at it there were some fading red marks. He also has atrial fibrillation and hypertension and is on aspirin and atenolol for these conditions. I have not done any investigations and the Ibuprofen I prescribed has not helped at all. I have told him I think he has neuralgia following an attack of shingles. He lives alone and the constant pain is making him feel very low at the moment. I am concerned about the risks of prescribing amitryptilline for fear of causing problems with his heart rhythm. Please can you recommend a suitable alternative.

Yours,

Creating dependency

In some cases practitioners use referral as a way of dealing with challenging patients who they believe to be demanding inappropriate forms of care. Whilst this can sometimes be the right course of action, particularly if the patient regards the practitioner as having insufficient experience or status to tackle their problem, it carries several risks. The most obvious harm is in using resources that should be spent on patients who are likely to benefit from them. Furthermore, it is not possible to guarantee that the practitioner to whom you refer the patient will desist from giving inappropriate care, particularly if the act of referral has reinforced the patient's expectation that it will be provided. Consider the case of a 45-year-old man with a strong clinical diagnosis of irritable bowel syndrome, who is found to have gallstones by an ultrasound scan. The prevalence of asymptomatic gallstones in the general population is around 15% so it is likely that his pain is not caused by the gallstones. However, if he is referred to a surgeon there is a real possibility he will have an unnecessary operation,[25] with the attendant risk of serious complications, including death.

In 1673 the French dramatist Moliere wrote a famous play called 'Le Malade Imaginaire', sometimes translated as 'The Hypochondriac'. He was calling attention to the fate of people, preoccupied by their health and who believe that they are always ill, when they meet unscrupulous doctors willing to exploit them by offering useless but expensive treatments. In the NHS, such patients are seen as a nuisance rather than a business opportunity because they become frequent attenders in primary care and are referred to many different hospital clinics in a fruitless attempt to diagnosis a physical disease. In one recent study they represented a third of all new referrals to a neurology clinic.[26] Hypochondriasis, hysterical conversion and somatisation disorder are classified as psychiatric illnesses but often by the time patients are referred to a specialist with the skill to manage such diseases the patients' beliefs are so strongly rooted they are very difficult to change.

A more recent, and we think better, term is the patient with 'medically unexplained symptoms', although patients may prefer the expression 'functional symptoms'.[27] The extent of the problem for secondary care was highlighted by a study of seven different specialties that showed *over half* of all patients seen in outpatients fulfilled criteria for medically unexplained symptoms.[28] Ideally the diagnosis should be made in primary care settings and effective treatment offered before referral is made to secondary care.[29] However, if this does not happen it is vital that doctors and nurses in secondary care recognise the true problem, to avoid reinforcing the illness-seeking behaviours that can lock patients into a cycle of dependence on health professionals.

Summary

The decision to refer a patient is an important one. Referral may transfer the care of the patient completely to another health professional, but in many cases the referring practitioner will continue to be involved in the care of the patient. Used wisely the referral can provide immense benefits for your patients and enhance your relationship with them. However, if the reasons for doing so are not properly thought through or the process used is defective the patient can come to serious harm.

Summary and closure

Research shows that there are important differences between the recall of patients and practitioners when interviewed immediately after a consultation.[30] The forgotten items may be of little significance – or they might be essential. Effective communication skills by the practitioner will result in a good rapport with patients which will make them feel they have been actively involved in planning their care. This is known to improve adherence to treatment and satisfaction but even in these circumstances the important messages will need to be reinforced.[31]

After reaching a shared understanding and explaining the care plan, provide the patient with a summary of the key points. One of the most effective ways of doing this is to ask patients to reflect back to you what they will be doing as a result of the consultation. This will confirm they have remembered what you wanted them to hear and will give you an opportunity to reinforce or correct the message.

Other means can help to convey information. Patient information leaflets are available for all common conditions and can be downloaded from the Internet. Patient organisations can offer more extensive information about specific conditions and this may be available in audio or video format for patients who prefer not to read books.

Discussing the arrangements for follow-up is a vital step. In first-contact care settings it is often 'open' – that is the decision whether and when to return is left for the patient to decide. In managing chronic disease the interval before the patient is seen again is usually decided by the practitioner. This is termed 'closed' follow-up and the date is decided at this time. In both cases the interval should be negotiated rather than imposed. Where closed follow-up involves the patient undertaking a negotiated activity, for example a dietary chart, it may be useful to reiterate the plan for the next appointment at the same time as negotiating the time. For example, 'shall we meet again in four weeks and look at the types of food you are eating and when?'.

Open follow-up must, however, be qualified. That is the patient should understand the expected course of the problem and the circumstances that should prompt them to return and when to do so. It can be useful to encourage the patient to reflect this plan back to you and if appropriate to allow them to write down the details. For example, if you prescribe a new medication for an on-going problem such as a hiatus hernia you should give an indication as to how long it might take for the patient's coughing symptoms to reduce and when to return if they do not. Even patients given closed follow-up should know when to contact the practice or hospital to be seen earlier than planned.

Conclusion

This chapter is the longest and most detailed in the book so far. This reflects the complexity of the task of deciding the content of the care plan and negotiating this with your patients. It is important to remember that your responsibility for the problems patients bring ends the moment they leave the room. If you have done your job well they will accept responsibility for carrying through the plan you have agreed with them. In Chapter 6 we move on from describing the consultation and your part in it, to discussing how you can learn better. Understanding these principles and those set out in the subsequent chapters will help you to be a more effective learner and to take on responsibilities as a teacher.

References

1. Mullen PD. Compliance becomes concordance. *Brit Med J.* 1997; **314**(7082), 691.
2. Kravitz RL, Hays RD, Sherbourne CD, DiMatteo MR, Rogers WH, Ordway L *et al.* Recall of recommendations and adherence to advice among patients with chronic medical conditions. *Arch Intern Med.* 1993; **153**(16), 1869–78.
3. Janz NK, Wren PA, Copeland LA, Lowery JC, Goldfarb SL, Wilkins EG. Patient-physician concordance: preferences, perceptions and factors influencing the breast cancer surgical decision. *J Clin Oncol.* 2004; **22**(15), 3091–8.
4. Kaplan SH, Greenfield S, Ware JE Jr. Assessing the effects of physician–patient interactions on the outcomes of chronic disease. *Med Care.* 1989; **27**(3 Suppl.), S110–27.
5. Cigarette Smoking. Slight fall in smoking prevalence. http://www.statistics.gov.uk/cci/nugget.asp?id=866 (accessed December 2005).
6. Prochaska JO, DiClemente CC, Norcross JC. In search of how people change. Applications to addictive behaviors. *American Psychologist.* 1992; **47**(9), 1102–14.
7. Alcohol-related deaths. Rates continue to rise. http://www.statistics.gov.uk/cci/nugget.asp?id=1091 (accessed December 2005).
8. Wang GJ, Volkow ND, Thanos PK, Fowler JS. Similarity between obesity and drug addiction as assessed by neurofunctional imaging: a concept review. *J Addict Dis.* 2004; **23**(3), 39–53.
9. Lee SSC, Cheung P-YP, Chow MSS. Benefits of individualized counseling by the pharmacist on the treatment outcomes of hyperlipidemia in Hong Kong. *J Clin Pharmacol.* 2004; **44**(6), 632–9.
10. Powell P, Bentall RP, Nye FJ, Edwards RHT. Randomised controlled trial of patient education to encourage graded exercise in chronic fatigue syndrome. *Brit Med J.* 2001; **322**(7283), 387.

11. Hannay D. *The Symptom Iceberg*. London: Routledge and Kegan Paul. 1979.
12. Blenkinsopp A, Bradley C. Over the counter drugs: patients, society and the increase in self medication. *Brit Med J*. 1996; **312**(7031), 629–32.
13. Little P, Gould C, Williamson I, Warner G, Gantley M, Kinmonth AL. Reattendance and complications in a randomised trial of prescribing strategies for sore throat: the medicalising effect of prescribing antibiotics. *Brit Med J*. 1997; **315**(7104), 350–2.
14. Reis S. Review: early mobilisation may be better than bed rest for medical conditions and after surgery. *Evid Based Med*. 2000; **5**(3), 76.
15. Evidence-based medicine. A new approach to teaching the practice of medicine. Evidence-Based Medicine Working Group. *JAMA*. 1992; **268**(17), 2420–5.
16. Sackett D *et al. Evidence-Based Medicine. How to Practice and Teach EBM* (2e). Harcourt, Edinburgh: Churchill Livingstone. 2000.
17. Xin X, He J, Frontini MG, Ogden LG, Motsamai OI, Whelton PK. Effects of alcohol reduction on blood pressure: a meta-analysis of randomized controlled trials. *Hypertension*. 2001; **38**(5), 1112–7.
18. Rosenfeld RM, Vertrees JE, Carr J, Cipolle RJ, Uden DL, Giebink GS *et al.* Clinical efficacy of antimicrobial drugs for acute otitis media: meta-analysis of 5400 children from thirty-three randomized trials. *J Pediatr*. 1994; **124**(3), 355–67.
19. Marcy MTG, Shekelle P *et al.* Management of acute otitis media: evidence report/technology assessment No. 15. *Southern California Evidence-Based Practice Centre*. 2001; Publication No. 01–E010.
20. Brown T. Somatization. *Medicine*. 2004; **32**(8), 34–5.
21. Gottlieb S. US commercial scanning clinics are closing down. *Brit Med J*. 2005; **330**(7486), 272.
22. Cant PJ, Yu DSL. Impact of the '2 week wait' directive for suspected cancer on service provision in a symptomatic breast clinic. *British Journal of Surgery*. 2000; **87**(8), 1082–6.
23. Tattersall MH, Butow PN, Brown JE, Thompson JF. Improving doctors' letters. *Med J Aust*. 2002; **177**(9), 516–20.
24. Jenkins S, Arroll B, Hawken S, Nicholson R. Referral letters: are form letters better? *Br J Gen Pract*. 1997; **47**(415), 107–8.
25. Berger MY, Olde Hartman TC, Van Der Velden JJ, Bohnen AM. Is biliary pain exclusively related to gallbladder stones? A controlled prospective study. *Br J Gen Pract*. 2004; **54**(505), 574–9.
26. Carson AJ, Ringbauer B, Stone J, McKenzie L, Warlow C, Sharpe M. Do medically unexplained symptoms matter? A prospective cohort study of 300 new referrals to neurology outpatient clinics. *J Neurol Neurosurg Psychiatry*. 2000; **68**(2), 207–10.
27. Stone J, Wojcik W, Durrance D, Carson A, Lewis S, MacKenzie L *et al.* What should we say to patients with symptoms unexplained by disease? The 'number needed to offend'. *Brit Med J*. 2002; **325**(7378), 1449–50.
28. Nimnuan C, Hotopf M, Wessely S. Medically unexplained symptoms: an epidemiological study in seven specialities. *J Psychosom Res*. 2001; **51**(1), 361–7.
29. Gordon GH. Treating somatizing patients. *West J Med*. 1987; **147**(1), 88–91.
30. Parkin T, Skinner TC. Discrepancies between patient and professionals recall and perception of an outpatient consultation. *Diabetic Medicine*. 2003; **20**(11), 909–14.
31. Partridge MR. The asthma consultation: what is important? *Curr Med Res Opin*. 2005; **21** (4 Suppl.), S11–7.

Suggestions

David

- Why is the patient concerned?
- Are there any risks in conceding to his request?
- Does the patient understand the nature of an ECG test?

- What is the evidence in favour of my diagnosis?
- How do I phrase my explanation?
- What is the evidence against the patient's feared diagnosis?
- How do I reassure him without appearing to be dismissive?
- Have I sufficient experience to manage this problem or should I refer him whatever the outcome?

Kylie-Ann

- Does she lack knowledge and maturity as she is only 16?
- Is her attitude due to discomfort in unfamiliar surroundings or is she naturally aggressive?
- How do I explore her understanding of the contraceptive pill in a way that is appropriate for her?
- Is she attending a family planning clinic because she is reluctant to use her GP surgery?
- Does she have relationship problems at home?

Derek

- How can I judge what stage he has reached in the 'Cycle of Change'?
- Will the patient claim that his lung disease has resulted from a different cause?
- Do I need to educate him about the reasons why smoking is harmful?
- Can I help him to list other positive benefits from giving up, such as cost of smoking, smell of smoke, taste of food?
- Has the patient succeeded but relapsed in the past?
- What do his close family and friends say to him about smoking?
- How do I counter negative thinking, such as fear of putting on weight?

General versus specific advice

- *Keep his temperature down:* When his temperature is above 39 °C take all his clothes off. Sit him on your knee and wipe his body all over, using lukewarm water and a flannel. Keep on doing this for 15 minutes. Check his temperature again. If it is not below 38 °C continue for a further 15 minutes. Carry on doing this until his temperature is below 38 °C.
- *Take enough exercise:* Each day, and at least five times a week when the weather is fair, walk for 30 minutes. Do this briskly, so that you feel slightly short of breath. If you get any chest pains, stop until they pass off but report them to your doctor. Cycling, dancing and swimming are reasonable alternatives. You can do your exercise spread through the day (for example in two spells of 15 minutes).
- *Drink plenty of fluids:* Make up some rehydration fluid using a 5 ml teaspoon of salt and 15 ml spoon of sugar in 1 litre of water. Drink frequent, small sips all the time, even if you are vomiting. Try to drink at least 2 litres today.

Chapter 6

Learning and assessment

Robert McKinley

Introduction

Since we got up this morning we have all learnt. We may have learnt that the new breakfast cereal we have tried is horrible, that public transport timetable changes mean that we can get to work more quickly or that our new colleague is not an easy person with whom to work. Although these things range from the trivial to the important, each may have caused us to change our behaviour, for example, what we have for breakfast, our routine for travel to work or the way in which we relate to a colleague.

Learning is a natural part of everyday life but once we start to think about how we learn it becomes difficult, and the more complex the behaviour we want to learn the more difficult it becomes. This chapter deconstructs some aspects of learning and presents a straightforward approach that has been developed by a group of nurses and doctors and which has been well evaluated by participants on courses run by them.[1-4] The following are examined:

- What learning is
- How the efficiency of learning can be improved
- The relationship between assessment and learning
- How to assess
- What is needed to make an assessment
- How assessments should feed back into learning.

A series of examples is looked at. Some will be drawn from everyday experience and will be used as 'metaphors' to illustrate professional issues. These will be embedded in the text. Venepuncture is used as the basis for a series of exercises to illustrate the text. Venepuncture was chosen because it is a simple procedure performed by most healthcare professionals which can be used to deconstruct the concepts discussed. Finally, a more complex example is used of a consultation between a nurse and a patient as the basis of an exercise to illustrate the process of assessing and enhancing consultation skills. Suggested answers to the exercises are provided but these are not definitive and some of our suggestions are intended to provoke discussion and debate.

Learning and assessment

What is learning?

For our purposes learning is defined as 'the process whereby we acquire an attribute not previously possessed or further develop an existing attribute'. Bloom and others contend that the external evidence of learning is a change in behaviour which is in turn driven by a change in one of the three domains of learning: the cognitive, the affective or the psychomotor.[5–8] In healthcare education we talk about knowledge, skills and attitudes which overlap with these domains but are not identical to them.[9] Although usually discussed as belonging to separate domains, many of the attributes we seek to learn are an amalgam of all three.

Exercise 1: Venepuncture – knowledge, skills and attitudes

- Using venepuncture as an example, list the knowledge, skills and attitudes that you believe a healthcare professional must possess to be competent to take blood.

	Necessary to be judged competent
Knowledge	
Skills	
Attitudes	

How do we identify what we need to learn?

When a student nurse commences pre-registration training it may be appropriate that they learn 'everything' and for the course to offer a uniform learning experience to all. Few, however, will have no relevant knowledge, skills or attitudes and such a blanket approach is seldom appropriate even with a novice. It is certainly highly inappropriate for practitioners who are well established on a lifelong learning path. It is therefore necessary to tailor the learning experience to the needs of the practitioner. For example, an experienced specialist nurse in diabetes who wishes to move into practice nursing may need to develop her knowledge of asthma and ischaemic heart disease but will already possesses the interview skills and ability to relate to patients that are required in practice nursing.

Efficient learning requires first that we discover what we are good at and which of our attributes we need to improve and how we should improve them. Although we can discover this for ourselves, and as reflective practitioners[10, 11] we should continually do so, it is sometimes necessary to ask another person's opinion. The process of finding out what we need to learn is called an evaluation or assessment of learning needs. We can make such an evaluation or assessment for ourselves or it can be conducted by a colleague or an educational supervisor.[12] Learning and assessment are therefore two sides of a single coin, inseparable and complementary. It is unfortunate that 'assessment' is often seen as synonymous with an examination with consequences, something which if not feared is still perceived as a threat, however minor, and a hurdle to be cleared rather than an inseparable component of effective, focused lifelong learning and professional development.

How do we assess?

A fundamental aspect of assessment is that the attribute is judged against something. This is a process we instinctively and frequently do in our roles as consumers, citizens and healthcare practitioners. For example, we observe public life and make our personal judgements of whether we agree or not with the actions of others. Similarly, we eat our food and make judgements about its quality. In some cases the judgement may reflect our internalised personal preferences and moral codes, i.e. our own internalised criteria, for example our preferences for 'sweet or savoury' foods, or our leanings in directions which others may call 'reactionary' or 'liberal'. Alternatively, our judgements may be against external criteria, for example a 'crisp apple with a tart taste – just like a good Granny Smith', which may or may not agree with another's personal criteria for a 'nice apple'.

What is important in this process is that the judgements being made are appropriate to what we are assessing. We would never dream of assessing the quality of an apple by judging its politics or the policies of public figures by how they taste. These are deliberately ridiculous examples, but is attempting to assess attitudes or practical skills in a written examination any more reasonable? Written tests of attitudes and some skills were widely used in the recent past and some are still in use today.

Making an assessment

In making any assessment we need to understand and apply the following concepts.

What is being assessed? (identify the domains)

Assessment of a healthcare practitioner requires an assessment of at least one aspect of the triad of knowledge, skills and attitudes.[9] Although they are inter-related, they are not often assessed together. This is understandable as knowledge has usually been tested by written assessments and skills usually (but not always) assessed by observation of aspects of practice. Unfortunately, attitudes are less often examined. This produces a 'hierarchy' of testing neatly encapsulated by Miller in his 'pyramid'[13] (*see* Figure 6.1 and the box below).

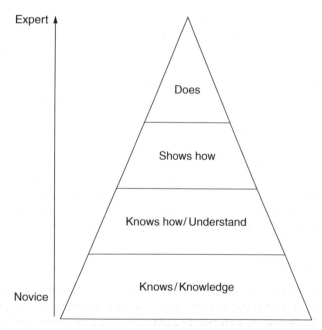

Figure 6.1: Miller's pyramid.

Miller's pyramid – applied to giving an intramuscular injection

'Knows'
- The healthcare practitioner possesses a body of knowledge.
  - Anatomy of the buttock, infection control, mode of action and the side-effects of the drug being injected, the patient may experience fear.

'Knows how'
- The practitioner can describe how they would apply their knowledge either as understanding of concepts or how they would perform an aspect of practice.
  - In writing explains injection should be given in outer, upper quadrant of the buttock, need for no touch technique, describes how to recognise an anaphylactic reaction and distinguish this from a faint by the symptoms and signs, describes how they would reassure the patient.

'Shows how'
- The practitioner demonstrates that they can perform an aspect of practice.
  - Under observation gives the injection in the correct site, prepares the skin and avoids contamination of the needle.
  - Explains procedure to patient whilst performing it in a reassuring manner.
  - Demonstrates taking a pulse and blood pressure and places a volunteer into the recovery position.

'Does'
- The healthcare practitioner applies their knowledge and skills in a professionally appropriate fashion in all encounters with patients to an acceptable standard. This is the ultimate 'test' of attitudes and professionalism.
  - Although rarely assessed in practice, using our example we could check the frequency of injection abscesses and the satisfaction of a random sample of patients who had been given injections by the practitioner.

As suggested in the box knowledge is the domain most tested at the foot of the pyramid and the domains of skills and attitudes form a larger proportion of what is tested in the transition from novice to expert, but all three can and should be assessed at all stages. It is useful therefore to think about a 'prism' or a three-dimensional Miller's triangle (*see* Figure 6.2).

Miller's 'Prism'

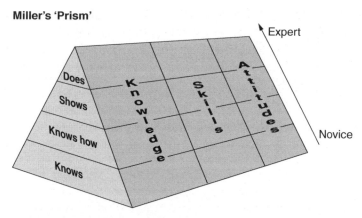

Schematic representation of the contribution of the domains of knowledge, skills and attitude to the layers of Miller's triangle with the accumulation of expertise.

Figure 6.2:   Miller's three-dimensional triangle.

Exercise 2: Venepuncture – components and methods of assessment

- Think about assessing a nurse taking a sample of blood.
- Write down what can be assessed in each of the 'layers' of Miller's triangle and how each action could be assessed.

	What could be assessed	Assessment method
'Knows'		
'Knows how'		
'Shows how'		
'Does'		

What is it assessed against? (the assessment criteria)

As we hinted in the introduction, an assessment cannot be conducted without a description of what is desired. For example, in the introduction we discussed some qualities of a particular variety of apple, a 'Granny Smith' that is typically bright green, hard to the touch, crisp to the bite and tart in taste which could be the criteria to judge such an apple. Generally, criteria for assessment should be as follows.

- *Objective:* they describe attributes that are externally evident and therefore accessible for assessment.
- *Explicit:* they exist in written form and are public so that all stakeholders (educators and trainers, learners, co-practitioners and service users) are aware of what qualities are being looked for in the assessment.
- *Valid:* the criteria must describe the attributes that are relevant and necessary for whatever is being assessed.[14] For example, in the assessment of the knowledge required to give an IM injection, it would neither be relevant nor valid to set an anatomy question in which practitioners were asked to describe the knee joint. Some practitioners may be able to do this very well and may also

have good knowledge of the anatomy of the buttock but we cannot safely assume that this is so. The other consideration is the depth of knowledge required. While knowledge of the surface landmarks and course of the sciatic nerve may be sufficient anatomical knowledge to give an injection safely in the buttock, a surgeon performing a hip joint replacement would need to know a great deal more. This example highlights a tension between the brevity and therefore utility of the criteria and whether they are sufficiently comprehensive to test the knowledge required for a particular practice context. As the number of criteria grow the assessment becomes more difficult to perform. Nevertheless, while reducing the number of criteria makes the assessment easier to do, it may reduce its validity because it no longer measures what the practitioner must know or be able to do, or the way in which they should conduct themselves.[15] There is no single objective test of whether a set of criteria is valid or not. It is a judgement of whether the tension between inclusiveness and practicality has been successfully resolved and that the items are those that must be assessed. This emphasises the importance of developing the assessment criteria in collaboration with stakeholders to ensure that essential elements are included.

What is assessed? (sample the attribute)

In order to assess anything it is necessary to sample it. The most obvious 'observation' is when an assessor watches someone perform an aspect of practice. We cannot safely conclude that practitioners are competent to give an intramuscular injection solely on the basis of marks in a written test. To know that they have reached the 'shows how' stage in Miller's pyramid they must be observed giving such an injection. Nevertheless, it must be recognised that a 'pencil and paper test' is also a means of observation, most often of knowledge, sometimes of understanding and even at times of certain skills. By and large, the sampling process chosen is different as the person moves between levels in Miller's pyramid.[9] At the base, sampling of 'knows' (knowledge) and 'knows how' (understanding) usually utilise pencil and paper tests; 'shows how' (competence) observation of practice and 'does' (performance) utilises audit and peer review by, for example, 360° assessment[16] and appraisal.

Exercise 3a: Venepuncture – criteria, methods and validity

- Refer back to your answers in Exercise 2 where you thought about what you could assess.
- Under the headings of knowledge, skills and attitudes write down the criteria that you would use to assess each aspect of the competence of a nurse in venepuncture. Check to make sure that each criterion is capable of assessment by stating how you would assess it.
- Then think about whether each of your criteria could be assessed at each level of Miller's pyramid.
- Finally, consider whether it is absolutely essential that every nurse demonstrates this criteria if they are to take blood samples, i.e. consider its validity (essential, optional, redundant).

	Criteria	Method of assessment	Miller's level: 'knows', 'knows how', 'shows', 'does', 'validity'	Validity (essential, optional, redundant)
Knowledge				
Skills				
Attitudes				

How do we assess? (judgement)

Observation does not lead to assessment. Assessment requires that the observer makes a judgement of the extent to which the observed performance meets the criteria. This judgement may be a simple 'right' or 'wrong', a judgement most frequently made when assessing an answer to a factual question. This may also apply to observation of performance in an area of practice when something is done which is clearly inappropriate. Nevertheless, things are not usually so clear-cut especially when observing complex skills in practice. Although there may be 'right' and 'wrong' ways of performing a procedure, there are also optimal and sub-optimal ways as well as ways which the observer does and does not like. There is therefore usually an element of subjectivity in such judgements. This is inevitable but can be minimised if the following precautions are taken. First, observers must make all judgements against the explicit public criteria for assessment. This helps to reduce the impact of idiosyncratic judgements driven by the personal preferences and practice of the assessors. Second, observers must also be self-aware and have considered and recognised how their own practice fits within the spectrum of acceptable and competent practice. Finally, they must judge the performance not by how *they* would perform the procedure but how the performance fits within a spectrum of competent and acceptable practice. This process requires observers to surrender autonomy and agree to make assessments against criteria that may not be their own. The invaluable benefit is that the judgements made have greater authority because they are based not on one person's personal preference but on a professional body of knowledge, attitudes and skills.

How good is it? (the standard)

The last stage in assessment is to make a judgement of the quality of the performance. It is not sufficient to describe what was observed but a judgement must be made of how the quality of what was observed relates to a standard. The standard may be internal or external to the performance. An internal standard relates to the performance alone and describes the relative strengths in the performance and the aspects of the performance that should be improved. The value of this approach to the person being assessed is that it shapes subsequent learning, focusing effort on areas that need to be improved rather than on existing strengths and should assist the practitioner to move to a higher overall standard. This is true irrespective of whether the person being observed is a novice or an expert.

On other occasions, a judgement is required about whether or not the performance observed is of sufficient quality for the practitioner to move to the next formal stage of professional development. For the learner this may mean progression to the next stage of study or progression from supervised to unsupervised practice or being ready to undertake extended roles under supervision or, eventually, without supervision. These judgements have major impacts on the practitioner and the practitioner's future clients. An explicitly stated and described external standard must therefore be used. This requires a statement of the standard that must be achieved for each stage of progression.

Exercise 3b: Venepuncture – criteria, judgement, standards and reflection on personal practice

- Using the list of criteria you wrote down in Exercise 3a, now consider whether you can make a yes/no judgement as to whether the learner possesses that attribute (Y/N) or whether you must make a judgement about whether it is optimally or sub optimally possessed or performed (O/S).
- Then consider whether each is a basic competence which any healthcare practitioner must possess or demonstrate or is likely to be a marker of an expert practitioner.
- Finally, consider whether you possess the knowledge implied by each of the criteria or reliably perform each aspect every time you carry out a venepuncture.

	Criteria	Type of judgement (Y/N or O/S)	Level of experience (E/N)	My own practice
Knowledge				
Skills				
Attitudes				

Exercise 4a: Observing a trainee performing venepuncture

You observe a trainee taking blood. She calls in her patient, Rashmi, a 75-year-old woman by name and, when she enters the room, introduces herself as Anita and asks Rashmi to take a seat and to roll up her left sleeve (which is closest to the desk). Anita checks the blood-test request form (for urea and electrolytes and full-blood picture) which is given to her by Rashmi and selects the correct sample tubes and needle and attaches the needle to the full-blood picture tube. She washes her hands and puts on gloves and fits the tourniquet correctly. She then gets up to collect cotton wool from the other side of the room. After identifying a visible vein towards the outside of the patient's arm and performing a competent venepuncture, she draws the full blood-picture sample, stabilises the needle, competently exchanges tubes, draws the Us and Es sample and takes the sample tube off the needle. She covers the venepuncture site with cotton wool and applies pressure as she withdraws the needle and then releases the tourniquet. She asks the patient to apply pressure while she disposes of the sharps and cotton wool appropriately. She then writes the patient's name on the sample bottles. Meanwhile the patient has flexed her elbow to hold the cotton wool in place. The trainee then applies a sticking plaster without inspecting the venepuncture site and tells the patient to remove it tomorrow morning. She then stands and opens the consulting room door and the patient stands, lifts her coat and handbag and leaves.

- List the strengths and opportunities for improvement displayed by this trainee.

You observe the trainee on multiple further occasions and her performance is very consistent displaying the same strengths and opportunities for improvement.

- Is she competent to perform the venepuncture in unsupervised practice?
- Why have you made this decision?

Summary: Issues in assessment

- *Criteria:* objective, explicit, valid
- *Sampling:* method
- *Judgement:* use criteria, be self-aware, be aware of spectrum of acceptable practice
- *Standards:* internal, external (explicit)

Quality in assessment

What makes a good assessment?

The attributes of an assessment process were described by Van der Vleuten.[17] He identified five attributes – reliability, validity, acceptability, feasibility and educational impact as listed and explained in the following box.

Five required attributes of an assessment process[18]

- *Reliability:* a measure of the variation in scores due to differences in performance between subjects and also the correlation of assessors rating the same performance. It is generally accepted that the reliability of a regulatory assessment must be at least 0.8.
- *Validity:* the degree to which an assessment is a measure of what should be measured. Although face validity of an assessment (the extent to which an assessment measures what it purports to measure) is often discussed, this should be augmented by discussion of whether what is

being assessed is what should be assessed. Validity therefore concerns both the instrument and assessment process and the challenge (cases) with which the candidate is tested. Ideally the content of the assessment should reflect the practitioner's own practice as closely as possible.

- *Acceptability:* is the degree to which the assessment process is acceptable to all stakeholders. In tests of practitioner competence the stakeholders are the practitioner being assessed, the assessors, the people who provide the clinical challenge (patients or simulators), the profession, future patients of that practitioner and society.
- *Feasibility:* the degree to which the assessment can be delivered to all those who require it within cost, staff and time constraints.
- *Educational:* the degree to which the assessment can assist the practitioner to improve their performance, usually through the provision of feedback on specific strengths and difficulties together with prioritised and specific strategies for improvement.

Van der Vleuten also identified that the relationship between these attributes is multiplicative; if one is missing (that is zero), the overall utility of the process is also zero. For example, an assessment with high reliability, acceptability, feasibility and educational impact that does not measure anything worthwhile (that is, it has zero validity) is a waste of time. For example if, in a post-IM injection course certification test the only anatomy question was about the anatomy of the knee, the test cannot tell you anything about possession of relevant anatomical knowledge and consequently whether course participants know where to give an IM injection in the buttock.

These five attributes are in tension. For example, one way of improving the reliability of the assessment is to reduce subjectivity and increase objectivity. This tends to force the assessment into assessing things that can be marked 'right' or 'wrong'. This obviously reduces the potential for examining nuance, subtlety and the interplay between practice and context. An assessment that ignores these subtleties has reduced validity. Another way in which to improve reliability is to standardise the assessments rather than using assessments based on observation of practice with real patients in the practitioner's workplace. Whilst standardisation may improve reliability,[17] the removal of the assessment from the workplace reduces validity, although there is much important work currently being done in the field of high fidelity simulation where simulations are made as realistic as possible.[19-23] Finally, good assessment requires extensive sampling. Extensive sampling results in more valid and more reliable assessments because the practitioner's skills have been sampled more widely. This, however, has a direct impact on the feasibility and the acceptability of the assessment because it can become both exhaustive and exhausting. There is no single 'correct' combination of attributes because the importance of each varies with the context of assessment.

How can these tensions be resolved?

There is no simple 'answer' to the problem of how the tensions between reliability, validity, feasibility, acceptability and educational impact can be resolved.

The solution is dependent on the context of the assessment. As we have hinted above, there are two principal reasons for carrying out assessments.

- To establish the current state of knowledge, skills and attitudes of practitioners being assessed with the aim of assisting them to improve. This is an educational process and these assessments are described as being educational or 'formative'.
- To make assessments for regulatory or summative purposes. Although this has traditionally been called 'summative' or 'endpoint' assessment, this is less appropriate today because increasingly practitioners are required to undertake assessments with regulatory impact, not just at the end of a period of training, but also whilst in practice to ensure that they remain competent to practice.

The demands of each type of assessment vary. Qualifying examinations, before graduation at the end of pre-registration training of nurses and doctors, are very 'high stakes' assessments for the practitioner, the institution and future patients. Making the correct pass/fail decisions is all-important and reliability of the assessment must be maximised. Maximising reliability often requires more extensive testing which reduces feasibility. On the other hand, during teaching in supervised practice, the goal of assessment is to identify strengths and opportunities for improvement. Educational impact becomes the primary objective. Ease of use (feasibility) and acceptability to the practitioner, teacher and patient and the validity of assessment are also of high importance. The reliability of pass/fail decisions is of lesser importance. Therefore extended observation is not needed, nor is it necessarily desirable on each occasion. Multiple episodes of 'mini-observation' are entirely appropriate and often the most effective method of assessment in this setting.

Educational versus regulatory assessment

Qualities

Educational assessment should be non-threatening and enabling. It requires an atmosphere of trust where the practitioner being assessed feels free to display not only strengths but also areas requiring improvement in the knowledge that the outputs of the assessment will only be used to assist them to perform better. Once a regulatory element is introduced, the practitioner almost invariably focuses on strengths and wishes to conceal weaknesses to minimise any threat that the assessment may pose to either career progression or continuation. Nevertheless, it is not possible to completely separate educational and regulatory assessment. If a practitioner requests an educational assessment by a colleague who then identifies serious deficiencies that call the practitioner's suitability for continuing independent practice into question, this cannot remain confidential and must be discussed with the practitioner's clinical governors.

Assessment criteria

Although the functions of educational and regulatory assessment should, as far as possible, be separated, it is highly desirable that the same assessment instruments are used in both. Use of a single set of valid criteria throughout the process of professional development from novice through to expert in both educational and regulatory assessments has important advantages. It ensures that the practitioner has been continuously assisted to address any areas requiring improvement and to reinforce their strengths and so that they move smoothly to a point where the final regulatory assessment is a step rather than a hurdle. This of course demands that what is assessed is actually what is important and reinforces the importance of the validity of the criteria against which the judgements are made.

Standards

It is not recommended that a novice should always be assessed against the whole panoply of criteria by which an expert would be assessed – at times it is more appropriate to use subsets of these criteria. Furthermore, the internal and external standards that are required also vary. For example, a performance identified as an area requiring improvement in an expert, might be judged as a strength if displayed to the same level of competence by a novice. Similarly, although an expert and a junior practitioner may be expected to perform a particular procedure competently, the junior practitioner would not necessarily be expected to do so in difficult conditions or under pressure. For example, contrast taking a venous blood sample from a well patient before elective surgery with doing the same from a patient who is in hypovolaemic shock as a result of major trauma.

Outputs

Although regulatory assessment is traditionally regarded as having a simple outcome (pass or fail) we argue that all assessments should have an educational facet. Any candidate who does not meet the required standard in a regulatory assessment should be given a statement of why the assessors reached this conclusion. This then forms the basis of remedial work to ensure that subsequent attempts are successful. We would also recommend that successful candidates be provided with feedback on the result – ideally a statement of their strengths and areas which could be improved – which should form the basis for their further professional development. This statement of learning is the ideal output of a summative assessment.

Assessment and learning

To connect assessment and learning, the assessor and learner need to identify and agree what needs to be learnt and how this can be addressed. We use a clinical metaphor, the diagnosis and prescription, to illustrate this process.

The educational diagnosis

This is a statement that summarises a practitioner's current level of learning and what needs to be learnt next. As an absolute minimum, after an educational assessment, the practitioner should be made aware of their relative strengths and opportunities for improvement. We would recommend that these statements of strengths and opportunities for improvement are phrased in terms of the criteria against which the judgement was made. This increases the professionalism of the assessment. Using appropriate terms that have been agreed by the organisation regulating the educational programme helps to ensure that judgement is only made on that which is important and valid. This reduces the risk of an individual assessor making judgements about factors that are not relevant and which may reflect their idiosyncratic preferences. Focusing on professionally desirable attributes 'depersonalises' the assessment allowing the practitioner to feel that conclusions reached are fair and based on a professional consensus. It also makes the feedback highly specific to the practitioner because it is based upon their personal strengths and areas in need of improvement that are unique to them.

Exercise 4b: Grouping strengths and opportunities for improvement

- Group each strength and opportunity for improvement you identified in Exercise 4a under the criteria for assessment of competence in venepuncture you developed in Exercise 3a.
- If any are left over consider whether they reflect your personal preferences or whether it is necessary for all healthcare professionals to possess them.

The educational prescription

This is a statement of how the practitioner should address what they need to learn next. The opportunities for improvement with recommendations as to how they can be addressed should be agreed between the assessor and practitioner. The advice offered needs to be prioritised so that the most important issues are identified and dealt with first. The guidance should also be specific so that the practitioner knows exactly what to do differently on the next occasion. It is good practice for the assessor to ask themselves, 'What exactly should this practitioner do next time to improve their performance most?' and the learner to ask their assessor, 'What exactly must I do next time to do this better?'. It is often easier to see what needs to be improved than how it can be improved. This is precisely why the CAIIN (*see* Chapter 9) includes a series of suggestions that the assessor (or reflective practitioner) can use as a starting point to identify appropriate strategies for the improvement of consultation competence.

Exercise 4c: Prioritising opportunities for improvement

- Rearrange your list for opportunities for improvement and the associated criteria of competence in Exercise 3 in the order of importance for improvement.
- For each opportunity for improvement try to write down exactly what the trainee should do the next time she takes blood to improve her performance.

This statement of prioritised opportunities for improvement and recommendations for improvement forms an educational prescription and diagnosis which, if implemented, should assist this trainee to avoid any omissions which give rise to concern about their suitability for independent practice and also to develop their competence across a broad range.

Exercise 5: Educational prescription and diagnosis in a consultation

A nurse training for a first-contact role has been consulted by Jane and her 7-year-old son, John. Jane reports that John has, 'a temperature and a cough'. The nurse quickly establishes a one-day history of a 'common cold' but no history suggestive of more serious illness. She performs a rapid competent examination and finds a temperature of 38.2 °C, normal tympanic membranes, mucopus in the nose, an inflamed pharynx, no cervical lymphadenopathy and a clear chest. She reassures Jane that John has a got the common cold and gives a full explanation of why antibiotics are not indicated and recommends paracetamol and fluids. Jane has listened carefully but just as she rises to leave asks, 'Are you sure?'. The nurse replies, 'Absolutely, antibiotics are not needed for a cold' but is left with the feeling that Jane has not been happy with her advice.

The supervisor notes that although the nurse has taken an appropriate history and conducted a competent and careful examination, she was abrupt and used closed questions. The nurse did not use clinical jargon but Jane was evidently not listening to the explanation about why antibiotics are not indicated.

Identify, using the CAIIN for primary care nurses:

- the nurse's consultation strengths
- opportunities for improvement that the nurse has displayed
- your educational diagnosis for this nurse
- the three most important opportunities for improvement for this nurse to address and the recommendations you would make to assist her to improve.

Conclusion

- Assessment and learning are inseparable.
- All assessments should be as objective as possible and made against valid, explicit criteria.
- All assessments require an appropriate sample of the knowledge, skills and/or attitudes being assessed.
- Assessors must surrender their personal preferences, use the agreed criteria and standards and judge not by their preferences but by that which the profession requires.
- There is no perfect assessment; all are compromises, some good, many not.
- Although regulatory and educational assessment should be separate they overlap at times. They should use the same criteria and similar methods.
- The educational diagnosis summarises the knowledge, skill and/or attitudes the practitioner already possesses and should acquire next.
- The educational prescription should summarise and prioritise exactly what the practitioner should do next to improve her knowledge, skills and/or attitudes.

References

1. Hastings AM, Lennon M, Redsell SA, Cheater FM. Evaluation of a consultation skills workshop using the Consultation Assessment and Improvement Instrument for Nurses. *Learning Health Social Care.* 2003; **2**, 201–12.
2. Preston-Whyte ME, Fraser RC, McKinley RK, Cookson J, Alun-Jones T. Hospital clinicians' views on training as examiners for undergraduate regulatory clinical examinations. *Med Educ.* 2000; **34**, 964.
3. Preston-Whyte ME, Fraser RC, McKinley RK. Teaching and assessment in the consultation. A workshop for general practice clinical teachers. *Med Teach.* 1993; **15**, 141–6.
4. Preston-Whyte ME, Fraser RC, McKinley RK. Teaching and assessment in the consultation. A hospital clinician's preparatory workshop for integrated teaching of clinical method to undergraduate medical students. *Med Teach.* 1998; **20**, 266–7.
5. Atherton JS. Learning and Teaching: Bloom's taxonomy. http://www.dmu.ac.uk/~jamesa/learning/bloomtax.htm (accessed November 2004).
6. Bloom BS (ed.). *Taxonomy of Educational Objectives: the classification of educational goals – Handbook I: cognitive domain.* New York: McKay. 1956.
7. Bloom BS. *Taxonomy of Educational Objectives: the classification of educational goals – Handbook II: affective domain.* New York: McKay. 1964.
8. Dave RH. *Developing and Writing Behavioural Objectives.* Armstrong RJ: Educational Innovators Press. 1975.
9. Court SD. The future training of consultant paediatricians. The knowledge, skills, and professional attitudes required of the consultant paediatrician. *Br J Med Educ.* 1969; **3**, 332–4.
10. Andrew ME. Reflection as infiltration: learning in the experiential domain. *J Adv Nurs.* 1996; **24**, 391–9.
11. Powell JH. The reflective practitioner in nursing. *J Adv Nurs.* 1989; **14**, 824–32.
12. Newble T, Cannon R. *A Handbook for Clinical Teachers.* Lancaster: MTP Press. 1983.
13. Miller GE. The assessment of clinical skills/competence/performance. *Acad Med.* 1990; **65**(Suppl.), S63–7.
14. Streiner DL, Norman GR. *Health Measurement Scales: a practical guide to their development and use.* Oxford: Oxford Medical Publications. 1989.
15. Van der Vleuten CP, Norman GR, De Graaff E. Pitfalls in the pursuit of objectivity: issues of reliability. *Med Educ.* 1991; **25**, 110–18.
16. Mason R, Zouita L, Ayers B. Assessing clinical competence and revalidation of clinicians. Results from pilot study using portfolio and 360 degrees questionnaire. *Brit Med J.* 2001; **322**, 1601.
17. Van der Vleuten CPM. The assessment of professional competence: developments, research and practical implications. *Adv Health Sci Educ.* 1996; **1**, 41–67.
18. McKinley RK, Fraser RC, Baker R. Model for directly assessing and improving clinical competence and performance in revalidation of clinicians. *Brit Med J.* 2001; **322**, 712–5.
19. Rethans JJ, Drop R, Sturmans F, Van der Vleuten C. A method for introducing standardized (simulated) patients into general practice consultations. *Br J Gen Pract.* 1991; **41**, 94–6.
20. Rethans JJ, Sturmans F, Drop R, Van der Vleuten C. Assessment of the performance of general practitioners by the use of standardized (simulated) patients. *Br J Gen Pract.* 1991; **41**, 97–9.
21. Rethans JJ, Martin E, Metsemakers J. To what extent do clinical notes by general practitioners reflect actual medical performance? A study using simulated patients. *Br J Gen Pract.* 1994; **44**, 153–6.
22. Kneebone R, Kidd J, Nestel D, Asvall S, Paraskeva P, Darzi A. An innovative model for teaching and learning clinical procedures. *Med Educ* 2002; **36**, 628–34.
23. Kneebone RL, Scott W, Darzi A, Horrocks M. Simulation and clinical practice: strengthening the relationship. *Med Educ.* 2004; **38**, 1095–102.

24. Robieux I, Eliopoulos C, Hwang P, Greenberg M, Blanchette V, Olivieri N *et al.* Pain perception and effectiveness of the eutectic mixture of local anesthetics in children undergoing venipuncture. *Pediat Res.* 1992; **32**, 520–3.
25. Robieux IC, Kumar R, Rhadakrishnan S, Koren G. The feasibility of using EMLA (eutectic mixture of local anaesthetics) cream in pediatric outpatient clinics. *Can J Hosp Pharm.* 1990; **43**, 235–6, xxxii.
26. Sinha PK, Manikandan S. Reducing venipuncture pain by cough trick. *Anesth Analg.* 2004; **99**, 952–3.
27. Dyson A, Bogod D. Minimising bruising in the antecubital fossa after venepuncture. *Br Med J (Clin Res Ed).* 1987; **294**, 1659.

Answers

Exercise 1: Venepuncture – knowledge, skills and attitudes

- Using venepuncture as an example, list the knowledge, skills and attitudes that you believe a healthcare professional must possess to be competent to take blood.

Necessary to be judged competent

Knowledge
- Principles of consent
- Type of sample required
  - plasma/serum
  - haematology
  - blood sugar, etc.
- Infection control
  - handwashing
  - gloves
- Venepuncture site
- Pain control
  - EMLA cream[24, 25]
  - 'cough trick'[26]
- Haemostasis
- Adverse event prevention
  - avoidance of arterial puncture
  - sticking plaster allergy
  - sample and form labelling

Skills
- Infection control
- Tourniquet application
- Vein selection
- Venepuncture technique
- Haemostasis

Attitudes
- Approach to the patient
  - offers choice of arm for venepuncture
  - offers choice of colour of sticking plaster
- Minimises discomfort

Exercise 2: Venepuncture – components and methods of assessment

- Think about assessing a nurse taking a sample of blood.
- Write down what can be assessed in each of the 'layers' of Miller's triangle and how each action could be assessed.

	What could be assessed	*Assessment method*
'Knows'	• Anatomy of the antecubital fossa • Principles of consent • Patient identification and specimen labelling • Infection control	• Multiple choice format questions
'Knows how'	• Describes correct ordering of procedure • Describes appropriate attitudes • Describes process of obtaining consent • Describes patient-centred care	• Short answer questions (multiple choice format)
'Shows how'	• Direct observation of taking blood	• Observation of simulation with vein pad • Observation with volunteer
'Does'	• Direct observation of usual practice • Supervisor/colleague report • Patient feedback	• Observation of practice with patients 360° feedback • Patient feedback • Bruising audit

Exercise 3a: Venepuncture – criteria, methods and validity*

- Refer back to your answers in Exercise 2 where you thought about what you could assess.
- Under the headings of knowledge, skills and attitudes write down the criteria that you would use to assess each aspect of the competence of a nurse in venepuncture. Check to make sure that each criterion is capable of assessment by stating how you would assess it.
- Then think about whether each of your criteria could be assessed at each level of Miller's pyramid.
- Finally, consider whether it is absolutely essential that every nurse demonstrates this criteria if they are to take blood samples, i.e. consider its validity (essential, optional, redundant).

	Criteria	Method of assessment	Miller's level: 'Knows', 'Knows how', 'Shows', 'Does', 'Validity'	Validity (essential, 'E', optional, 'O' redundant, 'R')
Knowledge	The learner can describe:			
	• the relationship of the brachial artery to the antecubital fossa and its importance			O
	• why the correct sample tube is required			E
	• the importance of legible sample labelling			E
	• the importance of legible clinical information on the request form	Written tests of knowledge	'Knows', 'Knows how'	E
	• the role of reducing interluminal pressure by tourniquet removal and elevation and extraluminal pressure in controlling bleeding			O
	• the role of hand-washing, skin preparation and no-touch infection control			E
Skills	The learner can demonstrate that they can:			
	• obtain consent			E
	• identify an appropriate vein for venepuncture			E
	• practise the principles of infection control	Direct observation with simulators, volunteers or patients	'Knows', 'Knows how', 'Shows'	E
	• select the correct sample tube			E
	• label the sample tube correctly and legibly			E

	• complete the investigation request correctly and legibly			E
	• perform the venepuncture and take a sample of blood			E
	• ensure haemostasis			E
Attitudes	Practitioner consistently demonstrates that they are:			
	• aware of the principles of consent			E
	• offers patient choice of arm for venepuncture			O
	• chooses appropriate vein for venepuncture	Direct observation, 360° feedback, Audit	'Knows', 'Knows how', 'Shows', 'Does'	E
	• offers patient choice of colour of sticking plaster			O
	• minimises patient discomfort			E
	• explains actions and reasons for them			O

*Correct performance of a skill may indicate possession of underlying knowledge and it may not. This can usually be checked by asking practitioners to explain why they choose to perform a task in that fashion. For example, it is likely that if a practitioner consistently avoids the medial side of antecubical fossa when taking blood they are aware that there is a greater risk of arterial puncture from sampling on that side but it may simply reflect habit rather than conscious awareness. This can be clarified by asking, 'Why did you choose to sample from that vein?'.

Exercise 3b: Venepuncture – criteria, judgement, standards and reflection on personal practice

- Using the list of criteria you wrote down in Exercise 3a, now consider whether you can make a yes/no judgement as to whether the learner possesses that attribute (Y/N) or whether you must make a judgement about whether it is optimally or sub optimally possessed or performed (O/S).
- Then consider whether each is a basic competence which any healthcare practitioner must be able to possess or demonstrate or is likely to be a marker of an expert (E) or novice (N) practitioner.
- Finally, consider whether you possess the knowledge implied by each of the criteria or reliably perform each aspect every time you carry out a venepuncture.

	Criteria	Type of judgement (Y/N or O/S)	Level of experience (E/N)	My own practice
Knowledge	The learner can describe:			
	• the relationship of the brachial artery to the antecubital fossa and its importance	Y/N	E	Yes
	• why the correct sample tube is required	Y/N	E	Yes
	• the importance of legible sample labelling	Y/N	N	Yes
	• the importance of clinical information on the request form and legibility	Y/N	N	Yes
	• the role of reducing interluminal pressure by tourniquet removal and elevation and extraluminal pressure in controlling bleeding	Y/N	E	Yes
	• the role of handwashing, skin preparation and no-touch infection control	Y/N	N	Yes
Skills	The learner can demonstrate that they can:			
	• obtain consent	O/S	N	Yes
	• identify an appropriate vein for venepuncture	O/S	N	Yes
	• practise the principles of infection control	O/S	N	Yes
	• select the correct sample tube	Y/N	N	Usually

	• label the sample tube correctly and legibly	O/S	N	Legibility can be a problem
	• complete the investigation request correctly and legibly	O/S	N	Legibility can be a problem
	• perform the venepuncture and take a sample of blood	O/S	N	Yes
	• ensure haemostasis	O/S		Yes
Attitudes	The practitioner demonstrates that they are:			
	• aware of the principles of consent	O/S	N	Yes
	• offers patient choice of arm for venepuncture	Y/N	E	Usually
	• chooses appropriate vein for venepuncture	Y/N	E	No – not available
	• offers patient choice of colour of sticking plaster	O/S	E	I try
	• minimises patient discomfort	O/S	E	Yes
	• explains actions and reasons for them	O/S	E	Yes

Exercise 4a: Observing a trainee performing venepuncture

• List the strengths and opportunities for improvement displayed by this trainee.

Strengths:
   • Calls patient by name
   • Introduces self
   • Clearly indicates what patient should do
   • Checks request form
   • Uses correct sample bottle and needle
   • Washes hands and uses gloves
   • Competent venepuncture
   • Applies pressure to stop bleeding
   • Asks patient to apply pressure to cotton wool
   • Labels sample tubes correctly

- Disposes of sharps correctly
- Applies plaster
- Gives patient instructions about wound care

Opportunities for improvement:
- Does not confirm patients' identity
- Does not explain process to patient or check patient's understanding
- Does not offer patient choice of venepuncture site
- Opens needle before washing hands and putting on gloves
- Applies tourniquet before ready to take sample
- Uses visible rather than palpable vein
- Removes needle before releasing tourniquet
- Does not ask patient to keep arm straight[27]
- Does not check that bleeding has ceased
- Does not give patient opportunity to ask questions

- Are they competent to perform the venepuncture in unsupervised practice?
  - No
- Why have you made this decision?
  - A consistent failure to confirm the patient's identity with the patient and cross-check this with the request form is a sufficiently serious omission to prevent progression to independent practice because any confusion which arose earlier in the chain of care will be perpetuated with potentially serious implications.

Exercise 4b: Grouping strengths and opportunities for improvement

- Group each strength and opportunity for improvement you identified in Exercise 4a under the criteria for assessment of competence in venepuncture you developed in Exercise 3a.
- If any are left over consider whether they reflect your personal preferences or whether it is necessary for all healthcare professionals to possess them.

Strengths:
- Understands which sample tube should be used
  - correct sample tube selection
- Some understanding of infection control
  - washed hands
  - used gloves
  - appropriate disposal of sharps and clinical waste
- Displayed knowledge of antecubital fossa anatomy
  - identified appropriate vein

- Some adverse events avoidance
  - risk of arterial puncture avoided
  - checks request form
  - legible patient details on sample tube
  - appropriate disposal of sharps and clinical waste
- Proficient venepuncture and sample drawing
- Gave patient instructions about wound care

Opportunities for improvement:
- Obtain consent
  - does not explain procedure and confirm patient knows what they are going to do
- Explain actions and reasons for them
  - does not ask the patient if they have any questions about the procedure
  - does not explain when and how the results are likely to be available
- Does not offer the patient a choice of arm for venepuncture
- Does not offer patient choice of colour of sticking plaster
- Avoidance of adverse events
  - does not confirm patient's identity with the patient
- Achieve homeostasis
  - does not select a palpable as opposed to visible vein for venepuncture, especially in an older person
  - does not release tourniquet before withdrawing needle
  - does not ask patient to keep arm straight while applying pressure
  - does not check for haemostasis before applying plaster

Not in criteria:
- Calls patient by name
- Introduces self

Exercise 4c: Prioritising opportunities for improvement

- Rearrange your list for opportunities for improvement and the associated criteria of competence in Exercise 3 in the order of importance for improvement.
- For each opportunity for improvement try to write down exactly what the trainee should do the next time she takes blood to improve her performance.

  - Avoidance of adverse events
    - always remember to check patient's identity and that the name on the sample form matches the patient's
  - Always obtain consent
    - always check that the patient knows what you are going to do and gives you permission to take blood

- Always ensure homeostasis
  - try to select a palpable as opposed to visible vein for venepuncture, especially in an older person
  - always release tourniquet before withdrawing needle
  - always ask patient to keep arm straight while applying pressure
  - check that bleeding has stopped before applying plaster
- Always explain actions and reasons for them
  - always check that the patient knows what you are going to do and gives you permission to take blood
  - remember to ask the patient if they have any questions about the procedure
  - give the patient an indication of when the results are likely to be available

Of minor importance in this context:

- Does not offer the patient a choice of arm for venepuncture
- Does not offer patient choice of colour of sticking plaster

---

Exercise 5: Educational prescription and diagnosis in a consultation

Identify, using the CAIIN for primary care nurses:

- the nurse's consultation strengths
- opportunities for improvement that they have displayed
- your educational diagnosis for this nurse
- the three most important opportunities for improvement for this nurse to address and the recommendations you would make to assist them to improve.
- This trainee's consultation strengths
  - listens attentively
  - exhibits well organised approach to information gathering
  - elicits physical signs correctly and sensitively
  - uses instruments in a competent and sensitive manner
  - formulates appropriate care plans
  - uses clear and understandable language
  - makes discriminating use of drug treatment
  - elicits relevant information from patient/clients
  - seeks relevant clinical signs
  - correctly interprets information gathered
  - applies clinical knowledge appropriately in the identification and management of the patient's/client's problem
- Opportunities for improvement they have displayed
  - allow patient to explain situation/problem fully
  - recognise patient's verbal cues
  - consider physical, social and psychological factors as appropriate

- negotiate care plans with patients/clients
- convey sensitivity to the needs of patients/clients
- Educational diagnosis
  - does not identify patient's/client's reasons for attendance and associated concerns and expectations because does not allow the patient to explain the situation/problem fully
  - does not consider social and psychological factors and incorporate them in the identified problem and negotiation of care plan with patient
- Three most important opportunities
  - Allow patient/client to explain situation/problem fully
    - resist the temptation to interrupt or distract the consultation
    - use open questions to begin with, e.g. 'How can I help?' followed by, 'Can you tell me more about that?'
  - Identify patient's/client's reasons for attendance and associated concerns and expectations
    - in every consultation you must be satisfied that you have established the patient's/client's reasons for consultation
    - ensure you know what the patient's/client's main concerns are. This may require direct enquiry about their view of the nature of the problem, its cause and possible effects.
    - ask the patient/client what they hope you can do for them unless this is evident already.
  - Consider physical, social and psychological factors as appropriate.
    - always bear in mind the patient's/client's problem with physical, psychological and social dimensions. For example, a mother of a child with a cold may be concerned about the possibility of other significant illness (meningitis) especially if the child has some symptoms in common with meningitis.

Chapter 7

Giving and receiving feedback

Rhona Knight

Introduction

'Mummy – you look beautiful, just like Cinderella.' My young son affirms me, as my husband and I are about to go out for the evening. This feedback as to my appearance is positive, gives me confidence and demands no change. On the other hand, while trying on a new dress and asking my husband what he thought, the response was less than positive. The dress did nothing for me, the colour made me look drained. Maybe I should try a similar dress but of a different colour? Or maybe even a completely different outfit? This feedback was supportive. I was OK as a person – the dress just didn't work on me. The feedback was constructive in that alternative ways forward were suggested. As a result the feedback preserved my self-esteem while at the same time it offered a challenge. Feedback does not always have this result, however. It also has the potential to be destructive. I remember as a young child being told off by an adult who was not a parent. The negative, unsupportive and unasked for feedback of, 'You are a wicked little girl' was etched on my mind for many years. This feedback attacked me as a person, undermined confidence and resulted in no obvious educational gain.

Feedback is intrinsically linked with growth and learning, whether it is on our latest Delia Smith creation or our work as practitioners. Feedback is at the heart of education.[1] The consultation is no exception. As lifelong learners we are all students of the consultation and we want to develop our skills within the consultation from just competent to expert.[2] For this we need feedback. As teachers of the consultation we want to promote and encourage growth and learning in our learners and for this we need to give feedback. We know our learners both want and appreciate it.[3, 4] It is for this reason that this chapter is devoted to feedback. The chapter looks at the principles of feedback and explores some basic tools of the feedback trade. It is not intended to be an academic treatise on the subject, but instead the chapter aims to give some practical approaches to feedback that the reader can take away and develop. The following areas are covered.

- What is feedback?
- Why bother with feedback?
- Key features of feedback.
- General principles of feedback.
- A feedback 'toolbox'.
- An exercise.

What is feedback?

'Feedback is an essential component of education and adult learning'.[5] But what do we mean by feedback? For some, minds will turn immediately to the control of the menstrual cycle; others will think of biofeedback technologies, for example those used by physiotherapists to train women in pelvic floor exercises. For those used to using microphones it is that awful screeching noise reminiscent of nails on a blackboard indicating that you are standing too close to the loudspeakers. In educational terms, feedback has been described as referring to information describing 'performance in a given activity that is intended to guide their future performance in that same or in a related activity'.[6] Another way to describe feedback is as follows.

> A two-way process in which an educational supervisor or group appropriately shares with the learner information based on observation, with the aim of enabling the learner to reach a defined goal.

This definition includes the four key elements needed for feedback:

- a learner
- a goal
- an observed episode
- an educational supervisor.

Do we need feedback?

In teaching consultation skills to students and qualified practitioners in primary and secondary care, good feedback is greatly valued. While for some this may be partly driven by an assessment process, for others the motivation is the desire to develop consultation skills. The need for feedback has been termed a 'hunger', and the hunger is for regular and constructive feedback.[7] Constructive feedback has also been shown to improve learning outcomes[8] and to help produce better marks in assessments, in a variety of educational settings.[9]

Key features of feedback

When feedback is analysed it can be found to have two basic components: support and challenge.[10] This can be illustrated in graphical form as shown in Figure 7.1. Any given feedback will fall into one of four quartiles, depending on its context and content.

In analysing each of the quartiles visual illustration is used and refers to four apt paintings by the artist Mark Chagall. Chagall, a 20th Century artist, famous for his religious and romantic paintings, was a Russian Jew. His art centred on the folklore of his childhood and he blended reality and the dream world in an exquisite way. Perhaps his bestknown work is 'La Mariee', the painting Anna Scott (Julia Roberts) gives to her beloved bookseller (Hugh Grant) in the film 'Notting Hill',[11] complete with its violin-playing goat.

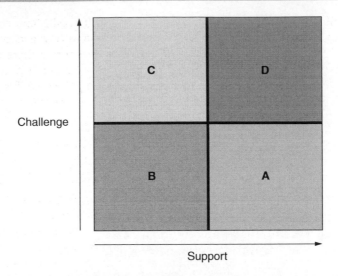

Challenge

Support

Figure 7.1: The two components of feedback – support and challenge.*

Low challenge–high support feedback

This kind of feedback is illustrated well in the picture 'Portrait with a glass of wine' painted in 1917–18, which hangs in the Musee National d'Art Moderne, Centre Georges Pompidou, Paris. In this picture we see a relaxed young gentleman being carried on the shoulders of a lady dressed in white. He raises his glass of wine in the air with a smile. He is being well supported, in fact he is being completely carried, but he is experiencing no challenge. Low challenge–high support feedback ('A' in Figure 7.1 above) could include comments such as:

'That was great, you did really well.'

'You made the patient feel at ease.'

'You listened and used silence very well.'

'That was brilliant.'

The comments are supportive and affirming but do not encourage change and development. They have the potential for building confidence but not of challenging growth. Low challenge–high support feedback has a role in various feedback contexts. One example would be where the learner is at 'survival level' as described by Neighbour in his hierarchy of educational imperatives.[12] This may happen at an early stage of consultation skills development, but may also be revisited at later stages when professional or domestic crises raise their head. It is also a useful method of feedback to an individual within a group setting, in the early stages of the life of a group, when many individuals can feel more vulnerable.

Low challenge–low support feedback

The painting 'The Sky of Paris', from a private collection, painted in 1973, shows a man and woman walking along hand in hand, with the Eiffel Tower in the background. It is a peaceful and relaxed scene. There is no challenge here and no support. When one looks at the picture in more detail one gets the impression that the mind of the man may well be on other things. And so it is with low challenge–low support feedback. The learner and teacher continue down a gentle learning journey, metaphorically hand in hand, not apparently going anywhere, where the feedback comments made by the supervisor would seem to indicate that her mind is not fully on the task at hand and give neither challenge or support. Low challenge–low support feedback ('B' in Figure 7.1 above) could include comments such as:

> 'That was fine.'

> 'Carry on – that seems to be working.'

> 'You completed the task in hand.'

On the principle that any feedback is better than nothing, these kinds of comments may have a role. They show the supervisor connecting with the learner, and as a mother it is a form of feedback I use when presented with homework to check, while I am also making dinner, doing the washing and encouraging one of the other children to get ready to go out. As an educational supervisor this kind of feedback may well have a role when it is in unprotected learning time and when the supervisor is also faced with other demands. If in fact the observed episode was generally fine, it conveys to the learner that there is nothing major to be concerned about and hence is better than no feedback at all. The dangers, however, include conveying a sense of apathy and lack of interest resulting in little motivation for improvement.

High challenge–low support feedback

To illustrate this form of feedback I have chosen the painting 'The promenade', completed in 1917, which is in the State Russian Museum in St Petersburg. Against a geometric background of greenhouses and meadowland and a white sky broken by the delicate blue leaves of a tree, a couple takes a walk. The only contact is that they are seen to hold hands. By this contact alone the lady is suspended in mid-air, in a way that appears to deny the laws of science. The scene is that of minimal support – by hand alone, but extremely high challenge. The situation is precarious and collapse seems inevitable. High challenge–low support feedback ('C' in Figure 7.1 above) is, apart from no feedback at all, probably the most dangerous form of feedback. It demands change to help the learner reach a defined goal, but does not affirm the learner in the process. It could include comments such as:

> 'Well you could have done that better, why didn't you focus more on the social background?'

> 'You missed out some essential things. You should have asked about what they thought was going on.'

> 'The patient gave a lot of verbal cues. You need to practise picking these up.'

For most learners, especially in the early stages of a learning relationship, this feedback is risky. It can de-motivate the learner, induce defensiveness and inhibit further learning. However, this form of high challenge–low support feedback may have a role in some learning relationships. One-to-one learning relationships that take place over a long period of time have the capacity to provide support by the nature of the relationship alone, and thus the interjection of a high challenge comment *may* be appropriate, when given within the context of that supportive background. An example of this is when my husband asks me to feedback on a teaching presentation he has prepared, usually with a brief request, 'What do you think?'. I have been known to respond, 'You need more pictures' or, 'These slides are too busy'. These responses are examples of minimalist, high challenge, low support feedback. I am assuming that my husband knows that the bits I don't comment on, I think are fine, and am relying on the long term supportiveness of the relationship to provide affirmation, while I challenge him in other areas. Low support–high challenge feedback is to be used with great care.

High challenge–high support feedback

'The Circus House', dating from about 1964, is one of many circus scenes painted by Chagall. It depicts a circus ring where a variety of artists are performing. The viewer's eyes are initially drawn to a dancer on horseback, and then, on her right, to an acrobat being held upside down in the air by a colleague. Looking to the top of the picture, a tightrope walker wends his way across the ring, and to the left of the picture a horse sits on a box playing a trumpet. All around the ring is the audience, watching and willing the artists to succeed in their tasks. This picture is full of challenge, as seen in the tasks being performed. It is also full of support. The support is not only portrayed as the physical support of the horse, the tightrope, the colleague and the box, but is also portrayed as emotional support, in the way the whole scene is held together by the watching audience. The high challenge and high support in this picture epitomises the most effective area of feedback in promoting growth and development ('D' in Figure 7.1 above). High challenge–high support feedback could include comments such as:

> 'Well done – you picked up on her anxiety and reflected it back – but do you think you got to the crux of the issue?'

> 'A good effort. You tried to explain what you thought was going on to him, but do you think he understood?'

> 'I liked the way you wrote down what you wanted her to do. Why did you choose that care plan?'

Whereas the unsupportive comment can result in 'paralysis' and induce defensiveness, the supportive comment affirms the learner and opens the door to further challenge. This form of feedback, although applicable to any stage of the learning journey perhaps works best once the teaching relationship has been established and learners have found their feet. High challenge–high support feedback fits in to Neighbour's hierarchy of educational imperatives[12] at the levels of recognition, self-esteem and autonomy.

General principles of feedback

Types of feedback

Three general categories of feedback have been described,[13] tailored to different requirements. The three categories are:

- brief feedback
- formal feedback
- major feedback.

Brief feedback describes an interjection within an observed learning situation. Unlike formal feedback it does not take place in protected time for feedback. An example of this could be that after observing the learner doing an incomplete examination, the teacher may say:

> 'Well done. You sensitively approached the patient *[supportive]*, however, to make sure you don't miss anything you might find it easier to do things this way *[challenging]*.'

Formal feedback is when protected time is put aside, to give feedback to the learner. This may vary in duration, but is usually a minimum of five minutes, and is a form of feedback that should feature regularly in a learning experience. It may take place, for example, after observation of a procedure, or after watching a video-recorded consultation.

Major feedback occurs when a reasonable amount of time is set aside to allow the learner to reflect on their performance, to receive feedback from a teacher and at a point in the learning cycle that allows for a plan to overcome weaknesses to be prepared. This may form part of an assessment process.

Guidelines for giving feedback

The literature is full of different guidelines for giving feedback. Perhaps the most useful eight top tips (listed in the box below) are described in the classic paper on feedback by Ende.[6]

Guidance for giving feedback[6]

Feedback should:

- be undertaken with teacher and learner working as allies, with common goals
- be well timed and expected
- be based on firsthand data
- be regulated in quantity and limited to behaviours that are remediable
- be phrased in descriptive non-evaluative language
- deal with specific performances, not generalisations
- offer subjective data, labelled as such
- deal with decisions and actions, rather than assumed intentions or interpretations.

Some readers may prefer King's criteria for feedback that are listed in the box below,[7] and those of you who use mnemonics, may find the following sentence helpful in remembering King's criteria: 'Do remember to be *Sensitive*, *Specific* and *Selective* in *Describing* and *Directing* your *Timely* feedback'.

> **Criteria for feedback**
>
> People are motivated when feedback is:
>
> - descriptive – of the behaviour rather than the personality
> - specific – rather than general
> - sensitive – to the needs of the receiver as well as the giver
> - directed – towards behaviour that can be changed
> - timely – given as close to the event as possible
> - selective – addressing one or two key issues rather than too many at once.

A synthesis of the two lists is preferred by some people and the following 'TEAM' guidelines can be recommended. In these the learner and teacher are working as a team with common goals.

> **T**iming: Is the timing suitable and appropriate? Is the learner expecting feedback? Is the time protected? Does the feedback relate closely in time to the observed episode?
> **E**nvironment: Is the environment appropriate? While some forms of brief feedback of necessity take place with a patient present, generally individual feedback, which is not part of group teaching, is best done in a private and safe environment without interruptions. The corridor, reception or coffee room usually does not offer this type of facility.
> **A**ppropriateness: Is the feedback appropriate? Is it based on observation? Is it descriptive? Is it specific? Is it sensitive to the learner? Does it make assumptions or judgements?
> **M**anageability: Is the feedback manageable? Is it about something that can be changed? Is it selective? Is there enough to work on? Is there too much?

A feedback 'toolbox'

Just as there is much written about guidelines for the content of feedback, so there is about methods of delivering feedback. In clinical education the best known are 'Pendleton's Rules' and the 'Calgary–Cambridge method'. These have been seen by many as being opponents in a fight symbolic of the annual University boat race that takes place on the Thames. The Oxford crew, coxed by psychologist Pendleton and rowed ably by clinicians Tate, Schofield and Havelock face the Cambridge crew of Draper and Silverman augmented by the Canadian Kurtz, from Calgary. Perhaps these are more usefully seen as two major tools in a toolbox, each useful in its own right, one more suited to some situations than the other. As teachers we need to know how to use these tools and to be able to adapt them for straightforward and more complex situations. However, any good toolbox will provide more than two tools. It is to this toolbox we will now turn.

Tool 1: Pendleton's rules

The Consultation: an approach to learning and teaching is the book that is referenced when 'Pendleton's Rules' for feedback are quoted.[14] The rules as first written recommended that feedback should:

- clarify matters of fact
- encourage the learner to go first
- consider what has been done well first
- make recommendations rather than state weaknesses.

These rules are used in giving feedback after a learner has been observed performing a consultation, which may be live or recorded on video. After observation, questions are only allowed to clarify points of fact. The learner then says what she thought was done well, followed by the teacher saying what was done well. The learner then indicates what was not done so well and what could be improved upon. This is followed by the teacher saying what was not done so well, suggesting possible improvements, ideally ending with a constructive and helpful discussion. One of the benefits of this approach is that positive feedback is an integral part of it. If we consider behavioural theory and parental experience, we can understand why this approach is enough to make the learner more likely to repeat the positive behaviour, or the child to say please and thank you next time. Thus when learners indicate that they do not need positive feedback and, instead, just want the areas that require improvement discussed, I find it is important to challenge them on this. Affirmation of positive areas is just as important as feedback on developmental areas, not only because it imparts confidence, but also it challenges the learner to continue the beneficial behaviours. One of the other advantages of this method is the safety and security the structure gives both learner and teacher. It is particularly well suited for giving feedback after a formal assessment.

The rules have become enshrined in clinical education as laws not to be broken. In the updated version of the book,[10] the authors indicate that the rules were initially written as an afterthought and were devised to address the problem of 'teaching by humiliation' prevalent in medical training at the time. They also highlight two issues to be considered in teaching consultation competence. The first is that judgements should be made against explicit criteria, which for the authors relate to the seven tasks of the consultation they describe in their book. In the case of readers here, the CAIIN competences are the criteria to be used. The second issue is that the rules are to be seen as general principles, and not as binding laws. They were designed to be learner-centred, and set within a contract that included both teacher and learner agendas, a designated time frame and defined roles and responsibilities.

Tool 2: The 'Calgary–Cambridge method'

This method is described in two papers published in *Education for General Practice*[15, 16] and the book *Teaching and Learning Communication Skills in Medicine*.[17] It centres on the concept of non-judgemental observational feedback relating to the learner's agenda. The two key concepts to be understood are Agenda Led Outcome Based Analysis (ALOBA) and 'SET-GO' feedback. Originally designed for use within a group viewing video-recorded consultations, the concepts can be readily adapted to various one-to-one learning situations, and to different consultation models.

Adapted principles of Agenda Led Outcome Based Analysis

At the beginning of the session the learner sets the scene, describes prior knowledge, and extenuating circumstances.

1. The learner identifies the problems experienced, and identifies what help she would like from the feedback session.

The observer encourages the learner to identify the problem areas of the consultation. The learner then chooses the area to spend time on, specifying what help they would like from the discussion.

2. The learner identifies what outcomes she was trying to achieve.

The learner indicates what she was aiming for in the area under discussion. By specifying the goals, problem solving is encouraged. In doing this, the learner could access the CAIIN competences.

3. The observer encourages self-assessment and self-problem-solving first.

The learner identifies possible strategies for reaching their specified goals. In doing this, the learner could access CAIIN recommended strategies.

4. The observer becomes involved in the problem-solving process.

The observer facilitates the process by agreeing or amending the strategies and solutions suggested by the learner. It is helpful to use the available strategies from the CAIIN where these apply.

5. Use descriptive feedback to encourage a non-judgemental approach.

See the SET-GO framework as described below. This enables specific feedback and avoids generalisations.

6. Provide balanced feedback.

The feedback should be both supportive and challenging. Where judgements are used, they should be balanced to include positive and negative comments. The focus should be on those aspects of the performance of greater importance.

7. Make offers and suggestions, provide alternatives.

The feedback is more likey to be accepted by the learner if the observer makes suggestions for consideration, as opposed to prescriptive comments. However, if the performance indicates the learner has important deficits these must be clearly pointed out.

8. Rehearse suggestions.

Rehearse and practise suggestions for improvement by role play. When acquiring or improving any skill, observation, feedback and rehearsal are required to effect change.

9. Be well intentioned, valuing and supportive.

The attitude and demeanor of the observer in providing the feedback plays an essential role in ensuring its acceptability. If the learner believes the observer wants them to improve, rather than treating the session as an opportunity to demonstrate their superiority, it will be much more effective.

10. Occasionally introduce teaching exercises and research evidence.

New elements of teaching can help to illustrate basic key consultation skills, particularly if these can be related to the evidence for their importance. It is important not to lose focus on the purpose of a feedback session, so this should be limited.

11. Structure and summarise learning so that an endpoint is reached.

A very useful question is, 'What three things will you take away from this session?'. After the learner responds the observer should summarise the session to ensure that the individual skills discussed have been incorporated into an overall conceptual framework.

SET-GO descriptive feedback

'SET-GO' is the acronym for a feedback method originally designed for analysis of video-recorded consultations. It can also be used in a directly observed consultation, when descriptive notes are kept of interactions within the consultation and their effects. SET-GO descriptive feedback has five parts and can be adapted for use with most methods of feedback. The learner and observer jointly watch a segment of a consultation or reflect back to a particular moment. For example, 'I'd like to take you back to when you told her she needed to lose weight'.

1. What I **S**aw.

The learner is asked to say what she has seen or remembered about what occurred. This statement must be descriptive, specific and non-judgemental. 'He folded his arms and looked down at his feet.'

2. What **E**lse did you see?

The learner says what happened next in descriptive terms. 'I asked him if he knew how harmful obesity is and he said you nurses always put everything down to me being fat.'

3. What do you **T**hink?

The learner is given the opportunity to acknowledge and problem solve. 'Perhaps I should have started by checking his weight and comparing it with previous readings.'

4. Clarify the **G**oal that the learner would like to achieve.

Together the learner and observer define what the learner is aiming for. 'I would like patients to recognise for themselves what needs to be done, rather than feel as if I am lecturing them.'

5. Look at **O**ffers of how to get there.

Observer and learner discuss the goal and together begin to problem solve. 'I could open the discussion of obesity by asking if he knows why he is getting more breathless climbing stairs.'

The 'Calgary–Cambridge method' of ALOBA and SET-GO can seem quite daunting and cumbersome initially, but it is worth learning how to use the tools. One of the benefits is that they encourage learners to analyse consultations in a more reflective way. This approach matches the Kolb Learning Cycle (*see* Chapter 8). Another benefit is that encouraging the learner to identify and prioritise learning needs helps develop skills for lifelong learning.

Tool 3: Non-judgemental feedback

The two methods described above represent the main tools used in feedback. However, there are additional tools needed to provide effective feedback. The first of these is the concept of non-judgemental feedback. This is feedback based on description. An example of judgemental feedback is, 'The start of the consultation was terrible; you didn't seem interested in her story at all'. A possible descriptive alternative could be, 'At the start of the consultation you were looking at the computer, which prevented eye contact'. Another example of judgemental feedback is, 'The start of the consultation was terrific, well done'. A non-judgemental alternative is, 'At the start of the consultation you lifted your head and looked at the patient and kept quiet while she spoke'. Judgemental feedback by its nature carries a judgement about what is good and what is bad. In the words of Silverman, Draper and Kurtz:

> Communication skills are neither intrinsically good nor bad, they are just helpful, or not helpful, in achieving a particular objective in a given situation. We need to address our comments as to 'what seemed to work' and 'what didn't seem to work' in relation to getting to where you were trying to go.[17]

Tool 4: Observation versus deduction

The next important concept is distinguishing between what is observed and what is deduced from an observation, i.e. separating behaviour from interpretation. It is also important for the teacher to remember that any deduction made is only a hypothesis, until confirmed by the learner. Observations could include: arms folded; legs crossed; speaking quickly; flushed; moving a lot; and breathing quickly. Deductions could include: bored; embarrassed; amused; disgusted. Therefore rather than the teacher saying to the learner, whom they observed to become slightly red faced and to move more, 'You were embarrassed', an alternative would be to say, 'I noticed at this stage in the consultation your face became red and you moved more in your seat, and I *wondered* if you might be *embarrassed*'. This allows the learner to confirm or refute the interpretation and to offer an appropriate alternative, for example irritation or anger.

Tool 5: Pi

The 'Pi' tool has two components: the **P**oint and the **I**llustration.[18] In giving prescriptive feedback to a learner it is useful to make the point and then back this up with an illustration. As in the example of brief feedback given above this may include showing the learner a particular examination technique. Another example for a learner, who has been observed to use a lot of closed questions at the start of the interview, could be, 'I would like you to ask more open questions at the beginning of the consultation' (POINT) and 'Why not ask the patient at the beginning "How can I help?" or "Tell me about it"' (ILLUSTRATION).

Most of us, if being asked to do something differently, find an example useful in helping us to understand the point that is being made, even if the suggested illustration is not the way we ultimately adopt.

Tool 6: PEE

The 'PEE' tool has three components: the **P**oint, the **E**xplanation and the **E**xample.[18] As with Pi above it is used in giving prescriptive feedback. The point or recommendation is made; the reason for the request is given; an example is outlined. For example, if the learner is seen to have difficulty in elucidating what her patients mean, a possible approach could be as follows.

- 'I would like you to try to clarify some of the key words patients use.' (**P**oint)
- 'Clarification is about checking you understand what the patient means. The patient's understanding is not always the same as yours.' (**E**xplanation)
- 'When the patient said she thought it was something sinister, you could ask her what she meant by sinister.' (**E**xample)

By using an example, the learner is given a suggestion as to how a goal can be reached, but more importantly is also given the reason why. This tool can work well as a short interjection as part of brief feedback and can also be part of a major or formal feedback session. As described above it is prescriptive and teacher-centred but it can also be turned around to be learner-centred, by the teacher enabling the learner to identify the point, to explore the explanation and to develop some possible examples.

Tool 7: Unacceptable behaviour

An area of feedback that concerns many of us is how to approach what is deemed to be unacceptable behaviour. Although this is an uncommon occurrence it does crop up frequently enough that we must know how to handle the situation. The feedback may concern matters such as inappropriate clothes, poor punctuality, unacceptable attitudes or even more serious issues. In feedback of this nature one of the priorities is to separate the person from the action. It is the behaviour you are addressing; not the nature or essence of the person. Because giving feedback in these situations is highly charged, it is useful to have a supportive structure. The suggestion below for tackling such issues comes from the West Midlands General Practice Deanery Modular Trainers' Course. It is a straightforward and practical approach.

1. Check the person is composed before you start.
2. Use a wake up, warning phrase, 'There is something very serious I have to say'.
3. Say very simply what is not right.
4. Give an example if necessary.
5. Relax the tone to allow for a positive response (usually an offer to improve ensues).
6. Respond to the offer positively – but define specific measurable outcomes.
7. Do not be drawn into a discussion or justification of the behaviour or your right to judge.
8. If complete rejection occurs, refer the problem to a higher level.

There are seven feedback tools in the toolbox, which can be added to as you continue in your teaching and learning career. Becoming familiar with the different tools is an important part of your role as a teacher. Just as a master craftsman uses tools in obvious ways and those you never considered before, so you will develop and learn to use the feedback tools as described here and in more individualised ways. However, to use any tool you need to learn how it works in your hands and how it works with the different materials placed before it, which takes time, practice, observation, reflection and feedback.

An exercise

Having spent some time looking at feedback it might be useful to get a piece of paper and pen and work through the following exercise.

Exercise: Feedback

- When did I receive feedback that was beneficial to me as a learner?
  – what was it that made that feedback beneficial?
- When did I receive feedback that was harmful to me as a learner?
  – what was it that made that feedback harmful?
- Consider a relationship in which you have given feedback.
  – what feedback did you give?
  – how did you give it?
  – how did the person respond?
  – what were you trying to achieve?
  – what did you do well?
  – what would you do differently next time?
- Consider your role as teacher.
  – how would you like to be given feedback on your teaching?
  – why?
- If you have time, might it be worth discussing your answers to these questions with a work colleague.
  – why?

Conclusion

The purpose of this chapter is to equip the learner as teacher to give feedback. It also aims to encourage the teacher as learner, to see how in everyday life we give and receive feedback, and that feedback is not something confined to the arena of education.

Feedback is essential for growth and development of all learners. It needs to include both challenge and support. With teacher and learner working as a TEAM (where the feedback Timing, Environment, Appropriateness and Manageability are considered) effective feedback is facilitated. Identifying and becoming familiar with different feedback tools allows teachers to develop their own expertise in feedback, and in turn, by modelling, to pass these on to the learner.

Learners who want to practise feedback need to find two or three situations, unrelated to their work, to try out the tools they are less familiar with, in a safe environment. Maybe it could be feedback to the girl behind the supermarket counter, your child's homework or a friend's new outfit ... the choice is yours.

References

1. Branch WT, Paranjape, A. Feedback and reflection: teaching methods for clinical settings. *Acad Med.* 2002; **77**, 1185–8.
2. Dreyfuss HL, Dreyfuss SE. *Mind over Machine.* New York: The Free Press. 1986.
3. Chambers R, Wall D. *Teaching Made Easy: a manual for health professionals.* Abingdon: Radcliffe Medical Press. 2000, p. 133.
4. Wall D, Macaleer S. Teaching the consultant teachers: identifying core content. *Med Educ.* 2000; **34**, 131–8.
5. Kogan JR, Bellini LM, Shea JA. Have you had your feedback today? *Acad Med.* 2000; **75**(10), 1041.
6. Ende J. Feedback in clinical medical education. *JAMA.* 1983; **250**, 777–81.
7. King J. Giving feedback. *Brit Med J Career Focus.* 1999; **318**, 2.
8. Rolfe I, McPherson J. Formative assessment: how am I doing? *Lancet.* 1995; **385**, 837–9.
9. Black P, William D. Assessment and classroom teaching. *Assess in Educ.* 1998; **5**, 7–73.
10. Pendleton D, Schofield T, Tate P, Havelock P. *The New Consultation.* Oxford: Oxford University. 2004. p. 75.
11. 'Notting Hill', Universal Pictures (UK) Ltd.
12. Neighbour R. *The Inner Consultation: how to develop an effective and intuitive consulting style (2e).* Abingdon: Radcliffe Medical Press. 2004.
13. Branch WT, Paranjape A. Feedback and reflection: teaching methods for clinical settings. *Acad Med.* 2002; **77**, 1185–8.
14. Pendleton D, Schofield T, Tate P, Havelock P. *The Consultation: an approach to learning and teaching.* Oxford: Oxford University. 1984. p. 75.
15. Silverman J, Draper J, Kurtz SM. The Calgary-Cambridge approach to communication skills teaching 1: Agenda-led outcome based analysis of the consultation. *Educ Gen Prac.* 1996; **7**, 288–99.
16. Silverman J, Draper J, Kurtz SM. The Calgary–Cambridge approach to communication skills teaching 2: SET-GO method of descriptive feedback. *Educ Gen Prac.* 1996; **8**, 16–23.
17. Kurtz SM, Draper J, Silverman J. *Teaching and Learning Communication Skills in Medicine (2e).* Abingdon: Radcliffe Medical Press. 2004.
18. West Midlands Modular Trainers' Course. 'Giving Feedback'. PowerPoint presentation. 2003.

Chapter 8

Devising and implementing the learning plan

John Fowler

Introduction

Chapter 7 explained how feedback could be provided to an individual learner following observation of clinical practice. In this chapter how best to bring about improved consultation performance from the perspective of the educator and the institution is considered. It is aimed at teachers, but all readers will find it useful to understand the principles described.

Clinical governance has put increasing pressure on nurses to consider ways that their current competences can be judged and improved. With the additional expansion and diversification of nursing roles, experienced nurses need to reflect on their practice and knowledge base, in order to identify development plans to take on these new and challenging roles. This form of independent consultation requires many similar, and some new, skills to those acquired through traditional nursing practice. How can we help nurses with substantial clinical experience adapt their existing ways of working and incorporate new knowledge and skills? Or indeed, should we? The reasons for doing it are twofold.

1. Practice should never remain static, all practitioners have a duty to develop and update their skills and knowledge and their consultation skills are no exception.
2. The nature of nurse consultations is changing rapidly, moving from a conversational assessment of patients' needs, usually based upon some form of daily activities model, to a more focused, timed-constrained encounter.

It is hoped that the new nurse consultations combine the best of both resulting in a focused assessment of health needs. Even in the traditional medical consultation there is an increasing emphasis on the move towards evidence-based patient choice,[1] which combines evidence-based practice and patient-centred negotiated choice.

Extending the skills of experienced nurses

Assisting experienced nurses to extend their consultation skills requires a different teaching approach to helping student nurses or inexperienced nurses acquire similar skills. Experienced nurses will already have developed and be confident with their own array of consultation skills. These will have developed over a number of years as a result of:

- current trends in the nursing profession, e.g. nursing process, patient-centred care
- developments regarding patient management systems, e.g. primary nursing planned pathways that have increased the nurses' role resulting in a greater degree of autonomous patient assessment
- general interpersonal skills that develop with experience based upon direct or indirect feedback from patients and colleagues.

Such nurses will have a wealth of experience gained from a variety of different clinical situations and be confident in their interactions with patients. However, a disadvantage of this expertise is that they may also be reluctant to expose their practice to outside scrutiny, fearing that they may not live up to their 'expert' reputation – in Rogerian terms they may feel psychologically unsafe.[2] Also some nurses may not welcome change or be open to new ways of working, instead feeling that they have developed a form of practice that works for them. This is quite different from teaching student nurses or medical students, who have limited experience and work in an environment in which they are exposed to and take on new ideas. They expect to have their practice closely observed and commented upon and to act and be treated like students.

Experiential learning cycle

The implementation of any learning plan needs to take cognisance of the above, otherwise experienced nurses may feel insulted or patronised. A skilled teacher will build upon the nurses' considerable expertise, be sensitive to the exposure of any flaws in their current consultation skills and find ways of helping them to improve their practices. The key elements that the teacher needs to use are the art and science of reflection combined with the nurses' clinical experiences of consultations. This combination of experience and reflection falls within the experiential learning theories epitomised by Dewey[3] and Kolb.[4] Experiential learning theories acknowledge the learning that occurs through active reflection upon experience. This differs from the more traditional view of learning that occurs through the impartment of 'knowledge' in a classroom lecture or textbook. Kolb's experiential learning theory, which he based on work by Lewin,[5] identifies four stages of the learning cycle.[4]

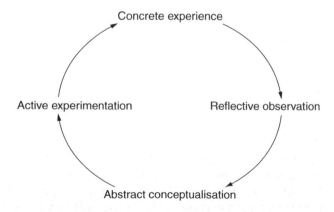

Figure 8.1: Four stages of the learning cycle identified by Kolb.[4]

Kolb's experiential learning cycle

Kolb suggests that people have an experience (concrete experience), which they then reflect upon (reflective observation). Following this they begin to identify rules that arise from that experience or impose rules from outside, on to their experience (abstract conceptualisation). This then results in them changing their way of working (active experimentation) which leads into a new experience (concrete experience) and the cycle continues. In terms of consultation skills, nurses use their experience of consultation skills, either real or via role play (concrete experience), reflect upon those experiences (reflective observation), formulate new ways of working (abstract conceptualisation) and then try the new ways in practice (active experimentation). The implication of Kolb's experiential learning theory for the attainment of consultation competence is that as skills develop they need to be reflected upon and incorporated within a practitioner's growing repertoire of advanced consultation skills.

Reflection and graduated reflection

One of the most effective ways of developing consultation skills is via the use of structured feedback based upon observation of practice and personal reflection.[6,7] Experience alone does not ensure learning occurs. It may result in learning at a superficial level or even learning of unsatisfactory practice.[8] A humorous, but arresting definition of an 'expert' is 'a person who makes the same mistake repeatedly, but with growing confidence he is right'! It is the combination of experience with reflection that results in the potential for a powerful learning mode.

There has been much discussion in the nursing and allied press for a number of years on the nature and importance of reflection.[9–11] Whilst there is widespread acceptance of reflection as a powerful learning tool, some people find it unhelpful and are more comfortable with traditional teacher-centred methods.[12] To overcome this reluctance to use reflection a graduated, reflective model can be used. With this, it is not a question of whether learners are reflecting but to what degree they incorporate reflection into their practice. The degree of incorporation varies with the:

- involvement of the learner
- focus of the experience
- tools used to enable reflection
- learner's role and expected behaviour.

Using a graduated reflection model a course can be structured in a progressive way starting with a low level of reflection and building (if time and the ability of the learners allows) to the maximum level.

Dewey[3] identified a number of qualities that a person needs in order to benefit from reflection as a learning method. The person requires an open mind, should be able to consider all aspects of an argument and take an active control over their education and practice. These qualities identified by Dewey fit well with that of the experienced nurse who is undertaking an independent practitioner consultation course. Provided that the attributes relating to teaching experienced nurses identified at the beginning of the chapter are acknowledged, and the practice of graduated reflection is used, then the combination of reflection based upon experience will enable an experienced nurse to further develop their consultation skills.

How then does the teacher combine the use of nurses' expertise in using graduated reflection whilst maintaining sensitivity to the exposure of their current performance to potential criticism? The first action is to allow a group of learners to get to know each other and to develop a degree of trust in the teacher. This should be done in relatively small groups where learners consider they are psychologically safe.[2] The members of the group need to be comfortable with each other and to feel that they are not in competition. The teacher should establish rules of confidentiality and demonstrate 'confident competence'. The next step is to introduce the first stages of graduated reflection (*see* box above). Initially learners should reflect upon situations in which they do not feel direct personal involvement. This could be watching a video-taped consultation of an area of clinical practice that is not their own. This allows them to reflect upon and discuss those consultation competences that are not dependent on expert knowledge or skill. These are more likely to be those involving interpersonal skills rather than problem solving. The next stage would be to introduce scenarios that are from the learners' area of clinical expertise, again preferably on videotape. The learners should reflect upon the consultation using some form of structured tool. Following this, graduated role play can be introduced with the learners working within their own area of expertise. This should include observation by the teacher and peers with structured feedback and discussion. This can be developed to include videotaping and analysis through discussion. Finally the learner should work in clinical practice and be observed by an experienced practitioner, and structured feedback and discussion should occur.

Graduated reflection

Person performing consultation	Focus of consultation behaviour	Tool for reflection	Learner
Stranger (1)	Neutral situation (1)	Discussion (1)	Observation (1)
Peer (2)	Similar to learners (2)	Observers feedback (2)	Role play (2)
Learner (3)	Actual practice (3)	Video feedback (3)	Real life (3)

Add together one score from each column
4 = minimum level of reflection
12 = maximum level of reflection

Building the challenge

Using a graduated exposure to reflection upon practice the learner can be moved from reflecting upon someone else's experience in a relatively detached and objective way to being videoed performing the consultation with discussion and analysis of the video consultation with peers and the course leader. The extent of the exposure will vary depending upon the following.

1. *The length and type of course:* it would not be possible to carry out full reflective exposure training in a half-day workshop. Building up to the use of video workshops would normally take time, which ideally would be structured as two hours a week for eight weeks.
2. *The skills of the teacher in using role play and video techniques:* teachers need training and supervision to use these techniques competently. It may be that two teachers are required in some stages of a consultation course: one practitioner who is experienced in consultations and one who is experienced in using role play and video techniques.
3. *Some learners will not want to be part of any role play workshop*: those who have experience or self-confidence can, in the hands of a competent teacher, be safely supported through the majority of role play and video techniques. Learners who have more than the usual fear of role play will go to almost any lengths not to be involved, including being absent on the day of the exercise. Obviously no learner should be compelled to learn using techniques that cause psychological distress. However, exemption of these learners might appear 'unfair' to others who feel uncomfortable with rather than distressed by such techniques. The teacher will also wish to consider whether this avoidance behaviour indicates self-awareness of a low level of competence.

There are a number of practical constraints including time, skills required of the teacher and the reluctance of some learners to participate that may justify limiting graduated exposure to the less intrusive stages. This can still be very useful to the learner and should not be seen as 'failure'. However, the use of the full method has a much greater impact in the development of consultation skills.

Although videotaping is more widely used and accepted in medical student teaching and GP training[13] it has also been successfully used in teaching nurse practitioners.[14] Wilma found that nurses who undertook a course based upon video-interaction analysis provided patients with more information, used more open-ended questions and were rated as more involved and less patronising than a control group.[15] The conclusion is that such methods are powerful tools that can assist people to refine their own behaviour in ways that traditional lectures and discussions cannot. They must, however, be used by skilled teachers in a planned and systematic way. The combination of the CAIIN with its specific competences and criteria of performance and a graduated exposure to reflection and self-analysis offers a powerful way to develop consultation skills.

Identifying and addressing learning needs

In order for nurses to identify their learning needs there must be a measure and standard of performance that they should attain. As described in Chapter 3 the CAIIN and the Leicester Assessment Package (LAP) from which it was derived are valid and reliable tools to assess consultation competence. If experienced nurses are given this list of categories and their component competences to discuss they will identify them as relevant to their consultations and will probably argue that they already exercise most of them in their daily work to a satisfactory standard. It may be that, because they are central to their work, experienced nurses would find it difficult to accept that they are not already skilled exponents of such skills. However, video-recording any practitioner (medical or nursing) conducting consultations in real life will certainly identify competences requiring improvement and even areas of serious weakness. Why might there be a discrepancy between what a nurse thinks she is doing and that which an experienced observer sees her to be doing? One or a combination of the following may be relevant.

1. The nurse has developed their current consultation skills in a different setting to that in which she is practising. The most common example of this is the nurse who has developed interviewing and relationship skills with patients from working in a hospital ward environment and who then begins working in a community setting. Another example would be that the consultation skills required by a clinical nurse specialist or consultant nurse will be different from those that the nurse has developed working in the more traditional nursing role. The categories of 'care planning' and 'problem solving' are most likely to prove challenging as they are heavily dependent on knowledge and clinical experience.

2. The further development of existing skills is not as easy as it may appear. It is often easier to learn a totally new skill rather than refine an existing one. Trying to make subtle alterations to a habitual skill demands that well-established behaviours be overridden. Kleinman refers to these barriers to change as 'similarity negative transfer'.[16]

3. Nurses are not used to having a defined length of time for consultations. In traditional settings nurses tend to relate to patients in a continuous way, acquiring information intermittently, as they interact with patients throughout a procedure or an eight-hour shift. The relationship between the patient and the nurse has time to develop; the patient is able to relax and builds up a degree of familiarity and trust with the nurse. The developing independent nurse practitioner is required to adopt a mode of consultation in which patients are booked in for a limited time, often 10–20 minutes, and then leave. The relationship has to be established quickly and information that is not collected during the consultation cannot be retrieved by 'nipping back' to the patient at a later time, to fill in a few blanks.

4. The nurse may have a different agenda to that of the patient or the health institution. For example a new patient may be booked to see a practice nurse for an initial consultation. The nurse's view of this may be to perform some baseline observations and offer necessary health promotion advice. The practice manager's perspective may be that this is one of 15 new patients who need 'clerking' and each has a nine-minute appointment with the nurse. The patient's perspective may be anything from 'the sooner I'm out of here the sooner I can get back to work' to 'I'm scared that this lump might be cancer'.

5. Some of the categories such as care planning, problem solving, health promotion, etc. require negotiation skills. This can be time consuming and possibly frustrating for practitioners who feel they know exactly what is required for patients. In a busy working environment nurses may adopt what they see as an efficient way of working – 'knowing what's best for the patient' at the expense of negotiating with and empowering the patient.

Simulated patients

The wealth and richness of experiential learning arises from the complexity of problems presented by patients, their views of these and the diversity of potential solutions. Ideally nurses, under the observation of experienced clinicians, would carry out consultations with real patients and then discuss their performance. This would be an optimal means of developing consultation skills. It may be difficult to video-record real-life consultation for practical reasons and ethical issues can limit the use of recordings in group teaching. A way to overcome this is by the use of simulated patients. The first step is to prepare a scenario. This comprises as much clinical information as necessary concerning the problem to be portrayed, in addition to all relevant background information. The degree of detail depends on the nature of the problem being portrayed.

This scenario is used in two ways.

- A nurse on the consultation course learns the scenario and role plays the patient. This has proved successful in our experience and allows useful discussion and learning to be generated. The technique does not require expensive resources and can easily be replicated for other groups. A limitation of this method is the degree of detail that a course participant is likely to be able to recall. It also depends on the nurse role playing the patient to do so in a realistic fashion. Unreasonable caricatures can quickly cause a teaching session to verge on the farcical, so careful preparation of the participants is needed.
- The use of paid actors who learn detailed clinical and background information about a patient and present this person to learners in role-play settings. The use of actors has a number of advantages; the 'performance' tends to be of a high quality with observers unable to detect which was the real patient and which was the actor. They can also present the same scenario in a consistent way to different learners, thus providing a reliable base on which to assess consultations. If the consultation is video-recorded different groups can use the scenarios in the initial stages of graduated reflection. Well-written scenarios can be transferred to other settings of care with minor adjustments and can contain several levels or degrees of challenge, depending on the expertise of the group of learners.

In Leicester a number of scenarios was developed to represent common consultation challenges. Actors portrayed these and the role of nurse was taken by volunteer nurse specialists. Working in groups of approximately ten learners, the video-recorded consultation formed the focus of the group's observation, reflection and analysis using the CAIIN tool. In the early stages of the graduated reflection the group watches the video and then each learner independently analyses and scores the consultation using the competences from the CAIIN tool. Under the guidance of a facilitator the participants discuss their individual thoughts and compare scores regarding the consultation. The use of an objective scoring system allows comparison of judgements to be made with individuals having to justify their decisions. In the early stages of graduated reflection this allows groups to discuss and compare analysis of consultations without engaging in stressful self-evaluation. Even if the course is to finish at this stage of graduated reflection the learners are still able to transfer a number of lessons from this type of simulation to their practice. The next stage is to involve the learner in a more direct and interactive way.

Peer interaction

Moving up the graduated experience and reflection continuum the next stage is to get the nurses on the course interacting as though they have taken part in the consultation. This is achieved by the small group observing and analysing a videoed consultation as above. Using the CAIIN the group makes a consensus summary of the strengths and weaknesses of the consultation. One member of the group volunteers to role play the nurse who undertook the consultation, another member of the group acts as an observer, whose role it is to give constructive feedback to the consulting nurse. If there is more than one group then the consulting nurse and the nurse giving feedback can switch groups. This ensures that the consulting nurse is unaware of the previous discussions. Most learners feel relatively comfortable with this level of role play and many find it a challenging and thought-provoking experience. It achieves two goals: first the learners are moved along the continuum of graduated reflection and second it allows them to experience and discuss the ways of giving and receiving feedback (*see* Chapter 7).

The next stage of peer interaction and deepening of reflection is for one learner to role play the consulting nurse whilst another plays the 'patient'. The learner's own area of work forms the focus of the consultation, e.g. a diabetic outpatient clinic. The 'patient', who need not be a diabetic specialist, is given a written brief regarding their symptoms, any particular concerns that she may have and necessary background information. The consulting nurse then performs the consultation under the observation of the rest of the group. By this stage of the course, the group should have bonded and trust and friendships developed, this will support the learners in this activity as the stress levels involved in role play begin to increase. The consultation proceeds using the CAIIN, with which the learners now have familiarity. Following the consultation the nurse is asked to summarise what she considers to be the main problems that the 'patient' is experiencing, how she reached that conclusion, why she chose the particular plan of care and if she felt that she had addressed all the issues in the patient's agenda. The 'patient' then gives feedback on her experience and whether all of her concerns had been identified. The observers then give their feedback, which often involves questions as to why the consulting nurse took a particular approach. This discussion can be particularly 'rich' when nurses from different areas of clinical practice are within the same group.

The next stage is to perform a similar exercise but to video-record the session. The session can be repeated as before but this time the video can be replayed and the consulting nurse asked to narrate the rational for certain questions and behaviours as the tape progresses. This can be expanded with the learner taking the tape away and 'writing up' the consultation. This could form part of the assessment strategy of the course.

The final stage of the graduated reflective exposure is for the learner to perform the consultation in their work situation using real patients. The consultations can be observed by a mentor and initial feedback and discussion can be promoted. If facilities exist and permission from patients can be gained then the consultations can be video-taped and the learner can self-analyse the consultations, possibly bringing one into the course group for discussion and group analysis. As before, such consultations can be formally 'written up' and form part of the summative assessment of the course.

A premise of this chapter is that the skill of the teacher lies in combining the recognition of nurses' considerable expertise, sensitivity to their concerns about exposure of their current consultation skills to scrutiny and the inclusion of 'reflective tips' regarding the development of future practice. Thus far, how the nurses' experiences can become the focus of reflection, whilst protecting the personal safety of the participants, has been discussed. The following section examines the way in which new ideas can be conveyed to the experienced nurse.

Strategies for improvement

With the increasing expansion of nurses' roles new clinical and assessment skills need to be developed and maintained. However, most nurses that attend post-registration consultation courses are already proficient in their area of specialty (e.g. pain control, asthma, colorectal diseases, etc.) and it is not the content expertise they lack but systematic consultation skills. If areas of weakness regarding physical procedures are identified then the learner needs to acquire those skills in the traditional way under the guidance of an appropriately qualified supervisor, depending on the type of skill required.

There is always a place for a structured and well-delivered lecture to introduce new ideas and evidence-based practices. However, within the context of reflective study and feedback from analysis of practice, lectures or even mini-lectures do not fit easily with the educational ethos that is created by learning in practice. Whilst they can introduce new ideas or consolidate facts they have limited use in changing behaviour. The authors of the CAIIN package suggest that consultations can be improved using a variety of techniques as follows:

- reflection
- reading to fill identified knowledge gaps
- self-analysis of video-taped consultations
- direct observation with feedback from a peer or mentor
- simulated recall with a teacher using video-taped consultations
- group teaching with simulated patients.

Building upon the graduated exposure reflection model there are various levels at which such strategies can be used.

1. Having a general discussion about consultations with learners identifying areas of difficulty from their own practice.
2. Observation of someone else's consultation, identifying the weaknesses and then using one or a combination of the above techniques to suggest improvements.
3. Be observed whilst role playing a consultation. With the aid of self-analysis and group feedback identify weaknesses and then use some, or a variety of the above strategies to make improvements. These new techniques can be taken back into the role-play situation and the consultation can be repeated.
4. Have a real consultation observed with subsequent feedback and develop improvements as above.
5. Video-record a real consultation and then using self-analysis and mentor feedback identify weaknesses and work on improvements as above.

The CAIIN documentation includes a number of practical suggestions for improvements that are linked to each of the competences. For example in the category

'Examination, diagnostic testing and practical procedures' there is a competence 'Performs technical procedure in a competent and sensitive manner'. If this has been identified as a weakness then linked to that competence are three potential recommended strategies for improvement that may be appropriate, depending on the nature of the deficiency.

1. Ask patients' permission to carry out the procedure.
2. Give an explanation of what you are doing to the patient.
3. If the procedure is likely to be uncomfortable perform it gently but efficiently.

These simple, objective guidelines can be very useful for the learner in their own self-reflections and individual learning. In a group setting they can be used to prompt discussion with learners giving suggestions for improvements. From the author's experience of conducting such sessions what works well is the inclusion of 'reflective tips' (*see* below).

Reflective tips

In the analysis and discussion following one of the consultation scenarios there are usually some areas in which the consulting nurse has met with difficulty. The first stage is to acknowledge the area of difficulty and ask if other members of the group have experienced similar problems. Those that have can then add to the discussion and widen or contextualise the area of difficulty. This reduces the pressure on the initial consulting nurse, as others identify with the problem. The next stage is to ask if anyone has any tips or suggestions, based upon experience, of what has worked for them as a solution to the problem. This idea of reflective tips is important for two reasons: first they are tips as opposed to definitive responses – at this level individuals are being helped to develop higher order skills by building upon their own personal strengths. What works for one person may not work, or be appropriate for another, thus it is a *tip* rather than a prescription. Second the tip or suggestion comes from a period of reflection by both the students in the group and the teacher; it should be based upon previous experience and adaptation of that experience to the current situation. In a group of experienced nurses there is nearly always someone who has encountered a similar situation and has found a useful solution.

The course leader can also add a tip or can suggest a solution written up in the literature, but which they have not used personally. If the problem the nurse has experienced is in helping the patient explain the problem in their own words the tip can be to, 'Use more open questions', linked to examples such as, 'Tell me more about the pain'; 'How did that make you feel?'. Other tips can be generated for the quiet, unresponsive patient, the overactive one, patients who have difficulty clearly identifying their problem, patients who may appear aggressive, etc. Tips and suggestions can also be formulated for other aspects of the consultation: what to do if you are unsure of the patient's diagnosis; what to do if the patient insists on an inappropriate form of treatment such as antibiotics for a cold.

The role of the teacher is to summarise the problem, call for tips from the participants and then summarise the suggestions so the learners can integrate them into their practice. If, for instance, the scenario identified that the consulting nurse was 'anticipating the patient's problem without giving sufficient opportunity for him to express himself', the tip might be, 'Try an open question at the beginning of the consultation such as, "How can I help you?"'. The learners can then be asked to incorporate this question into their consultations over the next week and report back the following week as to its effectiveness. Three or four tips could be given and dealt with each week in this way. The principle is to keep it simple and make it easy to remember.

In the final session learners can be asked to summarise how their consultation practices have changed over the duration of the course and what areas they are continuing to work on. The teacher can present the tips that have been given over the last few weeks as a summary. The learners can be asked to identify three core problems that they encounter when consulting with patients, and then to share them with each other in small groups. In discussion they can clarify potential solutions. Finally each learner will need to make an action plan, which could take the form of ongoing self-reflection to maintain consultation skills or an arrangement with one of their peers to observe each other on future occasions and to exchange feedback in the manner with which they are now familiar.

Summary

- The position of experienced practitioners needs to be appreciated when developing courses in consultation skills.
- Experienced practitioners will have considerable expertise to draw upon but may also have specific gaps in their knowledge and experience that are not immediately apparent.
- Experienced practitioners may be fearful of embarrassing themselves in front of peers.
- Lectures can be useful in presenting new knowledge or summarising key points but have little impact in changing behaviour.
- Experience, graduated reflection, analysis and feedback are the key to improving consultation performance.
- The concept of graduated reflection provides the underpinning structure of any course involving reflection, role play and observation (direct or via videotape) of clinical practice.
- Reflection and role play should be conducted in small groups.
- Feedback should be objective and structured.

References

1. Ford S, Schofield T, Hope T. Barriers to the evidence-based patient choice (EBPC) consultation. *Patient Educ Couns.* 2002; **47**(2), 179–85
2. Rogers C, Freiberg H. *Freedom to Learn (3e).* New York: Merrill. 1993.
3. Dewey J. *Experience and Education.* New York: Kappa Delta Pi, Collier books. 1938.
4. Kolb D. *Experiential Learning – experience as the source of learning and development.* New Jersey: Prentice-Hall. 1984.
5. Lewin K. *Field Theory in Social Sciences.* New York: Harper and Row. 1951.
6. Hastings A, Lennon M, Redsell S, Cheater F. Evaluation of a consultation skills workshop using consultation assessment and improvement instrument for nurses. *Learn Hlth Soc Care.* 2003; **2**(4), 202–12.
7. McKinley R, Frazer RC, Baker R. Model for directly assessing and improving clinical competence and performance in revalidation of clinicians. *Brit Med J.* 2001; **322**, 712–5.
8. Watson S. An analysis of the concept of experience. *J Adv Nurse.* 1991; **14**, 824–32.

9. Boud D, Keogh R, Walker D. *Reflection: turning experience into learning.* New York: Kogan Page. 1985.
10. Schon D. *The Reflective Practitioner.* London: Temple Smith. 1983.
11. Johns C. Professional supervision. *J Nurs Man.* 1993; **1**(1), 9–18.
12. Fowler J, Chevannes M. Evaluating the efficacy of reflective practice within the context of clinical supervision. *J Adv Nurse.* 1998; **27**, 379–82.
13. Cox J, Mulholland H. An instrument for the assessment of video tapes of general practitioners' performance. *Brit Med J.* 1993; **306**, 1043–6.
14. Bond S, Beck S, Cunningham WF, Derrick S, Healy B, Holdsworth S *et al.* Testing a rating scale of video-taped consultations to assess performance of trainee nurse practitioners in general practice. *J Adv Nurs.* 1999; **30**(5), 1064–72.
15. Wilma M, Caris-Verhallen M, Kerkstra A *et al.* Effects of video interaction analysis training on nurse–patient communication in the care of the elderly. *Patient Educ Couns.* 2000; **39**(1), 91–103.
16. Kleinman M. *The Acquisition of Motor Skill.* New Jersey USA: Princeton Book Company. 1983.

Chapter 9

Using the Consultation Assessment and Improvement Instrument for Nurses (CAIIN) in assessment

Adrian Hastings and Sarah Redsell

Introduction

This chapter is derived from the 'User's Guide' developed as support material for those using the CAIIN in formative and summative assessments. It uses the second version of the CAIIN, developed after validation for use with nurses in secondary care.[1] This version is equally applicable to primary care nurses.[2]

The CAIIN can be used:

- to enable student nurses to develop improved levels of consultation capability
- in continuing professional development (including clinical supervision)
- to develop and support new roles
- to identify and remedy poor professional performance
- for professional self-regulation.

The CAIIN consists of the following elements.

1. The seven categories of consultation competence and 37 component competences required by a nurse.
2. A recording form for the observer to make notes on each consultation seen.
3. Questions to be asked of nurses being observed.
4. Descriptors of levels of performance that facilitate the reliable allocation of grade levels or marks.
5. Recommended strategies for improvement.
6. Feedback summary forms.
7. Guidance on giving feedback.

Categories and criteria

The CAIIN

Interviewing (20%)

- Puts patients at ease
- Enables patients to explain situation/problem fully
- Listens attentively

- Seeks clarification of words used by patients as appropriate
- Demonstrates an ability to formulate open questions
- Phrases questions simply and clearly
- Uses silence appropriately
- Recognises patients' verbal and non-verbal cues
- Considers physical, social and psychological factors as appropriate
- Demonstrates a well-organised approach to information gathering

Examination, diagnostic testing and practical procedures (10%)

- Elicits physical signs correctly and sensitively
- Uses instruments in a competent and sensitive manner
- Performs technical procedures in a competent and sensitive manner

Care planning and patient management (20%)

- Formulates and follows appropriate care plans
- Reaches a shared understanding about the problem with patients
- Negotiates care plans with patients
- Uses clear and understandable language
- Educates patients appropriately in practical procedures
- Makes discriminating use of referral, investigation and drug treatment
- Arranges appropriate follow-up

Problem solving (15%)

- Accesses relevant information from patients' records
- Explores patients' ideas, concerns and expectations about their problem(s)
- Elicits relevant information from patients
- Seeks relevant clinical signs and makes appropriate use of clinical tests
- Correctly interprets information gathered
- Applies clinical knowledge appropriately in the identification and management of the patient's problem
- Recognises limits of personal competence and acts accordingly

Behaviour/relationship with patients (15%)

- Maintains friendly but professional relationships with patients
- Conveys sensitivity to the needs of patients
- Is able to use the professional relationship in a manner likely to achieve mutual agreement with the care plan

Health promotion/disease prevention (10%)

- Acts on appropriate opportunities for health promotion and disease prevention
- Provides appropriate explanation to patients for preventative initiatives suggested
- Works in partnership with patients to encourage the adoption of a healthier lifestyle

> Record-keeping (10%)
>
> • Makes an appropriate and legible record of the consultation
> • Records care plan to include advice and follow-up arrangements as appropriate
> • Enters results of measurements in records
> • Provides the names(s), dose and quantity of drug(s) prescribed to patients together with any special precautions

Observer recording form

The 'Observer recording' form (*see* below) is for use as an *aide-mémoire* for the observer. It is not designed to be retained as a permanent record. One form is completed for each consultation. It identifies the nurse and observer, the date of the assessment, the duration of the consultation and provides space to note the content of the consultation.

The main part of the form provides space divided into three sections to record the competences displayed during the consultation as strengths, those that are difficulties or omissions and the grade level or mark awarded in each category.

If a particular category of competence is not challenged in a consultation the observer should write 'n/a' (not applicable) in the relevant space. The commonest situation where this occurs is a consultation in which 'Examination, diagnostic testing and practical procedures' does not take place. This category is concerned with the technical ability of a nurse to conduct a physical examination (e.g. testing vibration sense in a diabetic patient using a sphygmomanometer), perform a diagnostic test (e.g. dipstick testing of urine) or to carry out a procedure such as connecting the patient to an intravenous line. It is important to note that the decision whether or not to perform a particular test or look for particular physical signs is a thinking skill and is assessed in the 'Problem solving' category.

Questions to be asked

Before the consultation starts the following question should be asked.

• What are your objectives for this consultation?

After the patient has left the following questions should be asked.

• What do you believe are the main problems this patient is experiencing?
• Why have you reached this conclusion?
• Why did you choose your care plan/patient management plan?
• Have you addressed all the issues in the patient's agenda?

These are the questions the observer should ask to explore the thinking underpinning the actions of the nurse. Clinical problem solving is an activity that takes place in the mind of the nurse during the consultation. This encompasses decisions about the likely cause of the problem presented by a patient as well as decisions about how to decide on the best care plan to address it. An observer can make judgements about why certain activities were done or not done, but

CONSULTATION ASSESSMENT AND IMPROVEMENT INSTRUMENT FOR NURSES – OBSERVER RECORDING FORM

Nurse: | Observer: | Date: | Number:

Content of consultation:

Start time:
Finish time:
Duration (mins):

Category	Strengths	Difficulties and omissions	Grade/mark
Interviewing			
Examination, diagnostic testing and practical procedures			
Care planning and patient management			
Problem solving			
Behaviour/relationship with patients/clients			
Health promotion/disease prevention			
Record-keeping			
Notes			

in order to understand the nurse's reasons fully it is necessary she has the opportunity to explain the thinking processes. For regulatory assessment it is important to ask the questions in a standardised way to ensure equity between candidates. In a teaching context the questions serve as a guide to the teacher and nurse as to the issues that need to be addressed.

Criteria for the allocation of grade level or percentage marks

Table 9.1 lists the criteria for the allocation of grade level or percentage marks.

Table 9.1: Criteria for the allocation of grade level or percentage marks.

Criteria	Grade level	Percentage marks
Consistently demonstrates a high standard of capability in all components	1	80% or above
Demonstrates a high standard of capability in most components and a satisfactory standard in all	2	70–79%
Demonstrates capability in all components to a satisfactory standard	3	60–69%
Demonstrates capability in most components to a satisfactory standard. Some minor omissions and/or defects in some components	4	50–59%
Demonstrates inadequacies in several components but no major omissions or defects	5	40–49%
Demonstrates major omissions and/or serious defects; clearly unacceptable standard overall	6	39% or below

The set of descriptors of performance shown in Table 9.1 facilitates conformity between different observers in assessing the level of performance. In single consultations sometimes only a small number of component competences may be challenged. For example, the problem may be relatively straightforward such as 'assessing a patient's fitness for surgery' but the demeanour of the patient may require particular strengths in 'behaviour and relationship with the patient'. If a patient mentions more than once that a relative had died and the nurse does not respond, this could be regarded as 'failing to recognise a verbal cue, ignoring social and psychological factors' and 'not conveying sensitivity' to the needs of the patient.

Normally grade levels are applied when the CAIIN is used for educational purposes. However, grade level should be seen as a code to represent the level of performance indicated by the descriptor to which it is attached. This needs to be understood by the nurses being observed, as they are likely to have received grades in previous assessments where those less than grade 'A' might have been regarded as having failed. In general terms competent nurses would expect to 'demonstrate capability in all components to a satisfactory standard' during an assessment.

Marks are used when it is necessary to rate a level of performance more precisely than when awarding grade levels. This is of most value in regulatory assessment and if it is desired to rank candidates in an order of merit. The percentage weightings reflect the relative importance of each consultation category. For example, 'Interviewing' the patient was regarded as more important than 'Examination etc.' by respondents in the validation research of the CAIIN.

Testing of the LAP, from which the original CAIIN for primary care nurses was developed, shows that it facilitates consistent judgements between markers in the assessment of the consultation performance of medical students[3] and of doctors.[4] As the methodology of the CAIIN is very similar it is reasonable to anticipate that it is equally reliable.

Recommended strategies for improvement

The CAIIN has been developed primarily as a tool for education and improvement. It is imperative therefore that it facilitates the provision of effective and practical solutions to identified difficulties in consultation performance. Alongside each competence are a number of recommended strategies (Table 9.2). When a nurse is observed to be having difficulties with a particular competence the strategies suggest practical ways in which they can improve their performance in the future. In some instances only one strategy may be appropriate, in others several may be necessary. Although the strategies are listed in the document against particular competences, they are not exclusive to these competences. If, in the view of an observer, a strategy linked to one component competence might be the best way to address a difficulty in another, it can be so used. Furthermore, the observer can suggest an identified strategy of their own if the document does not offer an appropriate one.

Table 9.2: Recommended strategies for improving consultation competence.*

Interviewing

Competence to be improved	Recommended strategy
Put patients at ease	If you have not met the patient before introduce yourself and explain your role Welcome the patient, e.g. by asking them what they prefer to be called, establishing eye contact, giving an indication where to sit etc. Review the patient's understanding of previous consultation(s) (if appropriate)
Enable patients to explain situation/problem fully	Resist the temptation to interrupt at the start of the consultation, although this may be necessary later if the patient becomes repetitive Use open questions to begin with, e.g.'How can I help?'; 'How did you feel about that?' Use prompts as appropriate, e.g. 'I see'; 'I understand; 'Tell me more about that' If a significant statement is made and the patient stops, repeat the last statement made by the patient, with a questioning tone to your voice

Table 9.2 (Continued)

Competence to be improved	Recommended strategy
Listen attentively	Demonstrate to the patient that you are listening by using appropriate body language and maintaining eye contact Avoid writing, or entering data on the computer, whilst the patient is talking to you Do not stop listening to the patient whilst you think about the next question to ask
Seek clarification of words used by patients as appropriate	If you do not understand what the patient means, ask them to explain/clarify If the patient uses a medical or technical term (e.g. constipation) make sure you understand exactly what they mean by it
Demonstrate an ability to formulate open questions	Use open questions such as 'How did that affect you?'; 'How do you think that happened?'. Avoid closing down the patient's explanation too early
Phrase questions simply and clearly	Avoid using 'leading' questions that invite only one answer, e.g. 'Your baby doesn't have diarrhoea does he?' Do not use 'double' or 'nested' questions, e.g. 'What is your pain like and how long have you had it?'; 'Is your appetite normal and have you lost weight?' Tailor the questions you ask to the level of the patient's ability to understand. Do not patronise or talk down to the patient Do not use technical jargon
Use silence appropriately	Try to tolerate the discomfort of appropriate silences. Resist the temptation to talk when the patient is thinking about their response If the patient is having difficulty telling the story or is distressed, allow time for them to regain composure
Recognise patients' verbal and non-verbal cues	Develop your awareness of words used by the patient that may indicate the need to probe further, e.g. 'My husband's at home all day now' Notice unusual words and/or surprising omissions and follow-up on these Be sensitive to behaviour that is incongruous, e.g. the patient who laughs when stating something serious Always consider the patient's demeanour and mood. Do they appear tense or relaxed, happy or sad?
Consider physical, social and psychological factors as appropriate	Always bear in mind that the patient's problem may have physical, psychological and social dimensions, e.g. a female patient offered major cardiac surgery may be worried about how her family will run the home in her absence and may delay/decline surgery. An elderly man admitted for a hernia operation may be worried about his disabled wife at home
Demonstrate a well-organised approach to information gathering	Have a clear plan for the interview but always address the patient's agenda If the patient has several issues to be discussed, deal with them in turn, indicating that you will return to each one Avoid moving on to care planning/patient management until you are satisfied you have gathered all the information you need from the interview and examination

Table 9.2 (Continued)

Examination, diagnostic testing and practical procedures

Competence to be improved	Recommended strategy
Elicit physical signs correctly and sensitively	Improve technique to elicit physical signs by reading about it or observing a recording of the technique Appropriately expose the part(s) to be examined with due sensitivity to the patient Ask for a demonstration and then practise under supervision
Use instruments in a competent and sensitive manner	Familiarise yourself with *(relevant)* instrument and practise its use under supervision
Perform technical procedures in a competent and sensitive manner	Ask patient's permission to carry out the procedure Give an explanation of what you are doing to the patient If the procedure is likely to be uncomfortable perform it gently but efficiently Do not undertake any procedure you may have doubt about your ability to perform

Care planning/patient management

Competence to be improved	Recommended strategy
Formulate and follow appropriate care plans	Formulate care plan to address the needs of an individual patient Provide sufficient explanation to enable the patient to make informed decisions about their care Think about how the patient can actively participate in decisions about their care and how they can help themselves
Reach a shared understanding about the problem with patients	Give the patient an explanation of your ideas about their problem tailored to their reason for consulting. If there is disagreement try to resolve this through discussion Ask the patient whether they have understood what you have said and give them sufficient opportunity to question you When appropriate ask the patient to relate what you have agreed If appropriate use leaflets and good quality Internet information to reinforce your explanation and advice
Negotiate care plans with patients	Before discussing what to do about the problem ensure you have a shared understanding of the problem Discuss with the patient your recommendations and ensure they have sufficient information to make informed decisions Allow patients to take an active role in their care planning, ensuring you have explained the risks/benefits of each strategy
Use clear and understandable language	Do not use technical jargon Tailor your explanation to the level of the patient's understanding Provide information in small portions particularly if it is distressing or complex

Table 9.2 (Continued)

Competence to be improved	Recommended strategy
Educate patients appropriately in practical procedures	Demonstrate the procedure and allow the patient supervised practice as appropriate Provide written information for the patient to take away with them Allow time to clarify areas of misunderstanding
Make discriminating use of referral, investigation and drug treatment	Remember to consider the need for referral and be aware of the reasons for and against any potential referral, whether to a hospital consultant or other members of the multi-disciplinary team Consider the need for investigation, and be aware of the reasons for and against any potential investigation Think about the reasons for and against prescribing a particular drug Always consider the major side-effects and/or interactions If in doubt about whether or what to prescribe, do not guess, consult written information sources or a colleague Ensure the patient understands how prescribed items should be taken, the expected impact and the principal side-effects to be expected
Arrange appropriate follow-up	If the problem is likely to resolve use 'open' follow-up. Let the patient decide whether they need to return, but give guidance as to the circumstances when appropriate If follow-up is necessary indicate the time during which likely changes will take place Ensure the patient understands when/where the next appointment will take place and the nature and purpose of that appointment Provide contact name and number, as appropriate

Problem solving

Competence to be improved	Recommended strategy
Access relevant information from patients' records	Scrutinise the key features of the patient's history before you see them, as appropriate. As a minimum, review the summary card/screen, current medication and last consultation During the consultation re-examine the record whenever this is likely to contain information you require, particularly if the patient is unsure of factual details
Explore patients' ideas, concerns and expectations about their problem(s)	In every consultation you must be satisfied that you have established the patient's reason(s) for the consultation. Even when the appointment is for review of a continuing problem ensure you have understood their ideas about it Ensure you know what the patient's main concerns are. This may require direct enquiry about their view of the nature of the problem, its cause and possible effects

Table 9.2 (Continued)

Competence to be improved	Recommended strategy
	If it has not been established ask the patient what they hope you can do for them
	If the patient has already stated their ideas, concerns or expectations try not to ask them again. It is better to reflect remarks they have made to confirm their true concerns
	Consider when is the most appropriate time to ask about a patient's expectations for treatment. If there is still a significant element of diagnostic uncertainty it is probably better to wait until you know what the problem is and how you think you are going to manage it, before exploring what the patient wishes to be done
Elicit relevant information from patients	Identify the key/important features of the patient's problem and concentrate your questions on these
	Use focused questions to fill the gaps in the information you are gathering
Seek relevant clinical signs and make appropriate use of clinical tests	Ask yourself which physical signs will help you to decide between competing diagnoses of the patients' problem
	Consider what question will be answered by the result of a 'clinical' test. Only conduct it if you know a useful course of action for a positive and a negative result
Correctly interpret information gathered	Take sufficient time to consider what the information you have gathered means and how you can apply it. Explain to the patient that you are taking 'time out' to think about their problem
	To help organise your thoughts summarise and reflect back to the patient what you have been told. This has two benefits: it will confirm to the patient that you have understood the problem, and it will clarify your thoughts
	Be prepared to check with books, 'on-line' sources, colleagues, particularly for single items of information
	Avoid over-interpretation of features in the history that might support a diagnosis or conclusion you have reached prematurely
	If you recognise a pattern of symptoms and signs that nearly fits a diagnosis, consider very carefully any feature that does not fit
Apply clinical knowledge appropriately in the identification and management of the patient's problem	If in doubt about the nature of the problem, stop and reconsider it from a different angle. It may help to use your knowledge of anatomy (e.g. a pain in the leg might come from a muscle, blood vessel or nerve) or pathology (e.g. could this problem be caused by infection or a tumour?)
	Improve your awareness of the key features of particular problems/diagnoses
	Utilise information sources to enhance your management/care plans

Table 9.2 (Continued)

Competence to be improved	Recommended strategy
Recognise limits of personal competence and act accordingly	Nobody knows everything. It is an excellent professional attribute to be able to recognise the limits of your competence Do not be afraid to tell the patient that you do not know something. They will usually appreciate your honesty When you recognise you have reached the limits of your competence, do not guess – seek appropriate help by asking a colleague, or consulting information sources

Behaviour/relationship with patients

Competence to be improved	Recommended strategy
Maintain friendly but professional relationship with patients	Adopt friendly, professional behaviour and demeanour relevant to the circumstances of the individual patient and consultation Be sensitive to the needs of individuals from different cultural groups
Convey sensitivity to the needs of patients	Try to consider what it would be like to be in the patient's shoes and respond appropriately within professional boundaries. Appropriate responses can include verbal (e.g. 'I can see you are angry'; 'I can understand that', 'I can see why you are distressed about it') and non-verbal acknowledgement of the patient's state
Be able to use the professional relationship in a manner likely to achieve mutual agreement with the care plan	Try to reach a shared understanding with the patient about the problem. If there is uncertainty about its nature you may need to explain the process by which you have reached your conclusions The patient's views about the problem and management should be explicitly acknowledged and decision-making shared, as appropriate

Health promotion/disease prevention

Competence to be improved	Recommended strategy
Act on appropriate opportunities for health promotion and disease prevention	Consider specific preventive interventions that could be made in any patient of a particular age and gender During consultations actively look for lifestyle issues alluded to by the patient or non-verbal cues, e.g. nicotine-stained fingers, smell of alcohol Remember there may be circumstances that might make a preventive intervention harmful, even though otherwise indicated Having identified legitimate preventive opportunities, be selective and prioritise these according to the evidence for their effectiveness and the circumstances of the particular patient Always establish the patient's motivation to change before giving advice. Be sensitive to patient's circumstances and beliefs

Table 9.2 (Continued)

Competence to be improved	Recommended strategy
Provide appropriate explanation to patients for preventive initiatives suggested	In initiating your choice of preventive action, always provide the patient with an opening, explanatory statement. Ascertain what the patient has tried previously before 'launching in' Elicit patient's response (including their level of awareness) and react accordingly Be prepared to provide evidence for the reasons for the intervention
Work in partnership with patients to encourage the adoption of a healthier lifestyle	There is no point in continuing to try and alter the behaviour of an informed patient who rejects the intervention First establish the level of motivation of the patient then negotiate an action plan with the patient. Do not preach or dictate Identify agreed targets; this may involve a series of interim targets Throughout any preventive initiative undertaken be positive about benefits. Adopt a supportive approach and provide encouragement and reinforcement Offer continuing support and review of progress through follow-up

Record-keeping

Competence to be improved	Recommended strategy
Make an appropriate and legible record of the consultation	The minimum information set is: date, summary of key features in history, significant examination findings, a diagnosis or problem definition (which should be coded if using computer records) Information recorded should be with patient consent
Record care plan to include advice, prescription and follow-up arrangements as appropriate	Note the advice given. Be careful to include agreed targets when the problem is to be reviewed When a prescription is issued note the drug, dose, quantity and specific information about major side-effects Note the investigations requested Indicate the follow-up arrangements agreed with the patient
Enter results of measurement in records	Note numerical values, e.g. weight, blood pressure immediately. Use a 'jotting' pad if necessary to avoid the need to search the record or computer for a specific card/screen Review the record you have made once the patient has left the consultation to ensure important measurements have been noted

Table 9.2 (Continued)

Competence to be improved	Recommended strategy
Provide the name(s), dose and quantity of drug(s) prescribed to patients together with any special precautions	Record the generic name of any drugs prescribed. Note any special precautions conveyed to the patient, e.g. 'alcohol is not permitted with this medication' and their reaction to the advice

*Please consult the Glossary on pages 154–156 if you are unsure about the meaning of terms used in these recommended strategies.

Whilst the information given in Table 9.2 provides specific and practical suggestions as to how to perform differently, it does not recommend the particular method of learning how to do so. A range of effective techniques for improving consultation performance exists. These include:

- reflection
- reading, etc. to fill identified knowledge gaps
- self-analysis of videotaped consultations
- direct observation with feedback from a peer or mentor
- simulated recall with a teacher using videotaped consultations
- group teaching with simulated patients.

Feedback summary

Feedback can be given verbally and/or in writing. An example of a suitable design of form is given in Table 9.3.

Table 9.3: Feedback summary form.

Name of Nurse	Date
Observer	Number of consultations
PRINCIPAL STRENGTHS	
PRIORITY STRATEGIES FOR IMPROVEMENT	
ANY OTHER COMMENTS	
OVERALL COMPETENCE	

INTERVIEWING (20%)	Mark/grade
Strengths Suggestions for improvement	
EXAMINATION, DIAGNOSTIC TESTING AND PRACTICAL PROCEDURES (10%)	Mark/grade
Strengths Suggestions for improvement	
CARE PLANNING/PATIENT MANAGEMENT (20%)	Mark/grade
Strengths Suggestions for improvement	
PROBLEM SOLVING (15%)	Mark/grade
Strengths Suggestions for improvement	
BEHAVIOUR/RELATIONSHIP WITH PATIENT (15%)	Mark/grade
Strengths Suggestions for improvement	
HEALTH PROMOTION/DISEASE PREVENTION (10%)	Mark/grade
Strengths Suggestions for improvement	
RECORD-KEEPING (10%)	Mark/grade
Strengths Suggestions for improvement	

It is invaluable to include specific examples of instances where a competence was demonstrated as a strength or difficulty. For example, if the nurse twice overlooked verbal cues you might note, 'The patient seen for a wound check said, "I have been tired lately"'. When using the CAIIN for educational assessment, grade levels rather than marks are normally used. As feedback plays such a vital part in the educational process, written feedback should be given to the nurse to facilitate self-learning leading to improved consulting capability. Sequential assessments can be used to chart progress over time. The CAIIN can also be adapted for regulatory use in which case grade levels can be converted to marks.

Giving and receiving feedback

This is discussed in detail in Chapter 7.

Procedure for using the CAIIN

Summary

Preparation

- Familiarise yourself with the overall procedures to be followed.
- Familiarise yourself with the required consultation competences and the criteria for the allocation of grade levels/marks.
- Agree with the nurse being assessed the purpose of the assessment and the number of consultations to be observed.
- Check the nurse is aware of the procedures during each consultation.

Observation

- Check the information available to the nurse from the record at the start of each consultation.
- Ask about her objectives for the consultation.
- Observe the consultation, including examination and tests.
- Record competences displayed as strengths or difficulties and note omissions.
- After the patient has left ask the questions to explore clinical reasoning.
- Check the record made.

Consideration

- Allocate grade levels/marks for performance in each consultation category challenged on the 'Observer recording' form.
- At the end of the observation phase scrutinise the 'Observer recording' forms for all consultations.
- Determine the overall grade level/mark for each consultation category and the final mark to reflect performance over the whole assessment.
- Decide on the key strengths and priorities for improvement.

Feedback

- Prepare the written feedback.
- Give verbal feedback, following the guidance in the document 'Giving and receiving feedback'.

These are the recommended procedures when the CAIIN is used in formal assessments, whether regulatory or formative. In such cases it will normally be most appropriate to use marks although grade levels can also be used. When a teaching session is in progress more flexibility may be allowed, but the competences remain an invaluable aid to learning consultation skills. Therefore, teaching will have most educational impact if is delivered within the framework of the CAIIN. When it is necessary to give feedback to nurses on their performance after a teaching session it is usually better to do so using the descriptor or code grade level.

1. It is essential that you first become thoroughly familiar with the content and function of all the forms before carrying out any assessments. You must be fully conversant with the detailed criteria against which you are judging a nurse's performance, as well as the descriptors for the award of particular marks or grade levels. This will optimise equity and comparability between multiple observers and those nurses being assessed.
2. Before the consultation starts scrutinise the information available to the nurse from the patient record.
3. Ask the question concerning objectives before the patient enters the room. This allows you to judge the nurse's ability to interpret prior knowledge of the patient and to organise the content and direction of the consultation.
4. Throughout the period of assessment use the 'Observer recording' form to make detailed notes on the nurse's performance in every consultation witnessed. If no record is kept it is very difficult to remember what took place during a series of consultations. Include both positive and negative features as well as omissions.
5. In all instances when the patient gives permission observe the nurse's ability to elicit physical signs when examining, using an instrument or carrying out a practical procedure.
6. If a particular category of consultation competence is not tested enter 'n/a' (not applicable) in the appropriate space. This is most likely to occur with the categories 'Examination etc.' and 'Health promotion/disease prevention'.
7. The mark awarded for the seven categories of consultation competence and the overall mark in each consultation require the exercise of professional judgement by the observer. They are influenced by the difficulty of the challenge and guided by reference to the criteria for the allocation of grade levels/marks. It is important to remember that all competences are unlikely to be challenged in every consultation.
8. Make a note of the duration of the consultation. In assessing whether the time taken is appropriate, due allowance must be made for any intervention(s) you have made. In this way you are able to assess the extent to which the candidate is efficient in the use of time in the consultation.
9. The four questions to be asked at the end of each consultation give nurses the opportunity to explain the reasons for their actions. They also serve as a check that issues the patient has brought to the consultation, which were not apparent at the start, have been detected and addressed. If the assessment is being conducted for regulatory purposes it is wrong to ask questions other than those defined or to provide feedback between consultations. This ensures that idiosyncratic observers do not bias the process, which would not be fair.
10. After each consultation you should check the record made in the patient's notes.
11. The final task to be carried out between consultations is to enter a mark/grade level in each box on the 'Observer recording' form to reflect your assessment

of the level of performance achieved, within each of the relevant categories. To arrive at this, the actual performance of the candidate needs to be compared with the criteria of consultation competences. The observer is not at liberty to consider any other criteria. Reference also needs to be made to the criteria for the allocation of grade levels/marks to assist in determining the appropriate mark/grade levels to be awarded.

12. Once the required number of consultations has been observed you should scrutinise all the recording forms and assess the nurse's performance as reflected by the grade levels/marks you have allocated in all seven categories of competence. For each of the categories the grade levels/marks awarded across all the consultations are collated into a final mark to reflect overall performance in all seven categories of competence in turn. It should be noted that the overall mark is *not* the average of the marks allocated to all the consultations. The observer should take account of the nature and difficulty of the clinical challenges presented and a final judgement may be, quite appropriately, disproportionately influenced by performance in challenging cases.

13. The observer should complete the feedback summary form using any comments made on the recording form for guidance. Make your comments as specific as possible, with due concentration on priority areas, since vague generalisations will be of little benefit to the nurse. This provides the nurse with detailed feedback on performance, an essential component of any assessment process, which will facilitate self-learning and improved consulting capability.

14. In is important to consider carefully the prioritisation of your comments. Those messages you consider to be most important should appear at the start of the feedback summary. If a nurse has a large number of strengths or difficulties the less important can be noted in the 'additional comments' section. These will provide an important record for future reference, but the feedback should focus on the key messages you wish the nurse to act on.

15. Once the written feedback has been prepared the observer is in a position to offer verbal feedback following the recommended procedures.

When the CAIIN is being used in regulatory assessment it is necessary to make a judgement about the number of patients and the range of challenges to be included. This depends on the purpose of the assessment and the clinical context in which the nurse works. No specific formula currently exists to determine this. If the CAIIN is to be used to judge whether nurses are fit to work as nurse practitioners at the end of training we would recommend observation of a minimum of eight consultations, where the multiple problems would be likely to represent the range of challenges to which they need to be able to respond. This figure is based on experimental evidence with the LAP.[4,5]

References

1. Redsell SA, Lennon M, Hastings AM *et al*. Devising and establishing the face and content validity of explicit criteria of consultation competence for UK secondary care nurses. *Nurs Educ Today*. 2004; **24**(3), 180–7.
2. Redsell SA, Hastings AM, Cheater FM *et al*. Devising and establishing the face and content validity of explicit criteria of consultation competence in UK primary care nurses. *Nurs Educ Today*. 2003; **23**(4), 299–306.

3. McKinley RK, Fraser RC, Van der Vleuten C *et al*. Formative assessment of the consultation performance of medical students in the setting of general practice using a modified version of the Leicester Assessment Package. *Med Educ.* 2000; **34**, 573–9.
4. Fraser RC, McKinley RK, Mulholland H. Consultation competence in general practice: testing the reliability of the Leicester Assessment Package. *Br J Gen Pract.* 1994; **44**(384), 293–6.
5. Fraser RC, McKinley RK, Mulholland H. Consultation competence in general practice: establishing the face validity of prioritised criteria in the Leicester Assessment Package. *Br J Gen Pract.*1994; **44**(380), 109–13.

Glossary

This glossary explains the meaning of terms that have been used in the book, in the context of describing and assessing effective consultations. The definitions are not necessarily those that would be found in a dictionary.

Acceptability	In relation to assessment of consultation skills the method must be acceptable to the practitioner, the assessor and to the patient
Category	A grouping of different competences that describe importance activities in different phases of the consultation
Clinical information	Information gained from talking with, examining and diagnostic testing of a patient
Clinical problem solving	The process of thinking about and interpreting clinical information to formulate a diagnosis or describe a problem and to decide a management/care plan
Competence	A specific skill required by a health professional to consult with patients. Each of them starts with a verb; that is they describe an action
Consultation	The meeting between a practitioner and a patient to discuss and assess the health concerns and problems of the patient
Criterion	A systematically developed statement that can be used to determine the level of performance in assessment
Doctor	A registered medical practitioner
Double questions	Instances when a practitioner asks a patient two questions at once. Usually patients will only answer the second, resulting in uncertainty about their response to the first
Feasibility	Whether a particular method of assessment is practical to use in terms of the time taken to train assessors and to carry it out
Focused questions	Questions that seek to elicit a specific piece of information, e.g. 'How often do you pass urine at night?'
Formative assessment	A diagnostic evaluation of the capability of a practitioner leading to advice on how to improve. The grade or mark awarded is not used to decide whether the practitioner has passed or failed a course of study
Key feature(s)	Those attributes of a disease condition that are usually present and whose absence would call into question the accuracy of a diagnosis
Leading questions	Questions that are phrased in such a way that the patient is strongly encouraged to give the expected answer
Learner	This term refers to a health professional at any stage in their career who is gaining a new skill, or improving an existing one
Near-patient testing	A 'near-patient' test is one conducted during the consultation, whose result is available for immediate interpretation and action, e.g. multi-function test strips for urinary tract infection as an alternative to MSU

Nested questions	These are instances where an open question is followed by a closed one. For example, 'Tell me what the headache is like, is it sharp?'. This limits the opportunity for a patient to tell their story using their own words
Normative	Conforming to an established standard
Nurse	Refers to a qualified nurse working in an autonomous or semi-autonomous role
Over interpretation	Having unwarranted confidence in the significance of a particular piece of information, e.g. assuming that frequency of passing urine means the patient inevitably has diabetes
Patient	The person consulting with a practitioner about their healthcare. Also refers to individuals consulting by proxy, e.g. parents, carers or partners
Pattern-recognition	When a practitioner believes that any cluster of symptoms and signs of a patient are a close enough fit to a recognised diagnosis
Practitioner	This term encompasses all health professionals working with patients. Used particularly when describing activities believed to be generic
'Prodigy'	Software, available on most primary care computer systems, which provides information and guidance in decision-making
Protocol	Agreed written guidance to a practitioner about the content of clinical care to be provided in particular circumstances. The majority of protocols in secondary care specify how chronic diseases should be managed, or how specialised clinics should operate. In primary care they can also be used to control the type and sequence of questions to be asked of a patient with acute illness
Rank	To place in order of priority
Regulatory assessment	An assessment that determines whether practitioners are competent to undertake duties, which form part of their recognised work
Reliability	An indication of the consistency of scores between assessors, or over a period of time
Secondary care nurse	This includes all categories of nurses working in semi-autonomous or autonomous roles (nurse practitioners, specialist nurses and nurse consultants)
Shared understanding	When a practitioner and a patient agree about the nature of the health problem of the patient, they have reached a shared understanding. This requires the practitioner to provide sufficient explanation of their reasons for their conclusions and for the patient to have the opportunity to explain their beliefs about the problem(s)
Standard	The percentage of events that should comply with the criterion
Student	Refers to a health professional undertaking initial training prior to attaining registration

Summative assessment	The determination of an individual's competence in order to decide whether or not a required level of competence has been reached
Systematic care	Care that is provided consistently to all patients with the same health problem. It usually involves the use of protocols, call/recall systems and audit
Technical jargon	Words that are understood by professionals in the field but which cannot be assumed to carry the same meaning for patients
Validity	An indication of how well an assessment actually measures what it is supposed to measure

Index

Page numbers in *italic* refer to tables, figures or worked examples.